THE MASTERS

THE *STRANGERS AND BROTHERS* NOVEL-SEQUENCE BY C. P. SNOW

STRANGERS AND BROTHERS

THE CONSCIENCE OF THE RICH

TIME OF HOPE

THE LIGHT AND THE DARK

THE MASTERS

THE NEW MEN

HOMECOMING

THE AFFAIR

C. P. SNOW is also the author of *THE SEARCH*

THE MASTERS

C. P. SNOW

NEW YORK

CHARLES SCRIBNER'S SONS

Cover drawing by Doreen Yarwood from
The Architecture of Britain © 1976

7 9 11 13 15 17 19 F/P 20 18 16 14 12 10 8 6

PRINTED IN THE UNITED STATES OF AMERICA
LIBRARY OF CONGRESS CATALOG CARD NUMBER 76-13428
ISBN 0-684-14744-0

IN MEMORY OF

G. H. HARDY

NOTE

I have not given a name to the college in this story; I have never liked geographical inventions such as Christminster, and have avoided them through the whole sequence of Lewis Eliot novels.

This fictional college stands upon an existing site, and its topography is similar to that of an existing college, though some of the details are different. That is the end, however, of my reference to a real institution. This history (which I have sketched in an appendix, in the hope that it may be interesting to some unfamiliar with Cambridge) has no factual connection with any real college, though the generalisations are as true as I can make them. The people have been composed from many sources; and, to the best of my belief, there has been no actual election in Cambridge or Oxford in recent times which followed the course of this imaginary one. There is a tradition of a last-minute change of fortune early in the century, and a well-authenticated one in Mark Pattison's Memoirs. It was G. H. Hardy who first drew my attention to the latter source, when I was originally contemplating this theme. To his memory I dedicate this book, in love and reverence.

C.P.S.

CONTENTS

THE MASTERS

I

A LIGHT IN THE LODGE

ONE

NEWS AFTER A MEDICAL EXAMINATION

The snow had only just stopped, and in the court below my rooms all sounds were dulled. There were few sounds to hear, for it was early in January, and the college was empty and quiet; I could just make out the footsteps of the porter, as he passed beneath the window on his last round of the night. Now and again his keys clinked, and the clink reached me after the pad of his footsteps had been lost in the snow.

I had drawn my curtains early that evening and not moved out. The kitchens had sent up a meal, and I had eaten it as I read by the fire. The fire had been kept high and bright all day; though it was nearly ten o'clock now, I stoked it again, shovelling coal up the back of the chimney, throwing it on so it would burn for hours. It was scorchingly hot in front of the fire, and warm, cosy, shielded, in the zone of the two armchairs and the sofa which formed an island of comfort round the fireplace. Outside that zone, as one went towards the walls of the lofty medieval room, the draughts were bitter. In a blaze of firelight, which shone into the sombre corners, the panelling on the walls glowed softly, almost rosily, but no warmth reached as far. So that, on a night like this, one came to treat most of the room as the open air, and hurried back to the cosy island in front of the fireplace, the pool of light from the reading lamp on the mantelpiece, the radiance which was more pleasant because of the cold air which one had just escaped.

I was comfortable in my armchair, relaxed and content.

There was no need to move. I was reading so intently that I did not notice the steps on the staircase, until there came a quick repeated knock on my door, and Jago came in.

"Thank the Lord I've found you," he said. "I'm glad you're in!"

Outside, on the landing, he kicked the snow from his shoes and then came back to the armchair opposite mine. He was still wearing his gown, and I guessed that they had sat a long time in the combination room. He apologised for disturbing me. He apologised too much, for a man who was often so easy.

But sometimes he found the first moments of a meeting difficult; that was true with everyone he met, certainly with me, though we liked each other. I had got used to his excessive apologies and his over-cordial greetings. He made them that night, though he was excited, though he was grave and tense with his news.

He was a man of fifty, and some, seeing that he had gone both bald and grey, thought he looked older. But the first physical impression was deceptive. He was tall and thick about the body, with something of a paunch, but he was also small-boned, active, light on his feet. In the same way, his head was massive, his forehead high and broad between the fringes of fair hair; but no one's face changed its expression quicker, and his smile was brilliant. Behind the thick lenses, his eyes were small and intensely bright, the eyes of a young and lively man. At a first glance, people might think he looked a senator. It did not take them long to discover how mercurial he was. His temper was as quick as his smile; in everything he did his nerves seemed on the surface. In fact, people forgot all about the senator and began to complain that his sympathy and emotion flowed too easily. Many of them disliked his love of display. Yet they were affected by the depth of his feeling. Nearly everyone recognised that, though it took some insight to perceive that he was not only a man of deep feeling, but also one of passionate pride.

At this time—it was 1937—he had been Senior Tutor of the college for ten years. I had met him three years before, in 1934, when Francis Getliffe, knowing that I wished to spend most of my time in academic law, proposed to the college that they should give me a fellowship. Jago had supported me (with his quick imagination, he guessed the reason that led me to change my career when I was nearly thirty), and ever since had borne me the special grateful affection that one feels towards a protégé.

"I'm relieved to find you in, Eliot," he said, looking at me across the fireplace. "I had to see you tonight. I shouldn't have rested if I'd had to wait until the morning."

"What has happened?"

"You know," said Jago, "that they were examining the Master today?"

I nodded. "I was going to ask at the Lodge tomorrow morning."

"I can tell you," said Jago. "I wish I couldn't!"

He paused, and went on:

"He went into hospital last night. They put a tube down him this morning and sent him home. The results came through just before dinner. It is utterly hopeless. At the very most—they give him six months."

"What is it?"

"Cancer. Absolutely inoperable." Jago's face was dark with pain. He said: "I hope that when my time comes it will come in a kinder way."

We sat silent. I thought of the Master, with his confidential sarcasms, his spare and sophisticated taste, his simple religion. I thought of the quarrels he and Jago had had for so many years.

Though I had not spoken, Jago said:

"It's intolerable to me, Eliot, to think of Vernon Royce going like this. I can't pretend that everything has been always easy between us. You know that, don't you?"

I nodded.

"Yet he went out of his way to help me last term," said Jago. "You know, my wife was ill, and I was utterly distracted. I couldn't help her, I was useless, I was a burden to everyone and to myself. Then one afternoon the Master asked me if I would like to go a walk with him. And he'd asked me for a very definite reason. He wanted to tell me how anxious he was about my wife and how much he thought of her. He must have known that I've always felt she wasn't appreciated enough here. It's been a grief to me. He said all he'd set out to say in a couple of dozen words on the way to Waterbeach, and it touched me very much. Somehow one's dreadfully vulnerable through those one loves." Suddenly he smiled at me with great kindness. "You know that as well as anyone alive, Eliot. I felt it when you let me meet your wife. When she's better, you must ask me to Chelsea again. You know how much I enjoyed it. She's gone through too much, hasn't she?" He went on: "That afternoon made a difference to all I felt for Royce. Do you wonder that it's intolerable for me to hear this news tonight?"

He burst out:

"And do you know? I went for another walk with him exactly a month ago. I was under the weather, and he jogged along as he always used to, and I was very tired. I should have said, I believe anyone would have said, that he was the healthier man."

He paused, and added: "Tonight we've heard his sentence."

He was moved by a feeling for the dying man powerful, quick, imaginative and deep. At the same time he was immersed in the drama, showing the frankness which embarrassed so many. No man afraid of expressing emotion could have been so frank.

"Yes, we've heard his sentence," said Jago. "But there is one last thing which seems to me more ghastly than the rest. For there is someone who has not heard it."

He paused. Then he said: "That is the man himself. They are not going to tell him yet."

I exclaimed.

"For some reason that seems utterly inhuman," said Jago, "these doctors have not told him. He's been given to understand that in two or three months he will be perfectly well. When any of us see him, we are not to let him know any different."

He looked into my eyes, and then into the fire. For a moment I left him, opened my door, went out into the glacial air, turned into the gyp room, collected together a bottle of whisky, a syphon, a jug of water. The night had gone colder; the jug felt as though the water inside had been iced. As I brought the tray back to the fireside, I found Jago standing up. He was standing up, with his elbows on the mantelpiece and his head bent. He did not move while I put the tray on the little table by my chair. Then he straightened himself and said, looking down at me:

"This news has shaken me, Eliot. I can't think of everything it means." He sat down. His cheeks were tinged by the fire. His expression was set and brooding. A weight of anxiety hung on each of those last words.

I poured out the whisky. After he took his glass, he held it for an instant to the firelight, and through the liquid watched the image of the flames.

"This news has shaken me," he repeated. "I can't think of everything it means. Can you," he asked me suddenly, "think of everything it means?"

I shook my head. "It has come as a shock," I said.

"You haven't thought of any consequences at all?" He gazed at me intently. In his eyes there was a question, almost an appeal.

"Not yet."

He waited. Then he said:

"I had to break the news to one or two of our colleagues

in hall tonight. I hadn't thought of it myself, but they pointed out there was a consequence we couldn't put aside."

He waited again, then said quickly:

"In a few weeks, in a few months at most, the college will have to elect a new Master."

"Yes," I said.

"When the time arrives, we shall have to do it in a hurry," said Jago. "I suppose before then we shall have made up our minds whom we are going to elect."

I had known, for minutes past, that this was coming: I had not wanted to talk of it that night. Jago was longing for me to say that he ought to be the next Master, that my own mind was made up, that I should vote for him. He had longed for me to say it without prompting; he had not wanted even to mention the election. It was anguish to him to make the faintest hint without response. Yet he was impelled to go on, he could not stop. It harassed me to see this proud man humiliating himself.

Yet that night I could not do as he wanted. A few years before I should have said yes on the spot. I liked him, he had captured my imagination, he was a deeper man than his rivals. But my spontaneity had become masked by now; I had been too much knocked about, I had grown to be guarded.

"Of course," I said, "we've got a certain amount of time."

"This business in the Lodge may go quicker even than they threaten," said Jago. "And it would be intolerable to have to make a rush election with the college utterly divided as to what it wants."

"I don't see," I said slowly, "why we should be so much divided."

"We often are," said Jago with a sudden smile. "If fourteen men are divided about most things, they're not specially likely to agree about choosing a new Master."

"They're not," I agreed. I added: "I'm afraid the fourteen will have become thirteen."

Jago inclined his head. A little later, in a sharp staccato manner, he said:

"I should like you to know something, Eliot. It was suggested to me tonight that I must make a personal decision. I must decide whether I can let my own name be considered."

"I've always taken it for granted," I said, "that whenever the Mastership fell vacant you'd be asked that."

"It's extraordinarily friendly of you to say so," he burst out, "but, do you know, before tonight I've scarcely thought of it for a single moment."

Sometimes he was quite naked to life, I thought; sometimes he concealed himself from his own eyes.

Soon after, he looked straight at me and said:

"I suppose it's too early to ask whether you've any idea whom you prefer yourself?"

Slowly, I raised my eyes to meet his.

"Tonight is a bit too early. I will come and tell you as soon as I am certain."

"I understand." Jago's smile was hurt, but warm and friendly. "I understand. I shall trust you to tell me, whoever you prefer."

After that we talked casually and easily; it was not till the college clock struck midnight that Jago left. As he went down the stairs, I walked across to my window and pulled the curtains. The sky had cleared, the moon was shining on the snow. The lines of the building opposite stood out simple and clear; on the steep roofs the snow was brilliant. All the windows were dark under the moon, except for the great bedroom of the Lodge, where the Master lay. There a light glowed, warm, tawny, against the stark brightness of the night.

The last chimes of twelve were still falling on the court. On the ground the snow was scarcely marked. Across it Jago was walking fast towards the gate. His gown blew behind him as he moved with light steps through the bitter cold.

TWO

THE MASTER TALKS OF THE FUTURE

When I woke next morning, the bedroom seemed puzzlingly bright. Round the edges of the blind a white sheen gleamed. Then, half-awake, I felt the chill against my face, remembered the snow, drew the bedclothes higher. Like a pain returning after sleep, the heavy thought came back that that morning I was obliged to call at the Lodge.

The quarters chimed, first from a distance away, then from Great St. Mary's, then from the college clock, then from a college close by. The last whirr and clang were not long over when, soft-footedly, Bidwell came in. The blind flew up, the room was all a-glare; Bidwell studied his own watch, peered at the college clock, uttered his sacramental phrase:

That's nine o'clock, sir."

I muttered. From beneath the bedclothes I could see his rubicund cunning peasant face, open and yet sly. He said:

"It's a sharp old morning, sir. Do you lie warm enough in bed?"

"Yes," I said. It was true. That bedroom, niche-like and narrow as a monastic cell, had not been dried or heated in five hundred years. When I returned to it from some of our food and wine, it seemed a curious example of the mixture of luxury and bizarre discomfort in which the college lived. Yet, in time, one missed the contrast between the warmth in bed and the frigid air one breathed, and it was not so easy to sleep elsewhere.

I put off ringing up the Lodge until the middle of the

morning, but at last I did so. I asked for Lady Muriel (the Master came from a Scottish professional family; in middle age he married the daughter of an earl), and soon heard her voice. It was firm and loud. "We shall be glad to see you Mr. Eliot. And I know my husband will be."

I walked across the court to the Lodge, and in the drawing-room found Joan, the Royces' daughter. She interrupted me, as I tried to sympathise. She said: "The worst thing is this make-believe. Why don't they tell him the truth?"

She was nearly twenty. In girlhood her face had been sullen; she was strong and clever, and longed only to be pretty. But now she was just at the age when the heaviness was lifting, and all but she could see that her good looks would soon show through.

That morning she was frowning in her distress. She was so direct that it was harder to comfort her.

Her mother entered; the thick upright figure bore towards us over the deep carpet, past the Chinese screens, past the Queen Anne chairs, past the lavish bric-à-brac of the long and ornate drawing-room.

"Good morning, Mr. Eliot. I know that we all wish this were a happier occasion."

Her manner was authoritative and composed, her eyes looked steadily into mine. They were tawny, full and bold; in their boldness lay a curious innocence.

"I only learned late last night," I said. "I did not want to bother you then."

"We only learned ourselves before dinner," said Lady Muriel. "We had not expected anything so drastic. There was a great deal to decide in a short time."

"I cannot think of anything I can do," I said. "But if there is——"

"You are very kind, Mr. Eliot. The college is being most kind. There may be matters connected with my husband's manuscripts where Roy Calvert could help us. In the meantime, you can do one great service. I hope you've already been told that my husband does not realise the true position. He believes that the doctors have overhauled him and found him pretty sound. He has been told that he has the trace of an ulcer, and he believes he will soon be well. I ask you to think before every word, so that you leave him with the same conviction."

"It won't be easy, Lady Muriel," I said. "But I'll try."

"You will understand that I am already acting as I ask you to act. It is not easy for me."

There was grandeur in her ramrod back. She did not give an inch. "I am positive," she said, "that we are doing right. It is the last comfort we can give him. He can have a month or two in peace."

"I completely disagree," Joan cried. "Do you think comfort is all he wants? Do you think he would take comfort at that price?"

"My dear Joan, I have listened to your views——"

"Then for God's sake don't go on with this farce." The girl was torn with feeling, the cry welled out of her. "Give him his dignity back."

"His dignity is safe," said Lady Muriel. She got up. "I must apologise to you, Mr. Eliot, for forcing a family disagreement upon you. You will not wish to hear more of it. Perhaps you would care to see the Master now."

As I followed Lady Muriel upstairs, I thought about her: how she was strong and unperceptive, snobbish and coarse-fibred, downright and brave. Beneath the brassy front there lingered still an inarticulate desire for affection. But she had not the insight to see why, even in her own family, she threw it away.

She went before me into the bedroom, which was as wide, and nearly as long, as the drawing-room below. Her words rang loudly in the great room. "Mr. Eliot has come to pay you a visit. I'll leave you together."

"This is nice of you," came the Master's voice from the bed. It sounded exactly as I had last heard it, before his illness—brisk, cheerful, intimate. It sounded like the voice of a gay and healthy man.

"I've told Mr. Eliot that you ought to be back at college meetings by the end of term. But he mustn't tire you this morning." Lady Muriel spoke in the same tone to me. "I shall leave you with the Master for half an hour."

She left us. "Do come and sit down," said the Master, and I brought a chair by the bedside. He was lying on his back, looking up at the ceiling, where there was embossed a gigantic coloured bas-relief of the college arms. He looked a little thinner, but the cheeks were still full; his dark hair was only just turning grey over the ears, his comely face was little lined, his lips were fresh. He was sixty-two, but that morning he looked much younger. He was in extraordinarily high spirits.

"It is a relief, you know," he said. "I'd imagined this might be something with an unpleasant end. I may have told you that I don't think much of doctors—but I distinctly enjoyed their conversation last night."

He smiled. "As a matter of fact, I feel a little more tired than you'd imagine. But I take it that's natural, after those people have been rummaging about. And I suppose this ulcer has been tiring me and taking away my appetite. I've got to lie here while it heals. I expect to get a little stronger every day."

"You may get some intermissions." From my chair I could see over the high bed rail, out of the single window; from the bed there was no view but the cloudless sky, but I could see most of the court under snow. My eyes stayed there. "You mustn't worry too much if you have setbacks."

"I shan't worry for a long time," he said. "You know, when I was nervous about the end of this, I was surprised to find how inquisitive one is. I did so much want to know whether the college would ever make up its mind about the beehives in the garden. And I did want to know whether our old friend Gay's son would really get the job at Edinburgh. It will be remarkable if he does. It will reflect the greatest credit on Mrs. Gay. Between you and me"—he passed into his familiar, intimate whisper—"it's an error to think that eminent scholars are very likely to be clever men."

He chuckled boyishly. "I shouldn't have liked not to know the answers. And I shouldn't have liked not to finish that little book on the early heresies."

The Master had spent much of his life working on comparative religion. Oddly, it seemed to have made not the slightest difference to his faith, which had stayed unchanged, as it were in a separate compartment, since he first learned it as a child.

"How long will it take you?"

"Only a couple of years. I shall ask Roy Calvert to write some of the chapters."

He chuckled again. "And I should have hated not to see that young man's magnum opus come out next year. Do you remember the trouble we had to get him elected, Eliot? Some of our friends show a singular instinct for preferring mediocrity. Like elects like, of course. Or, between you and me," he whispered, "dull men elect dull men. I'm looking forward to Roy Calvert's book. Since the Germans dined here, our friends have an uncomfortable suspicion that he's out of the ordinary. But when his book appears, they will be told that he's the most remarkable scholar this society has contained for fifty years. Will they be grateful to you and me and good old Arthur Brown for backing him? Will they be grateful, Eliot?"

His laugh was michievous, but his voice was becoming weaker.

As I got up to go, he said:

"I hope you'll stay longer next time. I told you, I expect to get a little stronger every day."

After I had said goodbye to Lady Muriel and Joan, I let myself out of the Lodge into the sunny winter morning. I felt worn out.

In the court I saw Chrystal coming towards me. He was a very big man, both tall and strongly muscled. He walked soft-footed and well-balanced.

"So you've seen him this morning?"

"Yes," I said.

"What do you think of it?"

"I'm sorry."

"I'm sorry myself," said Chrystal. He was crisp and brusque, and people often thought him hectoring. This morning he was at his sharpest. From his face alone one would have known that he found it easy to give orders. His nose was beak-like, his gaze did not flicker.

"I'm sorry myself," he repeated. I knew that he was moved. "Did you talk to him?"

"Yes."

"I shall have to do the same." He looked at me with his commanding stare.

"He's very tired," I said.

"I shouldn't think of staying."

We walked a few steps back towards the Lodge. Chrystal burst out:

"It's lamentable. Well, we shall have to find a successor, I suppose. I can't imagine anyone succeeding Royce. Still, we've got to have someone. Jago came to see me this morning."

He gave me a sharp glance. Then he said fiercely:

"It's lamentable. Well, it's no use our standing here."

I did not mind his rudeness. For, of all the college, he was the one most affected by the news of the Master. It was not that he was an intimate friend; in the past year, apart from the formal dinners at the Lodge, they had not once been in each other's houses; it was a long time, back in the days when Chrystal was Royce's pupil, since they spent an evening together. But Chrystal had hero-worshipped the older man in those days, and still did. It was strange to feel, but this bustling, dominating, successful man had a great capacity for hero-worship. He was a power in the college, and would have been in any society. He had force, decision, the liking for action; he revelled in command. He was nearly fifty now, successful, within the modest limits he set himself, in all he undertook. In the college he was Dean (a lay official of standing, though by this time the functions were dying away); in the university he was well known, sat on the Council of the Senate, was always being appointed to committees and syndicates. He made a more than usually comfortable academic income. He had three grown-up daughters, and had married each of them well. He adored his wife. But he was still capable of losing himself in hero-worship, and the generous, humble impulse often took the oddest forms. Sometimes he fixed on a business magnate, or an eminent soldier, or a politician; he was drawn to success and power on the grand scale —to success and power, which, in his own sphere, he knew so well how to get.

But the oldest and strongest of his worships was for Royce.

That was why he was uncontrollably curt to me in the court that morning.

"I must get on," he said. "We shall have to find a successor. I shall have to think out who I want. I'll have a word with Brown. And I should like five minutes with you."

As we parted, he said:

"There's something else Brown and I want to talk to you about. The way I see it, it's more important than the next Master."

THREE

A SMALL PARTY IN THE COMBINATION ROOM

The combination room glowed warm when I entered it that evening. No one had yet come in, and the lights were out; but the fire flared in the open grate, threw shadows on to the curtains, picked out the glasses on the oval table, already set for the after-dinner wine. I took a glass of sherry and an evening paper, and settled myself in an armchair by the fire. A decanter of claret, I noticed, was standing at the head of the table; there were only six places laid, and a great stretch of the mahogany shone polished and empty.

Jago and Winslow came in nearly together. Winslow threw his square into one armchair and sat in another himself; he gave me his mordant, not unfriendly grin.

"May I pour you some sherry, Bursar?" said Jago, not at ease with him.

"If you please. *If* you please."

"I'm dreadfully afraid I've spilt most of it," said Jago, beginning to apologise.

"It's so good of you to bring it," said Winslow.

Just then the butler entered with the dining-list and presented it to Winslow.

"We are a very small party tonight," he said. "Ourselves, the worthy Brown and Chrystal, and young Luke." He glanced at the decanter on the table. He added:

"We are a small party, but I gather that one of us is presenting a bottle. I am prepared to bet another bottle that we owe this to the worthy Brown. I wonder what remarkable event he is celebrating now."

Jago shook his head. "Will you have more sherry, Bursar?"

"If you please, my dear boy. *If* you please."

I watched him as he drank. His profile was jagged, with his long nose and nutcracker jaw. His eyes were hooded with heavy lids, and there were hollows in his cheeks and temples that brought back to me, by contrast, the smooth full face of the Master—who was two or three years younger. But Winslow's skin was ruddy, and his long, gangling body moved as willingly as in his prime.

His manners were more formal than ours, even when his bitter humour had broken loose. He was wealthy, and it was in his style to say that he was the grandson of a draper; but the draper was a younger son of a county family. Lady Muriel was intensely snobbish and Winslow had never got on with the Master—nevertheless, he was the only one of the older fellows whom she occasionally, as a gesture of social acceptance, managed to call by his Christian name.

He had a savage temper and a rude tongue, and was on bad terms with most of his colleagues. The Master had quarrelled with him long before—there were several versions of the occasion. Between him and Jago there was an absolute incompatibility. Chrystal disliked him unforgivingly. He had little to his credit. He had been a fine classic in his youth and had published nothing. As Bursar he was conscientious, but had no flair. Yet all the college felt that he was a man of stature, and responded despite themselves if he cared to notice them.

He was finishing his second glass of sherry. Jago, who was trying to placate him, said deferentially:

"Did you get my note on the closed exhibitions?"

"Thank you, yes."

"I hope it had everything you wanted."

Winslow glanced at him under his heavy lids. For a moment he paused. Then he said:

"It may very well have done. It may very well have done."

He paused again. "I should be so grateful if you'd explain it to me some time."

"I struggled extremely hard to make it clear," said Jago, laughing so as not to be provoked.

"I have a feeling that clarity usually comes when one struggles a little less and reflects a little more."

At that Jago's hot temper flared up.

"No one has ever accused me of not being able to make myself understood——"

"It must be my extreme stupidity," said Winslow. "But, do you know, when I read your notes—a fog descends."

Jago burst out:

"There are times, Bursar, when you make me feel as though I were being sent up to the headmaster for bad work."

"There are times, my dear Senior Tutor, when that is precisely the impression I wish to make."

Angrily, Jago snatched up a paper, but as he did so Brown and Chrystal came through the door. Brown's eyes were alert at once behind their spectacles; the spectacles sat on a broad high-coloured face, his body was cushioned and comfortable; his eyes looked from Jago to Winslow, eyes that were sharp, peering, kindly, and always on the watch. He knew at once that words had passed.

"Good evening to you," said Winslow, unperturbed.

Chrystal nodded and went over to Jago; Brown talked placidly to Winslow and me; the bell began to ring for hall. Just as the butler threw open the door, and announced to Winslow that dinner was served, Luke came rapidly in, and joined our file out of the combination room, on to the dais. The hall struck cold, and we waited impatiently for the long grace to end. The hall struck more than ever cold, when one looked down it, and saw only half-a-dozen undergraduates at the far end; for it was still the depth of the vacation, and there were only a few scholars up, just as there were only the six of us at the high table.

Winslow took his seat at the head, and others manoeuvred for position; Jago did not want to sit by him after their fracas, so that I found myself on Winslow's right hand. Jago sat by me, and Luke on the same side: opposite was Brown and then his friend Chrystal, who had also avoided being Winslow's neighbour.

Brown smiled surreptitiously at me, his good-natured face a little pained, for though he could master these embarrassments he was a man who liked his friends to be at ease: then he began to talk to Winslow about the college silver. My attention strayed, I found myself studying one of the portraits on the linenfold. Then I heard Jago's voice, unrecognisably different from when he replied to Winslow, talking to young Luke.

"You look as though things are going well in the laboratory. I believe you've struck oil."

I looked past Jago as Luke replied:

"I hope so. I had an idea over Christmas." He had been elected a fellow only a few months before, and was twenty-four. Intelligence shone from his face, which was fresh, boyish, not yet quite a man's; as he talked of his work, the words tripped over themselves, the west-country burr got stronger, a deep blush suffused his cheeks. He was said to be one of the most promising of nuclear physicists.

"Can you explain it to a very ignorant layman?"

"I can give you some sort of notion. But I've only just started on this idea." He blushed again cheerfully. "I'm afraid to say too much about it just yet."

He began expounding his subject to Jago. Chrystal made an aside to Brown, and asked across the table if I was free next morning. Winslow heard the question, and turned his sardonic glance on to Chrystal.

"The college is becoming quite a hive of activity," he said.

"Term starts next week," said Chrystal. "I can't leave things till then."

"But surely," said Winslow, "the appearance of the young

gentlemen oughtn't to obstruct the really serious purposes of our society? Such as rolling a log in the right direction?"

"I'm sure," Brown intervened, quickly but blandly, "that the Dean would never roll a log across the table. We've learned from our seniors to choose a quieter place."

We were waiting for the savoury, and someone chuckled.

"By the way," Winslow looked down the table, "I noticed that a bottle of claret has been ordered in the combination room. May I enquire whom we are indebted to?"

"I'm afraid I'm responsible." Brown's voice was soothing. "I ought to have asked permission to present a bottle, but I rather anticipated that. And I ought to have asked whether people would have preferred port, but I found out from the kitchens who were dining, and I thought I knew everyone's taste. I believe you always prefer claret nowadays?" he said to Winslow.

"If you please. If you please." He asked, the caustic note just on the edge of his voice: "And what remarkable event do you wish to celebrate?"

"Why, the remarkable event I wish to celebrate," said Brown, "is the appearance of Mr. R. S. Winslow in the Trial Eights. I don't think anyone has got in before me. And I know we should all feel that when the Bursar has a son at the college, and the young man distinguishes himself, we want the pleasure of marking the occasion."

Winslow was taken right aback. He looked down at the table, and gave a curiously shy, diffident smile.

"I must say this is handsome of you, Brown," he said.

"It's a privilege," said Brown.

We returned to the combination room, and took our places for wine. The table could hold twenty, and we occupied only one end of it; but the room was intimate, the glasses sparkled in the warm light, the silver shone, the reflection of the decanter was clear as it passed over the polished table. Luke filled our glasses, and, since Winslow's health was to be drunk, it was the duty of Jago, as the next senior, to propose it. He did it with warmth, his face alight. He was full of grace and friendliness, Brown's steady cordialty had infected him, he was at ease within this group at the table as he never could be with Winslow alone. "The Bursar and his son," he said.

"Thank you, Senior Tutor, thank you all. Thank you." Winslow lifted his glass to Brown. As we drank Brown's health, I caught his dark, vigilant eye. He had tamed Winslow for the moment: he was showing Jago at his best, which he very much wanted to do: he had brought peace to the table. He was content, and sipped his claret with pleasure. He loved good fellowship. He loved the arts of management. He did not mind if no one else noticed his skill. He was a shrewd and far-sighted man.

He was used to being thought of as just a nice old buffer. 'Good old Brown', the Master called him. 'The worthy Brown', said Winslow, with caustic dismissal: 'uncle Arthur' was his nickname among the younger fellows. Yet he was actually the youngest of the powerful middle-aged block in the college. Jago was just over fifty; Chrystal, Brown's constant friend and ally, was forty-eight, while Brown himself, though he had been elected a fellow before Chrystal, was still not quite forty-six. He was a historian by subject, and was Jago's junior colleague as the second tutor.

Winslow was talking, with a veneer of indifference, about his son.

"He'll never get into the boat," he said. "He's thought to be lucky to have gone as far as this. It would be pleasant for his sake if they made another mistake in his favour. Poor boy, it's the only notoriety he's ever likely to have. He's rather a stupid child."

His tone was intended to stay caustic—it turned indulgent, sad, anxiously fond. Brown said:

"I'm not prepared to agree. One might say that he doesn't find examinations very congenial."

Winslow smiled.

"Mind you, Tutor," he said with asperity, "it's important for the child that he gets through his wretched tripos this June. He's thought to stand a chance of the colonial service if he can scrape a third. Of course, I'm totally ignorant of these matters, but I can't see why our colonies should need third class men with some capacity for organized sports. However, one can forgive the child for not taking that view. It's important for his sake that he shouldn't disgrace himself in June."

"I hope we'll get him through," said Brown. "I think we'll just about manage it."

"We'll get him through," said Jago.

"I'm sorry that my family should be such a preposterous nuisance," said Winslow.

The wine went round again. As he put down his glass, Winslow asked:

"Is there any news of the Master tonight?"

"There can't be any," said Chrystal.

Winslow raised his eyebrows.

"There can't be any," Chrystal repeated, "until he dies. It's no use. We've got to get used to it."

The words were so curt and harsh that we were silent. In a moment Chrystal spoke again:

"We've got to get used to him dying up there. That is the fact."

"And him thinking he will soon be well," Jago said. "I saw him this evening, and I tell you, I found it very hard to sit by."

Chrystal said:

"Yes. I've seen him myself."

"He's quite certain he'll soon be well," Jago said. "That is the most appalling thing."

"You would have told him?"

"Without the shadow of a doubt."

"I'm surprised that you're so convinced," said Winslow, ready to disagree.

"I am utterly convinced."

"I don't like to suggest it, but I'm inclined to think that Dr. Jago may be wrong." Winslow glanced round the table. "If I'd had to make Lady Muriel's decision, I think I might have done the same. I should have thought: this will mean for him a few days or weeks of happiness. It's the last happiness he'll get—he ought to have it if it's in my power. Do any of you share my view?" Winslow's eyes fell on Chrystal, who did not reply: then on Brown, who said:

"I haven't thought it out."

"No," said Jago. "You're presuming where no one has a right to presume." His tone was deep and simple, no trace of awkwardness left. "There are a few things no one should dare to decide for another man. There are not many serious things in a man's life—but one of them is how he shall meet his death. You can't be tactful about death: all you can do is leave a man alone."

We were all watching him.

"Winslow," Jago went on, "you and I do not often see things with the same eyes. Neither you nor I have been friendly with Royce through most of our lives. We know that, and this is not a good time to pretend. But there is one thing we should never have disagreed about. We had a respect for him. We should have admitted that he always faced the truth, even when it was grim. We should have said that he was the last man among us to be drugged by lies when he was coming near his death."

Winslow was staring at his empty glass. Chrystal broke the silence:

"You've said things I should like to have said myself."

Silence came to the table again. This time Brown spoke:

"How long will it be before they have to tell him?"

"Three or four months," I said. "It may be sooner. They say it's certain to be over in six months."

"I can't help thinking of his wife," said Brown, "when she has to break the news."

"I'm thinking of the Master," said Chrystal, "the day he hears."

The coffee was brought in. As Winslow lit a cigar, Brown took the chance of bringing them to earth.

"I suppose," he said, "that the position about the Master will have to be reported to the next college meeting?"

"I'm clear that it must," said Chrystal.

"We have one, of course," said Brown, "on the first Monday of full term. I feel that we're bound to discuss the Mastership. It's very painful and delicate, but the college has got to face the situation."

"We can't elect while the Master is alive. But the college will have to make up its mind in advance," said Chrystal.

Winslow's temper was not smoothed. He was irritated by Jago's effect on the party, he was irritated by the competence with which Chrystal and Brown were taking charge. He said deliberately:

"There's a good deal to be said for discussing the wretched business this term. We can bring it to a point in some directions." His eyes flickered at Jago, then he turned to Brown as though thinking aloud. "There are one or two obvious questions we ought to be able to decide. Are we going outside for a Master, or are we going to choose one of ourselves?" He paused, and said in his most courteous tone: "I think several of the society will agree that there are good reasons for going outside this time."

I caught sight of Luke leaning forward, his face aglow with excitement. He was a sanguine and discreet young man, he had scarcely spoken at the table that night, he was not going to intervene now of all times, when Winslow was deliberately, with satisfaction, undermining Jago's hopes. But I thought that little had escaped young Luke: as acutely as anyone there, he was feeling the antagonism that crackled through the comfort-laden room.

"I didn't mean," said Brown, roundly but with a trace of hurry, "that the college could go nearly as far as that at the present time. In fact I'm very dubious whether it would be proper for a college meeting to do more than hear the facts about the Master's condition. That gives us a chance to talk the matter over privately. I'm afraid I should deprecate doing more."

"I agree with Brown," said Chrystal. "I shall propose that we take steps accordingly."

"You believe in private enterprise, Dean?" Winslow asked.

"I think the Dean and I believe," said Brown, "that with a little private discussion, the college may be able to reach a very substantial measure of agreement."

"I must say that that is a beautiful prospect," said Winslow. He looked at Jago, who was sitting back in his chair, his lips set, his face furrowed and proud.

Winslow rose from the head of the table, picked up his cap, made off in his long loose stride towards the door. "Good night to you," he said.

FOUR

A PIECE OF SERIOUS BUSINESS

I called at Brown's rooms, as we had arranged with Chrystal, at eleven o'clock next morning. They were on the next staircase to mine, and not such a handsome set; but Brown, though he went out each night to his house in the West Road, had made them much more desirable to live in. That day he stood hands in pockets in front of the fire, warming his plump buttocks, his coat-tails hitched up over his arms. His bright peering eyes were gazing appreciatively over his deep sofas, his ample armchairs, his two half-hidden electric fires, out to the window and the snowy morning. Round the walls there was growing a set of English water colours, which he was collecting with taste, patience, and a kind of modest expertness. On the table a bottle of madeira was waiting for us.

"I hope you like this in the morning," he said. "Chrystal and I are rather given to it."

Chrystal followed soon after me, gave his crisp military good-morning, and began at once:

"Winslow gave a lamentable exhibition last night. He makes the place a perfect bear-garden.

It seemed to me a curious description of the combination room.

"He's not an easy man," said Brown. "And he doesn't seem to be mellowing."

"He won't mellow if he lives to be a hundred," said Chrystal. "Anyway, it's precisely because of him that we want to talk to you, Eliot."

We sat down to our glasses of madeira.

"Perhaps I'd better begin," said Brown. "By pure chance, the affair started in my direction. Put it another way—if I hadn't been tutor, we mightn't have got on to it at all."

"Yes, you begin," said Chrystal. "But Eliot ought to realise all this is within these four walls. Not a word must leak outside."

I said yes.

"First of all," Brown asked me, sitting back with his hands folded on his waistcoat, "do you happen to know my pupil Timberlake?"

I was puzzled.

"I've spoken to him once or twice," I said. "Isn't he a connection of Sir Horace's?"

"Yes."

"I know the old man slightly," I said. "I met him over a case, two or three years ago."

Brown chuckled.

"Good," he said. "I was almost sure I remembered you saying so. That may be very useful.

"Well," he went on, "he sent young Timberlake to the college—he's a son of Sir Horace's cousin, but his parents died and Sir Horace took responsibility for him. The boy is in his third year, taking Part II in June. I hope to God he gets through. It will shatter everything if he doesn't. He's a perfectly decent lad, but a bit dense. I think he's just a shade less stupid than young Winslow—but it's a very very near thing."

"It's not a near thing between their seniors," said Chrystal. "I'll trade Winslow for Sir Horace any day."

"I was very much taken with Sir Horace when I met him." Brown liked agreeing with his friend. "You see, Eliot, Sir Horace came up for a night just about three weeks ago. He seemed to be pleased with what we were doing for the boy. And he especially asked to meet one or two people who were concerned with the policy of the college. So I gave a little dinner party. The Master was ill, of course, which, to tell you the truth, for this particular occasion was a relief. I decided it was only prudent to leave out Winslow. I had to ask Jago, but I dropped him a hint that this wasn't the kind of business he's really interested in. Naturally, I asked the Dean." He gave Chrystal his broad, shrewd, good-natured smile. "I think the rest of the story's yours. I left everything else to you."

"Sir Horace came up," said Chrystal, "and Brown did him well. There were only the three of us. I should have enjoyed just meeting him. When you think what that man's done—he controls an industry with a turnover of £20,000,000 a year. It makes you think, Eliot, it makes you think. But there was more to it than meeting him. I won't make a secret of it. There's a chance of a benefaction."

"If it comes off," Brown said, cautiously but contentedly, "it will be one of the biggest the college has ever had."

"Sir Horace wanted to know what our plans for the future were. I told him as much as I could. He seemed pleased with us. I was struck with the questions he asked," said Chrystal, ready to make a hero of Sir Horace. "You could see that he was used to getting to the bottom of things. After he'd been into it for a couple of hours, I'd back his judgment of the college against half our fellows. When he'd learned what he came down to find out, he asked me a direct question. He asked straight out: 'What's the most useful help any of us could provide for the college?' There was only one answer to that—and when there's only one answer, I've found it a good rule to say it quick. So I told him: 'Money. As much money as you could give us. And with as few conditions as you could possibly make.' And that's where we stand."

"You handled him splendidly," said Brown. "He wasn't quite happy about no conditions——"

"He said he'd have to think about that," said Chrystal. "But I thought it would save trouble later if I got in first."

"I'm not ready to shout till we've got the money in the bank," Brown said, "but it's a wonderful chance."

"We ought to get it—unless we make fools of ourselves," said Chrystal. "I know that by rights Winslow should handle this business now. It's his job. But if he does, it's a pound to a penny that he'll put Sir Horace off."

I thought of Sir Horace, imaginative, thin-skinned despite all his success in action.

"He certainly would," I said. "Just one of Winslow's little jokes, and we'd have Sir H. endowing an Oxford college on a very lavish scale."

"I'm glad you confirm that," said Chrystal. "We can't afford to handle this wrong."

"We mustn't miss it," said Brown. "It would be sinful to miss it now."

These two were the solid core of the college, I thought. Year by year they added to their influence; it was greater now than when I first came three years before. It had surprised me then that they should be so influential; now that I had lived with them, seen them at work, I understood it better.

They were both genuinely humble men. They were profoundly different, at the roots of their natures, but neither thought that he was anything out of the ordinary. They knew that others round them were creative, as they were not; Chrystal had once been a competent classic, was still a first-rate teacher, but had done nothing original—Brown wrote an intricate account of the diplomatic origins of the Crimean war soon after he graduated, and then stopped. They did not even think that they were unusual as men. Either would say that the Master or Jago or one or two others were the striking figures in the college. All they might add was that those striking figures did not always have the soundest judgment, were not the most useful at 'running things'.

For, though they were the least conceited of men, they

had complete confidence in their capacity to 'run things'. Between them, they knew all the craft of government. They knew how men in a college behaved, and the different places in which each man was weak, ignorant, indifferent, obstinate or strong. They never overplayed their hand; they knew just how to take the opinion of the college after they had settled a question in private. They knew how to give way. By this time, little of importance happened in the college which they did not support.

They asked very little more for themselves. They were neither of them ambitious; they thought they had done pretty well. They were comfortable and happy. They accepted the world round them, they believed it was good the college should exist, they had no doubt they were being useful in the parts they played. As they piloted their candidate through a fellowship election, or worked to secure this benefaction from Sir Horace, they gained the thrill that men feel at a purpose outside themselves.

They were both 'sound' conservatives in politics, and in religion conforming and unenthusiastic churchmen. But in the college they formed the active, if sometimes invisible, part of a progressive government. (College politics often cut right across national ones: thus Winslow, an upper class radical, became in the college extremely reactionary, and Francis Getliffe and I, both men of the left, found ourselves in the college supporting the 'government'—the Master, Jago, Chrystal, Brown—with whom we disagreed on most things outside.) To that they devoted their attention, their will, their cunning, and their experience. They had been practising it for twenty years, and by now they knew what could be done inside the college to an inch.

I had never seen a pair of men more fitted for their chosen job. They were loyal to each other in public and in private. If they brought off a success for the college, they each had a habit of attributing it to the other. Actually most men thought that, of the two, Chrystal was the dominating spirit. He had a streak of fierceness, and the manifest virility which attracts respect—and at the same time resentment—from other men. He also possessed the knack of losing his temper at the right moment, which made him more effective in committee. He was urgent and impatient and quick to take offence. He gave an immediate impression of will, and many of the college used to say: 'Oh, Chrystal will bring Brown along with him.'

I did not believe it. Each was shrewd, but Brown had the deeper insight. I had seen enough of both to be sure that, in doubt or trouble, it was Chrystal who relied on the stubborn fortitude of his friend.

"How much is it likely to be?" I asked. They glanced at each other. They thought I knew something about men, but was altogether too unceremonious in the way I talked of money.

"Sir Horace hinted," said Chrystal, with a suspicion of hush in his voice, "at £100,000. I take it he could sign a cheque for that himself and not miss it."

"He must be a very hot man," said Brown, who was inclined to discuss wealth in terms of temperature.

"I wonder if he is?" I said. "He must be quite well off, of course. But he's an industrial executive, you know, not a financier. Isn't it the financiers who make the really big fortunes? People like Sir H. don't juggle with money and don't collect so much."

"You put him lower than I do," said Chrystal, somewhat damped. "You're under-rating him, Eliot."

"I'm not letting myself expect too much," said Brown. "But if Sir Horace decided to raise £50,000 for us, I dare say he could."

"I dare say he could," I said.

They had asked me to join them that morning in order to plan the next move. They had heard nothing from Sir Horace since his visit. What could we do? Could we reach him again? Were any of my London acquaintances any use?

I thought them over, and shook my head.

"Is it a good idea anyway to approach him from the outside?" I asked. "I should have thought that it was very risky."

"I've felt that all along," said Brown.

"You may be right," said Chrystal sharply, irritated but ready to think again. "What do we do? Do we just wait?"

"We've got to rely on ourselves," said Brown.

"What does that mean?" said Chrystal.

"We've got to get him down again," said Brown. "And let him see us as we really are. Put it another way—we must make him feel that he's inside the picture. I don't say we wouldn't make things decent for the occasion. But we ought to let him realise the difficulty about Winslow. The more we take him into our confidence, within reason, the more likely he is to turn up trumps."

I helped him persuade Chrystal. Chrystal was brusque, he liked his own ideas to prevail, he liked to have thought of a plan first; but I noticed the underlying sense which brought him round. He could have been a moody man; his temper was never equable; but he wanted results so much that he had been forced to control his moods.

They agreed to try to attract Sir Horace to the feast in February. Brown was as realistic as usual. "I don't suppose for a moment that anything we can do will make a pennyworth of difference, once he's made up his mind. But it can't do any harm. If he's forgetting us, it might turn out useful to remind him that we're glad to see him here."

He filled our glasses again. Chrystal gave a satisfied sigh. He said:

"Well, we can't do any more this morning. We've not wasted our time. I told you, Eliot, I regard this as more important than the Mastership. Masters come and Masters go, and whoever we elect, everyone will have forgotten about it in fifty years. Whereas a benefaction like this will affect the college for ever. Do you realise that the sum I've got in my mind is over ten per cent of our capital endowment?"

"It would be a pity to miss it," said Brown.

"I wish we hadn't got this mastership hanging over us," said Chrystal. "One thing is quite clear. There's no reason to go outside. That's just a piece of Winslow's spite. We can find a Master inside the college easily enough. Jago would do. I was impressed with the way he spoke last night. He's got some of the qualities I want in a Master."

"I agree," said Brown.

"Other names will have to be considered, of course. I expect some people will want Crawford. I don't know about him."

"I agree," said Brown. "I'm not keen on him. I don't know whether Eliot is——"

"No," I said.

"He'll certainly be run. I don't know whether anyone will mention Winslow. You haven't seen a Master elected, have you, Eliot? You'll find some people are mad enough for anything. I'm depressed," said Chrystal, "at the whole prospect."

Soon afterwards he left us. Brown gave a sympathetic smile. "He's upset about poor Royce," he said.

"Yes, I thought that."

"You're very observant, aren't you?"

Brown added:

"I think Chrystal will get more interested when things are warming up a bit. I think he will." He smiled again. "You know, I don't see how this can possibly be an easy election. Chrystal says that there may be support for Crawford, and I suppose there's bound to be. But I should regard him as a disaster. He wouldn't lift a finger for any of us. I don't know what you feel, but I shall be inclined to stick in my heels about him."

"He wouldn't do it well," I said.

"I'm glad we're thinking alike. I wonder whether you've come down definitely for any one yet?"

His eyes were fixed on me, and I hesitated. Easily he went on:

"I should value it if you would keep me in touch, when you do know where you're coming down. My present feeling, for what it's worth, is that we ought to think seriously about Jago. I know people criticise him; I'm quite prepared to admit that he's not ideal; but my feeling is that we can't go far wrong with him."

"Yes."

"Do you agree, really?"

"Yes."

"Might you consider supporting him?"

"I'm not sure, but I think I shall."

His glance had stayed on me. Now he looked away, and said:

"I very much wanted to know how you would respond to his name. I'm not committed to him myself, of course. I've been held up a little by a personal matter which you'll probably think a trifle far-fetched."

"Whatever's that?"

"Well," said Brown, "if Jago were to be elected Master, the college would need a new Senior Tutor. And it seems to me possible that some people would want me to follow him in the job."

"It's a complete and utter certainty," I said. That was the truth.

"It's nice of you to say so, but I don't believe it's as certain as that. There are plenty who don't think much of me." Brown chuckled. "But I can't pretend it's not a possibility. Well then, you see the problem. Am I justified in trying to get Jago in as Master, when I may provide myself with a better job out of it?"

"There's no doubt of the answer——"

"Yes," said Brown, "I've arrived there myself, after thinking it over. If one always stopped supporting people whose election could bring one the slightest advantage, it would be remarkably silly. Put it another way—only a crank could really be stopped by such scruples." He burst into his whole-hearted, fat man's laughter.

"So I'm quite easy in my conscience about supporting Jago," he finished up. "But I'm still not ready to commit myself. He'd be a good Master, in my judgment. I'd put it a bit stronger, and say that he's the best Master in view. We don't want to run him, though, unless he's got plenty of support. It would do no good to anyone."

"Well," he said, with a smile good-natured, cunning and wise, "that's what I've been thinking. That's as far as I've got."

FIVE

SUCCESS AND ENVY

Jago came to see me that afternoon. He made no reference to our first talk, or to the conversation about the Mastership the night before; but he had manufactured an excuse to call on me. He had thought up some questions about my law pupils; neither he nor I was interested in the answers.

He had been driven to see me—so that, if I had anything to say, he would know at once. His delicacy revolted, but he could not prevent himself from spinning out the visit. Was I going to Ireland again? He talked, with unaccustomed flatness, about his native town of Dublin. Not that he showed the vestigial trace of an Irish accent. He was born in the Ascendancy, his stock was as English as any of ours; he had—surprisingly, until one knew his origin—the militant conservatism of the Anglo-Irish. His father had been a fellow of Trinity, Dublin, and Jago was the only one of the present college who had been born into the academic life.

He went on talking, still tied to my room, unable to recognise that I could say nothing that day. I thought that no one else in his position would have kept his dignity so well: whatever his excesses, that remained. Before he went away, he had to ask:

"Did I hear that you and Chrystal and Brown were colloguing this morning?"

"Yes. It was just a financial matter. They wanted a legal opinion."

He smiled off his disappointment.

"You three work much too hard," he said.

The college was slowly filling up. I heard that Nightingale and Pilbrow were back from vacation, though I had not yet seen them. And the next evening, a few minutes before hall, I heard a familiar step on my staircase, and Roy Calvert came in.

He had been working for three months in Berlin. With relief I saw that he was looking well, composed and gay. He was the most gifted man the college had produced for years; as the Master said, he had already won an international reputation as an Orientalist. Yet he was sometimes a responsibility. He was the victim of attacks of melancholy so intense that no one could answer for his actions, and there had been times when he could scarcely bear the thought of living on.

That night, though, I knew at a glance that he was rested. He was more as I first knew him, cheerful, lively, disrespectful and kind. He was my closest friend in Cambridge, and the closest I ever had. Thinking of the life he had led, the work he had got through, one found it hard to remember that he was not yet twenty-seven; yet in a gay mood, his eyes sparkling with malicious fun, he still looked very young.

We arrived a little late in the combination room, just in time to see Gay, with slow, shuffling steps, leading the file into hall. He was wearing an overcoat under his gown, so as to meet the draughty hall, and under the long coat there was something tortoise-like about his feet; but, when one looked at his face, there was nothing pathetic about him. His cheeks were red, his beard white, trimmed and sailor-like, his white hair silky and abundant; he carried his handsome head with arrogance and panache. He was nearly eighty, and the oldest fellow.

As he sat at the head of the table, tucking with good appetite into his food, Brown was trying to explain to him the news about the Master. Gay had not heard, or had forgotten: his memory was beginning to flicker and fade, he forgot quickly about the weeks and months just past. Brown was having some trouble in making it clear which Master he meant; Gay seemed to be thinking about the last Master but one.

"Ah. Indeed," said Gay. "Very sad. But I have some recollection that he had to live on one floor some little time ago."

"That wasn't the present Master," said Brown patiently. "I mean Royce."

"Indeed. Royce. You didn't make that clear," Gay reproved him. "He's surely a very young man. We only elected him recently. So he's going, is he? Ah well, it will be a sad break with the past."

He showed the triumph of the very old, when they hear of the death of a younger man. He felt half his age. Suddenly he noticed Roy Calvert, and his memory cleared.

"Ah. Do I see Calvert? Haven't you been deserting us?"

"I got back to England this morning."

"Let me see. Let me see. Haven't you been in Germany?"

"Yes," said Roy Calvert.

"I hadn't forgotten you," said Gay victoriously. "And where in Germany, may I ask?"

"Berlin."

"Ah. Berlin. A fine city. A fine university. I was once given an honorary degree of the university of Berlin. I remember it to this day. I remember being met at the Zoo station by one of their scholars—fine scholars they have in that country—and his first words were: 'Professor M. H. L. Gay, I think? The great authority on the sagas.' Ah. What do you think of that, Calvert? What do you think of that, Brown? The great authority on the sagas. They were absolutely the first words I heard when I arrived at the station. I had to demur to the word 'great' of course." He gave a hearty laugh. "I said: 'You can call me the authority on the sagas, if you like. The authority, without the great.' "

Brown and Chrystal chuckled. On Chrystal's left, Nightingale looked polite but strained. Roy Calvert's eyes shone: solemn and self-important persons were usually fair game to him, but Gay was too old. And his gusto was hard to resist.

"That reminds me," Gay went on, "about honorary degrees. Do you know that I've now absolutely collected fourteen of them? What do you think of that, Calvert? What do you think of that, Chrystal?"

"I call it pretty good," said Chrystal, smiling but impressed.

"Fourteen honorary degrees. Not bad, eh? From every civilised country except France. The French have never been willing to recognise merit outside their own country. Still, fourteen isn't so bad. And there's still time for one or two more."

"I should think there is," said Chrystal. "I should think there is. And I shall want to present a bottle in honour of every one of them, Gay."

Gay said the final grace in a ringing voice, and led us slowly back to the room. On the table, a bottle of port was ready for him; though the rest of us preferred claret, it was a rule that the college should drink port on any night when he came in to dine. As Chrystal helped him off with his overcoat, Gay's eye glittered at the sight of walnuts in a silver dish.

"Ah. Nuts and wine," he said. "Splendid. Nuts and wine. Is the Steward here? Congratulate him for me."

He rolled the port on his tongue and cracked nut after nut. His teeth were as sound as in youth, and he concentrated vigourously on his pleasure. Then he wiped his lips and said:

"That reminds me. Are any of us publishing a book this year?"

"I may be," said Roy. "If they can finish cutting the type for——"

"I congratulate you," said Gay. "I congratulate you. I

have a little work of my own coming out in the summer. I should not absolutely rank it among my major productions, but I'm quite pleased with it as a tour de force. I shall be interested to see the reception it obtains. I sometimes think one doesn't receive such a fair hearing when one is getting on in years."

"I shouldn't have thought you need worry," said Brown.

"I like to insist on a fair hearing," Gay said. "I'm not vain, I don't mind what they say against me, but I like to be absolutely assured that they're being fair. That's all I've asked for all along, ever since my first book.

"Ah. My first book." He looked down the table. His eyes had been a bright china blue, but were fading now. "That was a great occasion, to be sure. When the Press told me the book was out, I went round to the bookshops to see for myself. Then I walked out to Grantchester to visit my brother-in-law Dr. Ernest Fazackerley—my wife was his youngest sister, you know. And when I told him the great news, do you know that cat of his—ah, that was a cat and a half—he put up his two paws, and I could imagine for all the world that he was applauding me."

In a few minutes the butler brought a message that the Professor's taxi was waiting at the porter's lodge. This was part of the ritual each Thursday and Sunday night, for on those nights, in any weather, he left his house in the Madingley Road, and was driven down to the college for dinner. There was more of the ritual to come: Chrystal helped him into his overcoat again, he replaced his gown on top of it, and said goodnight to each of us one by one. Goodnights kept coming back to us in his sonorous voice, as he shuffled out of the room, with Roy Calvert to help him over the frozen snow.

"Those old chaps were different from us," said Chrystal, after they had gone. "We shan't do as much as that generation did."

"I'm not quite convinced that they were so wonderful,"

said Nightingale. There was a curious carefulness about his manner, as though he were concealing some pain in order not to embarrass the party. About his face also there was a set expression: he seemed to be discipling himself to behave well. His lips were not often relaxed, and lines of strain etched the fine skin. He had a mane of fair wavy hair, brushed across his brow. His face was drawn, but not weak, and when he was pleased there was charm in his looks.

"No one has ever explained to me," said Nightingale, "what there is original about Gay's work."

"I'll take you up on that, Nightingale," Chrystal said. "He's better known outside the college than anyone we've got. It will be time enough for us to talk when we've done as much."

"I agree," said Brown.

"If anyone sat down to his sagas for four hours a day for sixty years, I should have thought they were bound to get somewhere," said Nightingale.

"I wish I could feel sure there is one man among us," Chrystal retorted, "who'll have as much to his credit—if he lives to be Gay's age."

"From what the German professors have written," Brown put in, "I don't think there's any reasonable doubt that Calvert will make as big a name before he's done."

Nightingale looked more strained. "These gentlemen are lucky in their subjects," he said. "It must be very nice not to need an original idea."

"You don't know anything about their subjects," said Chrystal. He said it sharply but amicably enough, for he had a hidden liking for Nightingale. Another thought was, however, troubling him. "I don't like to hear old Gay criticised. I've got as great a respect for him as anyone in the college. But it is lamentable to think that we shall soon have to elect a Master, and the old chap will have his vote. How can you expect a college to do its business, when you've got people who have lost their memories but are only too willing to take a hand?"

"I've always thought they should be disfranchised," said Nightingale.

"No," said Brown. "If we cut them off at sixty-five or seventy, and didn't let them vote after that, we should lose more than we gained."

"What do you mean?"

"I think I mean this: a college is a society of men, and we have to take the rough with the smooth."

"If you try to make it too efficient," I said, "you'll suddenly find that you haven't a college at all."

"I thought you were a man of advanced opinions," said Nightingale.

"Sometimes I am," I said.

"I don't know where I come down," said Chrystal. He was torn, torn as he often was, torn as he would have hated anyone to perceive. His passion to domineer, his taste for clean efficiency, all his impulses as a party boss with the college to run, made him want to sweep the old men ruthlessly away—take away their votes, there would be so much less dead wood, they impeded all he wanted to do. Yet there was the other side, the soft romantic heart which felt Gay as larger than life-size, which was full of pious regard for the old, which shrank from reminding them that they were spent. "But I don't mind telling you that there are times when I consider the college isn't a fit body to be entrusted with its money. Do you really mean to tell me that the college is fit to handle a capital endowment of a million pounds?"

"I'll give you an answer," said Brown cheerfully, "when I see how we manage about electing a Master."

"Is anything being done about that?" Nightingale asked.

"Nothing can be done yet, of course," said Brown. "I suppose people are beginning to mention names. I've heard one or two already." As he talked blandly on, he was watching Nightingale. He was usually an opponent, he was likely to be so now, and Brown was feeling his way. "I think that Winslow may rather fancy the idea of Crawford. I wonder how you'd regard him?"

There was a pause.

"I'm not specially enthusiastic," said Nightingale.

"I'm interested to hear you say that," said Brown. His eyes were bright. "I thought it would be natural if you went for someone like Crawford on the scientific side."

Suddenly Nightingale's careful manner broke.

"I might if it weren't Crawford," he said. His voice was bitter: "There's not been a day pass in the last three years when he hasn't reminded me that he is a Fellow of the Royal, and that I am not."

"That's ridiculous," said Brown consolingly. "He's got a good many years' start, hasn't he?"

"He reminds me that I've been up for election six times, and this year is my seventh."

Nightingale's voice was harsh with envy, with sheer pain. Chrystal left all the talk to Brown.

"Well, I might as well say that at present I don't feel much like going for Crawford myself," said Brown. "I'm beginning to doubt whether he's really the right man. I haven't thought much about it so far, but I have heard one or two people speak strongly for someone else. How do you regard the idea of Jago?"

"Jago. I've got nothing against him," said Nightingale.

"People will feel there are certain objections," Brown reflected.

"Some people will object to anyone."

Brown smiled.

"They'll say that Jago isn't so distinguished academically as—for instance, Crawford. And that's a valid point. The only consideration is just how much weight you give to it. Put it another way—we're unlikely to get everything we want in one man. Do you prefer Jago, who's respectable on the academic side but not a flyer—but who seems admirably equipped in every other way? Or do you prefer Crawford, who's got other limitations that you've made me realise very clearly? Wouldn't those limitations be unfortunate in a Master?"

"I'm ready to support Jago," said Nightingale.

"I should sleep on it if I were you," said Brown. "But I value your opinion——"

"So do I," said Chrystal. "It'll help me form my own."

He and Brown went off together, and Nightingale and I were left alone.

"Come up to my rooms," said Nightingale.

I was surprised. He was the one man in the college whom I actively disliked, and he disliked me at least as strongly. There was no reason for it; we had not one value or thought in common, but that was true with others whom I warmly liked; this was just an antipathy as specific as love. Anywhere but in the college we should have avoided each other. As it was, we met most nights at dinner, talked across the table, even spent, by force of social custom, a little time together. It was one of the odd features of a college, I sometimes thought, that one lived in social intimacy with men one disliked: and, more than that, there were times when a fraction of one's future lay in their hands. For these societies were always making elections from their own members, they filled all their jobs from among themselves, and in those elections one's enemies took part—for example, Jago disliked Winslow far more intensely that I Nightingale, and at that moment he knew that, until the election was over, he was partially in Winslow's power.

We climbed a staircase in the third court to Nightingale's rooms. He was a teetotaller, the only one in the college, and he had no drink to offer, but he gave me a cigarette. He asked a few uninterested questions about my holidays. But though he tried, he could not keep to his polite behaviour. Suddenly he broke out:

"What are Chrystal and Brown up to about the Mastership?"

"I thought Brown had been telling us—at some length."

"I know all about that. What I want to hear is, has one of those two got his eye on it for himself?"

"I shouldn't think so for a minute," I said.

"We're not going to be rushed into that, are we?" he asked. "I wouldn't put it past them to try."

"Nonsense," I said. He was irritating me. "They made it clear enough—they'll run Jago."

"I'll believe that when I see it. I've never noticed them exert themselves much for anyone else. I've not forgotten how they squeezed Brown into the tutorship. I was two or three years junior, but there's no doubt I had the better claim."

Suddenly he snapped out the question:

"What are you going to do?"

I did not reply at once.

"Are you going to propose Chrystal as a bright idea at the last moment?"

He was intensely suspicious, certain that there was a web of plans from which he would lose and others gain. If I had told him I too was thinking of Jago, he would have seen meanings behind that choice, and it might have turned him from Jago himself. As it was, Jago's seemed the one name that did not arouse his suspicion and envy that night.

I looked round his sitting-room. It was without feature, it was the room of a man concentrated into himself, so that he had nothing to spend outside; it showed nothing of the rich, solid comfort which Brown had given to his, or the eccentric picturesqueness of Roy Calvert's. Nightingale was a man drawn into himself. Suspicion and envy lived in him. They always would have done, however life had treated him; they were part of his nature. But he had been unlucky, he had been frustrated in his most cherished hope, and now envy never left him alone.

He was forty-three, and a bachelor. Why he had not married, I did not know: there was nothing unmasculine about him. That was not, however, his abiding disappointment. He had once possessed great promise. He had known what it was to hold creative dreams: and they had not come off. That was his bitterness. As a very young man he had shown a spark of real talent. He was one of the earliest theoretical chemists. By twenty-three he had written two good papers on molecular structure. He had, so I was told, anticipated Heitler-London and the orbital theory; he was ten years ahead of his time. The college had elected him, everything seemed easy. But the spark burnt out. The years passed. Often he had new conceptions; but the power to execute them had escaped from him.

It would have been bitter to the most generous heart. In Nightingale's, it made him fester with envy. He longed in compensation for every job within reach, in reason and out of reason. It was morbid that he should have fancied his chances of the tutorship before Brown, his senior and a man made for the job; but it rankled in him after a dozen years. Each job in the college for which he was passed over, he saw with intense suspicion as a sign of the conspiracy directed against him.

His reputation in his subject was already gone. He would not get into the Royal Society now. But, as March came round each year, he waited for the announcement of the Royal elections in expectation, in anguish, in bitter suspiciousness, at moments in the knowledge of what he might have been.

SIX

STREETS IN THE THAW

It began to thaw that night, and by morning the walls of my bedroom carried dank streaks like the tracks of a snail. Lying in bed, I could hear the patter of drops against the window ledge. "Dirty old day underfoot, sir," Bidwell greeted me. "Mr. Calvert sends his compliments, and says he'd send his goloshes too, if he could persuade you to wear them."

I had scarcely seen Roy Calvert alone since he returned; he called in for a few minutes after breakfast on his way to pay visits round the town. "They'd better know I am alive." He grinned. "Or else Jago will be sending out a letter." It was one of Jago's customs to 'send out a letter' whenever a member of the college died; it was part of the intimate formality which, to Roy Calvert, was comic without end. He went out through the slush to pay his visits; he had a great range of acquaintances in Cambridge, and he arranged to visit them in an order shaped partly by kindness, partly by caprice. The unhappy, the dim, the old and passed over, even those whom anyone else found tedious and ordinary, could count on his company; while the important, the weighty, the established—sometimes, I thought in irritation, anyone who could be the slightest use to him—had to wait their turn.

Before he went out, he arranged for us both to have tea in the Lodge, where he was a favourite. He would go himself earlier in the afternoon, to talk to the Master. So at tea-time I went over alone, and waited in the empty drawing-room. The afternoon was leaden, the snow still lay on the court, with a few pockmarks at the edges; the fire deep in the room behind me was reflected in the heavy twilight. Roy Calvert joined me there.

It had been worse than he imagined, and he was subdued. The Master had been talking happily of how they would collaborate—the 'little book on the heresies'. This was a project of the Master's which Roy had been trying to avoid for years. Now he said that he would do it as a memorial.

When Lady Muriel came in, she began with her inflexible greetings, as though nothing were wrong in the house. But Roy took her hand, and his first words were:

"I've been talking to the Master, you know. It's dreadful to have to pretend, isn't it? I wish you could have been spared that decision, Lady Mu. No one could have known what to do."

She was taken aback, and yet relieved so that the tears came. No one else would have spoken to her as though she were a woman who wanted someone to guide her. I wished that I had been as straightforward.

She was already crying, she said that it was not easy.

"No one could help you," said Roy. "And you'd have liked help, wouldn't you? Everyone would."

He took care of her until Joan joined us, and then they began to argue about the regime in Germany. "Just so," said Roy, to each of Joan's positive statements. Both women knew that he had no liking for disputation; both laughed at the precise affirmative, which had once been affected but now was second nature.

Joan's tenderness for Roy was already near to open love, and her mother indulged him like a son. She must have known something of his reputation, the 'vineleaves in his hair' (as the Master once quoted), the women who pursued him. But she never said to Joan, as she had said about any other man whom her daughter brought to the Lodge, 'My dear Joan, I can't imagine what you can possibly *see* in him.'

I talked about Joan as we walked out of the Lodge into the dark, rainy night.

"That girl," I said, "is falling more in love with you."

He frowned. Like many of those who attract passionate love, there were times when he wanted to forget it altogether. And that night, despite his sadness over the Master, he felt innocent and free of the shadows.

"Come and help me do some shopping," he said. "I need to buy some presents at once."

We walked along Sidney Street in the steady rain. Water was swirling, chuckling, gurgling in the gutters; except by the walls, the pavements were clear of snow by now, and they mirrored the lights from the lamps and shop-fronts on both sides of the narrow street.

"We shall get much wetter." He smiled. "You always looked remarkable in the rain. I need to get these presents off tonight."

We went from shop to shop, up Sidney Street, down John's Street, Trinity Street, into the market place. He wanted the presents for his disreputable, unlucky Berlin acquaintances who lived above his flat in the Knesebeckstrasse, and he took great care about choosing them.

"That might do for the little dancer." I had heard of 'the little dancer', by the same title before. "She weighs 35 kilos," Roy commented. "Light. Considerably lighter than Arthur Brown."

In one shop, he suddenly asked, quietly, with complete intimacy, about Sheila, my wife. He knew the whole story of my marriage, and what I had to expect when I went each Tuesday to the Chelsea house. I was glad to talk. In the street, he looked at me with a smile full of affectionate sharp-edged pity. "Yet you go on among those comfortable blokes—as though nothing was the matter," he said. "I wish I could bear as much."

Without speaking, we walked past Great St. Mary's into

the market place. He could say no more, and, with the same intimacy, asked:

"About those comfortable blokes, old boy. Who are we going to have for Master?"

We were loaded with parcels, our coats were heavy with the damp, rain dripped from our faces.

"I think I want Jago," I said.

"I suppose there's a move for Crawford."

"I'm against that," I said.

"Crawford is too—stuffed," said Roy Calvert. "He'll just assume the job is due to him by right. He's complacent. I'd never vote for a man who was complacent."

I agreed.

"You know," he said, "old Winslow is the most unusual man among that lot. He bites their heads off, he's a bit of a bully, he's frightfully ill-adjusted. But no one on earth could call him tug. They wouldn't have him at any price."

"No one on earth could call Jago tug," I said. "He's the least commonplace of men."

"There are plenty of things in favour of Jago," said Roy. "But they're not the things we're going to hear."

"He stands a fair chance," I said.

"He's not a commonplace man, is he?" said Roy. "Won't he be kept out because of that? They'll never really think he's 'sound'."

"Arthur Brown is for him."

"Uncle Arthur loves odd fish."

"And Chrystal," I said, "thinks he can manage him. By the way, I'm very doubtful whether he's right."

"It will be extremely funny if he isn't."

We turned down into Petty Cury, and Roy said:

"The ones who don't want Jago won't take it quietly. They'll have a good deal to say about distinguished scholars —and others not so distinguished."

"I know more about that than they do," he added. I smiled at the touch of arrogance, unusual in him. I saw his face, clear in the light from a shop. He shook his head to get rid of some raindrops, he smiled back, but he was in dead earnest. He went on quietly: "Why won't they see what matters? I want a man who knows something about himself. And is appalled. And has to forgive himself to get along."

SEVEN

DECISION TO CALL ON JAGO

Roy Calvert and I kept coming back to the Mastership, as we talked late into the night. Before we went to bed, we agreed to tell Brown next day that we were ready to support Jago. "Sleep on it, sleep on it," said Roy, mimicking Brown's comfortable tones. The next morning Bidwell, after announcing the time and commenting on the weather, said: "Mr. Calvert's compliments, sir, and he says he's slept on it and hasn't changed his mind."

At five that afternoon, we found Brown in his rooms. His tea was pushed aside, he was working on some lists: but, continuously busy, he was always able to seem at leisure. "It's a bit early for sherry," he said. "I wonder if you feel like a glass of chablis? I opened it at lunch-time, and we thought it was rather special."

He brought out some glasses, and we sat in his armchairs, Brown in the middle. His eyes looked from one of us to the other. He knew we had come for a purpose, but he was prepared to sit there all evening, drinking his wine with enjoyment, and leave the first move to us.

"You asked me," I said, "to let you know, when I'd decided about the next Master."

"Why, so I did," said Brown.

"I have now," I said. "I shall vote for Jago."

"I shall also," said Roy Calvert.

"I'm very glad to hear it," Brown said. He smiled at me: "I had a feeling you might come round to it. And Roy——"

"It's all in order," said Roy, "I've slept on it."

"That's just as well," said Brown. "Because if not I should certainly have advised you to do so."

I chuckled. In his unhurried, ponderous fashion he was very good at coping with Roy Calvert.

"Well," said Brown, sitting back contentedly, "this is all very interesting. As a matter of fact, I can tell you something myself. Chrystal and I had a little talk recently, and we felt inclined to put Jago's name forward."

"Without committing yourselves, of course?" Roy enquired.

"Committing ourselves as much as it's reasonable to do at this stage," said Brown.

"There's one other thing I think I'm at liberty to tell you," he added. "Nightingale told me definitely this morning that he was of the same way of thinking. So at any rate we've got the nucleus of a nice little party."

How capably he had managed it, I thought. He had not pressed Jago on any one of us. Chrystal had been undecided, but patiently Brown drew him in. With Chrystal, with me, with Nightingale, he had waited, talking placidly and sensibly, often rotundly and platitudinously, while our likes and dislikes shaped themselves. Only when it was needed had he thrown in a remark to stir one of our weaknesses, or warm our affection. He had given no sign of his own unshakeable resolve to get the Mastership for Jago. He had shown no enthusiasm, he had talked with his usual fair-mindedness. But the resolve had been taken, his mind had been made up, the instant he heard that the Master was dying.

Why was he so resolved? Partly through policy and calculation, partly through active dislike of Crawford, partly through a completely uncalculating surrender to affection; and, as in all personal politics, the motives mixed with one another.

Most of all, Brown was moved by a regard for Jago, affectionate, indulgent and admiring; and Brown's affections were warm and strong. He was a politician by nature; since he was set on supporting Jago he could not help but do it with all the craft he knew—but there was nothing politic about his feeling for the man. Jago might indulge his emotions, act with a fervour that Brown thought excessive and in bad taste, 'let his heart run away with his head', show nothing like the solid rational decorum which was Brown's face to the world. Brown's affection did not budge. In the depth of his heart he loved Jago's wilder outbursts, and wished that he could have gone that way himself. Had he sacrificed too much in reaching his own robust harmony? Had he become too dull a dog? For Brown's harmony had not arrived in a minute. People saw that fat contented man, rested on his steady strength, and thought he had never known their conflicts. They were blind. He was utterly tolerant, just because he had know the frets that drove men off the rails, in particular the frets of sensual love. It was in his nature to live them down, to imbed them deep, not to let them lead him away from his future as a college worthy, from his amiable wife and son. But he was too realistic, too humble, too genuine a man ever to forget them. 'Uncle Arthur loves odd fish', said Roy Calvert, whom he had helped through more than one folly. In middle age 'Uncle Arthur' was four square in himself, without a crack or flaw, rooted in his solid, warm, wise and cautious nature. But he loved odd fish, for he knew, better than anyone, the odd desires that he had left behind.

"We've got the nucleus of a nice little party," said Brown. "I think the time may almost have come to ask Jago whether he'll give us permission to canvas his name."

"You don't think that's premature?" said Roy, anxiously solemn.

"He may find certain difficulties," said Brown, refusing to be put out of his stride. "He may not be able to afford it. Put it another way—he'd certainly drop a bit over the exchange. With his university lectureship and his college teaching work, as Senior Tutor he must make all of £1800 a year, and the house rent free. As Master he'll have to give up most of the other things, and the stipend of the Master is only £1500. I've always thought it was disgracefully low, it's scarcely decent. Of course, he gets the Lodge free, but the upkeep will run him into a lot more than the Tutor's house. I really don't know how he's going to manage it."

I was smiling: with Roy present, I found it harder to take part in these stately minuets. "Somehow I think he'll find a way," I said. "Look, Brown, you know perfectly well that he's chafing to be asked."

"I think we might be able to presuade him," Brown said. "But we mustn't be in too much of a hurry. You don't get round difficulties by ignoring them. Still, I think we've got far enough to approach Jago now."

"The first step, of course," he added, "is to get Chrystal. He may think we're anticipating things a bit."

He telephoned to Chrystal, who was at home but left at once for the college. When he arrived, he was short-tempered because we had talked so much without him. He was counter-suggestible, moved to say no instead of yes, anxious to find reasons why we should not go at once to Jago. Brown used his automatic tact; and, as usual, Chrystal was forming sensible decisions underneath his short pique-ridden temper (he had the kind of pique which one calls 'childish'—though in fact it is shown most clearly by grave and adult men). Suddenly he said:

"I'm in favour of seeing Jago at once."

"Shall I fix a time tomorrow?" said Brown.

"I'm against waiting. There's bound to be talk, I want to get our feet in first. I'm in favour of going tonight."

"He may be busy."

"He won't be too busy for what we're coming to say," said Chrystal, with a tough, pleasant, ironic smile.

"I'll ring up and see how he's placed," said Brown. "But we mustn't forget Nightingale. It would be nice to take him round as well." He rang up at once, on the internal exchange through the porter's lodge: there was no answer. He asked for a porter to go to Nightingale's rooms: the report came that his rooms were shut.

"This is awkward," said Brown.

"We'll go without him," said Chrystal impatiently.

"I don't like it much." Brown had a slight frown. "It would be nice to bring everyone in. It's important for everyone to feel they're in the picture. I attach some value to taking Nightingale round."

"I'll explain it to Nightingale. I want to get started before the other side."

Reluctantly, Brown rang up the Tutor's house. He was sure it was an error of judgment not to wait for Nightingale—whom he wanted to bind to the party. On the other hand, he had had trouble bringing Chrystal 'up to the boil'. He did not choose to risk putting him off now. He rang up, his voice orotund, confidential, cordial; from his replies, one could guess that Jago was welcoming us round without a second's delay.

"Yes, he'd like to see us now," said Brown, as he hung the receiver up.

"I can't say I'm surprised," said Chrystal, rising to go out.

"Wait just a minute," said Brown. "The least I can do is send a note to Nightingale, explaining that we tried to find him."

He sat down to write.

"It might help if I took the note round to Nightingale," said Roy Calvert. "I'll drop the word that I'm going to vote for Jago, but haven't gone round on the deputation."

"That's very thoughtful of you," said Brown.

"Not a bit of it," said Roy. "I very much doubt whether the next but one junior fellow ought to be included in such a deputation as this."

Chrystal did not know whether he was being serious or not.

"I don't know about that, Calvert, I don't know about that," he said. "Still, we can tell Jago you're one of us, can we?"

"Just so," said Roy. "Just so."

The Tutor's house lay on the other side of the college. and Brown, Chrystal and I began walking through the courts. Chrystal made a remark about Roy Calvert:

"Sometimes I don't know where I am with that young man."

"He'll be a very useful acquisition to our side," said Brown.

EIGHT

THREE KINDS OF POWER

In Jago's house we were shown, not into his study, but into the drawing-room. There Mrs. Jago received us, with an air of *grande dame* borrowed from Lady Muriel.

"Do sit down, Dean," she said to Chrystal. "Do sit down, Tutor," she said to Brown. "A parent has just chosen this time to call on my husband, which I feel is very inconsiderate."

But Mrs. Jago's imitation of Lady Muriel was not exact. Lady Muriel, stiff as she was, would never have called men by their college titles. Lady Muriel would never have picked on the youngest there and said:

"Mr. Eliot, please help me with the sherry. You know it's your duty, and you ought to like doing your duty."

For Mrs. Jago wanted to be a great lady, wanted also the attention of men, and was never certain of herself for an instant. She was a big, broad-shouldered woman, running to fat, physically graceless apart from her smile. It was a smile one seldom saw, but when it came it was brilliant, open, defenceless, like an adoring girl's. Otherwise she was plain.

That night, she could not keep up her grand manner. Suddenly she broke out:

"I'm afraid you will all have to put up with my presence till Paul struggles free."

"That's very nice for us all," said Arthur Brown.

"Thank you, Tutor," said Mrs. Jago, back for a second on her pedestal again.

She had embarrassed Jago's friends ever since he married

her. She became assertive in any conversation. She was determined not to be overlooked. She seized on insults, tracked them down, recounted them with a masochistic gusto that never flagged. She had cost her husband great suffering.

She had cost him great suffering, but not in the way one might expect. He was a man who gained much admiration from women. With his quick sympathy, his emotional power, he could have commanded all kinds of love. He liked the compliment, but he wanted none of them. He had loved his wife for twenty-five years. They had had no children. He loved her still. He could still be jealous of that woman, who, to everyone outside, seemed so grotesque. I had seen her play on that jealousy and give him pain.

But that was not his deepest suffering about her. They had married when he was a young don, and she his pupil. That relation, which can always so easily fill itself with emotion, had never died. He wanted people to recognise her quality, how gifted she was, how much held back by her crippling sensitiveness. He wanted us to see that she was gallant, and misjudged; he was burning to explain that she went through acuter pain than anyone, when the temperament she could not control drove his friends away. His love remained love, and added pity: and the sight of her in a mood which others dismissed as grotesque still had the power to take and rend his heart.

He suffered for her, and for himself. He loathed having to make apologies for his wife. He loathed all his imagination could invent of the words that were spoken behind his back—'poor Jago. . . .' But even those wounds to his pride he could have endured, if she had been happier. He would still, after twenty-five years, have humbled himself for her as for no one else—just to see her content. As he told me on the night we first knew the Master was dying, 'one is dreadfully vulnerable through those one loves'.

When Jago came in, his first words were to his wife.

"I'm desperately sorry I've been kept so long. I know you wanted to get back to your book——"

"It doesn't matter at all, Paul," she said with lofty dignity, and then cried out: "It only means that the Dean and the Tutor and Mr. Eliot have had to make conversation to me for half an hour."

"If they don't get a greater infliction than that this term," he said, "they'll be very lucky men."

"It's wretched for them that because of parents who haven't the slightest consideration——"

Gently Jago tried to steer her off, and show her at her best. Had she talked to us about the book from which we had drawn her? Why hadn't she mentioned what she told him at tea-time?

Then Chrystal said:

"You'll excuse us if we take the Senior Tutor away, won't you, Mrs. Jago? We have a piece of business that can't wait."

"Please do not think of considering me," she retorted.

This was a masculine society, and none of us would have considered discussing college business in front of our wives, not even in front of Lady Muriel herself. But, as we went out to Jago's study, I caught sight of his wife's face, and I knew she had embraced another insult. Jago would hear her cry 'they took the opportunity to say I wasn't wanted.'

Once in Jago's study, with Jago sitting behind his big tutorial desk, crowded with letters, folders, dossiers, Reporters, copies of the Ordinances, Chrystal cleared his throat.

"We've come to ask you one question, Jago," he said. "Are you prepared to be a candidate for the Mastership?"

Jago sighed.

"The first thing I want to say," he replied, "is how grateful I am to you for coming to speak to me. It's an honour to be thought of by such colleagues as you. I'm deeply touched.

He smiled at us all.

"I'm specially touched, if I may say so, to see Eliot with you. You two are old friends—we've grown up together. It isn't so much a surprise to find you're indulgent towards me. But you don't know how flattering it is," he said to me, "to be approved of by someone who's come here from a different life altogether. I'm so grateful, Eliot."

He was the more pleased, I thought, because I had hesitated, because I had not been easy to convince: it is not the whole-hogging enthusiasts for one's cause to whom one feels most gratitude.

"We shouldn't ask you," said Chrystal briskly, "unless we could promise you a caucus."

"I think it's only fair to tell you, before you give us your answer, that we haven't made any attempt to discover the opinion of the college," said Brown. "But I don't think we're going beyond our commission in speaking for one or two others besides ourselves. Calvert specially asked us to tell you that he will give you his vote, and, though I'm not entitled to bring a categorical promise from Nightingale, I regard him as having pledged his support."

"There's no doubt of that," said Chrystal.

"Roy Calvert, that's nice of him!" cried Jago. "But Nightingale—I'm astonished, Brown, I really am astonished."

"Yes, we were a bit surprised ourselves." Brown went on steadily: "There are thirteen of us, not counting the present Master. If we leave you out, and assume that another member of the society will be the other candidate, that gives eleven people with a free vote. It wants seven votes to get a clear majority of the society, and a Master can't be elected without, of course. Personally, I should regard five as a satisfactory caucus to start with. Anyway, it's all we're entitled to promise tonight, and if you think it's not enough we shall perfectly understand."

Jago rested his elbows on the desk, and leant forward towards us.

"I believe I've told each one of you separately that this

possibility came to me as an utter shock. I still feel that my feet aren't quite firm under me. But since it did seem to become a possibility I've thought it over until I'm tired. I had serious doubts as to whether I ought to do it, whether I wanted to do it, whether I could do it. I've had several sleepless nights this week, trying to answer those questions. And there's one thing I've become convinced of, even in the small hours—you know, when one's whole life seems absolutely pointless. I'm going to tell you without modesty, between friends. I believe I can do it. I believe I can do it better than anyone within reach. So, if you want me, I've got no choice."

"I'm glad to hear it, Jago," said Chrystal.

"Splendid," said Brown.

"As for the campaign," said Jago, with a brilliant smile, "I put myself at your disposal, and no one could be in better hands."

Chrystal took charge. "There'll be opposition," he said.

"You don't think I mind that, do you?" said Jago.

"You don't mind, but we do," said Chrystal sharply. "We're bound to, as we're taking the responsibility of running you. The opposition will be serious. It will come from an influential part of the college. They're the people I call the obstructors."

"Who are they, when it comes to the point?" said Jago, still exhilarated.

"I haven't started counting heads," said Chrystal. "But there's Winslow, for certain. There's old Despard——"

"Crawford, if he isn't a candidate," Brown put in.

"I don't believe he's in a particularly good position to be impartial," said Jago. "And as for the other two, I'm not depressed by their opposition. They're just two embittered old men."

"That's as may be," said Chrystal. "But they're also two influential old men. They get round, they won't let you in by default. I didn't mean to say we shan't work it. I think we've got a very good chance. But I wanted to warn you, this isn't going to be a walk-over."

"Thank you, Dean, thank you. Don't let me run away with myself." Jago was friendly, gracious, full of joy. "But I'm glad that we've got the younger man on our side. I wouldn't exchange those two old warriors for Calvert and Eliot here. If we can call on the young men, Dean, we can do something with the college. It's time we took our rightful place. We can make it a great college."

"We shall need money," said Chrystal, but his own imagination was stirred. "We're not rich enough yet to cut much of a dash. Perhaps we can get money. Yes——"

"It's inspiring to listen to you," Brown said to Jago. "But, if I were you, I shouldn't talk too much in public about your plans. People might think you were too ambitious. We don't want to put their backs up. I'm anxious that nothing you say in the next few months shall give them a handle against you."

I watched their heads, grouped round the desk, their faces glowing with their purpose—Brown's purple-pink, rubicund, keen-eyed, Chrystal's beaky, domineering, Jago's pale, worn with the excesses of emotion, his eyes intensely lit. Each of these three was seeking power, I thought—but the power each wanted was as different as they were themselves. Brown's was one which no one need know but himself; he wanted to handle, coax, guide, contrive, so that men found themselves in the places he had designed; he did not want an office or title to underline his power, it was good enough to sit back amiably and see it work.

Chrystal wanted to be no more than Dean, but he wanted the Dean, in this little empire of the college, to be known as a man of power. Less subtle, less reflective, more immediate than his friend, he needed the moment-by-moment sensation of power. He needed to feel that he was listened to, that he was commanding here and now, that his word was obeyed. Brown would be content to get Jago elected and influence him afterwards, no one but himself knowing how much he had done. That was too impalpable a satisfaction for Chrystal. Chrystal was impelled to have his own part recognised, by Jago, by Brown and the college. As we spoke that evening, it was essential for Chrystal that he should see his effect on Jago himself. He wanted nothing more than that, he was no more ambitious than Brown—but irresistibly he needed to see and feel his power.

Jago enjoyed the dramatic impact of power, like Chrystal: but he was seeking for other things besides. He was an ambitious man, as neither Brown nor Chrystal were. In any society, he would have longed to be first; and he would have longed for it because of everything that marked him out as different from the rest. He longed for all the trappings, titles, ornaments and show of power. He would love to hear himself called Master; he would love to begin a formal act at a college meeting 'I, Paul Jago, Master of the college . . .' He wanted the grandeur of the Lodge, he wanted to be styled among the heads of houses. He enjoyed the prospect of an entry in the college history—'Dr. P. Jago, 41st Master'. For him, in every word that separated the Master from his fellows, in every ornament of the Lodge, in every act of formal duty, there was a gleam of magic.

There was something else. He had just said to Chrystal 'we can make it a great college'. Like most ambitious men, he believed that there were things that only he could do. Money did not move him in the slightest; the joys of office moved him a great deal; but there was a quality pure, almost naïve, in his ambition. He had dreams of what he could do with his power. These dreams left him sometimes, he became crudely avid for the job, but they returned. With all his fervent imagination, he thought of a college peaceful, harmonious, gifted, creative, throbbing with joy and luminous with grace. In his dreams, he did not altogether know how to attain it. He had nothing of the certainty with which, in humility, accepting their limitations, Chrystal and Brown went about their aims, securing a benefaction from Sir Horace, arranging an extra tutorship, making sure that Luke got a grant for his research. He had nothing of their certainty, nor their humility; he was more extravagant than they, and loved display far more; in his ambition he could be cruder and more predatory; but perhaps he had intimations which they could not begin to hear.

NINE

QUARREL WITH A FRIEND

When I arrived in the combination room that evening, Winslow, Nightingale and Francis Getliffe were standing together. They had been talking, but as they saw me at the door there was a hush. Winslow said:

"Good evening to you. I hear you've been holding your adoption meeting, Eliot?"

Nightingale asked:

"Did you get all the reception you wanted?"

"It was very pleasant. I'm sorry you weren't there," I said. It was from him, of course, that they had heard the news. There was constraint in the air, and I knew that Francis Getliffe was angry. He had returned from Switzerland that day, deeply sunburned; his strong fine-drawn face—I thought all of a sudden, seeing him stand there unsmiling—became more El Greco-like as the years passed.

"Aren't you even going to see your candidate?" I asked Winslow. "Do you prefer to do it all by correspondence?" Sometimes he liked to be teased, and he knew I was not frightened of him. He gave an indulgent grin.

"Any candidate I approved of would be fairly succinct on paper," he said. "Your candidate, if I may say so, would not be so satisfactory in that respect."

"We are appointing a Master, you know, not a clerk," I said.

"If the college is misguided enough to elect Dr. Jago," said Winslow, "I shall beg to be excused when I sometimes fail to remember the distinction."

Nightingale gave a smile—as always when he heard a malicious joke. He said:

"My view is, he will save us from worse. I don't object to him—unless someone better turns up."

"It should not be beyond the wit of men to discover someone better," said Winslow. Though he had talked once of 'going outside', Brown assumed that he would 'come round' to Crawford; but he had not so much as mentioned the name yet.

"I don't see this college doing it. It always likes to keep jobs in the family. That being so, I'm not displeased with Jago," said Nightingale.

I heard the door open, and Chrystal walked up to shake hands with Francis Getliffe, who had not spoken since I came in.

"Good evening to you, Dean," said Winslow. I said, in deliberate candour:

"We were just having an argument about Jago. Two for, and two against."

"That's lamentable." Chrystal stared at Getliffe. "We shall have to banish the Mastership as a topic in the combination room. Otherwise the place won't be worth living in."

"You know what the result of that would be, my dear Dean?" said Winslow. "You would have two or three knots of people, energetically whispering in corners. Not but what," he added, "we shall certainly come to that before we're finished."

"It's lamentable," said Chrystal, "that the college can't settle its business without getting into a state."

"That's a remarkable thought," said Winslow. As Chrystal was replying tartly, the butler announced dinner: on the way in, Francis Getliffe gave me a curt word: "I want a talk with you. I'll come to your rooms after hall."

We were sitting down after grace when Luke hurried in, followed by Pilbrow, late as he had been so often in his fifty years as a fellow. He rushed in breathlessly, his bald head gleaming as though it had been polished. His eyes were brown and sparkling, his words tumbled over each other as he apologised: he was a man of seventy-four, with the spontaneity, the brilliance, the hopes of a youth.

Chrystal had not been able to avoid Winslow's side, but he talked diagonally across the table to Francis Getliffe.

"Have we fixed the date of the next feast, Getliffe?" he asked.

"You should have written it down in your pocket book, my dear Dean," said Winslow. Chrystal frowned. Actually, he knew the date perfectly well. He was asking because he had something to follow.

"February the 12th. A month tomorrow," said Francis Getliffe, who had during the previous summer become Steward.

"I hope you'll make it a good one," said Chrystal. "I'm asking you for a special reason. I happen to have a most important guest coming."

"Good work," said Francis Getliffe mechanically, preoccupied with other thoughts. "Who is he?"

"Sir Horace Timberlake," Chrystal announced. He looked round the table. "I expect everyone's heard of him."

"I am, of course, very ignorant of these matters," said Winslow. "But I've seen his name occasionally in the financial journals."

"He's one of the most successful men of the day," said Chrystal. "He controls a major industry. He's the chairman of Howard and Haslehurst."

From the other side of the table, Francis Getliffe caught my eye. The name of that company had entered his wife's life, and I knew the story. In the midst of his annoyance, he gave a grim, intimate smile of recognition.

Nightingale smiled.

"I suppose," he said, "he might be called one of these business knights."

"He's none the worse for that," retorted Chrystal.

"Of course he's none the worse for that," Pilbrow burst out from the lower end of the table. "I've never been much addicted to business men, but really it's ridiculous to put on airs because they become genteel. How else do you think anyone ever got a title? Think of the Master's wife. What else were the Bevills but a set of sharp Elizabethan business men? It would be wonderful to tell her so." He exploded into joyful laughter. Then he talked rapidly again, this time to Winslow, several places away at the head of the table. "The trouble with your ancestors and mine, Godfrey, isn't that they made money, but that they didn't make quite enough. Otherwise we should have found ourselves with titles and coronets. It seems to me a pity whenever I order things in a shop. Or whenever I hear pompous persons talking nonsense about politics. I should have liked to be a red Lord."

"Of course," he said, following his process of free association, "snobbery is the national vice. Much more than other things which foreigners give us credit for." He often talked so fast that the words got lost, but phrases out of Havelock Ellis bubbled out—*'le vice anglais'*, I heard.

Pilbrow was delighted with the comparison. When he had quietened down, he said:

"By the way, I've hooked an interesting guest for the feast too, Getliffe."

"Yes, Eustace, who is it?"

Pilbrow produced the name of a French writer of great distinction. He was triumphant.

In matters of art, the college's culture was insular and not well informed. The name meant nothing to most men there. But nevertheless they wanted to give Pilbrow the full flavour of his triumph. All except Chrystal and Nightingale. Chrystal was piqued because this seemed to be stealing Sir Horace's thunder; Sir Horace had been jeered at by Nightingale that night, and Chrystal was sensitive for his heroes; he also liked solid success, and a French writer, not even one he had heard of, not even a famous one, was flimsy by the side of Sir Horace. He was huffed to notice that I took this Frenchman seriously, and told Pilbrow how much I wanted to meet him.

Nightingale did what seemed impossible, and detested Pilbrow. He was full of envy at Pilbrow's ease, gaiety, acquaintance with all the cultivated world. He knew nothing of Pilbrow's artistic friends, but hated them. When Pilbrow announced the French writer's name, Nightingale just smiled.

The rest of us loved Pilbrow. Even Winslow said:

"As you know, Eustace, I understand these things very little—but it will be extremely nice to see your genius. I stipulate, however, that I am not expected to converse in any language but my own."

"Would you really like him next to you, Godfrey?"

"If you please. If you please."

Pilbrow beamed. All of us, even the youngest, called him by his Christian name. He had been a unique figure in the college for very long. He would, as he said, have made a good red Lord. And, though he came from the upper middle classes, was comfortably off without being rich (his father had been the headmaster of a public school), many people in Europe thought of him in just that way. He was eccentric, an amateur, a connoisseur; he spent much of his time abroad, but he was intensely English, he could not have been anything else but English. He belonged to the fine flower of the peaceful nineteenth century. A great war had not shattered his feeling, gentlemanly and unselfconscious, that one went where one wanted and did what one liked.

If nostalgia ever swept over him, he thrust it back. I had never known an old man who talked less of the past. Long ago he had written books on the Latin novelists, and the one on Petronius, where he found a subject which exactly fitted him, was the best of its kind; all his books were written in a beautifully lucid style, oddly unlike his cheerful incoherent speech. But he did not wish to talk of them. He was far more spirited describing some Central European he had just discovered, who would be a great writer in ten years.

He went round Europe, often losing his head over a gleam of talent. One of his eccentricities was that he refused to dress for dinner in a country under a totalitarian régime, and he took extreme delight in arriving at a party and explaining why. Since he was old, known in most of the salons and academies of Europe, and well-connected, he set embassies some intricate problems. He did not make things easier for them by bringing persecuted artists to England, and spending most of his income upon them. He would try to bring over anyone a friend recommended—'everything's got to be done through nepotism', he said happily. 'A pretty face may get too good a deal—but a pretty face is better than a committee, if it comes to bed.'

He had never married, but he did not seem lonely. I believed that there were days of depression, but if so he went through them in private. In public he was irrepressible, an *enfant terrible* of seventy-four. But it was not the exuberant side of him that I most admired; it was not that no one could think of him as old; it was that he, like other people who do good, was at heart as tough as leather, healthily self-centered at the core.

Chrystal came back to the feast.

"There's one thing we can't overlook. I've already warned my guest. I don't know how others feel, but I can't bring myself to like having a feast here with the Master dying in the Lodge. Still, we've got no option. If we cancel it, it gives the show away. But, if they've told the Master the truth before the time of the feast, we should have to cancel it. Even at an hour's notice. I shouldn't have much patience with anyone who didn't agree."

"I think we should all agree," said Winslow. "Which is a very surprising and gratifying event, don't you think so, Dean?"

He spoke with his usual caustic courtesy, and was surprised to find Chrystal suddenly rude. He had not realised, he still did not, that Chrystal had spoken with deep feeling and was shocked by the sarcastic reply. In turn, Winslow became increasingly caustic, and Nightingale joined in.

I noticed young Luke, the observant and discreet, watching this display of conflicts, and missing nothing.

There was no wine that night. Pilbrow left for a party immediately after hall; cultivated Cambridge parties were not complete without him, he had been attending them for over fifty years. Between the rest of us there was too much tension for a comfortable bottle. Winslow gave his 'Good-night to you', and sauntered out, swinging the cap, which, in his formal style, he was the only one of us to bring into the room. I followed, and Francis Getliffe came after me.

He said, the moment we were inside my sitting-room:

"Look, I'm worried about this talk of Jago."

"Why?"

"It's bloody foolish. We can't have him as Master. I don't know what you can be thinking about."

We were still standing up. A vein, always visible when he was angry, stood out in the middle of Francis's forehead. His sunburn made him look well, on the surface; but under the eyes the skin was darkened and pouched by strain. He had been doing two men's work for months—his own research, on the nature of the ionosphere, and his secret experiments for the Air Ministry. The secret was well kept, neither I nor anyone in the college knew any details until three years later, but he was actually busy with the origins of radar. He was tired and overloaded with responsibility. His fundamental work had not received the attention that he looked for, and his reputation was not yet as brilliant as we had all prophesied. He was seeing some of his juniors overtake him; it was hard to bear.

Now he was throwing every effort into a new research. It had not yet started smoothly. It was an intolerable nuisance for him to come back to this trouble over the Mastership. He did not want to think about it, he was overtaxed already with the anxieties of air defence and the gnawing doubt that his new thoughts about the propagation of waves would not quite work out. Plunged into the middle of this human struggle, he felt nothing but goaded irritation and impatience.

We had been friends since we first met, nearly ten years before—not intimate friends, but between us there was respect and confidence. We were about the same age: he was now thirty-four and I thirty-two. We had much the same views, and a good deal of experience in common. He had brought me to the college when I decided that I did not want to go on competing all out at the Bar. In my three years in the college, we had been allies, trusting each other, automatically on the same side in any question that mattered. This was the first time we had disagreed.

"I don't know what you can be thinking about," said Francis.

"He'd be a goodish Master," I said.

"Nonsense. Sheer bloody nonsense," said Francis. "What has he done?"

It was a harsh question, and difficult to answer. Jago was an English scholar, and had published articles on the first writings produced by the Puritan settlers in New England. The articles were sound enough: he was interesting on William Bradford's dialogue; but it was no use pretending to Francis Getliffe.

"I know as well as you that he's not a specially distinguished scholar," I said.

"The Master of the college must be a distinguished scholar," said Francis.

"I don't mind that as much as you," I said. "I'm not a perfectionist."

"What has he done?" said Francis. "We can't have a man who's done nothing."

"It's not so much what he's done as what he is," I said. "As a human being there's a great deal in him."

"I don't see it."

He had lost his temper, I was trying to keep mine. But I heard an edge coming into my voice.

"I can't begin to explain the colour red," I said, "to a man who's colour blind. You'd better take my word for it——"

"You get more fun out of human beings that I do," he said. "But I don't want to choose someone who gives you the maximum amount of fun. I just want a decent Master of this college."

"If you're trying to secure that by cutting out all human judgment," I said, "you'll make the most unforgivable mistake."

Francis walked three strides, three of his long, plunging strides, to the fire and back. His steps fell heavy in the quiet room.

"Look," he said, "how much are you committed?"

"Completely."

"It's sheer utter irresponsibility. It's the first time I've seen you lose your balance. You must have gone quite mad."

"When I say completely," I said, "I could get out of it if there were a reason. But there won't be one. Jago satisfies what I want better than anyone we shall find."

"Have you given a second's thought to the fact that he's an absurd conservative? Do you think this is a good time to elect conservative figure-heads, when we might get a reasonable one?"

"I don't like that any more than you——"

"I wish you showed more sign of not liking it in practice," Francis said.

"For this particular job," I said, "I can't believe it's vitally important."

"It's vitally important for every job where men can get into the public eye," said Francis. "You oughtn't to need me to tell you. Things are balanced so fine that we can't give away a point. These conservative fools are sticking out their chests and trying to behave like solid responsible men. I tell you, they'll either let us drift lock, stock and barrel to the Fascists; or they'll get us into a war which we shall be bloody lucky not to lose."

Francis spoke with a weariness of anger. He was radical, like many scientists of his generation. As he spoke, he was heavy with the responsibility that, in two or three years at most, he and his kind would have to bear. He looked so tired that, for a second, I was melted.

"You needn't tell me that, you know, Francis," I said. "I may be voting for Jago, but I haven't changed altogether since we last met."

His sudden creased smile lit up his face, and then left him stern again.

"Whom do you want?" I asked.

"The obvious man. Crawford."

"He's conceited. He's shallow. He's a third-rate man."

"He's a very good scientist. That's understating the case."

I had never heard a contrary opinion. Some people said that Crawford was one of the best biologists alive.

Francis went on:

"He's got the right opinions. He isn't afraid to utter them."

"He's inconceivably self-satisfied——"

"There aren't many men of his standing with radical views. Anything he says, he says with authority behind him. Can't you see that it might be useful to have a Master of a college who is willing to speak out like that?"

"It might be very useful," I said. The quarrel had died down a little; I was listening to his argument. "It might be very useful. But that isn't all we want him for. Think what Crawford would be like inside the college."

I added: "He'd have no feeling. And no glow. And not a scrap of imagination."

"You claim all those things for Jago?"

"Yes."

"One can't have everything," said Francis.

I asked:

"Will Crawford be a candidate?"

"If I have anything to do with it."

"Have you spoken to Winslow yet?"

"No. I count him in for Crawford. He's got no option," said Francis.

Yes, I thought. Winslow had talked vaguely of going outside, he had ostentatiously mentioned no name. Those were the symptoms of one who hoped against hope that he would be asked himself: even Winslow, who knew how much he was disliked, who had been rejected flatly at the last election, still had that much hope. But everyone knew that he must run Crawford in the end.

"I don't see any other serious candidate," said Francis. He asked, suddenly and sternly: "Lewis, which side are you on?"

It was painful to quarrel. There was a silence.

"I'm sorry," I said. "I can't manage Crawford at any price. I see your case. But I still think this is a job where human things come first. So far as those go, I'm happy with Jago."

Francis flushed, the vein was prominent.

"It's utterly irresponsible. That's the kindest word I can find for it."

"We've got to differ," I said, suppressing the first words that came.

"I can't for the life of me understand why you didn't wait before you decided. I should have expected you to discuss it with me."

"If you'd been here, I should have done," I said.

"No doubt you've talked to other people."

"Of course."

"It will be hard," he said, "for me to think you reliable again."

"We'd better leave it," I said. "I've stood as much as I feel like standing——"

"You're going on with this nonsense?" he shouted.

"Of course I'm going on with it."

"If I can find a way to stop it," he said, "I promise you I shall."

TEN

FIRST COLLEGE MEETING OF TERM

Trunks piled up in the college gateway, young men shouted to each other across the court, the porters' trucks groaned, ground and rumbled on their way round the stone paths. The benches in hall were filled, there was a surge of noise before and after grace; feet ran up and down stairs, all evening long. At night the scratchings behind the walls were less insistent; the kitchens were full of food now, and the rats, driven out to forage in the depth of the vacation, were going back. A notice came round, summoning a college meeting for next Monday, the first Monday of full term.

The meeting was called for 4:30, the customary time, just as each alternate Monday was the customary day; the bell pealed, again according to custom, at four o'clock, and Brown came down his staircase, Francis Getliffe and Chrystal walked through the gate, I looked round for my gown, all of us on our way to the combination room. The room itself looked transformed from when it was laid for wine at night; a blotter, a neat pile of scribbling paper, an inkwell, pens and pencils, stood in each place instead of glasses; covered with paper, the table shone white, orderly, bleak; the curtains were not drawn, though the wall lights were switched on, and through the windows came the cold evening light. The room seemed larger, and its shape was changed.

Its shape was changed partly because another table, almost as long as the main one, was brought in specially for these occasions. This table was covered with a most substantial tea —great silver teapots and jugs, shining under the windows, plates of bread and butter, white, brown, wholemeal, bread with currants in it, bread with raisins in it, gigantic college cakes, black with fruit and already sliced, tarts, pastries, toasted tea cakes under massive silver covers. It was for this tea that the bell pealed half an hour before the meeting; and it was for this tea that we came punctually when we heard the bell.

Old Gay was already there. He seemed to have been there a considerable time. The rest of us stood round the table, holding our cups, munching a teacake, reaching out for a tart; but Gay had drawn up a chair against the table, and was making a hearty meal.

"Ah. How are you getting on, Chrystal?" he said, looking up for a moment from his plate. "Have you had one of these lemon curd tarts?"

"I have," said Chrystal.

"I congratulate you," said Gay promptly.

In a moment he looked up again.

"Ah, I'm glad to see you, Calvert. I thought you'd left us. Have you had any of this excellent stickjaw cake?"

"I was wondering whether it was too heavy for me," said Roy Calvert.

"I must congratulate the Steward. Winslow, I congratulate you on the remarkably fine tea you've given us."

"My dear Professor," said Winslow, "I was a most uninspired Steward: and I gave up being so five-and-twenty years ago."

"Then congratulate the new Steward for me," said Gay, quite unabashed, picking out a chocolate éclair. "Tell him from me that he's doing splendid work."

We stood round, occupied with tea. Everyone was in the room except Crawford; snatches of conversation kept reaching me and fading away. Chrystal and Brown had a quiet word, and then Chrystal moved to the side of the Master's Deputy, Despard-Smith, who was listening with a solemn, puzzled expression to Roy Calvert. Chrystal plucked the sleeve of his gown, and they backed into the window: I heard a few words in Chrystal's brisk whisper—'Master . . . announce the position . . . most inadvisable to discuss it . . . dangerous . . . some of us would think it improper.' As in all the whispered colloquies before meetings, the s's hissed across the room.

The half hour struck. Despard-Smith said, in his solemn voice—"It is more than time we started," and we took our places in order of seniority, one to the right, and one to the left of the chair. Round the table clockwise from Despard-Smith's left hand, the order became—Pilbrow, Crawford (whose place was still empty), Brown, Nightingale, myself, Luke, Calvert, Getliffe, Chrystal, Jago, Winslow, Gay.

There was one feature of this curious system of seating: it happened at that time to bring side by side the bitterest antipathies in the college, Jago and Winslow, Crawford and Brown, Nightingale and myself.

Despard-Smith looked round the table for silence. His face looked grey, lined, mournful above his clerical collar, grey above his black coat. He was seventy, and the only fellow then in orders, but he had never held a living; in fact, he had lived continuously in college since he entered it as a freshman fifty-one years before. He had been second wrangler in the days of the old mathematical tripos, and had been elected immediately after, as was often the practice then. He did no more mathematics, but became bursar at thirty and did not leave go of the office until he was over sixty. He was a narrow, competent man who had saved money for the college like a French peasant and, at any attempts to spend, predicted the gravest catastrophe. He had the knack of investing any cliché with solemn weight. At seventy he still kept a curious brittle stiff authority. He prided himself on his sense of humour: and, since he was also solemn and self-assured, he accordingly became liable to some of Roy Calvert's more eccentric enquiries.

It lay in the Master's power to name his own deputy: and

Despard-Smith had been appointed by the Master under seal in December, at the beginning of his illness—probably because the Master, like all the older fellows, could not struggle free from the long years in which Despard-Smith as bursar had held the college down.

"I shall now ask for the minutes," he said. He stuttered on the 'm': he sometimes stuttered slightly on the operative word: it added to his gravity and weight.

Everyone there was anxious to come to the question of the Mastership. Some were more than anxious: but we could not do it. Custom ordained a rigid order of business, first college livings and then finance. The custom was unbreakable. And so we settled down to a desultory discussion about who should be offered a country living worth £325 a year. It carried with it a rectory with fourteen bedrooms. In the eighteenth century it had been worth exactly the same figure, and then it had been a prize for which the fellows struggled. Now it was going to be hard to fill. Despard-Smith considered that a contemporary of his might listen to the call; Roy Calvert wanted it for a young Anglo-Catholic friend.

The college was inclined to think that Despard-Smith's contemporary might be a trifle old. As for Roy's nominee, he never stood a chance, though Roy pressed him obstinately. Roy never got the ear of a college meeting. He became too ingenious and elaborate; *tête-à-tête* with any of these men, he was perceptive, but when they were gathered together he became strangely maladroit. But Arthur Brown himself could not have manoeuvered a job for an Anglo-Catholic. At the bare mention Jago, who was in fact an eloquent agnostic, invariably remembered that he had been brought up an Irish protestant. And all the other unbelievers would follow him in a stampede and become obdurate low churchmen.

So it happened that afternoon. The college would not take either of the names.

At that point, Crawford came in, and slipped quietly but noticeably into his place. He moved sleekly, like a powerful man who has put on weight.

"My apologies, Mr. Deputy," he said. "As I informed you, I had to put in an appearance at the faculty board."

Despard-Smith gloomily, competently, recapitulated the arguments: it appeared to be 'the sense of the meeting' that neither of these men should be offered the living, and the question would have to be deferred until next meeting: it was, of course, deplorable: had Dr. Crawford any advice to give?

"No, Mr. Deputy, I have no observations to make," said Crawford. He had a full, smooth voice, and a slight Scottish accent. He assumed that he would be listened to, and he had the trick of catching the attention without an effort. His expression stayed impassive: his features were small in a smooth round face, and his eyes were round and unblinking. His hair was smoothed down, cut very short over the ears; he had lost none of it, and it was still a glossy black, though he was fifty-six. As he spoke to the Deputy, he wore an impersonal smile.

The financial business did not take long. The college was selling one of its antique copyholds at twenty years' purchase; the college owned property in all the conceivable fashions of five hundred years; some early gifts had, by their legal form, kept their original money value and so were now more trouble than they were worth. When it came to property, the college showed a complete lack of antiquarian sentimentality.

"If that is all," said Despard-Smith with solemn irritation, "perhaps we can get on. We have not yet dealt with our most serious piece of business. I cannot exaggerate the catastrophic consequences of what I have to say."

He stared severely round from right to left. Luke, for one moment free from scribbling notes for minutes, had been whispering to Roy Calvert. He blushed down to his neck: he, and the whole room, became silent.

Despard-Smith cleared his throat.

"The college will be partly prepared for the announcement which it is my painful duty to make. When the Master asked me to act as his deputy less than two months ago, I fully expected that before this term was over he would be back in the s-saddle again. I little imagined that it would fall to me to announce from this chair the most disastrous news that I have been informed of in my long association with the college." He paused. "I am told," he went on, "upon authority which cannot be denied that the Master will shortly be taken from us."

He paused again, and said:

"I am not qualified to express an opinion whether there is the f-faintest hope that the medical experts may be proved wrong in the event."

Crawford said:

"May I have permission to make a statement, Mr. Deputy?"

"Dr. Crawford."

"Speaking now not as a fellow but as one who was once trained as a medical man, I must warn the society that there is no chance at all of a happy issue," Crawford said. He sat impassively, while others looked at him. I saw Jago's eyes flash at the other end of the table.

"You confirm what we have been told, Dr. Crawford, that the Master's days on earth are n-numbered?"

"I must confirm that," said Crawford. He was a physiologist, best known for his work on the structure of the brain. His fingers were short and thick, and it was surprising to be told that he was an experimenter of the most delicate manual skill.

"We are all bound to be impressed by Dr. Crawford's statement," said Despard-Smith.

"I must add a word to it," said Crawford. "The end cannot be long. The college must be prepared to have lost its head by the end of the Easter term."

"Thank you for telling us the worst."

"I considered it my duty to tell the college all I knew myself," said Crawford.

He had said nothing novel to most of us; yet his immobile certainty, Despard-Smith's bleak and solemn weight, the ritual of the meeting itself, brought a tension that sprang from man to man like an electric charge.

After a silence, Winslow said:

"Dr. Crawford's statement brings the whole matter to a point. I take it that with your permission, Mr. Deputy, the college will wish to discuss the vacancy we shall soon be faced with."

"I don't understand," said Chrystal at his sharpest.

"I thought I made myself fairly clear," said Winslow.

"I don't understand," said Chrystal. This kind of obstinate pretence of incomprehension was one of his favourite techniques at a meeting. "I should like us to be reminded of the statue governing the election of a Master."

"I wonder," said Brown, "if you would be good enough to read it, Mr. Deputy?"

"I'm in the hands of the m-meeting," said Despard-Smith.

"Why are we wasting time?" said Francis Getliffe.

"I should like the statute read," snapped Chrystal.

Winslow and Crawford exchanged glances, but Despard-Smith opened his copy of the statutes, which lay in front of him on the table, and began to read, half-intoning in a nasal voice:

"When a vacancy in the office of Master shall become known to that fellow first in order of precedence he shall summon within forty-eight hours a meeting of the fellows. If the fellow first in order of precedence be not resident in Cambridge, or otherwise incapable of presiding, the duty shall pass to the next senior, and so on. When the fellows are duly assembled the fellow first in order of precedence attending shall announce to them the vacancy, and shall before midnight on the same day authorise a notice of the vacancy and of the time hereby regulated for the election of the new Master, and cause this notice to be placed in full sight on the chapel door. The time regulated for the election shall be ten o'clock on the morning on the fifteenth day from the date of the notice if the vacancy occur in term, or on the thirtieth day if it occur out of term."

When he had finished, Gay said sonorously:

"Ah. Indeed. Very interesting. Very remarkable. Fine price of draughtsmanship, that statute."

"It makes my point," said Chrystal. "The college as a college can't take any action till the Mastership is vacant. There's no question before us. I move the next business."

"This is formalism carried to extreme limits," said Winslow angrily. "I've never known the Dean be so scrupulous on a matter of etiquette before——"

"It's completely obvious the matter must be discussed," said Francis Getliffe.

"I'm sure the Dean never intended to suggest anything else, Mr. Deputy," said Brown with a bland and open smile. "If I may take the words out of his mouth, I know the Dean hopes—as I feel certain we all do—that we shall discuss every possible element in the whole position, so that we finally do secure the true opinion and desire of the college. The little difference of opinion between us amounts to nothing more than whether our discussion should be done in a formal college meeting or outside."

"Or, to those of us who haven't the gift for softening differences possessed by Mr. Brown, whether we shall dissolve immediately into cabals," said Winslow with a savage, caustic grin, "or talk it out in the open."

"Speaking now as a fellow and not as a former medical man," said Crawford, "I consider that the college would be grossly imprudent not to use the next few months to resolve on the dispositions it must make."

"But that's agreed by everybody," I put in. "The only question is, whether a formal college meeting is the most suitable place."

"Cabals versus the open air," said Winslow, and Nightingale smiled.

Despard-Smith was not prepared for the waves of temper that were sweeping up.

"I cannot remember any p-precedent in my long association with the college," he said.

Suddenly Pilbrow began speaking with great speed and earnestness:

"The college can't possibly have a meeting about a new Master. . . . When the man who ought to be presiding is condemned. . . . I've never known such an extraordinary lack of feeling."

He finished, after his various starts, with complete lucidity. But the college had a habit of ignoring Pilbrow's interventions, and Chrystal and Winslow had both begun to speak at once when Jago quietened them. His voice was not an orator's: it was plummy, thick, produced far back in his throat. Yet, whenever he spoke, men's glances turned to him. He had his spectacles in hand, and his eyes, for once unveiled, were hard.

"I have no doubt," he said, "that we have just listened to the decisive word. This is not the first time that Mr. Pilbrow has represented to some of us the claims of decent feeling. Mr. Deputy, the Master of this college is now lying in his Lodge, and he has asked you to preside in his place. We know that we must settle on someone to succeed him, however difficult it is. But we can do that in our own way, without utterly offending the taste of some of us by insisting on doing it in this room—in a meeting of which he is still the head." When he sat back the room stayed uncomfortably still.

"That settles it," said Roy Calvert in a clear voice.

"I moved the next business ten minutes ago," said Chrystal, staring domineeringly at Despard-Smith. "I believe Mr. Brown seconded it. Is it time to vote on my motion? I'm ready to wait all evening."

The motion was carried by seven votes to four. For: Philbrow, Jago, Brown, Chrystal, myself, Calvert, Luke. Against: Winslow, Crawford, Nightingale, Getliffe.

Neither Despard-Smith nor Gay voted.

ELEVEN

VIEW FROM ROY CALVERT'S WINDOW

At Hall after the meeting, Winslow was grumbling about Jago's last speech—'high-minded persons have a remarkable gift for discovering that the requirements of decent feeling fit in exactly with what they want to do'. I thought about how we had voted. The sides were sorting themselves out. Nightingale had voted with the opposition: was that merely a gesture of suspiciousness against Chrystal and Brown? He was the most uncomfortable of bedfellows. Despard-Smith would presumably vote for Crawford. What about old Gay? He might do anything. I fancied Pilbrow would decide for Jago. It looked encouraging.

Two days afterwards, a note came round:

'Those who are not disposed to vote for the Senior Tutor may like to discuss candidates for the Mastership. I suggest a meeting in my rooms at 2.30 on Friday, Jan. 22. G.H.W.'

Winslow had had his note duplicated in the bursary, and sent it to each fellow. There was a good deal of comment. "The man's got no manners," said Chrystal. "He's always doing his best to make the place a beargarden." Brown said: "I've got a feeling that the college won't be a very happy family for the next few months." Jago said: "I shall manage to hold my tongue—but he's being needlessly offensive."

Although Roy Calvert and I were waited on by the same servant, his rooms were to be found not in the first court proper, but in a turret over the kitchen. His sitting-room commanded a view of the second court and the staircase up which Winslow's visitors must go. I arrived there after lunch on the Friday afternoon; Roy was standing at his upright desk, reading a manuscript against a lighted opalescent screen.

"I've kept an eye across the way," he said. "No one has declared himself yet.

"I need to finish this," he went on, looking back at the screen. "There's a new martyr in this psalm."

He read for a few minutes, and then joined me by the window. We looked across, through the mist of the raw January afternoon, to the separate building which contained the sets not only of Winslow, but also of Pilbrow and Chrystal. It was a building of palladian harmony; Eustace Pilbrow had lived in it for fifty years, and said that it was still as tranquil to look at as when he saw it for the first time.

It was twenty-five past two.

"High time the enemy appeared," said Roy.

Just then Winslow came lounging along the path from the first court. He wore no overcoat, but, as usual when in college on business, a black coat and striped trousers. As he lounged along, his feet came down heavily at each step; one could guess from his gait that he had unusually big feet.

"He's declared himself, anyway," said Roy. "He'd be sold if no one else turned up."

Roy was on edge in his own fashion, though he was not given to anxiety. Waiting for critical news of his own, he felt instead of anxiety a tingle of excitement. He felt it now, watching for news of Jago's chances.

We saw Winslow disappear in the mouth of his staircase.

"He's extremely tiresome." Roy smiled. "But I like the old stick. So do you."

A moment later, Despard-Smith, in clerical hat and overcoat, walked across the front of the building from the third court.

"That was only to be expected," I said.

"If he weren't able to express his view," said Roy, "it would be nothing short of catastrophic."

Francis Getliffe came quickly the way Winslow had come, in his long plunging strides.

"Now *he* ought to know better," said Roy.

"He's got some good reasons."

"He's getting stuffier as he gets older."

The half-hour struck. Very slowly, along the same path, came Gay. One foot shuffled slowly in front of the other; he was muffled up to the throat, but his cheeks shone very red, his beard very white.

"How in God's name did he decide?" I cried in disappointment.

He took minutes to make his way across the court. He was almost there when we saw Nightingale come along from the third court and join him.

"Judas?" said Roy.

They talked for a moment; we saw Nightingale shake his head, and walk away in our direction.

"Apparently not," I said.

Then, from the first court, Crawford walked smoothly into view. He was late, he was moving fast, but he gave no appearance of hurry. Roy whistled 'Here comes the bride' until he slipped up Winslow's staircase.

"I wonder," said Roy suddenly, "if old Winslow is still hoping. I wonder if he expects to be asked to stand this afternoon."

"People hope on," I said, "long after they admit it to themselves."

"Just so," said Roy. "In this case until they're seventy." (Under the statutes, seventy was the retiring age for the Master.)

No one else came. The court was empty.

"Is that the whole party?" said Roy. "I believe it is."

We waited, and heard the quarters chime. We waited again.

"If this is all, old boy," cried Roy, "it's in the bag."

We still stood there, looking over the court. The mist was deepening. An undergraduate brought in a girl, and they passed out of sight towards the third court. All of a sudden a light shone from Winslow's room. It made the court seem emptier, the afternoon more raw.

"They've only collected five," said Roy. "Not many. They've lost face."

Crawford came out again into the court. Again quickly but without hurry, he walked towards the first court. We could see down on to his face as he approached. He looked utterly impassive.

"Asked to retire," I said.

"I wonder what he thinks his chances are," said Roy. He added: "One thing—Winslow knows the worst now. His last chance has gone."

"I'm sorry for some of our friends," I said, "if they sit next to him tonight."

"I'd better get there early," said Roy. "I can look after myself."

I smiled. We gazed, as the afternoon darkened, at the one window lighted in the quiet building. At last Roy turned away. "That is that," he said. "It's pretty remarkable, old boy. We seem to be home."

"I think I'd better tell Arthur Brown," I said. Roy's telephone stood by his bedside, and I went there and talked to Brown. "How do you know how many turned up?" I heard Brown saying, cautious and inquisitive as ever. "How can you possibly have found out?"

I explained that we had been watching from Roy Calvert's window. Brown was satisfied, and asked for the names again. "Our party seems to be hanging together," he said. "But I think, to be on the safe side, I'll give a little luncheon soon. I say, Eliot, I'm sorry about old Gay. I should like to know who got at him. We've let them steal a march on us there."

"But it's pretty good," I said.

"I must say it looks perfectly splendid." For a second Brown had let himself go. Then the voice turned minatory again: "Of course, you'll remember it's much too early to throw your hats in the air. We haven't even got a paper majority for Paul Jago yet. We must go carefully. You mustn't let people feel that we think it's safe. It would be a wise precaution if you and Calvert didn't let on that you know who turned up this afternoon."

I told Roy, who gave a malicious chuckle.

"Good old Uncle Arthur," he said. "He must be the only person on this earth who regards you as an irresponsible schoolboy. It gives me great pleasure."

He rang down to the kitchens for tea and crumpets, and we ate them by the fire. When we had finished and I was sitting back with my last cup of tea, Roy glanced at me with a secretive grin. From a drawer he produced, as though furtively, a child's box of bricks. "I bought these yesterday," he said. "I thought they might come in useful. They won't be necessary unless Winslow shows us a new trick or two. But I may as well set them out."

He always had a love for the concrete, though his whole professional life was spent with words. Another man would have wirtten down the fellows' names, but Roy liked selecting fourteen identical bricks, and printing on them the names from Royce to Luke. The brick marked Royce he put by itself without a word. His expression lightened as he placed the two bricks Jago and Crawford together. Then he picked up Gay, Despard-Smith, Winslow and Getliffe, and arranged them in a row. He left the other seven in a huddle —'until everyone's in the open. It ought to be a clear majority.'

I had to give two supervisions from five to seven, and when the second was over went straight to the combination room. There Crawford was sitting by the fire alone, reading the local paper. He nodded, impersonally cordial, as I went over to the sherry table. When I came back, glass in hand, to the armchairs, Crawford looked at me over the top of his paper. "I don't like the look of the war, Eliot," he said. 'The war' was the civil war in Spain.

"Nor do I," I said.

"Our people are getting us into a ridiculous mess. Every Thursday when I go up to the Royal I try to call on someone or other who is supposed to be running our affairs. I try to make a different call each week and persuade them to see a little military sense. It's the least one can do, but I never come away feeling reassured. Speaking as one liberal to another, Eliot, and without prejudice to your subject, I should feel happier if we had a few men of science in the House and the Foreign Office."

For a few minutes he talked about the winter campaign in Spain. He had made a hobby of military history, and his judgment was calm and steady. Everything he said was devastatingly sensible.

Then Jago entered. He started as he saw Crawford, then greeted him with effusiveness. He was more uncomfortable than I had ever seen him—more uncomfortable, I suddenly realised, because he had heard the good news of the afternoon. He felt guilty in the presence of the less lucky one.

Crawford was unperturbed.

"I think we'd better abandon our military researches for tonight, Eliot," he said. "I believe the Senior Tutor isn't specially interested in war. And certainly doesn't share our sympathies about the present one. He'll realise we were right in time."

He got up from his chair, and stood facing Jago. He was several inches shorter, but he had the physical presence that comes through being able to keep still.

"But I am glad of the chance of a word with you, Jago," he said. "I was thinking of sending you a note. That won't be necessary if we can have three minutes. I understand that Eliot is committed to support you, and so I can speak in his presence."

"By all means," said Jago. "I am in your hands. Go ahead, my dear man, go ahead."

"This afternoon," said Crawford, "I was asked to let myself be a candidate for the Mastership. Those who asked me did not constitute a numerical majority of the college, but they represent a sound body of opinion. I saw no reason to hesitate. I don't approve of people who have to be persuaded to play, like the young woman who just happens to have brought her music. I told them I was ready to let my name go forward."

He was confident, impervious, conceited, self-assured. On the afternoon's showing he was left without a chance, but he seemed in control of the situation.

"I'm very grateful to you for telling me," said Jago.

"It was the least I could do," said Crawford. "We are bound to be the only serious candidates."

"I wish both the candidates," said Jago, with a sudden smile, "reached the standard of distinction set by one of them."

"That's as may be," Crawford replied. "There will be one question for us two to decide together. That is, what to do with our own personal votes. We ought to reach a working agreement on that. It is conceivable that the question may become important."

Then he said that he was dining in another college, and left us, with a cordial, impersonal goodnight.

Jago sighed and smiled.

"I'd give a good deal for that assurance, Eliot!"

"If you had it," I said, "you'd lose something else."

"I wonder," Jago cried, "if he's ever imagined that he could possibly be wrong? Has he ever thought for a minute that he might possibly disgrace himself and fail?"

Not in this world of professional success, power, ambition, influence among men, I thought. Of his mastery in this world Crawford was absolutely and impenetrably confident. Nothing had ever shaken him, or could now.

But I guessed that in his nature there was one rift of diffidence. He had a quiet, comely wife and a couple of children—while Jago would go home after dinner to his tormented shrew. Yet I guessed that, in time past, Crawford had been envious of Jago's charm for women. Jago had never been frightened that he might not win love; he had always known, with the unconscious certainty of an attractive man, that it would come his way. It was an irony that it came in such a form; but he stayed confident with women, he was confident of love; in fact, it was that confidence which helped him to devote such tenderness and such loving patience upon his wife. Whereas Crawford as a young man had wondered in anguish whether any woman would ever love him. For all his contented marriage—on the surface so much more enviable than Jago's—he had never lost that diffidence, and there were still times when he envied such men as Jago from the bottom of his heart.

TWELVE

JAGO WALKS ROUND THE COURT

The evening after Winslow's caucus, Brown asked me to join him and Chrystal, and when I went into Brown's room, they were busy talking. Brown said to me:

"I suggested we should meet here because it's a bit more private than the combination room. And I happen to have a glass of manzanilla waiting for you. We think it's rather helpful to a bit of business."

Brown gave me my glass, settled himself, and went on:

"I regard it as desirable to strike while the iron's hot. I can't forgive myself for letting them snatch old Gay from in front of our noses. We must have our little lunch before we lose anyone else."

"I'm with you," said Chrystal.

"I think they've shown more enterprise than we have," said Brown, "and we've got out of it better than we deserved."

"If I were Crawford, I shouldn't thank Winslow much," said Chrystal. "He's just run amok. He's done them more harm than good. If Crawford had us to look after him, there'd be no need to have an election."

"Well," said Brown, "I shall be happier when we've got our party round a lunch table."

"We must make them speak," said Chrystal.

"You'll preside," said Brown, "and you can make everyone say that he's supporting Jago."

"Why should I preside?"

"That's your job. I regard you as the chairman of our party." Brown smiled. "And we ought to have this lunch on Sunday. The only remaining point is whom do we ask. I was telling the Dean"—he said to me—"that I haven't been entirely idle. I haven't let the other side get away with everything. I think I've got Eustace Pilbrow. We certainly ought to ask him to the lunch. He's never been specially interested in these things, and he's not enormously enthusiastic, but I think I've got him. Put in another way: if Jago were a bit of a crank politically—saving your presence, Eliot—I believe Eustace would support him up to the hilt. As it is, I'm quite optimistic."

"That only leaves young Luke," said Chrystal. "Everyone else has got tabs on them. So I reckon at present."

"Obviously we invite the other three, Pilbrow, Nightingale and Roy Calvert," said Brown. "The question is, Eliot, whether we invite young Luke. I must say that I'm rather against it."

"He only needs a bit of persuasion," Chrystal said sharply. "Either side could get him for the asking. He's a child."

In the months since Luke became a fellow, I had not got to know him, except as an observant, intelligent, discreet and sanguine face at hall and college meetings. Once I had walked round the garden with him for half an hour.

"I wonder whether you're right," I said to Chrystal. "It may not be as easy as you think."

"Dead easy for us. Dead easy for Winslow," said Chrystal.

"I agree," said Brown. "I believe the Dean's right."

"That's why," he went on, "I'm against inviting him." His face was flushed, but stubborn and resolute. "I want to say where I stand on this. I won't be a party to over-persuading Luke. He's a young man, he's not a permanency here yet, he's got his way to make, and it would be a damned shame to hamper him. At the very best it won't be easy for the college to keep him when his six years are up: we've got one physicist in Getliffe, and it will be hard to make a case for another as a fixture." (Roy Calvert and Luke were research fellows appointed for six years: when that period ended, the college could keep them or let them go. It was already taken for granted that a special place must be found for Roy Calvert.) "It stands to reason that Luke has got to look to Crawford and Getliffe. They're the scientists, they're the people who can help him, they're the people who've got to make a case if the college is ever going to keep him. You can't blame him if he doesn't want to offend them. If I'd started as the son of a dockyard hand, as that boy did, though no one would ever think it, I shouldn't feel like taking the slightest risk. I'm certainly not going to persuade him to take it. Whichever side he comes down on, I say that it isn't for us to interfere."

"Look," I said, "Francis Getliffe is a very fairminded man——"

"I give you that," said Brown. "I'm not saying that voting for Jago would necessarily make a scrap of difference to Luke's future. But he may feel that he's making an enemy. If he does, I for one wouldn't feel easy about talking him round."

"You've got a point there," said Chrystal.

"The furthest I feel inclined to go," said Brown, "is to send him a note saying that some of us have now decided to support Jago. I'll tell him we're meeting on Sunday to discuss ways and means, but we're not inviting people who still want time to make up their minds."

"I'm sorry to say," said Chrystal, "that I think you're right."

There we left it for the evening. It was easier to understand their hold on the college, I thought, when one saw their considerate good-nature, right in the middle of their politics. No one could run such a society for long without a degree of trust. That trust most of the college had come to place in them. They were politicians, they loved power, at many points they played the game only just within the rules. But they set themselves limits and did not cross them. They kept their word. And in human things, particularly with the young, they were uneasy unless they behaved in a fashion that was scrupulous and just. People were ready to believe this of Brown, but found it harder to be convinced that it was also true of his friend. They saw clearly enough that Chrystal was the more ruthless: they did not see that he was the more tender-hearted.

In this particular instance, as it happened, they did not evoke the response that they deserved. Luke sat next to me in hall that night. For a couple of nights past he had been less sanguine and bright-eyed than usual: I asked about his work.

"It seems to be describing a sine curve," he said. I had to recollect that a sine curve went up and down.

He went on: "Sometimes I think it's all set. Sometimes I think it's as useless as the Great Pyramid. I'm in the second phase just now. I'm beginning to wonder if I shall ever get the wretched thing out."

He was depressed and irritable, and just then happened to hear Brown quietly inviting Roy Calvert to lunch in order 'to give Jago's campaign a proper start'.

"What is all this?" Luke asked me. "Is this the reply to Winslow's meeting?"

"Roughly," I said.

"Am I being asked?"

"I think," I said, "that Brown felt you hadn't yet made up your mind."

"He hasn't taken much trouble to find out," said Luke. "I'll have it out with him afterwards."

Passing round the wine in the combination room, he was quiet and deferential to the old man, as he always was. I was beginning to realise the check he imposed on his temper. An hour later, as Brown and I left the room and went into the court, Luke came rapidly behind us.

"Brown, why haven't I been invited to this bloody caucus?"

"It isn't quite a caucus, Luke. I was just going to write to explain——"

"It's a meeting of Jago's supporters, isn't it?"

"One or two of us," said Brown, "have come to the conclusion that he's the right man. And——"

"So have I. Why hasn't someone spoken to me about it? Why haven't I been told?"

It was raining, and we had hurried through the court into the gateway, for Brown was on his way home. We stood under the great lantern.

"Why, to tell you the truth, Luke, we thought you might naturally want to vote for Crawford. And we didn't want to put any pressure on you."

"I'm buggered if I vote for Crawford," cried Luke. "You might have given me credit for more sense. Jago would make one of the best Masters this college has ever had."

So Luke appeared for the Sunday lunch in Brown's rooms, once more effacing himself into discretion again, dressed with a subfusc taste more cultivated than that of anyone there except Roy Calvert. Unobtrusively he inhaled the bouquet of his glass of Montrachet.

Brown had placed Chrystal at one end of the table, and took the other himself. After we had sipped the wine, Brown said contentedly:

"I'm glad most of you seem to like it. I thought it was rather suitable. After all, we don't meet for this purpose very frequently."

Brown's parties were always modest. One had a couple of glasses of a classical wine, and that was all—except once a year, when his friends who had a taste in wine were gathered together for an evening. This Sunday there was nothing with lunch but the Montrachet, but afterwards he circulated a bottle of claret. "I thought we needed something rather fortifying," said Brown, "before we started our little discussion."

We were content after our lunch. Pilbrow was a gourmet, young Luke had the sensuous gusto to become one; Chrystal and Roy Calvert and I enjoyed our food and drink. Pilbrow was chuckling to himself.

"Much better than the poor old Achaeans——" I distinguished among the chuckles. We asked what it was all about, and Pilbrow became lucid:

"I was reading the *Iliad*—Book XI—again in bed—Pramnian wine sprinkled with grated goat's cheese—Pramnian wine sprinkled with grated goat's cheese——Oh, can anyone imagine how *horrible* that must have been?"

Six of us went on enjoying our wine. Meanwhile Nightingale sat over a cup of coffee, envying us for our pleasure, trying to be polite and join in the party.

In time Brown asked Chrystal whether we ought not to make a start with the discussion. There was the customary exchange of compliments between them: Chrystal wondered why he should act as chairman, when Brown himself was there: Brown felt the sense of the meeting required the Dean. At last, the courtesies over, Chrystal turned sharply to business. He wished us each to define our attitude to the Mastership, in order of seniority; he would wind up himself. So, sitting round the littered table after lunch, we each made a speech.

Pilbrow opened, as usual over-rapidly. But his intention was clear and simple. He was sorry that Jago had some reactionary opinions: but he was friendly, he took great trouble about human beings, and Pilbrow would vote for him against Crawford. It was a notable speech for a man of seventy-four; listening with concentration, I was surprised how little he was attended to. Chrystal was spinning the stem of a glass between his fingers; even Brown was not peering with acute interest.

Brown was listened to by everyone. For the first time, he spoke his whole mind about Jago, and he spoke it with an authority, a conviction, a round integrity, that drew us all together. Jago would make an outstandingly good Master, and his election would be a fine day's work for the college. Put it another way: if the college was misguided enough to elect Crawford, we should be down twice: once by getting a bad Master, once by losing a first-class one. And the second point was the one for us to give our minds to.

Nightingale made a circuitous attack on Crawford, in the course of which he threw doubts, the first time I had heard him or anyone else suggest them, on Crawford's real distinction as a scientist. 'His work may be discredited in ten years, any work of his sort may be, and then the college would be in an awkward situation.' The others round the table became puzzled and hushed, while Nightingale smiled.

I developed Pilbrow's point, and asked them what human qualities they thought they wanted in a Master. For myself, I answered: a disinterested interest in other people: magnanimity: a dash of romantic imagination. No one could doubt Jago had his share of the last, I said, and got a laugh. I said that in my view he was more magnanimous than most men, and more interested in others.

Roy Calvert took the same line, at greater length, more fancifully. He finished with a sparkle of mischief: 'Lewis Eliot and I are trying to say that Jago is distinguished as a man. If anyone asks us to prove it, there's only one answer—just spend an hour with him. If that isn't convincing it isn't our fault—or Jago's.'

Luke said no more than he was sure Jago would be a splendid Master, and that he would vote for him in any circumstances.

Chrystal had made a note on the back of an envelope after each speech. Now he summed up, brusque, giving his usual hint of impatience or ill-temper, competent and powerful. He had wanted to be certain how far the party were prepared to commit themselves. Unless he had misunderstood the statements, Brown, Nightingale and Luke were prepared to vote for Jago without qualification! Eliot and

Calvert would support him against any candidate so far mentioned; Pilbrow promised to support him against Crawford. "Have I got anyone wrong?" he asked sharply.

Brown and I were each watching Nightingale. No one spoke. One by one, we nodded.

"That's very satisfactory as far as it goes," said Chrystal. "I'm not going to waste your time with a speech. I can go at least as far as Pilbrow, and I think I find myself with Eliot and Calvert. I'm for Jago against Crawford and any other names I've heard. I'm not prepared to go the whole way with Brown just yet. I don't think Jago is an ideal candidate. He's not well enough known outside. But he'll do."

He looked across the table at Brown.

"There's a majority for Jago in this room," he said. "I don't think there's anything more to do this afternoon."

We were all stimulated, there was a glow of success and conspirators' excitement round the table. Brown and Chrystal told of the moves which had gone on before the present Master was elected. I learned for the first time that Jago had tried, in that election, to get together a party for Winslow. I asked whether they were remembering right. "Oh yes," said Brown, "they hadn't got across each other so badly then. I shouldn't have said they were ever specially friendly, though, should you?" he asked Chrystal.

The talk kept to elections of past Masters. Pilbrow began to laugh.

"I've just thought——" then he added with complete clarity: "In my almost infinite period as a fellow, I've never even been mentioned as a possible candidate. And I've never taken the slightest useful part in getting one elected. That's a long-distance record no one can ever beat." He went on laughing. He did not care. He was known, admired, loved all over Europe; he had great influence in letters; but nothing could make him effective at a college meeting. It was strange—and I thought again of Roy Calvert at the last meeting—that those two, both very natural men, should not be able to project themselves into a committee. Perhaps they were too natural. Perhaps, for influence in the affairs of solid men, one had to be able to send, as the Master said, the 'old familiar phrases reverberating round'. Neither Pilbrow nor Roy Calvert could do that without laughing. To be an influence in any society, in fact, one can be a little different, but only a little; a little above one's neighbours, but not too much. Pilbrow did much good, Roy Calvert was often selfless; but neither of them was humble enough to learn the language of more ordinary men.

But, even if they had tried their hardest, neither of them could ever have been the power that Brown or Chrystal was. Groups of men, even small groups, act strangely differently from individuals. They have less humour and simpler humour, are more easy to frighten, more difficult to charm, distrust the mysterious more, and enjoy firm, flat, competent expositions which a man by himself would find inexcusably dull. Perhaps no group would ever let itself be guided by Roy Calvert.

In the same way, the seven of us sitting at the table through the winter afternoon became more enthusiastic for Jago than any of us taken alone: our pleasure was simple, our exhilaration intense. Even Nightingale caught it. We were together, and for an hour everyone surrendered to the excitement; Jago would win, we wanted Jago, and all seemed bright.

The kitchen porters brought in tea at four o'clock. The excitement broke; we split into twos and threes; muffin in hand, Chrystal talked quietly to me about Sir Horace's visit a month hence. Then, as had been arranged, Jago came into the room.

"Good afternoon, Dean. Good afternoon, Brown. You mustn't let me interrupt. I expect you haven't finished your business. I should be so sorry to interrupt."

He was restless with anxiety, and at his worst. Chrystal stood up, stiff and dominating. If Jago was to be Master, he wanted it clear between them that he had brought it about. His expression was hard, almost threatening.

"We've finished, Jago," he said. "I can tell you that we've had a satisfactory meeting."

"Just so," said Roy Calvert, trying to soothe Jago's nerves.

"I mustn't ask about your secrets," said Jago. His smile was vivid but uneasy. There was a lull, and then Pilbrow asked about some old member in the Foreign Office. Would he help about a refugee? Was he approachable? What was he like?

"You'll find his general attitude utterly unsatisfactory according to your views," said Jago. "He's what the Dean and Brown and I would consider sound."

"Sound," Pilbrown said. "You'll lose the bloody empire and everything else, between you. Sound."

"I was going to say, however much we're on different sides, we're none of us above doing a job for a friend. I should be very much upset if——"

He promised to write that night about Pilbrow's refugee, and Pilbrow, mollified, asked about others at the Foreign Office. Jago was still on edge, eager to say yes, eager to keep the conversation alive. Did he know H—? A little. Sir P—J—? Reluctantly, Jago said no. Did he know P—?

"Do I know P—?" cried Jago. "Do I know P—, my dear Eustace? I should think I do. The first time I met him, he asked my advice about a minister's private life!"

He stayed in that vein, at his most flamboyant, until the party broke up. Roy Calvert and Brown knew the reason, and Roy, as though in fun, actually in kindness, laughed at him as if it were a casual tea-party and gave Jago the chance to score off him in reply. Jago took it, and amused us, especially Nightingale, with his jokes at Roy's expense. But the anxiety returned, and with it his flow of extravagance. Chrystal did not respond much, and went away early; then Pilbrow and Luke. Nightingale seemed to be enjoying himself, and I began to listen to the quarters, each time they chimed outside. So long as he stayed, Jago could not ask.

At last he went. The door closed behind him, and Jago turned to Arthur Brown with a ravaged look. "Well?"

"Well," said Brown comfortably, "if the election had been this afternoon, you would have got in nicely."

"Did everyone here——"

"Everyone you've seen said that, as things stood at present, they were ready to vote for you."

"That's wonderful." Jago's face lit up the room. "That's wonderful."

His smile was still radiant, but became gentler as he added:

"I'm touched to think of dear old Eustace Pilbrow throwing away his prejudices and being ready to support me. I don't suppose we've agreed on a single public issue since I became a fellow. We've disagreed on everything two men could disagree on. Yet he is willing to do this for me."

"You ought to be touched about young Luke," said Brown. "He's the most enthusiastic supporter you've got. And he's acting against his own interests."

"Ah, I think I'm better with young men than with people my own age." He added, with a flash of extraordinary directness and simplicity: "I don't have to show off to them, you see."

Roy caught my eye. His smile was sharp.

Then Brown spoke:

"I don't want to be a skeleton at the feast, because I've been feeling very gratified myself, but I think it would be remiss not to remind you that the thing's still open." Brown settled himself to give a caution. "You oughtn't to let yourself think that we're completely home. If the election had come off today, as I told you, you would be Master. But you realise that these people can't give a formal pledge, and one or two actually made qualifications. I don't think they were important qualifications, but you mustn't think it's absolutely cut-and-dried. The picture might just conceivably alter—I don't think it's at all likely, but it might—before things happen to the present Master as they must."

"But you're satisfied?" said Jago. "Are you satisfied? Will you tell me that?"

Brown paused, and said deliberately:

"Assuming that the college was bound to be rather split, I consider things couldn't look much healthier than they do today."

"That's quite good enough for me." Jago sighed in peace, and stretched his arms like a man yawning. He smiled at the three of us. "I'm very grateful. I needn't tell my friends that, I think."

He left us, and we stood up and walked towards the window. It was a clear winter evening, the sky still bright in the west. The lamps of the court were already lit, but they seemed dim in that lucid twilight. The light in the Master's bedroom was already shining.

"I hope I didn't say too much," said Brown to Roy Calvert and me. "I think it's all right. But I'm not prepared to cheer until I hear the votes in the chapel. Some of us know," he said to me, with his wise, inquisitive smile, "that you've got astonishing judgment of men. But, if you'll believe anyone like me, there are things you can only learn through having actually been through them. I've seen elections look more certain than this one does to-day, and then come unstuck."

I was beginning to watch Jago walk slowly round the court.

"You see," said Brown, "we haven't much weight in our party. Pilbrow doesn't count for very much, and you're too young, Roy, and Eliot hasn't been here long enough. I suppose Chrystal and I are all right, but we could do with a bit more solid weight. Put it another way: suppose another candidate crops up. Someone who was acceptable to the influential people on the other side. I think it's just imaginable that Chrystal would feel we hadn't enough weight to stand out against that. He might feel obliged to transfer. You noticed that he covered himself in case that might happen. I don't say it's likely, but it's just as well to keep an eye open for the worst."

Jago was walking very slowly round the court, past the door of the Lodge, past the combination room window, past the hall, back under Brown's window. He walked slowly, luxuriously, with no sign of his usual active, jerky step. He began to walk round again, and as he turned we saw his face. It was brilliant with joy. He looked at the grass as though he were feeling: '*my* grass'. He trod on the path, and then strayed, for the love of it, on the cobbles; '*my* path, *my* cobbles'. He stood for a long moment in the middle of the court, and gazed round him in exaltation: '*my* college'.

He glanced at the lighted window in the Lodge, and quickly turned his head away.

"He looks happy, doesn't he?" said Arthur Brown, in a steady, affectionate, protective tone. "He takes everything so much to heart. I only hope we manage to get him in."

II
WAITING

THIRTEEN

PROGRESS OF AN ILLNESS

The light in the Master's bedroom shone over the court each night; the weeks passed, and we still had to pay our visits, talking of next year's fellowships and how soon it would be before he could come into hall. Chrystal could not bear it, and made some ill-tempered excuse for not going into the Lodge. Hearing the excuse and taking it at its face value, Lady Muriel was contemptuous: 'I always knew he was common,' Roy Calvert reported her as saying.

Roy had become Lady Muriel's mainstay. He was the only man from whom she would ask for help. It fell to him to spend hours at the Master's bedside, keeping up the deception—and afterwards to sit with Lady Muriel in the great drawing-room, listening to doubts and sorrows that she could never manage to articulate.

Roy loved them both, and did it for love, but he was being worn down. For any of us, this service would have been nerve-racking; for Roy, with melancholia never far away, it was dangerous. But it was he who had to watch the Master's astonishment as, after weeks of pseudo-recovery, he found himself getting thinner and more exhausted.

We all knew that soon Lady Muriel would have to tell him the truth. Many of us wanted her to do it, just to be saved the pretence at the bedside. Men as kind as Brown and Pilbrow could not help thinking of themselves, and wanted to be saved embarrassment even at the cost of agony for the Master and his wife. Theirs was the healthy selfishness which one needs for self-protection in the face of death. If one sees another's death with clear eyes, one suffers as Roy Calvert was suffering. Most of us see it through a veil of our own concerns: even Brown wanted Lady Muriel to tell the Master, so that Brown himself need no longer screw up his self-control before he went into the Lodge. Even Brown wanted her to tell him—but not before the feast, with everything arranged to receive Sir Horace Timberlake. As Brown said, with his usual lack of humbug: "It can't make things worse for the Master if we have the feast. And we may not find another chance of getting Sir Horace down. So I hope Lady Muriel doesn't have to break the news till afterwards."

As the day of the feast came near, that hope became strong all over the college. Some of us were ashamed of it; one's petty selfishnesses are sometimes harder to face than major sins. Yet we did not want to have to cancel the feast. As though by common consent, although we did not discuss it, not a hint was dropped in the Lodge. They were not likely to have remembered the date, or to have heard of Sir Horace's visit. We were too much ashamed to mention it. Lady Muriel must be left, we thought, to choose her own time.

The feast was fixed for Shrove Tuesday, and on the Sunday before I met Joan Royce in the court, both of us on our way to the Jagos for tea. She made a pretext for bringing in Roy's name with the first words she spoke: and I thought how we had all done the same, in love.

The Jagos kept open house for fellows at Sunday teatime, but when we arrived they were still alone. Mrs. Jago welcomed us with a greater assumption of state than ever: she had been telling herself that no one wished to see her, that Jago's house was deserted because of her. In return, she mounted to great heights of patronage towards Joan and me.

Jago was patiently chaffing her—he was too patient, I thought—as he handed us our cups. The tea, like all the amenities which Mrs. Jago chose, was the best in college; her taste was as fine as Brown's, though not as rich. Joan, who was not domesticated but enjoyed her food, asked her about some shortbread. Mrs. Jago was feeling too umbraged to take the question as a compliment. But then, by luck, Joan admired the china.

"Ah, that was one of our wedding-presents," said Mrs. Jago.

"I suppose," said Joan thoughtfully, "there are some arguments in favour of a formal wedding."

Mrs. Jago forgot her complaint, and said with business-like vigour:

"Of course there are. You must never think of anything else."

"She means," said Jago, "that you'll miss the presents."

Mrs. Jago laughed out loud, quite happily:

"Well, they were very useful to us, and you can't deny it."

"To tell you the truth," said Joan, "I was thinking the same myself."

Jago's eyes were glinting with sadistic relish.

"You two!" he said. "You pretend to like books. But you can't get away from your sex, neither of you. How dreadfully realistic women are."

They both liked it. They liked being bracketed together, the ageing malcontent and the direct fierce girl. They were both melted by him; his wife, for all her shrewishness, still could not resist him, and Joan smiled as she did for Roy.

Then the two women smiled at each other with a curious tenderness, and Mrs. Jago asked gently and naturally about the Master's state.

"Is he in any pain?"

"No, none at all. Nothing more than discomfort sometimes."

"I'm relieved to hear that," said Mrs. Jago.

Joan said:

"He's losing weight each day. And he's getting a little weaker. My mother knows that the truth oughtn't to be kept from him any longer."

"When will she tell him?"

"Almost at once."

Jago and I exchanged a glance. We did not know, could not ask, whether that meant before Tuesday.

"It must be a terrible thing to do," said Mrs. Jago.

"It's worse for them both now," said Joan, "than if she had told him that first night. I'm sure she should have done. I'm sure one should not hold back anything vital—we're not wise enough to know."

"That's a curious remark," said Jago, "for a girl your age. When I was twenty, I was certain I knew everything——"

"You're a man," said Joan, hitting back after his gibe. "Men grow up very late."

"Very late," said Jago. He smiled at her. "But I've grown up enough now to know how completely right you are about—your mother's mistake. She should have told him then."

"I hope I shouldn't have shirked telling you, Paul," said Mrs. Jago, "if it had happened to you."

"I should be surer of your courage," said Jago, "than I should of my own."

She smiled, simply and winningly. "I hope I should be all right," she said.

Perhaps she would always rise, I wondered, to the great crisis of their life. I wondered it still, after Joan left suddenly to go to a party and Mrs. Jago was once more affronted. When Joan had gone out, Jago said:

"There's fine stuff in that young woman. I wish she didn't look so sulky. But there's wonderfully fine stuff in her."

"I dare say there is," said Mrs. Jago. "But she must learn not to show that she's so bored with her entertainment."

"It's ten to one that she's going to this party on the off-chance that Roy Calvert will be there," I said.

"I hope she gets him," said Jago. "She would supply everything he lacks."

"No woman ought to get him," cried Mrs. Jago. "He's too attractive to be tamed."

Jago frowned, and for a second she was pleased. Then she

began to nag. She had been cherishing snubs all afternoon, and now she let them out. Lady Muriel, cried Mrs. Jago, was too much a snob, was too much above the wives of the fellows, for anyone like herself to know the inside of the Lodge.

She could not very well ask Joan: but how did Jago expect her to make plans for furnishing it ready for them to move in?

It was then I wondered again how she would rise to the great moments.

"I can't think, Paul," she was saying, "how you can expect me to have the Lodge fit to live in for six months after we move. I shall be a burden on you in the Lodge anyway, but I want a fair chance to get the place in order. That's the least I can do for you."

It would be awkward if she spoke in that vein to others, I thought, as I walked back to my rooms. Nothing would give more offence, nothing was more against the rules of that society: I decided Brown, as manager of Jago's caucus, must know at once. As I was telling him, he flushed. "That woman's a confounded nuisance," he said. For once he showed real irritation. Jago would have to be warned, but of all subjects it was the one where Jago was least approachable. "I'm extremely vexed," said Brown.

His composure had returned when he and Chrystal called on me after hall.

"It's nothing to do with the Mastership," he said affably. "We just want to make sure that we've got everything comfortable for Sir Horace."

"Can you give us a line on his tastes?" said Chrystal.

"We noticed last time that he took an intelligent interest in his dinner," said Brown. "We thought you might have picked up some points that we missed."

They were competent and thorough. They took as much trouble over putting up Sir Horace as over the campaign for the Mastership. No detail was too trivial for them to attend to. I could not help at all: anything I could have told them they had docketed and acted on already. Chrystal asked me to have Sir Horace to breakfast on the Wednesday morning.

"He'll have got tired of our faces by then," he said. "I want him to feel he's moving about without us following him." He gave his tough smile. "But I don't intend him to get into the wrong hands."

"Winslow was asking," said Brown, "whether Sir Horace was down for any particular purpose. And if not why we should upset the seating arrangements for the feast. He wondered whether we had mistaken Sir Horace for a person of distinction."

"Winslow is *amusing,*" said Chrystal. He made the word sound sinister. "Anway," he added, "things are pretty well tied up for Sir Horace now."

"If we get him down, that is," said Brown. "There are forty-eight hours before Tuesday, and the last I heard from the Lodge wasn't very reassuring."

I told them what Joan had said that afternoon.

"I'm not ready to say we've got Sir Horace down here," said Brown, "until I see the feast begin and him sitting at table."

"It's lamentable," said Chrystal.

There was a rap on the door. With surprise I saw Nightingale come in. He was looking harassed, pale and intent. In a strained effort to keep the proprieties, he said goodnight to me, and asked if I minded him intruding. Then he addressed himself to Brown.

"I looked in your rooms last night and tonight. You weren't there, so I had to try your friends."

"Ah well," said Brown, "you've found now."

"Is it anything private?" I said. "We can easily leave you together."

"It may be private," said Nightingale. "But it's nothing that Chrystal and you won't know."

He had sat down, and leant over the arm of his chair towards Brown and Chrystal.

"I want to find out," he said, "how the offices will go round, once Jago is Master."

Chrystal looked at him, and then at Brown. There was a pause.

"Well, Nightingale," said Chrystal, "you know as much as we do."

"No, not quite," said Nightingale.

"You know as much as we do, Nightingale," Chrystal repeated. "The only office that can possibly be affected is a tutorship. You know as well as we do that tutors are appointed by the Master."

"You're only telling me pieces out of the statutes," said Nightingale. "I can read them for myself."

"I'm telling you the position."

"I know all about that. Now I want to know how everything has been arranged behind the scenes." Nightingale smiled, with the dreadful suspiciousness of the unworldly: it is the unworldly who see neat, black, conscious designs hidden under all actions.

"I take you up on that, Nightingale," said Chrystal, but Brown interrupted him.

"If Jago becomes Master, as we hope, you'll find that he'll have a completely open mind about the appointment. Not a word has been said—either by him or anyone else."

"That's the fact," said Chrystal. "The normal practice is for the Master to ask for advice——"

"I know all about that," said Nightingale again.

"But he needn't follow it." Chrystal's temper was very near breaking. "I've known cases where it wasn't followed. If you're asking me what Jago will do, I can only tell you what I think. It won't take you very far. I assume he will make Brown Senior Tutor. That doesn't need saying. For the other tutor he'll have to look round."

"No, it doesn't need saying," said Nightingale, looking at Brown.

"It would be an outrage if it did need saying. Anyone in his senses would offer Brown that job if he had the chance," I burst out angrily.

For a moment Nightingale was quiet. Then he said:

"I'll take your word for it that the other tutorship isn't ear-marked yet. I want you to know that I expect to be considered for it myself."

We looked at him. He went on:

"I'm a long way senior of all the people without offices in this college. Except for Crawford who doesn't need them. I've been done out of every office since I was elected. I want to prevent it happening again."

Brown said, knowing that he had to be soothed:

"I'm sure you can be absolutely certain that Jago will consider you very seriously. Put it another way: your standing in the college means that you're bound to be the first person considered. So now I shouldn't worry if I were you, until the vacancy has really happened."

"I've been fobbed off like that before," said Nightingale. "It's too vague by half."

"No one can be any more definite," said Chrystal crisply.

"Is that as much as you can tell me?" Nightingale asked, half-threatening, half-pleading.

"It is," said Chrystal.

"I don't think anyone could possibly go any further," said Brown, anxious to conciliate him. "We couldn't conceivably commit Jago in any shape or form. You must see that that is quite unreasonable. If, when he had to make the appointment, he happened to ask our advice (as I dare say he might feel inclined to do), you can rest assured that we are the last persons to overlook your claim. We can guarantee that you'll receive an absolutely fair hearing."

"It's not good enough," said Nightingale.

"I'm sorry," said Chrystal.

"I'm very sorry indeed," said Brown. "We're really going to the extreme limit, you know. I don't quite see what more we can possibly do."

"I see what I can do."

"What's that?"

"I shall go and tackle Jago myself," said Nightingale.

It was late, too late for him to go round that night, I thought with relief, but he left at once.

FOURTEEN

COMMEMORATION OF BENEFACTORS

I woke early next morning, and lay listening to the series of quarter chimes, thinking of the alignment in the college. The parties had stayed constant since the two caucus meetings: no one had changed sides, although Francis Getliffe and Winslow had made an attempt to seduce Eustace Pilbrow. That was the only open attempt at persuasion so far made. Roy Calvert and I had wanted to have a go at old Gay, but Brown said wait. Both sides, in fact, were holding back; it was taken for granted that one or two in each caucus were waverers, but it was not yet time to attack them. In secret, Brown felt content because Pilbrow had been approached too early.

But, from the beginning, Nightingale had been our weakest spot. Waiting for Bidwell to announce nine o'clock that morning, I doubted whether we should ever hold him. How could one handle him in his present state? Last night he had wanted a promise. He would not be satisfied with less.

Looking down into the court after breakfast, I saw Jago walking through. I thought he should be warned at once, and so went down to meet him. I asked if he had seen Nightingale recently. He said no, and asked me why.

"He's coming to see you," I said.

"What for?"

"He wants you to promise that, when you become Master, you'll offer him the tutorship."

Jago's face was shadowed with anger: but, before he had

done more than curse, we heard a tapping from one of the ground-floor windows. It was Brown beckoning us in.

He was standing in the bedroom of the set which the college used for guests. There was a fire burning in the grate, and he had put some books on the bedside table. One of them was a large history of the college, and another a volume of reminiscences of Cambridge in the eighteenth century.

"What ever are you doing, Brown?" said Jago.

"I'm just seeing that things are ready for Sir Horace tomorrow night."

Jago exclaimed.

"I think it's a mistake to have it too luxurious," Brown explained. "People like Sir Horace might get a wrong idea. They might think we weren't completely poverty stricken. So one's got to be careful. But I think there's no harm in seeing that the room is reasonably decent."

"You oughtn't to be doing it," said Jago. Angry at the news of Nightingale, his hurt pride broke out here. "The college oughtn't to be an antiquarian hotel for wealthy men. And I don't like seeing them waited on by their betters."

"For God's sake don't tell Chrystal that," Brown said quickly, looking flushed and troubled. "I don't mind. I'm always ready to accept things. But some people aren't. I don't mind what you think of Sir Horace, though mark you I'm quite convinced you're wrong. But, even if you were right, I should be prepared to use the instruments that providence puts in our hands." He smiled at Jago with concern. "Oh, by the way, I was going to talk to you this morning about another of those instruments—actually our friend Nightingale."

"I've just mentioned it," I said.

"I've never heard of such insolence," Jago said fiercely.

"You must be statesman-like," said Brown.

"He's the last person I should think of making tutor."

"I hope you won't consider it necessary to tell him so," said Brown.

"I should dearly like to."

"No. You can be perfectly correct—without giving him the impression that the door is absolutely closed. Remember, indignation is a luxury which we can't afford just at present."

"We're not all as sensible as you, my dear friend." But Jago's temper was simmering down, and shortly after he asked us who should be tutor. "If I am lucky enough to be elected," he said, "I think I shall feel obliged to offer it to Getliffe." Brown did not believe Francis would look at it (Brown was always inclined to see reasons why it was difficult for men to take jobs): he had only taken the stewardship under protest, he was 'snowed under' with his two kinds of research.

"Then it looks," said Jago, "as if I should have to come to you, Eliot."

"I couldn't do it without giving up my practice in London," I said. "And I can't afford to do that yet."

"It's going to be difficult," said Jago.

"Don't meet trouble half-way," said Brown, settling down to give a caution. "We can cross that bridge when we come to it. And I know you won't take it amiss if I say something that's been rather on my mind. It would be quite fatal to give people the impression that the Mastership was a foregone conclusion."

"I'm sorry. I'll be very careful," said Jago with an easy, repentant smile.

"And you won't mind my saying one more thing. Will you make sure that everyone connected with you is careful too?"

Jago's smile left him on the instant. He stiffened, and replied with a dignity that was unfriendly, lofty and remote:

"I am already sure of that."

Soon he went away and Brown gave me a rueful look.

"Confound the woman. We can only hope that he'll talk to her in private. People do make things difficult for themselves. When I talk about the instruments of providence, and then think of Nightingale and that woman, I must say that I sometimes feel we might have had better luck. It's not going to be an easy row to hoe, is it?" He looked round the room again, and marshalled the books in a neat line.

"Ah well," he said, "I think I've got things shipshape for Sir Horace. I fancied it might encourage him if he read a bit about the history of the college. Always provided that we get him here. I suppose there's no fresh news from the Lodge this morning?"

There was, in fact, no fresh news that day. On the morning of Tuesday, the day of the feast, we learned that the Master had still not been told. Sir Horace had arrived by car at teatime, Brown told me in the evening, just as I was beginning to dress. "I think it's all right," said Brown. "I think it's reasonably certain now that we shall get safely through the feast."

He added that Jago had so far contrived to evade Nightingale.

The chapel bell began to peal at a quarter past six. From my window I saw the light over the chapel door bright against the February dusk. Some of the fellows were already on their way to the service. This was the commemoration of benefactors, and in the 'thirties the only service in the year to which most of the fellows went.

That change, like many others in the college, had been sharp and yet not paraded. In Gay's young days, the fellows were clergymen who went to chapel as a matter of course; chapel was part of the routine of their lives, very much like hall. Sixty years after, most of the fellows were agnostics of one kind or another. Despard-Smith officiated at the ordinary services in chapel, the Master went regularly, Brown and Chrystal at times. Many of us attended only at commemoration. I put a gown over my tail-coat, and went myself that night.

Everyone was there except the doctrinaire unbelievers, Winslow and Francis Getliffe. By Roy Calvert's side stood Luke, who would have liked to keep away and was there simply not to offend. Crawford came in smoothly, a C.B.E. cross glinting under his white tie. On the coats of several men, when they pulled their gowns aside, glittered medals of the 1914-18 war. It struck me how inexplicable a thing was bravery. Nightingale was wearing a D.S.O. and an M.C. and bar, Pilbrow rows of medals of miscellaneous Balkan wars. They were both brave men, by any human standard. Who would have picked them out for courage, if he did not know the facts?

Brown and Chrystal entered, with Sir Horace Timberlake between them. They had decided it would be pleasant for Sir Horace to hear benefactors commemorated. He was the only man in chapel without a gown; one noticed his well-kept, well-washed, well-fed figure in his evening suit; his face was smooth, fresh, open and he had large blue eyes, which often looked ingenuous; he was older than Chrystal or Jago, but the only line in his face was a crease of fixed attention between his eyes. The chapel was full. Rain pattered against the stained glass windows, but no radiance came through them at night, they were opaque and closed us in like the panelled walls. On this winter night, as the chapel filled with fellows, scholars and the choir, it contracted into a room small, cosy and confined.

We sang a psalm and a hymn. Gay's sonorous voice rang out jubilantly from the backmost stall. Despard-Smith, aged and solemn in his surplice, intoned some prayers in a gloomy voice: and, in a prose version of the same voice, he read the list of benefactions. It was a strange jumble of gifts, going back to the foundation, arranged not in value but in order of receipt. A bequest from the sixth Master to provide five shillings for each fellow at the audit feast was read out at inexorable length, sandwiched between a great estate and the patronage of the college's most valuable living. It was strange to hear those names and to know that some of the benefactors had listened to the beginning of that higgledy piggledy list and had wished their own names to follow. I thought how the sound of 'Next,——, twelfth Master, who left to the college five hundred pounds, together with his collection of plate' would affect Jago that night—Jago, who was sitting there with the threat of Nightingale still on his mind.

But the only response I actually heard was from Gay, who at the end, as we went into the ante-chapel, said resoundingly:

"Ah. I congratulate you, Despard. A splendid service, splendid. I particularly liked that lesson 'Let us now praise famous men.' Perhaps we hear slightly too much nowadays about praising the obscure. Often very fine people in their way, no doubt, but they shouldn't get all the praise."

In little groups we hurried through the rain to the combination room. Some of our guests were already waiting there, and they asked about the Master, for that news was all round Cambridge. In the gossipy closeness of the university, other high tables kept hearing on and off about the progress of the illness and the choice of his successor.

"No change," said Chrystal sharply to the room. "They've not told him yet. They can't avoid it soon."

The combination room was becoming crowded, and men were pushing past us, sherry glass in hand, to get a sight of the order of seating. I had already seen it; it was unfamiliar, simply because Chrystal had insisted that Sir Horace must sit at the principal table. Winslow had already seen it also; but he came in late that evening, and studied it again with a sour face.

Chrystal plucked him by the gown.

"Winslow, may I introduce Sir Horace Timberlake?"

"If you please. If you please."

Winslow greeted Sir Horace with his usual sarcastic courtesy. The conversation spurted and floundered. Sir Horace turned uneasily to the chapel service.

"I was very much impressed by your service, Mr. Winslow. There was nothing showy about it, you know what I mean?"

"Indeed?" said Winslow.

"I thought the chapel was very fine," Sir Horace persisted. "It's a very good bit of eighteenth century panelling you've got—I suppose it must be eighteenth century, mustn't it?"

"I'm sure you're right, Sir Horace," said Winslow. "But you're bound to be a far better authority than I am. I've only been inside the chapel to elect masters."

Immediately after, Winslow asked Sir Horace to excuse him, so that he could join his guest, who had just arrived, together with Pilbrow and his French writer. Sir Horace looked downcast.

Jago did not enter the combination room until just on eight o'clock. Although he had a guest with him, the Master of another college, Nightingale approached him at once. I heard him say: "I should like a word with you tonight, Jago." Jago replied, his tone over-friendly, upset, over-considerate:

"I'm extremely sorry. I'm up to the ears with work. I'm completely booked for tonight." He paused, and I heard him go on unwillingly: "Perhaps we could fix something for tomorrow?"

FIFTEEN

NEGOTIATIONS AFTER A FEAST

The wall lights in the hall were turned off for the feast, and the tables were lit by candles. The candle light shone on silver salts, candlesticks, great ornamental tankards, and on gold cups and plates, all arranged down the middle of the tables. Silver and gold shone under the flickering light; as one looked above the candlesticks, the linen fold was half in darkness and the roof was lost.

In order to seat Sir Horace as Chrystal insisted, Winslow had been brought down from the high table, and so had Pilbrow and Pilbrow's French writer. I sat opposite Winslow and started to talk across the table to the Frenchman. He was, as it turned out, very disappointing.

I recalled the excitement with which I heard Pilbrow was bringing him, and the cultural snobbery with which we had piqued Chrystal and dismissed Sir Horace. How wrong we were. An evening by Sir Horace's side would have been far more rewarding.

The Frenchman sat stolidly while Pilbrow had a conversational fling. "Pornograms," Pilbrow burst out. "An absolutely essential word—Two meanings. Something written, as in telegram. Something drawn, as in diagram." The Frenchman was not amused, and went on talking like a passage from his own books.

But, if he did not enjoy himself, others made up for it. All through the feast we heard a commentary from Gay, who sat at the end of the high table, not far away from us.

"Oysters? Excellent. You never did relish oysters, did you,

Despard? Waiter, bring me Mr. Despard-Smith's oysters. Capital. I remember having some particularly succulent oysters in Oxford one night when they happened to be giving me an honorary degree. Do you know, those oysters slipped down just as though they were taking part in the celebration.

He did not follow our modern fashion in wines. Champagne was served at feasts, but it had become the habit to pass it by and drink the hocks and moselles instead. Not so Gay. "There's nothing like a glass of champagne on a cold winter night. I've always felt better for a glass of champagne. Ah. Let me see, I've been coming to these feasts now for getting on for sixty years. I'm happy to say I've never missed a feast through illness, and I've always enjoyed my glass of champagne."

He kept having his glass filled, and addressed not only the end of his own table, but also ours.

"My saga-men never had a meal like this. Grand old Njal never had such a meal. My saga-men never had a glass of champagne. It was a very hard, dark, strenuous life those men lived, and they weren't afraid to meet their fates. Grand chaps they were. I'm glad I've been responsible for making thousands of people realise what grand chaps they were. Why, when I came on the scene, they were almost unknown in this country. And now, if a cultivated man does not know as much about them as he knows about the heroes of the Iliad, he's an ignoramus. You hear that, Despard? You hear that, Eustace? I repeat, he's an ignoramus."

We sat a long time over the port and claret, the fruit and coffee and cigars. There were no speeches at all. At last—it was nearly half past ten—we moved into the combination room again. Roy Calvert was starting some concealed badinage at the expense of Crawford and Despard-Smith. Like everyone else, he was rosy, bright-eyed and full of well being. Like everyone except Nightingale, that is: Nightingale had brought no guest, was indifferent to food, and always hated drinking or seeing others drink. He stood in the crush of the combination room, looking strained in the midst of the elation. Winslow came up to Gay, who was making his way slowly—the press of men parted in front of him—to his special chair.

"Ah, Winslow. What a magnificent feast this has been!"

"Are you going to congratulate me on it?" asked Winslow.

"Certainly not," said Gay. "You gave up being Steward a great number of years ago. I shall congratulate the man responsible for this excellent feast. Getliffe is our present steward. That's the man. Where is Getliffe? I congratulate him. Splendid work these young scientists do, splendid."

Chrystal and Brown did not mean to stay long in the combination room: it was time to get down to business. They caught Jago's eye and mine. We said goodbye to our guests, and followed the others and Sir Horace up to Brown's rooms.

"I wonder," said Brown, after he had established Sir Horace in a chair by the fire, "if anyone would like a little brandy? I always find it rather settling after a feast."

When each of us had accepted our drink, Sir Horace began to talk: but he was a long time, a deliberately long time, in getting to the point. First of all, he discussed his 'nephew', as he called young Timberlake, who was actually his second cousin.

"I want to thank all you gentlemen, and particularly Mr. Brown, for what you've done for the boy. I'm very grateful for all your care. I know he's not first class academically, and there was a time when it worried me, but now I've realised that he's got other qualities, you know what I mean?"

"I don't think you need worry about him," said Brown.

"He's an extremely good lad," said Jago, overdoing it a little. "Everyone likes him. It's a miracle that he's not hopelessly spoiled."

"I'm interested to hear you say that," said Sir Horace. "I

haven't got the slightest worry on that account. I've always been certain about his character. I saw that his mother took all the trouble she could about his education in that respect."

"I'm sure that we all regard him as doing you the greatest credit," said Brown.

"And speaking with due respect as a stupid sort of person in front of first-class minds, character does count, don't you agree with me?"

"There are times, Sir Horace," Jago broke out, "when I think young men like your nephew are our most valuable products. The first-class man can look after himself. But the man of personality who isn't much interested in learning—believe me, they're often the salt of the earth."

"I'm glad to hear you say that, Dr. Jago."

So it went on. Sir Horace pursued the subjects of his nephew, education, character versus intelligence, the advantages of the late developer, the necessity of a good home background, enthusiastically and exhaustively. Jago was his chief conversational partner, though Brown now and then put in a bland, emollient word. Chrystal tried once or twice to make the conversation more practical.

"I must apologise for the old chap I introduced to you," said Chrystal.

"Mr. Winslow?" said Sir Horace, who did not forget names.

"Yes. He's one of our liabilities. He's impossible. By the way, he's the Bursar, and if he weren't so impossible we should have asked him to meet you. In case we had a chance of continuing where we left off last time."

"Every organisation has its difficult men, you know," Sir Horace replied. "It's just the same in my own organisation. And that's why"—he turned to Jago—"I do attach the greatest importance to these universities turning out——" Indefatigably he continued to exhaust the subject of education. I wanted to see Brown and Chrystal successful, I wanted to go to bed, but I was also amused. Sir Horace was showing no effects of wine; he was tireless and oblivious of time. He was as much a master of tactics as Brown and Chrystal, and he was used to men trying to pump him for money. It was like him to cloud his manoeuvres behind a smoke screen of words, and when he was using this technique he did not much mind what he said. He called it 'thinking aloud'. Often, as was the case that night, he talked a lot of humbug. He was genuinely fond of his nephew, and was himself diffident in societies like the college which he did not know. But his own sons had real ability, and that was what Sir Horace valued. The idea that he had a veneration for stupid men of high character, or thought himself to be anything but intelligent, was absurd—and alone, in cold blood, he knew it was absurd.

Even Jago's vitality was flagging. Brown's eyes were not as bright as usual, Chrystal had fallen silent. The midnight chimes had sounded some time before. In the short lulls between Sir Horace's disquisitions, one heard the rain tapping on the windows. Sir Horace had worn us all down, and went on uninterrupted. Suddenly he asked, quite casually:

"Have you thought any more of expanding your activities?"

"Certainly we have," said Chrystal, coming alertly to life.

"I think someone suggested—correct me if I'm wrong—that for certain lines of development you might need a little help. I think you suggested that, Mr. Chrystal."

"I did."

"We can't do anything substantial placed as we are," said Brown. "We can only keep going quietly on."

"I see that," Sir Horace reflected. "If your college is going to make a bigger contribution, it will need some financial help."

"Exactly," said Chrystal.

"I think you said, Mr. Chrystal, that you needed financial help with no conditions attached to it. So that you could develop along your own lines. Well, I've been turning that over in my mind. I dare say you've thought about it more deeply than I have, but I can't help feeling that some people wouldn't be prepared to exert themselves for you on those terms. You know what I mean? Some people might be inclined to see if financial help could be forthcoming, but would be put off at just making it over to you for general purposes. Do you agree with me or don't you?"

Brown got in first:

"I'm sure I should be speaking for the college in saying that it would be foolish—it would be worst than that, it would be presumptuous—only to accept money for general purposes. But you see, Sir Horace, we have suffered quite an amount from benefactions which are tied down so much that we can't really use them. We've got the income on £20,000 for scholarships for the sons of Protestant clergymen in Galway. And that's really rather tantalising, you know."

"I see that," said Sir Horace again. "But let me put a point of view some people might take. Some people—and I think I include myself among them—might fancy that institutions like this are always tempted to put too much capital into bricks and mortar, do you know what I mean? We might feel that you didn't need to put up a new building, for instance."

"It's the go ahead colleges who are building," said Chrystal. "Take some examples. There are two colleges whose reputation is going up while we stay flat——"

Chrystal showed great deference to Sir Horace, a genuine humble deference, but he argued crisply. Just as Sir Horace's tactics formed behind a cloud of vague words. Chrystal's and Brown's were hidden in detail. Sharp, precise, confusing details were their chosen weapon. Complete confidence in the value of the college: their ability to treat Sir Horace as a far more gifted man, but at the same time to rely on the absolute self-confidence of the college as a society: their practice at handling details so that any course but their own became impossible: those were the means they opposed to Sir Horace's obstinate imagination.

The argument became lively, and we all took a hand. Sir Horace shook his head:

"I'm sorry, Mr. Chrystal. For once I don't agree with you."

"I'm sorry too," said Chrystal, with a tough, pleasant, almost filial smile.

Sir Horace had guessed completely right. If the college secured a benefaction, Chrystal and Brown were eager to put up a building: they were eager to see the college of their time—*their* college—leave its irremovable mark.

At the beginning Brown had, as he used to say, 'flown a kite' for compromise, and now Chrystal joined him. Clearly, any college would welcome thankfully a benefaction for a special purpose—provided it could be fitted into the general frame. Sir Horace was assenting cordially, his eyes at their most open and naïf. All of a sudden, he looked at Chrystal, and his eyes were not in the least naïf. "I also shouldn't be very happy about thinking of financial help which might be used to release your ordinary funds for building," he said in his indefatigable, sustained, rich-sounding, affable voice. "I can imagine other people taking the same line. They might be able to think out ways of preventing it, don't you agree with me? If people of my way of thinking got together some financial help, I'm inclined to believe it would be for men. This country is short of first-class men."

"What had you in mind?" asked Brown.

"I'm only thinking aloud, you know what I mean. But it seems to an outsider that you haven't anything like your proper number of fellowships. Particularly on what I might call the side of the future. You haven't anything like enough fellowships for scientists and engineers. And this country is dead unless your kind of institutions can bring out the first-rate men. I should like to see you have many more young scientific fellows. I don't mind much what happens to them, so long as they have their chance. They can stay in the university, or we shall be glad to take them in industry. But they are the people you want—I hope you agree with me."

"That's most interesting," said Jago.

"I'm afraid you're doubtful, Dr. Jago."

"I'm a little uncertain how much you want to alter us." Jago was becoming more reserved. "If you swamped us with scientific fellows—you see, Sir Horace, I'm at a disadvantage, I haven't the faintest idea of the scale of benefaction you think we need."

"I was only thinking aloud," said Sir Horace. In all his negotiations, as Chrystal and Brown perfectly understood, an exact figure was the last thing to be mentioned. Sums of money were, so to speak, hidden away behind the talk: partly as though they were improper, partly as though they were magic. "Imagine though," Sir Horace went on, "people of my way of thinking were trying to help the college with—a fairly considerable sum. Do you see what I mean?"

"A fellowship," said Chrystal briskly, "costs £20,000."

"What was that, Mr. Chrystal?"

"It needs a capital endowment of £20,000 to pay for a fellowship. If you add all the perquisites."

"I fancied that must be about the figure," said Sir Horace vaguely. "I imagine that a few people could see their way to providing a few of those units——" His voice trailed off. There was a pause.

"If they were giving them for fellowships in general," said Chrystal at last, "it would be perfect. There are no two ways about that. If the fellowships were restricted to science——"

"I am interested to hear what you think, Mr. Chrystal."

"If they were, it might raise difficulties."

"I don't quite see them."

"Put it another way," said Brown. "On the book, today, Sir Horace, we've got four scientific fellows out of thirteen. I wouldn't maintain that was the right proportion, we should all agree it wasn't enough. But if we changed it drastically at a single stroke, it would alter the place overnight. I should be surprised if you regarded that as statesman-like."

"Even the possibility of a benefaction is exciting," said Jago. "But I do agree with my colleagues. If the fellowships were limited to one subject, it would change the character of our society."

"You will have to change the character of your society in twenty years," said Sir Horace, with a sudden dart of energy and fire. "History will make you. Life will make you. You won't be able to stop it, Dr. Jago, you know what I mean?"

He had heard from the others that Jago was likely to be the next Master, and all the evening had treated him with respect. Sir Horace was charmed, Jago had for him the fascination of the unfamiliar, he wanted to be sure of Jago's unqualified approval. Brown and Chrystal he was more used to, he got on well with them, but they were not foreign, exciting, 'up in the air'.

All of us were waiting for a concrete bargain. Sir Horace, however, was willing to let a talk like this fade inconclusively away. He said:

"Well, I can't tell you how valuable I've found it to have all your opinions. It's most stimulating, I hope you agree with me? It gives us all plenty to think about."

He relished the power of giving or withholding money. It was always a wrench for him to relinquish it. He liked men waiting on him for a decision. There was sometimes a hidden chuckle beneath the anti-climax. Like Chrystal, he loved the feel of power.

It was after two o'clock, but he returned happily to the talk on education. He had great stamina and no sense of time, and another hour passed before he thought of bed.

SIXTEEN

AN HOUR OF PRIDE

When I went into my sitting-room next morning, half-an-hour before my usual time, there was Sir Horace, bright and trim and ready for his breakfast. He had had less than five hours' sleep, but he was as conservational as ever. He referred to our common acquaintances, such as Francis Getliffe's brother; he asked questions about the men he had met the night before. He was much taken with Jago. "There's an unusual man," said Sir Horace. "Anyone could see that in five minutes. Remarkable head he's got. Will he be your next Master?"

"I hope so."

"Brown and Chrystal want him, don't they?"

I said yes.

"Good chaps, those." Sir Horace paused. "If they were in industry, they'd drive a hard bargain."

I put in the thin edge of a question. But, though he had begun the day so talkative and affable, Sir Horace was no more communicative than the night before. His intention became masked at once in a loquacious stream about how much his nephew owed to Brown's tutoring. "I want him to get an honours degree. I don't believe these places ought to be open to the comfortably off, unless the comfortably off can profit by them," said Sir Horace, surprisingly unless one knew his streak of unorganised radicalism. "I hope you agree with me? If this boy doesn't get his honours degree, I shall cross off the experiment as a failure. But he'd never have touched it if it hadn't been for Brown. I'll tell you frankly, Mr. Eliot, there have been times when I wished the boy didn't require so much help on the examination side."

We had not long finished breakfast when Roy Calvert came in. They had met for a moment after the feast. Sir Horace was automatically cordial. Then he went to the window, and looked out at the court, lit by the mild sunshine of a February morning.

"How peaceful it all is," Sir Horace observed. "You don't realise what a temptation it would be to quit the rough-and-tumble and settle down here in peace."

He smiled with his puzzled, lost, friendly look, and Roy smiled back, his eyes glinting with fun.

"I don't think we do," said Roy. "I'll change with you, Sir Horace."

"You wouldn't get such peace."

"I don't know. Are some of your colleagues on speaking terms? Ours just manage it. Should you call that specially peaceful?"

Sir Horace laughed uneasily; he was not used to affectionate malice from young men half his age. But he had an eye for quality. Up to that moment he had placed Roy as an ornament and a flâneur; now he captured his interest, just as Jago had done. He began asking Roy about his work. He was mystified by most of Roy's explanation, but he felt something here that he had not met. I saw him studying Roy's face when it was not smiling.

Soon he was asking if he could be shown Roy's manuscripts. They went off together, and I did not see them until midday. Then Roy ran up the stairs to say that the 'old boy' was going; he fetched Brown and Chrystal and we all met at the side door of the college, where the car was garaged. The chauffeur had just arrived, and Sir Horace was standing by the car in a tremendous fur coat, looking like an Imperial Russian general.

"I'm sorry I've not seen anything of you this morning, Mr. Chrystal," said Sir Horace. "I've had a very interesting time looking at Mr. Calvert's wonderful things. There were several points last night I should like to explore with you again, you know what I mean? I very much hope we shall have the opportunity some time."

The car drove off, Sir Horace waving cordially. As it turned out of sight, Roy Calvert asked:

"Is he going to unbelt?"

"Don't ask me," said Chrystal. He added loyally: "Of course, men in his position have to make a hundred decisions a day. I expect he looks on this as very small beer—and just puts it off until he's got important things finished. It's unfortunate for us."

"I'm not giving up hope yet," said Brown, robust against disappointment. "I can't believe he'd lead us up the garden path."

"It would be funny if he did," said Roy. "And took a series of dinners off us. Never getting to the point."

"I don't call that funny, Calvert," Chrystal said irritably.

"I believe it may come right," said Brown. He added, in a hurry: "Mind you, I shan't feel inclined to celebrate until I see a cheque arrive on the bursary table." He said aside to Chrystal: "We've just got to think of ways and means again. I should be in favour of letting him lie fallow for a month or two. In the meantime, we shall have time to consider methods of giving him a gentle prod."

The sky was cloudless and china-blue, there was scarcely a breath of wind. The sun was just perceptibly warm on the skin, and we thought of taking a turn round the garden before lunch. Roy Calvert and Chrystal went in front. They were talking about investments. Roy was the only child of a rich man, and Chrystal liked talking to him about money. Brown and I followed on behind. Our way to the garden was overlooked by the windows of the tutor's house, and as we walked I heard my name called in Jago's voice.

I stayed on the path, Brown strolled slowly on. Jago came out from his house—and with him was Nightingale.

"Can you spare us a moment, Eliot?" Jago cried. His tone was apologetic, almost hostile.

"Of course."

"Nightingale and I have been discussing the future of the college. Naturally, we all think the future of the college depends on the men we attract to college offices." Jago's words were elaborate, his mouth drawn down, his eyes restless. "So that we've been speculating a little on which of our colleagues might consider taking various college offices."

"These things have a way of being settled in advance," said Nightingale.

"I hope it doesn't embarrass you to mention your own future," Jago had to go on.

"Not in the slightest," I said.

"I know it's difficult. No one can pledge themselves too far ahead. But I've just been telling Nightingale that, so far as I know, you wouldn't feel free to think of a college office in the next few years."

"I shouldn't. I can be ruled out," I said.

"Why? Why can we rule you out?" Nightingale broke out in suspicion.

I had to give a reason for Jago's sake.

"Because I don't want to break my London connection. I can't spend two days a week in London and hold an office here."

"Your two days must be exceptionally well paid." Nightingale smiled.

"It's valuable for the college," said Jago with an effort to sound undisturbed, "to have its young lawyers taught by a man with a successful practice."

"It seems to be rather vauable for Eliot." Nightingale smiled again. But his suspicions had temporarily abated, and he parted from us.

"Good God," muttered Jago, as Nightingale disappeared at the bottom of his staircase.

"I hope you contained yourself," said Brown, who had been waiting for us to join him. We all three walked towards the garden.

"I was very tactful," said Jago. "I was *despicably* tactful, Brown. Do you know that he doubted my word when I said that Eliot here couldn't take a tutorship if it was offered him? He said he might believe it if he heard it from Eliot himself. I ought to have kicked the man out of my study. Instead of that, I inflicted him on Eliot, so that he could have the satisfaction of hearing it. I am so sorry, Eliot."

"You had to do it," I said.

"I call it statesman-like," said Brown.

"I call it despicable," said Jago.

The garden was quiet with winter, the grass shone emerald in the sunlight, the branches of the trees had not yet begun to thicken. In the wash of greens and sepias and browns stood one blaze of gold from a forsythia bush. Roy and Chrystal were standing under a great beech, just where the garden curved away to hide the inner 'wilderness'.

"God forgive me," said Jago bitterly, as we stepped on to the soft lawn. "I've never prevaricated so shamefully. The man asked me outright what my intentions were. I replied—yes, I'll tell what I replied—I told him that it might put us both in a false position if I gave a definite answer. But I said that none of those I knew best in the college could possibly take a tutorship. That's where your name came in, Eliot. He insisted on discussing you all one by one."

"I hope you let him," said Brown.

"I let him."

"I hope you didn't give him the impression that you'd never offer him the job," said Brown.

"I should be less ashamed," said Jago, "if I could think I had."

Jago was angry and anxious. He was angry at what he had been forced to do: anxious that it might not be enough. But, most of all that morning in the sunny garden, he was angry, bitterly angry, at the insult to his pride. He had lowered himself, he had thrown his pride in front of his own eyes and this other man's, and now, ten minutes later, it had arisen and was dominating him. He was furious at the humiliation which policy imposed: was this where ambition had taken him? was this the result of his passion? was this the degradation which he had to take?

Brown would not have minded. A less proud man would have accepted it as part of the game: knowing it, Jago looked at his supporter's kind, shrewd and worldly face, and felt alone. The shame was his alone, the wound was his alone. When he next spoke, he was drawn into himself, he was speaking from a height.

"I assure you, Brown, I don't think you need fear a defection," he said, with a mixture of anxiety, self-contempt, and scorn. "I handled him pretty well. I was as tactful as a man could be."

SEVENTEEN

"WE'RE ALL ALONE"

After lunch that day Roy Calvert stopped me in the court. His lips twitched in a smile.

"Everyone was worried whether we should have the feast, weren't they?" he said.

"Yes."

"Just so. Well, I heard a minute ago that it wasn't necessary. Joan and her mother never intended to tell him before the feast. They'd marked down the date weeks ago. They knew the old boy was coming down to unbelt—which he didn't—and they decided that we mustn't be disturbed. Isn't that just like the appalling sense of women?"

I could not help laughing.

"We've been sold," said Roy. "Not only you and me—but all those sensible blokes. We've been absolutely and completely and magnificently sold."

But, though he was smiling, he was already sad, for he had guessed what was to happen that day. I did not see him again all afternoon and evening. His name was on the dining list for hall, but he did not come. Late at night, he entered my room and told me that he had been with Lady Muriel for hours. She had broken the news to the Master early in the afternoon.

I was distressed not only on their account, but on Roy's. He was beginning to have the look and manner which came upon him during a wave of depression. And I was not reassured when, instead of telling me anything that had been said in the Lodge, he insisted on going to a party. For, as he and I knew too well, there was a trace of the manic-depressive about his moods. I was more afraid for him in a state of false hilarity than in sadness.

However, he was genial at the party, although he did not speak of the Master until we had returned to college and were standing in sight of the Lodge windows. It was well into the small hours, but one light was still shining.

"I wonder," Roy said, "if he can sleep tonight."

We stood looking at the window. The court was quiet beneath the stars.

Roy said:

"I've never seen such human misery and loneliness as I did today."

Beside the fire in his sitting-room, he went on telling of the Master and Lady Muriel, and he spoke with the special insight of grief. Theirs had not been a joyous marriage. The Master might have brought happiness to many women, Roy said, but somehow he had never set her free. As for her, there was a terrible story that, when the Master was engaged to her, an aunt of hers said to him: "I warn you, she has no tenderness." That showed what her façade was like, and yet, Roy had told me and I believed him, it was the opposite of the truth. Perhaps few husbands could have called her tenderness to the surface, and that the Master had never done. She had given him children, they had struggled on for twenty-five years. "She's never had any idea what he's really like," said Roy. "Poor dear, she's always been puzzled by his jokes."

Yet they had trusted each other; and so, that afternoon, it was her task to tell him that he was going to die. Roy was certain that she had screwed herself up and gone straight to the point. "She's always known that she's failed him. Now she felt she was failing him worst of all. Because anyone else would have known what to say, and she's never been able to put one word in front of another."

Occasionally we had imagined that the Master saw through the deception, but it was not true. The news came as a total shock. He did not reproach her. She could not remember what he said, but it was very little.

"It's hard to think without a future." That was the only remark she could recall.

But the hardest blow for her was that, in looking towards his death, he seemed to have forgotten her. "I was less use than ever," Lady Muriel had cried to Roy.

It was that cry which had seared Roy with the spectacle of human egotism and loneliness. They had lived their lives together. She had to tell him this news. She saw him thinking only of his death—and she could not reach him. It did not matter whether she was there or not.

After she had gone out, and Joan had visited him for a few minutes, he had asked to be left to himself.

Roy said:

"We're all alone, aren't we? Each one of us. Quite alone."

Later, he asked:

"If she was miserable and lonely today, what was it like to be him? Can anyone imagine what it's like to know your death is *fixed?*"

EIGHTEEN

RESULT OF AN ANXIETY

After his demand on Jago, Nightingale seemed to be satisfied or to have lost interest. Brown's explanation was that he was enough open to reason to realise that he could go no further; for his own practical ends, it was sensible to stop. Brown did not let us forget Nightingale's practical ends: "He may be unbalanced," said Brown, "he may be driven by impulses which I am sure you understand better than I do, but somehow he manages to give them a direction. And that concerns me most. He wants some very practical things, and he's going to be a confounded nuisance."

That was entirely true. I learned a lot about men in action, I learned something of when to control a psychological imagination, from Arthur Brown. But it was also true that Nightingale was right in the middle of one of those states of anxiety which is like a vacuum in the mind: it fills itself with one worry, such as the tutorship; that is worried round, examined, explored, acted upon, for the time being satisfied: the vacuum is left, and fills immediately with a new worry. In this case it was the March recommendations of the council of the Royal Society: would he get in at last? would his deepest hope come off?

This anxiety came to Nightingale each spring. It was the most painful of all. And it seemed sharper because, unlike his worry over the tutorship, there was nothing he could do to satisfy himself. He could only wait.

Crawford had just been put on the council of the Royal Society for the second time, owing to someone dying. Crawford told us this news himself, with his usual imperturbability. Nightingale heard him with his forehead corrugated, but he could not resist asking:

"Do you know when the results will be out?"

Crawford looked at his pocket-book.

"The council will make its recommendations on Thursday March —." He told Nightingale the date. "Of course, they're not public for a couple of months after. Is there anyone you're interested in?"

"Yes."

The intense answer got through even to Crawford.

"You're not up yourself, are you?"

"Yes."

"I'm afraid I didn't realise it," said Crawford, making an unconcerned apology. "Of course your subject is a long way from mine. I don't think I've heard anything about the chemists' list. If I did, I'm afraid I paid no attention. If I knew anything definite, I should be tempted to tell you. I'm not a believer in unnecessary secrecy."

Francis Getliffe had been listening to the conversation, and we went out of the room together. As the door closed behind us, he said:

"I wish someone would put Nightingale out of his misery."

"Do you know the result?"

"I've heard the lists. He's not in, of course. But the point is, he's never even thought of. He never will get in," said Francis.

"I doubt if anyone could tell him," I said.

"No," said Francis.

"When are you going to get in, by the way?" I asked, forgetting our opposition, as though our ease had returned.

"I shan't let myself be put up until I stand a good chance. I mean, until I'm certain of getting in within three or four years. I'm not inclined to go up on the off-chance."

"Does that mean the first shot next year?"

"I'd hoped so. I'd hoped that, if I was put up next year,

I was bound to be elected by 1942. But things haven't gone as fast as they should," he said with painful honesty.

"You've been unlucky, haven't you?"

"A bit," said Francis. "I might have got a shade more notice. But that isn't the whole truth. I haven't done as much as I ought."

"There's plenty of time," I said.

"There's got to be time," said Francis.

None of us, I thought, was as just as he was, or made such demands on his will.

About three weeks later, as I went into the porter's lodge one day after lunch, I heard Nightingale giving instructions. A special note in his tone caught my attention: it occurred to me that it must be the day of the Royal results. "If a telegram comes for me this afternoon," he repeated, "I want the boy sent to my rooms without a minute's delay. I shall be in till hall. Have you got that? I don't want a minute's delay."

The afternoon was harshly cold; the false spring of February had disappeared, and before tea-time it was dark, the sky overhung with inky clouds. I stayed by my fire reading, and then sent for tea before a pupil arrived. As I waited for the kitchen porter, I stood looking out of the window into the court. A few flakes of snow were falling. Some undergraduates came clanking through in football boots, their knees a livid purple, their breath steaming in the bitter air. Then I saw Nightingale walking towards the porter's lodge. The young men were shouting heartily: Nighingale went past them as though they did not exist.

In a moment, he was on his way back. He had found no telegram. He was walking quite slowly: the cold did not touch him.

In hall that night his face was dead white and so strained that the lines seemed rigid, part of the structure of his brow. Every few seconds he put a hand to the back of his head, and the tic began to fascinate Luke, who was sitting next to him. Several times Luke looked at the pale, grim, harassed face, started to speak, and then thought better of it. At last his curiosity was too strong, and he said:

"Are you all right, Nightingale?"

"What do you mean, all right?" Nightingale replied. "Of course I'm all right. What do you think you're talking about?"

Luke blushed, but would not be shouted down.

"I thought you might have been overworking. You were looking pretty tired——"

"Overworking," Nightingale said. "I suppose you think that's the worst thing that can happen."

Luke shrugged his shoulders, muttered a curse under his breath and caught my eye. He had a rueful, self-mocking sense of humour; his work was in a hopeful phase, and he lived at the laboratory from nine in the morning until it closed at night. It was hard to have his head bitten off for laziness.

We were already through the soup and fish when Crawford came into hall. He slipped into the seat next mine, but before he sat down called up the table to Winslow:

"My apologies for being late. I've had to attend the council of the Royal. And this weather wasn't very good for the train."

He ate his way methodically through the first courses and had caught us up at the sweet. All the time Nightingale's eyes were fixed on him with a last desperate question of anxiety. But Crawford was untroubled and, having levelled up in eating, talked reflectively to me. It was like him that his conversation did not alter with the person he was addressing; if there was anything he wanted to deliver, I served to receive it as well as Francis Getliffe.

"Selecting people for honorific purposes is a very interesting job. But it's not as easy as you might suppose. As a matter of fact, I was thinking of the choice of Fellows of the Royal—which I happen just to have been concerned with.

Speaking as a man of science, I should be happier if there were sharper criteria to help us make the choice. I'm not meaning the choice is made unfairly: no, I should say that on the conscious level they're as fair as human choices can be. But the criteria are not sharp, and it's no use pretending they can be. 'Original work of distinction'—how can you compare one man with a new theory on the interior of the stars with someone else who has painstakingly measured the movements of a fish?"

The rest had finished the meal, Winslow was waiting to say grace, but Crawford finished saying what he had to say. On our way into the combination room, he suddenly noticed Nightingale, and called out:

"Oh, Nightingale. Just a minute."

We passed on, leaving the two of them together. But we heard Crawford's audible, impersonally friendly voice saying clearly:

"No luck for you this time."

They followed us at once. Most of those dining went away without sitting down to wine, but Crawford said that he had had a busy day and needed a glass of port. So Winslow and I shared a bottle with him, and listened to his views on the organisation of science, the place of the Royal Society, the revolution in scientific technology. Nightingale hung on to every word.

Crawford enjoyed talking; some were put off by his manner and could not bear to listen, but they lost something. He had not the acute penetrating intellect of Roy Calvert; in an intelligence test he would not have come out as high as, say, the Master or Winslow; and he had no human insight at all. But he had a broad, strong, powerful mind, not specially apt for entertaining but made to wear.

Nightingale sat outside the little circle of three round which the bottle passed. Since he learned the news, his expression was still taut with strain, but his eyes had become bright and fierce. There was nothing crushed about him;

his whole manner was active, harsh, and determined as he listened to Crawford. He listened without speaking. He did not once give his envious smile. But, once as I watched him, his eyes left Crawford for an instant and stared inimically at mine. They were feverishly bright.

When I went away, the three of them were still at the table, and Crawford and Winslow were emptying the bottle.

The next evening, half an hour before dinner, I heard Francis Getliffe's firm, plunging, heavy step on the stairs. He used to call in often on his way to hall, but he had not done so since our quarrel.

"Busy?" he said.

"No."

"Good work." He sat in the armchair across the fire, took a cigarette, cleared his throat. He was uncomfortable and constrained, but he was looking at me with mastery.

"Look, Lewis, I think it's better for me to tell you," he said. "Your majority for Jago has been broken."

He was triumphant, he enjoyed telling me—yet he felt a streak of friendly pity.

"Who's gone over?" I said, but I did not need to ask.

"Nightingale. He told Crawford himself last night. Winslow was there too."

I blamed myself for having left them together, with Nightingale in that condition. Then I thought that was not realistic: it could have made no difference. And I did not want to show concern in front of Francis Getliffe.

"If it weren't for the vote, which is a nuisance," I said, "I should wish you joy of him."

Francis gave a grim smile.

"That makes it 6—5. Neither side has a clear majority. I hadn't reckoned on that. I don't know whether you had."

NINETEEN

"A NICE LITTLE PARTY"

As soon as Francis Getliffe left me, I rang up Brown. He said that he was kept by a pupil, but would get rid of him and come. The moment he entered, I told him the news.

"So that's it," said Brown. He accepted it at once.

"Things happen as they must," he added in a round, matter-of-fact tone. "They've gone pretty smoothly for us so far. We've got to be ready for our set-backs. I don't say this isn't a confounded nuisance, because it obviously is. Still, repining won't get us anywhere, and there's plenty to do if we're going to retrieve the position."

"I shall be astonished," I said, "if Nightingale changes sides again."

"I expect you're right," said Brown. "But we've got other people to look after too, you know. Mind you," he went on, with a trace of irritation, "I always thought we handled Nightingale badly. We ought to have taken him round to Jago's that first afternoon. It would have been well worth waiting for him. I was wrong not to stick in my heels."

But Brown did not spend much time blaming Chrystal or himself. He was thinking realistically of what it meant 6—5 now. For Crawford—Winslow, Despard-Smith, Getliffe, Gay and Nightingale. For Jago—Brown, Chrystal, Calvert, Eliot, Pilbrow and Luke. "It's bad to lose a clear majority. It affects your own party," Brown reflected. "Just at the moment, I should guess they're more confident than we are. We must take care that a rot doesn't set in."

"Shall you do anything tonight?"

"No," said Brown. "We've got to wait. We needn't tell

Jago yet. There's no point in worrying him unnecessarily. You see, we've only learned this from the other side. It explains a dig Winslow gave Chrystal today, by the way. But we shall be well-advised not to take any action until we hear from Nightingale himself. Remember, he's always tried to do the proper thing, and he's bound to let Jago know. A decent man couldn't just cross over without sending some sort of explanation. And there's always the bare chance that he may think better of it."

For once, Brown's patience guided him wrong. Gossip was going round the college that night and next morning; apparently Nightingale had already spoken with venom against Jago and 'his clique'. Jago had heard nothing of it, but I received accounts from several sources, differing a good deal from one another. Brown spoke to Chrystal, went back on his tactics laid down the previous night, and decided it was time to 'have it out'. They were planning to get Nightingale alone after hall, as though by chance. As it happened, Saturday, that very night, was made for their purpose. The number of men dining varied regularly with the days of the week; Sunday was always a full night—'married men escaping the cold supper at home', old Despard-Smith used to complain. Saturday, on the other hand, was a sparse one, usually only attended by bachelors living in college. That particular Saturday happened to be specially sparse, for Despard-Smith had a cold, and there was a concert in the town which removed Pilbrow and also Roy Calvert, who was escorting Mrs. Jago. Chrystal and Brown put their names down to dine that night, and there arrived in hall only the thee of us, Nightingale and Luke.

Nightingale was silent during dinner. Brown kept up a stream of comfortable, unexacting conversation, but all the time, through the amiable remarks on college games, his glance was constantly coming back to Nightingale's defensive mask.

"How long is it since you saw the Lent races, Nightingale?" Chrystal asked directly.

"I haven't time for anything like that," said Nightingale. They were his first words since we sat down.

"You'll make yourself ill," said Chrystal, with genuine sympathy. "Come on the towpath with me next week. It will do you good."

"I can look after myself," said Nightingale. Up to that night, he had held on to his politeness, but now it slipped away.

"I've heard that before," said Chrystal. "Listen to me for once."

Nightingale's eyes were blank, as he sat there, exposed to Chrystal's crisp voice and Brown's rich, placid one: he knew what to expect.

Luke left immediately after hall. His work was occupying him more than ever, and he said that he had to work out some results. Whether or not it was because of his precocious tact I did not know. Brown said:

"Well, that does make us a nice little party."

He ordered a bottle of claret and took his place at the head of the table. Nightingale was still standing up. He started to move towards the door. He was leaving, without saying goodnight. We were exchanging glances: suddenly he looked back at us. He turned round, retraced his steps, sat down defiantly at Brown's right hand. There was something formidable about him at that moment.

The decanter went round, and Brown warmed his glass in his hands.

"Has Jago been dining recently? I haven't seen him all the week," Brown asked casually.

"He's not been here any of the nights I have," I said.

"I've only dined once this week," said Chrystal. "He wasn't here."

Nightingale stirred his coffee, and did not reply.

"Has he coincided with you, Nightingale?" Brown asked.

"No."

"That reminds me," said Brown in the same conversational tone. "I've been meaning to ask you for some time. How are you feeling about the Mastership now?"

"How are you?" Nightingale retorted.

"I'm still exactly where I was," said Brown. "I'm quite happy to go on supporting Jago."

"Are you?" Nightingale asked.

"Why," said Brown, "I hope you haven't had any second thoughts. At least, not enough to upset your commitments——"

"Commitments!" Nightingale broke out. "I'm not going to be bound because I made a fool of myself. I can tell you, here and now, I've thought better of it."

"I'm very sorry to hear it," said Brown. "But perhaps we——"

"And I can tell you I've good reasons to think better of it. I'm glad I had my eyes opened before I'd done the damage. Do you think I'm going to vote for a man who's taking it for granted that he's been elected and is behaving like the Master before the present one is dead? And whose wife is putting on airs about it already?" He stopped, and asked more virulently: "Do you think I'm going to put up with a Master who's backed by people who are getting the college a bad name——?"

"Who do you mean?" I was infuriated.

"I mean your friend Calvert, for one."

"Anything you say about him is worthless," I said.

"There are one or two others," said Nightingale, "who live apart from their wives. It's not for me to say whether they want to keep their liberty of action——"

"Stop that," said Chrystal, before I could reply. "You're going too far. I won't have any more of it, do you hear?"

Nightingale sank back, white-faced. "I'm glad I've explained to you my reasons for changing," he said.

What were his true motives, I thought, as I stared at him through my own anger. He was possessed by envy and frustration. Crawford talking unconcernedly of the 'Royal', making it sound like a club to which one belonged as a matter of course, turned the knife in the wound as if he were jealous in love and had just heard his rival's name. So did Chrystal and Brown, looking happy and prosperous in their jobs, going about to run the college. So did the sound of Mrs. Jago's voice, asking the number of bedrooms in the Lodge or the kind of entertainment that undergraduates preferred. So did the sight of Roy Calvert with a girl. And Nightingale suffered. He did not suffer with nobility, he did not accept it in the grand manner, which, though it does not soften suffering, helps to make the thought of it endurable when the victim is having a respite from pain. Nightingale suffered meanly, struggling like a rat, determined to wound as well as be wounded. There was no detachment from his pain, not a glimmer of irony. He bared his teeth, and felt release through planning a revenge against someone who 'persecuted' him. He never felt for a day together serene, free and confident.

I could understand his suffering. One could not miss it, for it was written in his face. I was not moved by it, for I was cut off by dislike. And I could understand how he struggled with all his force, and went into action, as he was doing now, with the intensity of a single-minded drive. He had the canalised strength of the obsessed.

But I could not begin to know why his envy had driven him first away from Crawford, now back to him. Had he, that night of the Royal results, found in Crawford's assurance some sort of rest? Was Crawford the kind of man he would, in his heart, have liked to be?

I could not see so far. But I was sure that, as Arthur Brown would remind me, there was a kind of practical veneer on his actions now. When he thought of what he was doing, he gave practical self-seeking reasons to himself. He probably imagined that Crawford would help get him into the Royal next year. He had certainly decided that Jago would not give him the tutorship, would do nothing for him. His calculation about Crawford was, of course, quite ridiculous. Crawford, impersonal even to his friends, would be the last man to think of helping, even if help were possible. Nevertheless, Nightingale was certain that he was being shrewd.

Chrystal was saying:

"You ought to have told us you were going over."

"Ought I?"

"You owed it to us to tell us first," said Chrystal.

"I don't see why."

"I take you up on that, Nightingale. You can't pledge yourself to one candidate and then promise to vote for another. It's not the way things are done."

"If I stick to the etiquette, no one else does. I'm not going to penalise myself any more," said Nightingale.

"It's not the way to do business."

"I leave business to your clique," Nightingale replied. He rose and, without saying goodnight, went towards the door. This time he did not turn back.

"That's that," said Chrystal. "I don't know what's happening to Nightingale."

"Well, there it is," said Brown.

"Shall we get him back?" Chrystal asked.

"Not a hope in hell," I said.

"Why are you so sure?"

"I must say," said Brown, "that I'm inclined to take Eliot's view. It's much safer to regard the worst as inevitable, because then it won't do us any harm if we turn out to be wrong. But that apart, I confess I shall be surprised if we see Nightingale back again."

"You may be right," said Chrystal.

"I haven't a doubt," I said.

"Have you summed him up right?" asked Chrystal, still wanting to disbelieve.

"I'm ready to rely on Eliot's judgment," said Brown.

"In that case," said Chrystal, changing round briskly, "we ought to see Jago at once."

"Do you want to?" For once Brown shrank from a task.

"No. But we can't leave him in the dark."

"I suppose it would be rather tempting providence——"

"If we don't tell him tonight," said Chrystal, "some kind friend will do him the service tomorrow or next day. It's lamentable, but it will come better from us."

"I must say that it's going to be abominably unpleasant."

"I'll go by myself," said Chrystal. "If you prefer that."

"Thank you." Brown smiled at his friend, and hesitated. "No, it will be better for him if we all go. It will let him realise that he's still got most of his party intact."

Brown and I wanted an excuse for delaying, even if only for ten more minutes, in the combination room. It was Chrystal, buoyed up by action, never despondent when he could get on the move, who forced us out.

TWENTY

THE DEPTH OF AMBITION

As we already knew, Jago was alone. We found him in his study reading. His eyes flashed as soon as he saw us; every nerve was alert; he welcomed us with over-abundant warmth. Chrystal cut him short by saying:

"We've got some bad news for you."

His face was open in front of us.

"You must be prepared for changes to happen both ways," said Brown, trying to cushion the blow. "This isn't the last disturbance we shall get."

"What is it?" Jago cried. "What is it?"

"Nightingale has gone over," said Chrystal.

"I see."

"You mustn't let it depress you too much," Brown said. "It was always a surprise to me that you ever attracted Nightingale at all. Put it another way: you can regard Nightingale as being in his natural place now, and you can think of the sides being lined up very much as we might have expected beforehand."

Jago did not seem to hear the attempt to comfort him.

"I suppose he's done it because I didn't promise him the tutorship. I couldn't. It was a wretched position to be flung into. It was utterly impossible. I suppose it's too late to mend matters now. It's difficult to make a move——"

Brown was looking at him with an anxious glance.

"Forget Nightingale," Brown broke in very quickly. "Count him out."

"If I'd offered him the tutorship it would have held him." There was a passionate appeal in Jago's voice.

"I doubt it very much," I said.

"If I could only have made something like a promise."

"Jago," said Chrystal, "if you had promised that man the tutorship, you might have gained one vote—but you would have lost six others. So you can rest easy."

"Are we letting him go without an effort?" cried Jago. "Is it utterly impossible to persuade him back?"

"We think so," said Chrystal.

Jago's whole expression was racked.

"Shall I see him?" he said.

"No," said Chrystal.

"I don't think it would help much." Brown's tone was as firm as Chrystal's, though he went on with a friendly explanation: "He's an obstinate man. It might only carry things from bad to worse. There's no one so bitter as a turncoat, you know. I think it's very much safer to regard him as an enemy from now on."

"If you don't," said Chrystal, "I can't answer for the consequences."

He and Brown looked solid, earthy men of flesh and bone against Jago at that moment. Jago's face seemed only a film in front of the tortured nerves. Yet they were telling him, as each of us in the room perfectly understood without a definite word being spoken, that he must make no attempt —by any suggestion of a promise—to bring Nightingale back.

He had wanted us to encourage him by a hint: he had been appealing for a piece of machiavellian advice 'you oughtn't to make Nightingale a promise: but there's no harm in his thinking you have done so: he'll be disappointed later, that's all'. If we had given him the most concealed of hints, he would have rushed to Nightingale, used every charm of which he was capable, safeguarded himself verbally perhaps but in no other way. If he could have made a bargain with Nightingale, whatever it meant letting Nightingale think he had been promised, he would have made it that night. It needed Chrystal's threat to stop him at last.

Just as he had been more angry than the others at Nightingale's first approach, now he was tempted to stoop lower than they would ever do. In the garden, on the February morning when Nightingale asked for the tutorship, he thought with disgusted pride—was this how ambition soils one? But that was when his ambition seemed still in his hands. Now it was in danger of being taken away: ashamed, beside himself, tormented, he was tempted to cheat, steal and lie.

He heard Chrystal's threat. He looked at the firm, uncompromising face. Then at mine. Then, for a longer time, at Arthur Brown's, distressed, kindly, but unwavering.

Suddenly Jago's own face changed. He was thinking of himself without mercy. He was sickened by the temptation.

"Shall I withdraw from the election?" he asked with a kind of broken dignity.

Brown smiled in affectionate relief, and showed the depth of his relief by an outburst of scolding.

"You mustn't swing from one extreme to the other. We've still got an excellent chance. We've lost your most unreliable supporter, that's all. You're still in the lead. You must keep a sense of proportion."

"I agree with Brown," said Chrystal. His tone was not so warm as Brown's, but toughly reassuring. Jago smiled at us, a smile without defence.

"We shall have to reconsider some of our dispositions," said Brown, more contentedly than he had spoken that night. "You needn't worry, you can leave the staff work to us. The other side have got weak spots too. Eliot and Calvert have wanted to tap them, but I think Eliot agrees that it's still premature. The great thing at present is to take good care not to have any more confounded defections. I don't know whether you others agree with me, but I should say there was just one more vulnerable spot in our party."

"I take it you mean old Eustace Pilbrow," said Jago.

"He's a weak spot," said Chrystal. "He's always being got at by some crank or other."

He turned Winslow and Getliffe down when they spread themselves to persuade him," Brown said. "I believe we can keep him steady. He's very fond of you, providentially."

"I can never quite believe it," Jago replied. "But——"

Chrystal broke in:

"When I look round, he seems to me the only weak spot. The rest are safe."

Jago said:

"I believe you three are safe because you know the worst about me. If any of you left me now, I shouldn't only lose the Mastership. I should lose the confidence you've given me."

Chrystal repeated: "The rest are safe. There's no other weak spot. They'll never break five of your votes. You can bank on them."

Jago smiled.

"Well," said Brown, "the essential thing for the present is to make sure of Pilbrow. If we hold him, we can't lose. Six votes for you means that they can't get a majority, since Crawford is fortunately debarred from voting for himself. Though I confess I feel uncharitable enough to think that he would consider it a reasonable action. And that reminds me that you and Crawford will soon have to settle how you're going to dispose of your own votes. They may be significant."

"They're certain to be, now," said Chrystal.

"Crawford sent a note this very day suggesting a talk. I was mystified——"

"The other side have got on to it too. They must have realised how much his vote and yours mean"—Brown was bright-eyed with vigilance—"as soon as this confounded man told them he was ratting."

"I'm compelled to discuss it if he wishes to," said Jago. "I can't decently do less than that."

"But go carefully whatever you do. Examine any proposal he puts forward. It may seem harmless, but it's wiser not to commit yourself at once. Whatever you do, don't say yes on the spot." Brown was settling down to an exhaustive, enjoyable warning: then his expression became more brooding.

"There's something else you ought to guard against." He hesitated, Jago did not speak, and sat with his head averted. Brown went on, speaking slowly and with difficulty:

"We shouldn't be reliable supporters or friends unless we asked you to guard against something which might damage your prospects irretrievably. Put it another way: it has helped to lose us Nightingale, and unless you stop, it might do you more harm than that."

Jago still did not speak.

Brown continued:

"I know we didn't manage Nightingale very cleverly, any of us. We've made him angry between us. And one mistake we fell into that infuriated him was—I gave you a hint before—he thought some of us were acting as though you had the Mastership in your pocket. That's bound to be dangerous. I don't like doing it, but I'm compelled to warn you again." He hesitated for some moments, then said: "There seem to have been some women talking over the tea-cups."

Brown was embarrassed but determined and intent. He looked at Jago, whose head had stayed bent down. Brown remembered that morning when, at a hint far slighter than this, Jago had drawn himself aloof and answered with a hostile snub. It had taken all Brown's stubborn affection to try again—and to try on this night, when Jago had suffered a bitter disappointment, had lost his self-respect, had condemned himself.

"I am grateful for your friendship," said Jago without looking up. "I will accept your advice so far as I can."

Suddenly he glanced at Brown, his eyes lit up.

"I want to ask one thing of my friends," he said quietly. "I trust you to take care that not a sign of these strictures reaches my wife. She would be more distressed than I could bear."

"Will you have a word with her yourself?" Brown persisted.

I thought Jago was not going to reply. At last he said: "If I can do it without hurting her."

As we heard him, we seemed within touching distance of a deep experience. We were all quiet. None of us, not even Brown, dared to say more. Not even Brown could speak to him in this way again.

Soon afterwards, Mrs. Jago came in from the concert, with Roy Calvert attending her. Ironically, she was happier than I had ever seen her. She had been exalted by the music, she had been mixing with fashionable Cambridge and people had talked to her kindly, she had been seen in the company of one of the most sought-after young men in the town.

She flirted with Roy, looking up at him as he stood by her chair with his heels on the fender.

"Think of all the young women you might have taken out tonight."

"Women are boring when they're too young," said Roy.

"We should all like to believe that was true," she said.

"You all know it's true," he said. "Confess."

His tone was playful, half-kind, half-gallant, and, just for a moment, she was basking in confidence. She neither asserted herself nor shrieked out apologies. A quality vivacious, naïve, delicate, scintillated in her, as though it were there by nature. Perhaps it was the quality which Jago saw when she was a girl.

It was a strange spectacle, her sitting happily near to Roy. Her black evening dress made her look no slighter, and her solid shoulders loomed out of her chair: while Roy stood beside her, his shoulders pressed against the mantelpiece, his toes on the carpet, his figure cleanly arched.

She smiled at her husband.

"I'm positive you haven't had such a perfect evening," she said.

"Not quite," said Jago, smiling fondly back.

TWENTY-ONE

PROPAGANDA

Since Lady Muriel broke the news, the Master had wished to see none of his friends, except Roy. But towards the end of term, he began to ask us one by one to visit him. The curious thing was, he was asking us to visit him not for his own sake, but for ours. "I don't think," Roy said sadly, "he wants to see anyone at all. He's just asking out of consideration for our feelings. He's becoming very kind." He knew that we should be hurt if he seemed indifferent to our company. So he put up with it. It was a sign of the supreme consideration which filled him as his life was ending.

It was strange to go into his bedroom, and meet the selflessness of this dying man. It was stranger still to leave him, and return into the rancour of the college.

For Nightingale had already become a focus of hate, and had started a campaign against Jago. It was a campaign of propaganda, concentrated with all his animosity and force. He was devoting himself to finding usable facts; and each night, unless one of Jago's active friends was near, he would grind them out.

The sneers did not aim at Jago himself, but at those round him. First his wife. Nightingale brought out, night after night, stories of her assuming that the Lodge was already hers: how she had inquired after eighteenth-century furniture, to suit the drawing-room: how she had called for pity because she did not know where they were going to find more servants. He jeered at her accent and her social origin: 'the suburbs of Birmingham will be a comedown after Lady Muriel'.

That particular gibe made Brown very angry, but probably, both he and I agreed, did little harm.

Others were more insidious. Nightingale harped away about her absurd flirtations. It was true. They had been common in the past. They were the flirtations of a woman with not a shred of confidence in her attractions, trying to prove them—so much more innocent, yet sometimes more unbalanced, than the flirtations which spring up through desire.

After Mrs. Jago, Nightingale's next point of attack was Jago's supporters and friends, and most of all Roy Calvert. I came in for a share of obloquy, but the resentment he felt for me seemed to become transferred to Roy. Roy's love affairs—for the first time they were discussed across the combination room table. Joan's name was mentioned. Someone said she would soon be engaged to Roy. Engaged? Nightingale smiled.

This gossip went seething round. Despard-Smith said one night in my hearing:

"Extraordinary young man Calvert is. I'm worried about him. I saw him in the court this afternoon and, after what I've heard recently, I asked if he was thinking of marriage. He made a most extraordinary reply. He said: 'The Calverts are not the marrying kind. My father was, of course, but he was an exception'. I'm worried about the young man. I'm beginning to be afraid he has no sense of humour." Despard-Smith frowned. "And I'm beginning to wonder whether, in his own best interests, he oughtn't to be advised to apply for a post in the British Museum."

The propaganda began to endow Jago's side with a colour of raffishness. It was a curious result, when one thought of Brown and Chrystal, the leaders of the party and the solidest people in the college. Nevertheless, that was the result, and we in Jago's party were ourselves affected by it. In a short time, Nightingale had driven the two sides further apart. By the end of term, high table was often uncomfortable to dine at. Men formed the habit of looking at the names of those down for dinner, and crossing off their own if there were too many opponents present. It became less a custom to stay for wine after hall.

Among the gossip and faction, there was one man who stayed impervious. Crawford was not sensitive to atmosphere. He sat down self-assuredly to dinner with a party consisting entirely of Jago's supporters; he talked to me with sober, complacent sense about the state of Europe; he offered Roy Calvert a glass of sherry in the combination room, and gave his opinions of Germany. Either Crawford did not hear Nightingale's slanders or he took no notice of them. Once I heard Nightingale speak to him in a low voice in hall.

"I'm afraid," said Crawford, cordially, loudly, but without interest, "that I'm very stupid when it comes to personalia."

After the last college meeting of the term, which had been dull but cantankerous, Crawford said, as we were stirring to go:

"Mr. Deputy, may I be allowed to make an unusual suggestion?"

"Dr. Crawford."

"I should like your permission to retire with the Senior Tutor for five minutes. We shall then possibly be in a position to make a joint statement."

Jago and Crawford left the room, and the rest of us talked, smoked, or doodled. On my right hand Nightingale turned ostentatiously away, and I chatted to Luke about his research. He had been chasing a red herring, he said: the last month's work was useless; it was like a 'blasted game of snakes and ladders'; he had just struck a gigantic snake. Then Jago and Crawford returned. They were talking as they entered, Jago excited, his eyes smiling, Crawford self-contained, his expression quite unmoved. None of us, after the Saturday night at Jago's, had heard whether Crawford's invitation had come to anything. Chrystal was annoyed, Brown concerned that Jago might commit a tactical mistake.

Crawford slid into his seat.

"Mr. Deputy."

"Dr. Crawford."

"Speaking as a fellow, I assume that I'm out of order in referring to the impending vacancy," said Crawford. "But if we dissolve ourselves into an informal committee, I suggest that difficulty can be overcome. Perhaps I can take the transformation as completed." He gave a broad smile, enjoying the forms of business, as he always did. "Speaking then as a member of this informal committee, I can go on to suggest that it may be useful if the Senior Tutor and I make a statement of intention."

He stared impassively at Despard-Smith.

"I take it," Crawford went on, "that we are not going beyond reasonable common knowledge in regarding ourselves as candidates when the vacancy in the mastership occurs. Further, I take it, from such expressions of current feeling as reach me, that we are justified in regarding ourselves as the most likely candidates. Finally, I take it that it is also reasonable common knowledge that a clear majority has not yet found itself to express the will of the college. In the circumstances, the votes which the Senior Tutor and I dispose, by virtue of being fellows, may be relevant. We have discussed whether we can reach agreement between ourselves on the use we make of them. The greatest measure of agreement we can reach is this: we do not feel it incumbent upon us to intervene in the college's choice. We do not consider ourselves justified in voting for one another. As matters stand at present, we shall abstain from voting."

There was a silence.

"Ah. Indeed," said Gay. "Very well spoken, Crawford. I congratulate you."

Jago said:

"I should like to add a word to my colleague's admirable précis. I am sure we should both choose to be frank with the society."

Crawford gave a cordial assent.

"We both feel uncomfortably certain," said Jago, with a malicious smile, "that the other would not be our natural first choice. I know my colleague will correct me if I am misrepresenting him. We don't feel that it's reasonable for us to give our votes to each other, against our own natural judgment, just because we appear to be the only candidates."

"Exactly," said Crawford.

They were drawn close in their rivalry. Even as they said they would not vote for the other, they felt an inexplicable intimacy. They found real elation in making a statement together; they enjoyed setting themselves apart from the rest of us. It was not the first time I had noticed the electric attraction of rivalry: rivals, whether competing for a job, opposing each other in politics, struggling for the same woman, are for mysterious moments closer than any friends.

As we left the meeting, Chrystal and Brown drew me aside.

"Jago is *amusing,"* said Chrystal angrily. "How can he expect us to get him in if he plays this sort of game without warning?"

"I don't suppose he had any option," said Brown in a soothing tone. "It looks pretty certain on the face of it that Crawford just sat smugly down and said nothing on earth would make him vote for Jago. I'm satisfied Jago did the best thing in the circumstances by giving no change himself."

"We ought to have been told. It's lamentable," said Chrystal. "It looks as though we shall never get a majority for either. They've just presented us with a stalemate. There are times when I feel inclined to wash my hands of the whole business."

"I can't follow you there." Brown was for once short with his friend. "This looks like a tight thing, I give you that. But there's one advantage. I don't see how Crawford can possibly get a majority now."

"What use is that? If we can't get a majority ourselves."

"If we're certain of avoiding the worst, I shall be happier.

And we haven't started serious persuasion yet," said Brown firmly. "The first thing is to close our own ranks."

Chrystal agreed, a little shamefacedly, but left it to Brown to spend an hour with Pilbrow that night. For a fortnight, ever since Nightingale's defection, Brown had been trying to arrange a talk with Pilbrow. But Pilbrow's round of concerts and parties did not allow him much free time; and he was bored with college politics, and was not above dissimulating to avoid them. This day, at the college meeting, Brown had pinned him down.

I rather wished I had accompanied Brown myself, for I was Pilbrow's favourite among the younger fellows. He was attracted by Roy Calvert, but could not understand his political ambivalence; he could not understand how anyone so good-hearted could have friends of influence in the third Reich. Whereas the old man knew that I was on the left of centre, and stayed there.

I wished decidedly that I had gone, when Brown told me what Pilbrow had said. I knew at once that Brown was not quite at ease.

"I think he'll come up to scratch," Brown said. "But I must say he's getting crankier as he grows older. Would you believe it, but he wanted me to sign a letter about the confounded Spanish war? I know you support that gang of cutthroats too, Eliot. I've never been able to understand why you lose your judgment when it comes to politics.

"Well," he went on. "I hope he didn't take it amiss when I turned him down. I've never known Eustace Pilbrow to bear a grudge. And he made just the same kind of promise as he made at our caucus. He's still for Jago, just because he's rather fond of him." He told me, word for word, what Pilbrow had said. It was, as Brown admitted, 'on the target' for an old man. He had replied in the same terms to the other side, telling them that he preferred Jago for personal reasons. It seemed satisfactory.

Yet Brown was wearing a stubborn frown. "He's further

away from this election than any of us," he said. "I wish we could bring him more into the swim of things."

He added:

"Still, I don't see how he can help coming up to scratch." He reflected. "One thing I'm sure of. The other side aren't going to humbug the old man against his will. I've never realised before how obstinate he is. And that takes a load off my mind."

TWENTY-TWO

THE SCENT OF ACACIA

Then something happened which none of us had reckoned on. The course of the Master's disease seemed to have slowed down. Just after the Easter vacation, we began to suspect that the election might not be held that summer. Sitting in the combination room, the smell of wisteria drifting through the open window, we heard Crawford expound: in his judgment, the Master would not die until the early autumn. He had been just as positive in forecasting a quick end, I remembered, but he commented on the new situation without humbug. "Speaking as a friend of Royce's, I take it one should be glad. He's only in discomfort, he's not in pain, and I get the impression that he's still interested in living. I expect he'd prefer to go on even as he is than have anyone accelerate the process. Speaking as a fellow, it upsets our arrangements, which is a nuisance and I'm not going to pretend otherwise," said Crawford. "I had hoped we should have made all our dispositions by next academic year, and it doesn't look like that now."

Imperturbably, Crawford gave us a physiological explanation of the slowing-down of the disease.

After that news, the air was laden with emotion. Each time I passed the wisteria in the court, I thought of the Master, who, Roy said, was amused at his reprieve: that odour was reaching him for the last time in his life. The college smelt of flowers all through the early summer: I thought of Joan, eating her heart out with love, and Roy, so saddened that I was constantly afraid.

As the news went round that the Master would live

months longer, the college became more tense. Some people, such as Chrystal, were glad to forget the election altogether. Chrystal's interest passed entirely to the negotiations with Sir Horace, which had not gone much further since the night of the feast; Sir Horace wrote frequently to Brown, but the letters were filled with questions about his nephew's chances in the Tripos; occasionally he asked for a piece of information about the college, but Brown saw no hope of 'bringing him to the boil' until the boy's examination was over. Brown himself was coaching him several hours a week during that term. "I don't know," he said, "whether Sir Horace is ever going to turn up trumps. But I do know that our prospects vanish, presuming they exist at all, if our young friend has to go down without a degree."

But Chrystal, along with Pilbrow, was an exception in shelving the Mastership. With most men, the antagonism became sharper just because of the delay. Nerves were on edge, there was no release in any kind of action, there seemed no end to this waiting. Nightingale's gossip about Roy went inexorably on. It infected even Winslow, who normally showed a liking for Roy. Winslow was heard to say, "I used to think that my colleagues were more distinguished for character than for the more superficial gifts of intelligence. The Senior Tutor appears to have chosen supporters who seem determined to remove part of that impression."

The gossip came round to Roy, though we tried to shield him. His spirits had been darker since the way he comforted Lady Muriel, and now, as he heard how he was being traduced, there were nights when he sank into despondency. Usually he would have cared less than most men what others said, but just then the sky had gone black for him. His was a despondency which others either did not notice or passed over; it would have struck no one as specially frightening, except him and me. Often we walked round the streets at night. The whole town smelt of gilliflower and lilac. The skies were luminous, windows were thrown open in the hot

May evenings. I tried to lift Roy from sadness, if only for a minute: almost imperceptibly, he shook his head.

Nightingale was making other attacks, not only those on Roy. One night towards the end of May, Luke asked if he could talk to me. I took him up to my room, and he burst out: "I've had about as much as I can stand of this man Nightingale. I'm beginning to think I've been quiet in this college for almost long enough. One of these days I shall do the talking, and by God they'll get a surprise."

"What's Nightingale done now?"

"He's as good as told me that unless I switch over to Crawford they'll see that I'm not made a permanency."

"I shouldn't pay too much attention——"

"Do you think I should pay attention? I told him as politely as I could—and I wished I hadn't got to be so blasted polite—that I'd see him damned first. Do they think I'm the sort of lad they can bully into going through any bloody hoop?"

"They probably do," I smiled, though I was angry myself. I was growing very fond of him. When he was angry, he was angry from head to toe, angry in every inch of his tough, square, powerful body. It was the same with every mood—his hopes or disappointments about his work, even his passionate discretion. He threw the whole of his nature into each of them. On this night he was angry as one whole human interger of flesh and bone. "They probably do. They're wrong."

"They'll be surprised how wrong they are," Luke fumed. "I should like to be kept in this college, it's much nicer than the old dockyard, but do they think they've only got to whistle and I'm theirs? They can do their damnedest, and I shan't starve. A decent scientist will get some sort of job. They're just trying to blackmail me because I'm afraid to lose my comforts."

I told him that 'they' could only be Nightingale himself. I could not believe that Francis Getliffe knew anything of this move, and I said that I would confront him with it. Luke, still angry, went off to his laboratory in the summer evening.

I should have spoken to Francis Getliffe the following night, but I found that he had left Cambridge (the examinations had begun, and lectures were over for the year) for some Air Ministry experiments. He was not expected back for a fortnight, and so I told Brown about Luke.

"Confound those people," he said. "I'm a mild man, but they're going too far. I'm not prepared to tolerate many more of these outrages. I don't know about you, but it makes me more determined to stick in my heels against Crawford. I'm damned if I'll see them get away with it."

We each found ourselves holding the other side *collectively* responsible for Nightingale's doings. Just as young Luke stormed about what 'they' had threatened, so did Arthur Brown: and I felt the same. There were times when we all saw the other side through a film of enmity. We forgot who they were and what they were truly like. We were becoming victims of something like war hysteria. And that happened to Brown, who was as sensible, tolerant and level-headed as a man can be: it happened to me, who was not a partisan by nature.

At that time we were a little ashamed of ourselves, and I thought, when I next saw Brown, that he was going a roundabout way to atone. "I'm wondering about enlarging the claret party this year." Brown's claret party took place each year at the beginning of June. "I'm inclined to think it would be rather statesman-like. After all, we've got to live with the present society even if we slide Jago in. Mind you, I'm all against trying to make arrangements with the other side over the election. But I should regard it as reasonable to remind them that we're still capable of enjoying their company. It would be a decent gesture to invite some of them to the party."

And so the claret party consisted of Winslow, Crawford,

Pilbrow, Roy Calvert, me and Brown himself. Like so much of that summer, it tantalised me. The night was tranquil, the college had never looked more beautiful. I should be lucky if I had the chance to drink wine so good again. But Roy's melancholy had got worse, and all the time I was fearing one of his outbursts. Most of that night, I could think of nothing else.

Twice I managed to signal to Roy that he must keep quiet. He was enough in control of himself to do so, though he was affected by the sight of another unhappy man. For Winslow was worried by his son's examination, which had just finished. As soon as the party began, Brown asked him how the boy had got on, and Winslow snubbed him:

"My dear Tutor, I cannot answer for the prospects of the semi-illiterate. I hope the wretched youth managed to read the questions."

Roy heard the sadness in that answer, and it nearly touched the trigger of his own. But, to my momentary relief, we settled down to wine. It was ten o'clock, but the sun had only just set, and over the roof opposite Brown's window there was a brilliant afterglow. From one of the May week balls, we could just hear the throbbing of a band. There was the slightest of breezes stirring, and on it came the scent of acacia from the court beneath.

Pilbrow took charge of the party. He was an authority on wine, and had been Brown's master. His bald head gleamed in the fading light, shone when, towards midnight, Brown switched on the lamps; the ruddy cheeks flushed, but otherwise Pilbrow did not change at all as one decanter after another was left empty. He fixed one of us with a lively brown eye and asked what we noticed at each sip—at the beginning, middle and end of each sip. The old man rang all the changes possible with ten bottles of claret. When we were half-way through, he said with extreme firmness:

"I don't think any of you would ever be quite first-class. I give our host the benefit of the doubt——"

"I don't claim it," said Brown. "I shall never be anything like as good as you."

Meanwhile, Roy had been drinking faster than the rest of us. The dangerous glint had come into his eyes. He began to talk to Winslow—and it was then I had to signal. Roy's smile was pathetic as he fell into silence.

Winslow was speaking again about his son, this time in a different tone.

"I shall be relieved," he said with humility, "if the examiners let him through."

"Oh, they'll let him through," said Brown.

"I don't know what will happen to him if they don't," said Winslow. "He's a stupid child. But I believe there's something in him. He's a very nice person. If they gave him a chance now, I honestly believe he may surprise you all in ten years' time."

No one there had heard Winslow speak so openly. It was some moments before he regained his sardonic tone. Then he made himself say to Brown:

"My dear Tutor, you've had the singular misfortune to teach the foolish creature. I drink to you in commiseration."

Brown insisted on drinking to young Winslow's success.

"Let me fill your glass. Which shall it be? You've gone a bit light on the Latour '24."

We each had ten glasses in front of us, labelled to match the decanters. Brown selected the right one from Winslow's set.

"That will do very nicely. If you please. If you please."

Crawford surveyed the glasses, the decanters, the gleam of crystal and silver, the faces all flushed, the scene of luxury and ease. Out of the window there was still a faint glow in the west. Girls' laughter came up from the court, as a party moved out of college to a ball.

"It's very hard to realise what the world is really like tonight—when one's enjoying your hospitality, Brown," he announced. "Speaking as a scientific observer, I should have to say that the world tonight is more unstable than it's ever been in human experience. But it's impossible to believe that, sitting with the present spectacle in front of us."

"That's always so," said Pilbrow unexpectedly. "I've been caught in two revolutions, or not exactly caught, but . . . One sees a woman in the garden by the railway line, just digging on a sunny morning. One can't believe that it's actually *begun*."

"One can't believe tonight," said Crawford, "that one ought to be fighting against this mess Brown's political friends are plunging us into. I expect I shall remember very vividly tomorrow morning."

"Yes! Yes!" cried Pilbrow, his eyes gleaming like buttons. He joined in Crawford's reflections, as the decanters were put away one by one. He talked about the 'mess'; he was off to the Balkans in three weeks to see for himself. At the age of seventy-four, he was as excited as a boy about his expedition. Brown had had a moment's anxiety when he saw how Pilbrow was vigorously applauding Crawford. But now the old man was safely talking of his travels and Brown was rubicund; though Roy was silent, Winslow subdued, Brown felt that this party had been a success.

After the party, Roy and I walked in the garden. The breeze had dropped, and on the great beeches no leaf stirred. The full moon hung like a lantern, and the scent of acacia pierced the air. Roy was very quiet, and we walked round in silence. Then he said, as though it were a consolation: "I shall sleep tonight."

When he was in a phase of depression, I had known him insomniac for four or five nights together. He would lie open-eyed through the minutes of a night, and then another, having to face his own thoughts. Until, his control broken, he would come to my room and wake me up: should we drive over to George Passant and make a night of it? Or to our friends in London? Or should we go for a walk all night?

The melancholy, the melancholy shot through with sinister gaiety, had been creeping upon him during the past few weeks. He could not throw it off, any more than a disease. When it seized him, he felt that it would never go.

We walked round, not talking, in a night so warm that the air seemed palpable. I thought that we had been lucky to escape that party scot free. I did not know how to stop him damaging himself.

I thought that, so long as I lived, I should be mocked by the scents of that summer. They might have come along with peace of mind, the wisteria, the gilliflower, the lilac, the acacia.

TWENTY-THREE

AFFLICTION

I had expected an outbreak from Roy at the claret party, but, when it did come, I was not prepared.

It was a fortnight later, a Saturday morning, and I woke early. There was a college meeting that day to consider examination results. Some were already published, sent round to tutors, stuck in the tailors' windows; most did not come out till this Saturday.

I knew that the envelopes reached the porters' lodge by a quarter to nine, so I did not wait for Bidwell's ritual awakening. I walked through the court in the cloudless morning, and found a large packet addressed to me. I was opening it when Brown entered the lodge, panting a little, still wearing trouser clips after cycling in from his house.

"I hope we haven't had too many disasters," he said. He opened his own envelope, spread the sheets on the counter.

"Thank God for that!" he exclaimed in a moment. "Thank God for that!"

"What's happened?"

"Young Timberlake's got through. They've given him a third. Which between you and me, is probably slightly more than abstract justice required. Still, I think Sir Horace will be satisfied. If the young man had crashed, it might have been the most expensive failure in the history of the college. I'm breathing a great deal more freely, I can tell you."

His cleverest pupil had been given a starred first. "I always said he was our next real flier," said Brown triumphantly.

He turned back, pencil in hand, to tick off the names on the history sheet. In a moment he gave a shrill whistle.

"I can't find Dick Winslow's name. He seems to have failed absolutely. They don't seem even to have allowed him the ordinary degree. They don't seem to have made him any allowance at all. It's scarcely credible. I think I'd better ring up the examiners straight away. I did once find a name left off a list by mistake."

He put through his call, and came back shaking his head.

"Absolutely hopeless," he said. "They say they just couldn't find any signs of intelligence at all. Well, I knew he was dense, but I shouldn't have believed that he was as dense as that."

The meeting was called for half-past eleven. As the room filled up, one kept hearing whispers about young Winslow. In the midst of the bustle, men asked each other if they had heard. Some were speaking in malice, some in good nature, some in a mixture of the two. At last Winslow himself entered, heavy-footed, carrying his cap but not swinging it in his normal fashion. He was looking down, and went straight to his place.

"Ah, good morning, Winslow," cried Gay, who had not grasped the news.

"Good morning to you," said Winslow. His voice was deadened. He was immersed in his wretchedness.

Despard-Smith was just opening the meeting when Gay said:

"I have a small presentation to make, before we begin our discussion on these excellent agenda. I wish to present to the society, for inclusion in the library, this copy of my latest publication. I hope and expect that most fellows have already bought it. I hope you've bought yours, Brown? I hope you have, Crawford?"

He rose precariously to his feet, and laid a copy in front of Despard-Smith.

"As a matter of fact, I haven't yet," said Crawford. "I've noticed one or two reviews."

"Ah. Reviews," said Gay. "Those first reviews have a lukewarm tendency that I don't like to see."

Suddenly, distracted from Winslow, I saw how nervous the old man was about his book's reception. Gay, the least diffident of men, had never lost that nervousness. It did not die with age: perhaps it became sharper.

The meeting began at last. There was only two minutes' business over livings, but under finance there were several items down. Despard-Smith asked the Bursar if he would 'take us through' his business.

Winslow's head was sunk down.

"I don't think it's necessary," he muttered. He did not raise his eyes. Everyone was looking at him.

Then it came to Jago to describe the examination results. He passed from subject to subject in the traditional Cambridge order, mathematics, classics, natural sciences. . . . Most people at the meeting knew only a handful of the young men he was talking about; but his interest in each was so sharp that he kept a hold upon the meeting. He came to history. The table was very quiet. "One brilliant and altogether deserved success," he said in his thick voice. "Some of us know the struggle that young man had to come here at all. I'm prepared to bet, Mr. Deputy, that he's going to write his name in the story of this college." Then with a grin, he said how much the society ought to congratulate Brown on squeezing Timberlake through. Jago then studied his papers, and paused. "I think there's nothing else to report about the historians." Very quickly, he turned to the next subject.

It was intended as chivalry, perhaps as more. I could not tell how Winslow received it. He still sat with his head sunk down. There was no sign that he had heard anything of the meeting. He did not speak himself: even for a formal vote, he had to be asked.

We broke off at one o'clock for a cold lunch, and most people ate with zest. Winslow stood apart, with his back to the room. I saw Roy's eyes upon him, glinting with wild pity.

Since the party, his depression had grown heavier still, and he had kept himself alone. I was at once anxious as I saw him watching Winslow, but then someone offered him a decanter of wine and he refused. I thought that he was taking care, and I had no sense of danger.

When we resumed the meeting, Jago dealt with the results of the preliminary examinations. There were inquiries, one or two rotund criticisms, some congratulations.

"Of course," said Despard-Smith, summing up, "for a scholar of the college only to get a third class in a university examination is nothing short of s-scandalous. But I think the general feeling of the college is that, taking the rough with the smooth, we can be reasonably satisfied with the achievements of the men. I gather that is your opinion, Senior Tutor?"

"I should go further. We ought to be proud of them."

"You don't dissent, Tutor?" Despard-Smith asked Brown.

"I agree with my senior colleague," said Brown. "And I should like to draw the college's attention to the remarkable results that the Dean has once more secured."

Before the meeting ended, which was not long after, I was set thinking of Despard-Smith's use of the phrase 'the men'. That habit went back to the '90's: most of us at this table would say 'the young men' or 'the undergraduates'. But at this time, the late 1930's, the undergraduates themselves would usually say 'the boys'. It was interesting to hear so many strata of speech round one table. Old Gay, for example, used 'absolutely', not only in places where the younger of us might quite naturally still, but also in the sense of 'actually' or even 'naturally'—exactly as though he were speaking in the 1870's. Pilbrow, always up to the times, used an idiom entirely modern, but Despard-Smith still brought out slang that was fresh at the end of the century—'crab', and 'josser', and 'by Jove'. Crawford said 'man of science', keeping to the Edwardian usage which we had abandoned. So, with more patience it would have been possible to construct a whole geological record of idioms, simply by listening word by word to a series of college meetings.

This one closed. The fellows filed out, and I waited for Roy. Winslow was still sitting at the table, with the order-book and files in front of him; he seemed not to have the spirit to move. The three of us were left alone in the room. Roy did not glance at me or say a word: he went straight to Winslow, and sat down by his side.

"I'm dreadfully sorry about Dick," he said.

"That's nice of you."

"And I am dreadfully sorry you've had to sit here today. When one's unhappy, it's intolerable to have people talking about one. It's intolerable to be watched."

His tone was full of pain, and Winslow looked up from the table.

"You don't care what they say," Roy cried, "but you want them to leave you alone. But none of us are capable of that much decency. I haven't much use for human beings. Have you, Winslow, have you? You know what people are feeling now, don't you? They're feeling that you've been taken down a peg or two. They're remembering the times you've snubbed them. They're saying how arrogant and rude you've been. But they don't matter. None of us matter."

His voice was very clear, throbbing with a terrible elation. Winslow stared at him.

"There is something in what they say, young man," he said.

"Of course there is. There's something in most things that they say about anyone." Roy laughed.

I went round the table to stop him. Roy was talking about the slanders on himself. I had him by the shoulder, but he shook me off. He told Winslow there was something in what Nightingale said.

"Would you like to know how much there is in it?" he cried. "We're both miserable. It may relieve you just a bit."

Winslow raised his voice:

"Don't trouble yourself, Calvert. It's no concern of mine."

"That's why I shall do it." There was a sheet of blank paper in front of Winslow. Roy seized it, and began to write quickly. I took hold of his arm, and jogged his pen. He cursed. "Go away, Lewis. I'm giving Winslow a little evidence." His face was wild with pure elation. "This is only for Winslow and me." He wrote more, then signed the page. He gave it to Winslow with a smile.

"This has been a frightful day for you," Roy cried. "Keep this to remind you that people don't matter."

He said good afternoon, and went out of the room.

"This is distressing," said Winslow.

"He'll calm down soon."

"I never had any idea that Calvert was capable of making an exhibition of himself. Is this the first time it has happened?"

I had two tasks. I had to safeguard Roy as much as I could. And I had to think of politics. I told some of the truth, and some lies. I had never seen Roy lose control until this afternoon, I said. It was a shock to me. Roy was upset over the Master: it had worn his nerves to breaking-point to see such suffering.

"He's a considerable scholar, from all they say," said Winslow. "I had my doubts about him once, but I've always found him an engaging young man."

"There's nothing whatever to worry about."

"You know him well," said Winslow. "I expect you're right. I think you should persuade him to take a good long holiday."

Winslow was studying the sheet of paper. At last he said: "So there is something in the stories that have been going round?"

"I don't know what he has written there," I said. "I've no doubt that the stories are more highly painted than the facts. Remember they've been told you by people who envy him."

"Maybe," said Winslow. "Maybe. If those people have this ammunition, I don't see how Master Calvert is going to continue in this college. The place will be too hot to hold him."

"Do you want to see that happen?"

"I'm comparatively indifferent about the young man. He can be amusing, and he's a scholar, which is more than can be said for several of our colleagues." Winslow stared at me. "I'm comparatively indifferent, as I say. But I'm not indifferent about the possibility of your candidate becoming Master."

"You mean," I said, "that if you let other people see Calvert's note, you could make a difference to Jago's chances?"

"I did mean that," said Winslow.

"You can't do it," I said.

"Why not?"

"You can't do it. You know some of the reasons that brought Calvert to the state he was in this afternoon. They're enough to stop you absolutely, by themselves."

"If you'd bring it to a point——"

"I'll bring to a point. We both know that Calvert has lost control of himself. He got into a state pretty near despair. And he wouldn't have got into that state unless he'd seen that you were unhappy and others were pleased at your expense. Who else had any feeling for you?"

"It doesn't matter to me one way or the other," said Winslow.

Then I asked:

"Who else had any feeling for your son Dick? You knew that Calvert was upset about him. Who else had any feeling for your son?"

I was taking advantage of his misery. Winslow looked as though he had no strength left. He stared down at the table, and was silent for a long time. At last, in a flat, exhausted mutter, he said:

"What shall I do with this?" He pointed to the sheet of paper.

"I don't mind," I said.

"Perhaps you'd better have it."

Winslow did not so much as look when I burnt the paper in the grate.

TWENTY-FOUR

ARGUMENT IN THE SUMMER TWILIGHT

I went straight from Winslow to Roy's room. Roy was lying on his sofa, peaceful and relaxed.

"Have I dished everything?" he asked.

He was *happy*. I had seen the course of his affliction often enough to know it by heart. It was, in fact, curiously mechanical. There was first the phase of darkness, the monotonous depression which might last for weeks or months: then that phase passed into another, where the darkness was lit up by flashes of 'gaiety'—gaiety which nearly overcame him at Brown's party, and which we both dreaded so much. The phase of gaiety never lasted very long, and nearly always broke into one frantic act, such as he had just committed. Then he felt a complete release.

For months, perhaps for longer, he knew that he was safe. When I first knew him well, in his early twenties, the melancholy had taken hold of him more often. But for two or three years past the calm and beautiful intervals had been winning over the despair. That afternoon he knew that he would be tranquil for months to come.

I was tired and weighed down. Sometimes I felt that the burden on me was unfair, that I got the worst of it. I told him that I should not always be there to pick up the pieces.

He was anxious to make amends. Soon he asked:

"I haven't dished Jago, have I?"

"I don't think so."

"How did you work it? You're pretty competent, aren't you?"

I shook my head.

"It didn't need much working," I said. "Winslow may like to think of himself as stark, but he isn't."

"Just so," said Roy.

"I had to hit below the belt, and it wasn't pretty," I said. "He hates Jago. But it isn't the sort of hate that takes up much of one's life. All his real emotions go into his son."

"Just so," said Roy again. "I think I'm lucky."

"You are."

"I couldn't have borne putting paid to Jago's chances," said Roy. "I'll do what I can to make up for it, old boy. I shall be all right now."

That evening in hall Roy presented a bottle in order to drink Jago's health. When he was asked the occasion, so that Luke could enter it in the wine book, Roy smiled and said precisely:

"In order to atone for nearly doing him a disservice."

"My dear Roy," cried Jago, "you couldn't possibly do me a disservice. You've always been too kind to me. It even makes me forgive you your imitations."

It was not only at the claret party that Roy mimicked Jago; he could not resist the sound of that muffled, sententious, emphatic voice; most of those round the table that night had heard him, and even Despard-Smith grinned.

As we went out that night, Arthur Brown reflected:

"You heard the reason Roy Calvert gave for presenting a bottle? Now I wonder exactly what he meant by it. Put it another way: a few years ago, whenever he said anything that wasn't straightforward, I used to expect one of his queer tricks. But I don't worry much about him now. He's become very much more stable. I really believe that he's settling down.

I did not disagree. It was better for Brown to speculate amiably, just as fellows in the future, studying the wine book, might wonder what that singular entry could mean.

I told Brown that I was taking action to protect Luke.

Francis Getliffe had returned for the meeting that morning, and his wife Katherine had asked me to dinner later in the week, for the first time since our quarrel in January. I intended to use the opportunity: it would be easy to let drop the story of Nightingale's threat, and it was too good a chance to miss.

When I arrived for dinner at their house in the Chaucer Road they welcomed me as in the old days. As Francis poured out sherry and took his wife a glass, he seemed less fine-drawn than in college. He looked at her with love, and his restlessness, his striving, his strenuous ambition, all died away; his nerves were steadied, he was content to the marrow of his bones. And she was happy through and through, with a happiness more continuous than a man could know.

The children were in bed. She talked of them with delight, with a pretence of not wanting to bore me. As she indulged her need to linger over them, she sat with matronly comfort in her chair; it seemed a far cry from the excited, apprehensive, girl of eighteen whom I met in her father's house at Bryanston Square nearly ten years before. I had been taken there by her brother Charles, the most intimate friend of my London days: it was the first big house I ever entered.

She talked of the past and her family, as we sat at dinner. Had I seen her brother recently? Then with great gusto, the nostalgia of a happy woman, she recalled days at her father's country house when Francis and I had both been staying there.

After dinner we moved into the garden at the back of the house. There we sat in the last of the light, as the western sky turned from flaming yellow to a lambent apple-green. The air caressed our faces. And languorous and heavy in the warm night wafted the scent of syringa, which brought back, with a voluptuous pain, the end of other summer terms.

Drowsy in the scented air, I was just going to drop a hint

about Luke when, to my astonishment, Katherine got in before me.

"I have been wanting a word with you, Lewis."

"Have you?"

"You do agree that Francis is right about the Mastership, don't you? It is essential for us to have a liberal-minded Master, don't you agree?"

So they had invited me to play the same game. I was curiously saddened, as one is saddened when the gulf of marriage divides one from a friend. Once Katherine had listened to each word that her brother and I spoke, she had been friend and disciple, she saw things with our eyes. Now she was happy with her husband, and everyone else's words were alien.

"I think Francis is quite wrong," I said.

"If we get saddled with a reactionary Master," said Francis, "Lewis will be responsible."

"That's unfair."

"Be honest, man," said Francis. "If you did what we should have expected you to do, Crawford would walk in. Several people would come over with you."

"I must say," Katherine broke in, "it seems rather gross, Lewis. This is important, don't you admit that it is important? And we've got a right to expect you not to desert our side. It's no use pretending, it does seem pretty monstrous to me."

I knew they felt that I was being ungrateful. When I was in distress, so that I wanted a refuge to hide in, Francis had set to work to bring me to the college. He had done it with great delicacy, for three years they had felt possessively pleased whenever I dined at their house—and now, at the first major conflict, I betrayed him. I thought how much one expects from those to whom one does a good turn; it takes a long while to learn that, by the laws of human nature, one does not often get it.

"Look," I said to Katherine, "your brother Charles has

got as much insight as anyone I've ever known. When you let yourself go, you're nearly as good. You know something of Crawford and Jago. Tell me, which is the more remarkable man?"

There was a pause.

"Jago," she said reluctantly. Then she recovered herself, and asked: "But do you want a remarkable man as Master, don't you admit that other things come first?"

"Good work," said Francis. "Lewis likes human frailty for its own sake."

"No," I said. "I like imagination rather than ordinariness."

"I'm afraid at times," said Francis stiffly, "that you forget about the solid virtues."

"If you prefer it," I spoke with anger, "I like self-torment rather than conceit."

They were profoundly out of sympathy with me, and I with them. We knew each other well enough to know there was no give on the other side. They became more obdurate in resisting any claim I made for Jago: my tongue got harsher when I replied about Crawford.

"Anyway," said Katherine at last, "*she* is appalling."

"She's pathetic," I said. "There's much humanity in her."

"That's monstrously far-fetched, don't you admit it?"

"If you'd watched Jago take care of her, you might understand what I've been telling you about him," I said.

"She'd be an intolerable nuisance in the Lodge," said Katherine.

"We're not electing her," I said. "We're electing her husband."

"You can't get out of it as though she didn't exist," said Francis.

For a moment we broke off the argument. Without our having noticed the light go, the garden now lay in deep twilight; the apple green sky had changed to an illuminated, cerulean blue; the first stars had come out.

It was then that I spoke of Luke—not, as I had planned, in the way of friendly talk, but at the moment when we had got tired of our barbed voices.

"I resent some of the comments that your side have made about her," I said. "But I don't want to talk about that now. There's something more important. It's another piece of tactics by one of your side. Did you know that Nightingale has been trying to coerce young Luke?"

"What do you mean?" said Francis.

I gave them the story.

"Is this true?" cried Francis. "Are those the facts?"

"I've told you exactly what Luke told me," I said. "Would you believe him?"

"Yes," said Francis, with no warmth towards me, angry with me for intruding this complaint, and yet disturbed by it.

"If you believe him," I said, "then it's quite true."

"It's nasty," Francis broke out. I could only see him dimly in the crepuscular light, but I was sure that his face had flushed and that the vein in his forehead was showing. "I don't like it. These things can't be allowed to happen. It's shameful." He went on: "I needn't tell you that nothing of this kind will affect Luke's future. I ought to say that his chances of being kept by the college can't be very strong, so long as I stay. But that has nothing to do with this shameful business. Luke's very good. He ought to be kept in Cambridge somehow."

"He's a very nice boy," said Katherine. She was not three years older, but she spoke like a mature woman of a child.

"By the way, it won't make the slightest difference to the election," I said. "Luke may be young, but he's not the first person one would try to cow. But I wanted to make sure you knew. I wasn't ready to sit by and see him threatened."

"I'll stop it," said Francis with angry dignity. "I'll stop

it," he repeated. Yet his tone to me was not softened, but harder than it had been that night. His whole code of behaviour, his self-respect, his uprightness and sense of justice, made him promise what he had done; and I was certain, as certain as I should be of any man, that he would carry it out. But he did not embrace me for making him do so. I had caused him to feel responsible for a piece of crooked dealing; it would not have mattered so much if I had still been an ally, but now it stiffened him against me. "You ought to remember," he said, "that some of your side are none too scrupulous. I'm not convinced that you've been too scrupulous yourself. Didn't you offer Nightingale that you wouldn't be a candidate for the tutorship, if only he'd vote for Jago? While you know as well as I do that Nightingale stands as much chance of becoming tutor as I do of becoming a bishop."

Soon after I thanked them for dinner and walked back into the town through the midsummer night. We had parted without the glow and ease of friendship. Walking back under the stars, at the mercy of the last scents of early summer, I remembered a May week five years before, on just such a night as this. Those two and I had danced in the same party; we had loved our partners, and there had been delight to spare for our friends. Yet, a few minutes past, I had said goodnight to Francis and Katherine with no intimacy at all. Was it only this conflict between us? Or was it a sign of something inevitable, like the passing of time itself? The memory of anyone one had truly loved stayed distinct always and with a special fragrance, quite unaffected by the years. And the memory of one's deepest friendships had a touch of the same magic. But nothing less was invulnerable to time, or chance, or one's private trouble. Lesser friendships needed more care than the deepest ones; they needed attention and manners—and there were times, in the midst of private trouble, when those one could not give. Was it my fault that I could not meet Francis and Katherine as I once did?

TWENTY-FIVE

AN OBSERVER'S SMILE

Throughout the long vacation most of the fellows did not go far away. We all knew that, as soon as the Master died, there would be a last series of talks, confidences, negotiations, until the day of the election, and we wanted to be at hand. Only two went out of England. Roy Calvert was giving a course of lectures in Berlin, and had to leave by the end of July; he went in cheerful spirits, promising to fly back at a day's notice if I sent for him. Pilbrow had departed for the Balkans shortly after Brown's claret party, and no one had heard a word from him since. He had guaranteed to return in time for the election, but when I last saw him he had no thoughts to spare for college conflicts.

During the summer no one changed his party. The bricks in Roy Calvert's room did not require moving; the score was still 6—5 for Jago, but not a clear majority of the whole 13 electors. Brown kept on persuading us to wait before we tried an attempt on Gay, or any other move. Chrystal, however, did make the first signs of an approach about Jago, one night when the old man was dining; he found him aware of the position but stubborn, and so went no further. In fact Chrystal was frustrated for lack of action, and his temper became shorter; they had heard nothing fresh from Sir Horace, apart from a long, effusive letter thanking Brown for his nephew's success. In that letter, for the first time, there appeared no encouraging hints about the college's future at all, and Chrystal and Brown were at a loss.

At the end of August the Master sent for me. He had a

special message he wanted to give me, and he told me, almost as soon as I arrived, that I was to remind him of it if he rambled. He wanted to give me the message before I went.

His face was now an old man's. The flesh was dried and had a waxy sheen. His eyes were sunken. Yet his voice was a good imitation of its old self, and, with his heightened insight, he knew the tone which would distress me least. And he spoke, with his old sarcastic humour, of his reasons for changing the position of his bed. It stood by the window now.

"I prefer to lie here," said the Master, "because I got tired of the remarkable decoration"—he meant the painted college arms—"which we owe to the misguided enthusiasm of one of my predecessors who had somewhat grandiloquent tastes. And, between you and me, I also like to look out of the window and see our colleagues walking about in twos and threes." He smiled without sadness and with an extraordinary detachment. "It makes me wonder how they are grouping themselves about the coming vacancy."

I looked into the emaciated, wasted, peaceful face. "It is surprisingly easy to face that kind of fact," he said. "It seems quite natural, I assure you. So you can tell me the truth. How much has been done about choosing my successor? I have only heard that Jago might be in the running—which, between ourselves, I could have guessed for myself. Will he get it?"

"Either he or Crawford."

"Crawford. Scientists are too bumptious." It was strange to hear him, even when so many of the vanities of self had gone, clinging to the prejudice of a life-time.

I described the present position of the parties. It kept his attention and amused him. As I spoke, I did not feel anything macabre about his interest; it was more as though an observer from another world was watching the human comedy.

"I hope you get Jago in," he said. "He'll never become

wise, of course. He'll always be a bit of an ass. Forget that, and get him in."

Then he asked:

"I expect there's a good deal of feeling?"

"Yes," I said.

"It's remarkable. People always believe that, if only they support the successful candidate, they've got his backing for ever. It's an illusion, Eliot, it's an illusion. I assure you, one feels a certain faint irritation at the faces of one's loyal supporters. They catch one's eye and smirk."

A recollection of the Getliffes' garden came to me, and I said:

"Gratitude plays some queer tricks."

"Gratitude isn't an emotion," he said, watching the human comedy. "But the expectation of gratitude is a very lively one."

His mind was very active, but began to leap from point to point.

"Tell me," he said. "Did they think I was going to die before this?"

"Yes."

"They cxpected to get the election over before next academic year?"

"Yes."

He *smiled.*

Soon after his mind began to wander, and I had to remind him about his message. Setting his will, his thoughts drifting, he forced himself to remember. At last it came back. He talked of Roy Calvert, his protégé and pupil, who had already outstripped him. He praised Roy's work. He wanted me to promise to look after him.

TWENTY-SIX

STALEMATE

At the beginning of October, the great red leaves of Virginia creeper flamed on the walls and blew opulently about the court. In the garden the leaves blazed on the trees. The mornings were misty, the days bright in a golden haze; in the evenings, the lights in the streets and the college were aureoled in the autumnal mists. In the evenings, a light still shone from the great bedroom of the Lodge.

The fellows came back from their September holidays: the freshmen waited in queues on Brown's staircase and walked round the courts in search of Jago's house. The college became noisy, the streets trilled with cycle bells as young men rode off to games in the afternoon. High table filled up: Brown presented a bottle to greet the new academic year: the whole society had returned to residence, except for Pilbrow and Roy Calvert.

It was only a few days later that Roy Calvert came back. He ran up my staircase one afternoon, looking very well. He had been free of depression since June, often he had managed to forget it. I had never seen him so settled. He was anxious to amuse me, concerned to help Brown and his other friends, eager to intrigue for Jago.

Tension in the college soon mounted again. Winslow had recovered some of his bite, and Nightingale ground away at his attacks with the stamina of a passion. Whispers, rumours, scandals, came to us at second or third hand. Roy Calvert figured in them less than in the summer; his actual presence as he was that autumn, equable, full of high spirits, prepared to devote himself to the shyest diner at high table, seemed to take away their sting—though once or twice I saw Winslow regarding him with a caustic glance. But the slanders were fuller than ever of 'that impossible woman'. Nightingale had the intuitive sense of propaganda that one sometimes finds in obsessed men; he knew how to reiterate that phrase, smiling it out when anyone else would have got tired; gradually all his outcries gathered round her. Even the sober members of his side, like Winslow and Francis Getliffe, were heard to say 'it's unthinkable to have that woman in the Lodge', and Brown and Chrystal were perturbed in private and did not know how to reply.

Brown, Roy and I considered how to stop every hole by which these slanders might get through to Jago. We were as thorough as we knew how to be; but there were nights when Jago sat silently in hall, his face white, ravaged. The long anxiety had worn him down, his outbursts of nervous emotion were more unpredictable. But it was the sight of him, his face engraved with his own thoughts, intolerably vulnerable, that distressed us most.

Did he know what was being said? Neither Roy nor I had any doubt.

The Master was spending more time asleep now; one still saw his room lit up when one came back to college on those hazy October nights under the serene and brilliant moon. An Indian summer had visited the town, and the buildings rested in the warmth. It made Jago's pallor more visible, as he walked through an evening so tranquil that the lines of the palladian building seemed to quiver in the haze.

It was strange to leave the combination room, and walk into such an evening. But the strain was growing more acute. There had been only one action which took away from it in the slightest; Francis Getliffe had been as good as his word, and, by what means I did not know, had stopped the threats to Luke.

One night when Brown and I were both dining, Chrystal

sharply asked if we could spare half-an-hour after hall. Brown and I each looked at him; we knew from his expression that he had something active to propose. I thought Brown even at that moment was a shade uneasy; but he took us to his rooms, and opened a bottle of hock, saying: "I've a feeling it will be rather refreshing in this weather."

He went on to talk of Sir Horace. At the end of the long vacation, they had persevered with schemes to get in touch with him again; finally they settled that Brown should write a letter, telling Sir Horace that they had been discussing his nephew's future and wondered whether it would not be wise for him to have a fourth year—'not necessarily reading for a Tripos'—Brown said he could not endure that risk again. This letter had been sent and evoked several telephone calls from Sir Horace. For once they had got him undecided. He nearly sent the young man back, and then thought again; in the end he decided against, but there was a long telephone conversation, thanks of unprecedented cordiality, and a half-promise to visit the college during the winter.

Brown was willing to speculate on that visit, but for the first time Chrystal brushed all talk of Sir Horace aside.

"We've shot our bolt there. It's up to him now," he said. "I want to hear your views about this mess we're in."

"You mean we haven't succeeded in making things safe for Jago?"

"It's not our fault. I don't accept any blame," said Chrystal. "But we're in a mess."

"Well," said Brown. "We've still got a lead of one. It's 6—5, providing Pilbrow troubles to come back. There's always a chance we might win someone over at the last minute. I've always thought there might be a chance with Gay."

"I didn't get any change from him. I regard him as fixed," said Chrystal.

"Well then, it's 6—5."

"And 6—5 is stalemate. It's lamentable."

"I'm certain our wisest course," said Brown firmly, determined to get in first, "is to sit tight and see how things pan out. Funny things may happen before we actually get into the chapel. I know it's a confounded nuisance, but we've got to sit tight and have some patience. We're not in such a bad position."

"I don't agree," said Chrystal. "The place is more like a beargarden than ever. And it's stalemate. I don't see how you can hope to make any progress."

"It's worth trying Gay again," I said.

"You'll be wasting your time. I rule him out," said Chrystal.

"At the very last," I said, "we ought to try old Despard. We haven't shown our hand completely."

"You can try," said Chrystal with scorn.

He went on:

"I see it like this. The present position is the best we can hope for. We may lose a vote. We shan't gain one. Do you take me up on that? We can't expect anything better than the present voting."

"I don't admit that it's certain," said Brown, "but I should regard it as a probability."

I agreed.

"I'm glad you see it the same way," said Chrystal. "Where does it get us?"

"If the voting does stay in the present position," Brown replied, "and I admit we haven't any right to expect better, then the decision goes to the Visitor, of course."

By statute, if the fellows could not find a clear majority of their number for one candidate, it was left for the Visitor to appoint. The Visitor had always been, right back to the foundation, the bishop of a northern diocese. I was sure, by the way, that Brown and Chrystal must have thought of this possibility as soon as Jago's majority was broken. I had myself at moments, though it took time for any of us to believe that a stalemate was the likely end.

"What happens then?" said Chrystal, pressing his point.

"I shouldn't like to guess," said Brown. "I suppose the greatest danger is that he would prefer the one who is more distinguished outside the college."

"He couldn't appoint Jago," said Chrystal. "He's not a churchman, and he hasn't got any reputation for his work."

"Surely Crawford's politics would be against him," I remarked.

"I wish I were absolutely certain of that," said Brown. "Isn't the Bishop a bit of a crank himself? Isn't he one of those confounded Churchill men who want to make trouble? I've heard that he's not sound. We can't rely on him to do the statesman-like thing."

"He'll never give it to Crawford," Chrystal announced. "Everyone knows that he's an unbeliever too. He's never kept it dark. I can't credit that he'd give it to Crawford. You can rule that out."

"I very much hope you're right. It's extremely reassuring to hear," said Brown, smiling but with his watchful eyes on his friend. "I'm becoming quite reconciled to the idea of the Visitor."

"I don't intend you to be. In my view, he's certain to bring in an outsider."

Chrystal spoke with assurance, almost as though he had inside knowledge. In fact, I suspected later that he had actually heard something from the other side.

It puzzled me, and it also puzzled me that he had asked me to join him and Brown that evening. Normally he would have discussed it in secret with Brown, and they would have decided their policy before any of the party, or anyone else in the college, had a chance to know their minds. It puzzled me: I could see that it disconcerted Brown. But soon I felt that Chrystal knew, right from the beginning, that he and Brown were bound to disagree. In his curiously soft-hearted way, Chrystal fought shy of a scene; he did not want to quarrel; he was afraid of the claims of friendship.

So he had asked me to be present. He had avoided an

intimate scene. He could not have borne to be prevented. He had seen a chance to act, and all his instincts drove him on.

He said: "He's certain to bring in an outsider. That would be the biggest disaster."

"I don't agree with you there," said Brown. "I could tolerate most outsiders in front of Crawford."

"I'm sorry," said Chrystal. "I like to know whom we're getting. If it came to the worst, I should prefer the devil we know. With Crawford, we should be certain where we were from the start. No, I don't want an outsider. I don't want it to go to the Visitor."

"Nor do I," I said. I turned to Brown. "It would mean that we had lost it for Jago."

"I see that," said Brown reluctantly.

"It's just conceivable the Visitor might put Crawford in," I said. "But he'd never give us Jago over Crawford's head. Jago's junior and less distinguished. If it goes to the Visitor, it will either be Crawford or a third person."

"I don't see any way out of that," said Brown.

"There isn't," said Chrystal. "But there's one thing we've never tackled. There are the two candidates themselves. I come back to them. We've got to force them to vote for each other."

"Well," said Brown, "I don't for the life of me see how you're going to do that. You can't expect Crawford to make a present of the Mastership to Jago. That's all you're asking him to do. I don't see Crawford suddenly becoming a public benefactor."

"Wait a minute," said Chrystal. "Suppose he's convinced that a stalemate means that he's out. He knows there's only one vote in it. As you said, funny things happen in elections. Don't you think he might gamble? It's the only chance he's got. It only means he has to win another vote. He may." Chrystal looked with his full commanding eyes at

Brown, and repeated: "He may. Someone may cross over. Are you dead certain of Pilbrow?"

"No. But I shall be disappointed if we can't hold him."

"I repeat," said Chrystal, "Crawford knows it's pretty even. He knows this way is his only chance. Why shouln't he chance it?"

"What about Jago?"

"If we brought it off, we should be presenting him with a decent chance of victory on a plate," said Chrystal fiercely. "I shouldn't have much use for Jago if he raised difficulties."

"That's all very well," Brown was frowning, "but they're both strong men in their different fashions. And they've gone out of their way to tell us definitely that they refuse to vote for each other."

"We'll threaten them with a third candidate."

Chrystal's plan was simple. The college was divided between two men, and did not wish for an outsider. It had a right to ask those two to save them from an outsider. Just one step was needed—for the 'solid people' on both sides to get together and threaten to switch to a third candidate if the other two refused. Chrystal had already heard something from Getliffe and Despard-Smith; they were no happier about the Visitor than he was; he was convinced that they would take part in his plan.

"I don't like it," said Brown.

"What's the matter?" Chrystal challenged him.

"I like being as friendly with the other side as I can. But I don't like arrangements with them. You never know where they lead."

They were speaking with all the difference of which they were capable. Brown, the genial, the peace-maker, became more uncompromising the more deeply he was probed. Both his rock-like stubbornness and his wary caution held him firm. While Chrystal, behind his domineering beak, was far more volatile, more led by his moods, more adventurous and willing to take a risk. The long stagnation had bored him;

he was, unlike Brown, not fitted by nature for a conflict of attrition. Now all his interest was alive again. He was stimulated by the prospect of new talks, moves, combinations and coalitions. He was eager to use his nerve and will.

"It's worth trying," said Chrystal. "If we want to win, we've got no option."

"I'm convinced we ought to wait."

"It ought to be done tomorrow."

"I shall always feel that if we hadn't rushed things about seeing Jago, we might have Nightingale in our pocket to this day," said Brown.

It was the first time I had heard him reproach his friend.

"I don't accept that. I don't think it's a fair criticism. Nothing would have kept Nightingale sweet. Don't you think so, Eliot?"

"Yes," I said.

Chrystal asked me another question:

"Do you agree that we ought to have a discussion with some of the other side?"

"Can you bring it off?" I replied. "If not, I should have thought it was better not to try. We shall have exposed ourselves."

"I'll bring it off," said Chrystal, and his voice rang with zest.

"Then it might win the Mastership for Jago," I said.

"It's worth trying," said Chrystal. "It must be tried."

Brown had been watching me as I answered. Then he watched Chrystal, and sank into silence, his chin set so that one noticed the heavy, powerful jowl. He thought for some time before he spoke.

"I'll join a discussion if you arrange one. I don't like it but I'll join in." He had weighed it up. He saw that, with skill and luck, it might turn out well for Jago. He saw the danger more clearly than anyone there. But he was apprehensive that, if he did not join, Chrystal might make an overture on his own account.

He added:

"I shan't feel free to express myself enthusiastically if we do meet the other side. Unless they put it all plain and above board. And I shall not want to bring any pressure on the two candidates."

"So much the better. If you and I disagree, they'll feel there isn't a catch in it," said Chrystal, with a tough, active, friendly smile.

TWENTY-SEVEN

CONFERENCE OF SIX

Next morning Chrystal was busy paying visits to some of the other side. He saw Brown and me before lunch, and announced that he had arranged a conference for the coming Sunday night. There was a crowd dining that Sunday, and I heard Despard-Smith's usual grating protest—'all avoiding the cold supper at home'; the number of diners that night helped to disguise the gap when six of us left after hall, but even so I wondered whether any suspicious eyes had noticed us.

We walked through the second court to Chrystal's rooms. It was an autumn night of placid loveliness; an unlighted window threw back a reflection of the hunter's moon; our shadows were black before us, and the old building rested in the soft radiance of the night.

It was warm, but Chrystal had a bright fire burning. His sitting room was comfortable, rather in the fashion of a club; on a small table, a pile of periodicals was stacked with Chrystal's unexpected, old-maidish tidiness; upon the walls stood out several cases with stuffed birds inside, which he had shot himself.

"Do you want to bring chairs by the fire?" said Chrystal. "Or shall we get round the table?"

"I suggest round the table, if you please," said Winslow. "Your fire is so remarkably hospitable, my dear Dean. Almost excessively hospitable for this particular night, perhaps."

Chrystal did not reply. He seemed resolved from the beginning not to be drawn by Winslow. With a plan in his mind, his temper had become much more level. So we sat round the table away from the fire—Despard-Smith, Winslow and Francis Getliffe on one side, Brown and I on the other. Before Chrystal took the chair at the head, he said he could not offer us Brown's variety of drinks, and filled for each of us a stiffish tumbler of whisky.

We all drank, no one had begun to talk, while Chrystal packed and lit his pipe. Suddenly he said:

"We've reached a stalemate over this election. Do you agree?"

"It looks like it," said Francis Getliffe.

"How do you all regard it?" said Chrystal.

"I regard it as disastrous," Despard-Smith replied. His expression was lugubrious, his voice solemn; but he had already nearly finished his glass, and he was watching each word and movement on our side of the table.

"It makes me think slightly less warmly than usual," said Winslow, "of the mental equipment of some of my colleagues."

"That is *amusing,*" said Chrystal, but he did not pronounce the word with his customary venom. "But it doesn't get us anywhere, Winslow. We shan't get far if we start scoring points off one another."

"I associate myself with you, Dean," said Despard-Smith, with bleak authority.

"I am still unenlightened as to where we are trying to get," said Winslow. "Perhaps others know the purpose of this meeting better than I do."

"It's simple." Chrystal looked at the three of them. "This election may go to the Visitor. Are you content?"

"The possibility hadn't escaped us," said Winslow.

"I expect that most of us have thought of it occasionally," said Brown. "But somehow we haven't really believed that it would happen."

"I have found it only too easy to believe," said Despard-Smith.

"Are you content?" asked Chrystal.

"To be honest," said Winslow, "I could only answer that —if I knew the mysterious ways in which the Bishop's mind would work."

"I should consider it a c-catastrophe," said Despard-Smith. "If we can't settle our own business without letting the Bishop take a hand, I look upon it as a scandalous state of affairs."

"I'm glad to hear you say that," said Chrystal. "Now I'm going to put our cards on the table. If this election does go to the Visitor, I've got a view as to what will happen. It won't mean your candidate getting in. It won't mean ours. It will mean a third party foisted on us."

"What do you think?" Francis Getliffe asked Despard-Smith.

"I'm reluctantly bound to say that the Dean is right," said Despard-Smith. He spoke, like Chrystal a few days before, as though he had the certainty of inside knowledge. I wondered if he had discovered anything through his clerical acquaintances. I wondered also if it was from him that Chrystal had picked up the hint. They were supporting each other at this table. And Despard-Smith's support was still, at the age of seventy, worth having. He was completely certain of his judgment. He poured himself another large whisky, and delivered an unshakable opinion. "I deeply regret to say it," said the old clergyman, "but the Dean is right. The way the Bench is appointed nowadays is of course disastrous. The average is wretchedly low. Even judged by that low average, this man doesn't carry a level dish. He can be relied upon to inflict some unsuitable person upon us."

"Do you want that?" said Chrystal vigorously.

"I don't," said Francis Getliffe.

"I don't myself," said Chrystal.

"It doesn't sound specially inviting," I said.

Winslow gave a sarcastic smile.

"It somewhat depends," he said, "whether one would

prefer either of our candidates to an unknown. I dare say some of you might. It may not be a completely universal view."

"You mean there may be people who won't mind it going to the Visitor, Winslow," said Chrystal. "If they're determined to keep one of the candidates out at any costs."

"Precisely, my dear Dean," said Winslow.

Brown looked from Winslow to Chrystal: his eyes were sharp but troubled as they moved from his opponent to his ally.

"I think the time has almost come to explain where we stand," he said. "My own position hasn't altered since last January. I'm convinced that Jago is the right man for us, and so I've never thought any further. I think I can say that Crawford wouldn't be my second choice, if I'm forced to speak off-hand."

"My dear Brown," said Winslow, "Jago wouldn't be my third choice. I don't find it easy to decide what number of choice he actually would be."

"That being my position," said Brown, "I shouldn't be averse to passing the decision to the Visitor, if we couldn't scrape up a majority for Jago."

"My reason is the exact opposite," said Winslow. "But I find myself surprisingly in agreement with the Tutor. I shan't worry if the Bishop has to use his wisdom."

"I shall," I said. "For once I disagree with Brown. I'd rather have either of those two than anyone in the field. I'd certainly rather have either than anyone the Bishop is likely to choose."

"Good work," said Francis Getliffe, in a quick, comradely manner, as in the days when we were always on the same side. "I'm with Eliot there. I'm not in favour of Jago, but I'd rather put up with him than the Bishop's nominee."

We all turned to Despard-Smith. He took a long sip from his glass, and said with deep solemnity: "I too find myself among the Laodiceans." He added, so gravely that no one took account of the anti-climax: "I've never been ready to buy a p-pig in a poke."

"Yes," said Chrystal. "Well, none of you will be surprised to hear how I feel." He was addressing himself to Brown. "I'm not voting for Jago to keep Crawford out. I'm voting for him because I think he's the better man. But either will do." He went on: "So that's four of us flat against letting it go to the Visitor. I regard that as enough reason to explore a bit further."

Brown was looking flushed and concerned, but he said:

"I have made my reservations, but I am sure we should all like to hear what the Dean has in mind. We all know that it's bound to be valuable." He was uneasy, I knew, but his affability covered him. I wondered whether it was friendship for Chrystal or party loyalty which had caused him to give help at this point. Almost certainly both—it was like him to mix policy and warmheartedness without thinking, it was just that mixture which made him so astute.

"Would you like to stay and hear it, Winslow?" said Despard-Smith.

"If you please," Winslow said indifferently. "If you please."

"Right," said Chrystal. "First of all I want to count heads. I regard Jago as having five votes certain as far as votes can be certain in a college—I mean three of us here and our two young men, Calvert and Luke. Pilbrow has promised to vote several times—but I'm not going to mince matters either way. He may even not come back, he's not specially interested in this election."

"That's fair enough," said Francis Getliffe with a sudden creased smile.

Chrystal went on:

"I regard your side as having four votes certain. Yourselves and Nightingale. Nightingale can't cross over again, or he'll make the place too hot to hold him. You're also counting on Gay, but I set him off against Pilbrow. He may have forgotten the name of your candidate before the election. He may vote for himself."

"I have no doubt," said Despard-Smith, "that Gay will weigh his vote."

"No, we've got to be fair," said Francis Getliffe. "We can't rely on him. Chrystal has been quite objective."

"Remarkably so," Winslow added. "But what does it all lead to? Bring it to a point, my dear Dean."

"I shall get there in one minute," said Chrystal. "But I didn't want to hide the facts. Jago is in the stronger position. There are no two ways about it. I don't want to hide it: if I did, you would have a right to think I was going in for sharp practice. What I'm going to suggest may put Jago in. It will almost certainly put one of the two in. It will save us from the Visitor." He paused and then said with extreme crispness:

"I suggest that we make ourselves clear to the two candidates. We tell them that four of us—or five or six if Brown or Winslow like to come in—will not tolerate this matter going to the Visitor. We tell them that they must vote for each other. It's the only way to bring a majority within reach. If they refuse, we say that we'll form a majority for another person. This will be someone *we* decide on. Not an outsider fobbed off on us by the Bishop. If we're forced to have a third candidate, we'll choose him ourselves." Chrystal broke into a smile. "But it will never come to that."

"I must say that it's a beautiful thought," said Winslow.

"It doesn't look unreasonable," said Francis Getliffe.

"I take it that it hasn't escaped you, Dean," said Winslow, "that your candidate commands a probable six votes—and Crawford's will neatly get him home?"

"I went out of my way to explain that," said Chrystal. "I said perfectly clearly that it might happen. I repeat: this is a way to escape the Visitor. So far as I can see, it's the only way."

"That may very well be true," said Francis Getliffe.

"I cannot remember any step of this kind during my association with the college. It is a grave step even to consider. It is absolutely unprecedented," said Despard-Smith. "But I feel we owe it to the college to consider the suggestion with the utmost seriousness. To let the Visitor s-saddle us with some incubus of his own would in my judgment be an unmitigated disaster."

From those first moments it was certain that Despard-Smith and Francis would support Chrystal's move in the long run. Their first response was 'yes!', however much they wrapped it round later. They seemed to be saying yes spontaneously even though it looked like giving Jago the game. They seemed to have lost their heads. Yet they were each of them strong-willed and hard-headed men.

I had no illusion that they were not calculating the chances. They thought, rightly or wrongly, that this was the best move for Crawford, although I could not imagine how they arrived at it.

I felt more than ever certain that they must have learned at least some piece of gossip about the Bishop's intention. They must have become quite certain that, if the Bishop had the power, Crawford would stand no chance. For a second, I suspected also that they had some information, unknown to us, about one of Jago's side. But later I doubted it. It did not seem that they had any well-backed hope. It seemed most likely that in secret they were sure of Gay, and had a vague hope of Pilbrow and even (so I gathered with incredulity from a chance remark) of Roy Calvert, some of whose comments Despard-Smith took literally and misunderstood. So far as I could detect, they knew nothing definite that we did not know.

Those seemed their motives on the plane of reason. But they were also moved by some of the inexplicable currents that sweep through any intricate politics. Despard-Smith and Francis, just like Chrystal and I myself, suddenly panicked at the idea of an outsider for Master. It was as though our privacy were threatened: magic was being taken from us: this intimate world would not be so much in our power. It was nonsense when we thought of it in cold blood, but we shied violently from the mere idea. And also we enjoyed—there was no escaping the satisfaction—the chance of asserting ourselves against our candidate. There are some hidden streaks in any politics, which only flash to the surface in an intense election such as this. Suddenly they leap out: one finds to one's astonishment that there are moment when one loves one's rival—despises one's supporters—hates one's candidate. Usually these streaks do not make any difference in action, but in a crisis it is prudent to watch them.

Despard-Smith let fall some solemn misgivings and qualifications; Francis Getliffe was guarded, though anxious to seem open to reason; but Chrystal knew he had won them over. He took it as a triumph of his own. And in fact it had been an impressive display. For the first time in this election, he had thrown his whole will into the struggle. He had something definite to achieve; and, even against men as tough as his opponents, his will told.

The talk went on. Winslow said:

"Even the idyllic spectacle of the lion lying down with the lamb does not entirely reconcile me to the Dean's ingenious idea."

Later, Brown finished up for the night:

"In any case, before I come to any conclusion, I shall certainly want to sleep on it."

"That goes without saying," said Despard-Smith. "It would be nothing less than s-scandalous for any of us to commit ourselves tonight."

I was surprised to hear a couple of days later that Winslow had decided to join. He had talked to his party: what had been said, I did not know: I was uneasy, but I noticed that so was Francis Getliffe. I was surprised that Winslow had not pushed his dislike of Jago to the limit. Was there a shade of affection, underneath the contempt? Once Jago had supported him: was there some faint feeling of obligation? Or was it simply that, despite his exterior, despite all his attempts to seem it, Winslow was really not a ruthless man?

Winslow's decision made it hard for Brown to stay outside. He felt his hand was forced, and he acquiesced with a good grace. But he was too cautious, too shrewd, too suspicious and too stubborn a man to be pleased about it. "I still don't like it," he confided to me in private. "I know it improves Jago's chances, but I can't come round to liking it. I'd rather it had come later after we'd had one stalemate vote in the chapel. I'd rather Chrystal was thinking more about getting Jago in and less about shutting the Visitor out. I wish he were a bit stronger against Crawford."

"Nevertheless," Brown added, "I admit it gives Jago a great chance. It ought to establish him in as strong a position as we've reached so far. It gives him a wonderful chance."

The six of us met again, and drafted a note to the two candidates. Despard-Smith did most of the writing, but Brown, for all his reluctance to join the 'memorialists' (as Despard-Smith kept calling us), could not resist turning a sentence or two. After a long period of writing, rewriting, editing and patching up, we agreed on a final draft:

'In the view of those signing this note, it is most undesirable that the forthcoming election to the Mastership should be decided by the Visitor. So far as the present intentions of fellows are known to us, it seems that neither of the candidates whose names we have heard mentioned is supported by a clear majority of the college. We accordingly feel that, in conformity with the spirit of college elections and the desire of the college that this forthcoming election shall be decided internally, it would assist our common purpose if each candidate voted for the other. If they can see their way to take this step, it is possible that a clear majority may be found to declare itself for one or other

candidate. If, on the other hand they find themselves unable to cast their votes in this manner, the signatories are so convinced of the necessity of an internal decision that they feel compelled to examine the possibility of whether a third candidate can be found who might command a clear majority of the college.

A T D-S
G H W
A B
C P C
F E G
L S E
Oct. 29, 1937'

"In other words," said Chrystal, "there'll be the hell of a row." He winked. There was often something of the gamin about him.

TWENTY-EIGHT

CLOWNING AND PRIDE

The note was sent to all fellows. It caused great stir at once, and within a few hours we learned that Jago and Crawford wished to meet the six. Roy Calvert said: "I must say it's a coup for Chrystal." Jago had said nothing to Brown or me, not a telephone message, not a note. Later that day, Roy brought news that Jago was brooding over the ultimatum. He was half-delighted, so Roy said, because of his chances—and also so much outraged that he intended to speak out.

The two candidates arranged to meet us after hall, at half-past eight. Both came in to dinner, and Jago's face was so white with feeling that I expected an outburst straightaway. But in fact he began by *clowning*. It was disconcerting, but I had seen him do it before when he was strung up and about to take the centre of the stage. He pretended—I did not know whether it was a turn or a true story—that some undergraduate had that afternoon mistaken him for an assistant in a bookshop. "Do I look like a shop assistant? I'm rather glad that I'm not completely branded as a don."

"You're not quite smart enough," said Roy, and in fact Jago was usually dressed in an old suit.

Jago went on with his turn. No one noticed the change in him when we were sitting in the combination room.

Word had gone round that the 'memorialists' were to confer with Crawford and Jago, and so by half-past eight the room was left to us. The claret was finished, and Crawford lit a cigar.

"I think we can now proceed to business, Mr. Deputy," he said.

"Certainly," said Despard-Smith.

"Our answer is a tale that's soon told." Crawford leaned back, and the end of his cigar glowed. "The Senior Tutor and I have had a word together about your ultimatum. We haven't any option but to accept it."

"I'm very glad to hear it," said Chrystal.

"If there are no other candidates, we shall vote for each other," said Crawford imperturbably. "Speaking as a private person, I don't think one can take much exception to what you want us to do. I think I do take a mild exception to the way you've done it, but not so strongly as my colleague. However, that's past history, and it's neither here nor there." He smiled.

Jago leaned forward in his chair, and slight as the movement was, we all looked at him. "For my part, I wish to say something more," he said.

"I should leave it alone," said Crawford. "What's done can't be undone. You'll only take it out of yourself."

In fact, Jago was looking tired to breaking-point. His face had no colour left, and the lines were deep—with sombre anger, with humiliation, with the elation that he might be safe again.

"It's good of you," said Jago to Crawford, "but I should be less than honest if I didn't speak. I take the strongest exception to the way this has been done. It was unnecessary to expose us to this kind of compulsion. Apparently you"—his eyes went round the table—"consider that one of the two of us is fit to be your Master: I should have hoped that you might in the meantime treat us like responsible persons. I should have hoped that was not asking too much. Why couldn't this have been settled decently amongst us?"

"We don't all share your optimism, my dear Senior Tutor," said Winslow.

"We were anxious to get everything in order," said

Brown, eager to smooth things down. "We didn't want to leave any loose ends, because none of us know how much time we've got left."

"That's no reason for treating Crawford and me like college servants," said Jago.

"Since when have college servants been required to vote for each other?" Winslow asked.

Jago looked at him. His anger appeared to quieten. His white and furrowed face became still.

"You are taking advantage of my position as a candidate," he said. "A candidate is fair play for any kind of gibe. You know that he's not at liberty to speak his mind. No doubt he deserves any gibes you care to offer him. Anyone who is fool enough to stand for office deserves anything that comes his way."

Winslow did not reply, and no one spoke. Crawford smoked impassively on, but all our attention was on Jago. He dominated the room.

"You have taught me that lesson," he said. "I shall vote for Crawford at the election."

As we were leaving, Jago spoke in a low voice to Chrystal:

"I should like to say something to you and Brown and Eliot."

"We can go back," said Chrystal. So, standing in the combination room, Jago faced three of his supporters.

"I should have been told about this." His voice was quiet, but his anger had caught fire again.

"I passed the word along as soon as we had decided to push forward," said Brown.

"I should have been told. I should have been told at the first mention of this piece of—persuasion."

"I don't see why," said Chrystal.

"When I find my party is negotiating behind my back——"

"This isn't a party matter, Jago," Chrystal broke in. "It's a college matter."

"I'm sorry," said Jago, in a tone as brusque as Chrystal's, "but I'm not used to having my actions dictated. Before my friends arrange to do so, I expect them to tell me first."

"Perhaps the circumstances are a little unfortunate," said Brown, "but I'm inclined to suggest that we're all losing our sense of proportion. I think you're forgetting that something very notable has been achieved. I'm not saying that it's all over bar the counting of the votes, but I do put it to you that things look brighter than they have done since Nightingale got angry with us. You're standing with a clear majority again, and the sensible course for us all is to keep it intact until we walk into the chapel."

He went on:

"I expect you know that you owe it entirely to the Dean. Put it another way: the Dean is the only man who could have forced a vote out of the other side. It was a wonderful night's work."

Beneath the round, measured, encouraging words there was strength and warning. Jago knew they were intended for him. He gazed into Brown's eyes; there was a pause, in which I thought I saw a quiver pass through his body; then he said:

"Your heads are cooler than mine. You must make allowances, as I know you're only too willing to do. I know Chrystal appreciates that I admire everything he does. This was an astonishing manoeuvre, I know. I'm very grateful, Chrystal."

"I'm glad it came off," Chrystal replied.

I walked back with Jago to his house to fetch a book. He scarcely spoke a word. He was at the same time elated, anxious, and bitterly ashamed.

I was thinking of him and Crawford. That night, Crawford had been sensible, had even been kind to his rival. I could understand the feeling that he was the more dependable. It was true. Yet, of the two, which was born to live in men's eyes?

And Jago knew it. He knew his powers, and how they were never used. The thought wounded him—and also made him naked to life. He had been through heartbreak because of his own frailty. He had seen his frailty without excuses or pity. I felt it was that—not his glamour, not his sympathy, not his bouts of generous passion—it was that nakedness to life which made me certain we must have him instead of Crawford. He was vulnerable in his own eyes.

Why had he never used his powers? Why had he done nothing? Sometimes I thought he was too proud to compete—and also too diffident. Perhaps at the deepest level pride and diffidence became the same. He could not risk a failure. He was born to be admired from below, but he could not bear the rough-and-tumble, the shame, the breath of the critics. His pride was mountainous, his diffidence intense. Even that night he had been forced to clown before he sacrificed his enemies. He despised what others said of him, and yet could not endure it.

There was one other thing. Through pride, through diffidence, he had spent his life among men whose attention he captured without an effort, with whom he did not have to compete. But it was the final humiliation if they would not recognise him. That was why the Mastership lived in his mind like an obsession. He ought to have been engaged in a struggle for great power; he blamed himself that he was not, but it sharpened every desire of his for this miniature power. He ought to have been just Paul Jago, known to all the world, with no title needed to describe him, his name more glowing than any title. But his nature had forced him to live all his life in the college: at least, at least, he must be Master of it.

TWENTY-NINE

"A VACANCY IN THE OFFICE OF MASTER"

In November we heard that the Master was near his death.

On December 2nd, Joan told Roy Calvert: "The doctor has just told us that he's got pneumonia. This is the end." As we were going into hall on December 4th, the news was brought that the Master had just died. Despard-Smith made an announcement to the undergraduates, and there was a hush throughout the meal. In the combination room afterwards coffee was served at once, and we listened to a simple and surprising eulogy from old Despard-Smith.

"I shall miss him," he said. "He was a very human man."

Soon, however, he and Winslow and Brown were occupied with procedure.

"I am no longer Deputy," said Despard-Smith. "I ceased to be Deputy the moment the Master died. The statutes are explicit on this point. The responsibility for announcing the vacancy passes to the senior fellow. I must say I view with apprehension having to rely on Gay to steer us through this business. It places us in a very serious position.

They studied the statutes again, but they had done so frequently in the past weeks, and there was no way out. The governing statute was the one which Despard-Smith had read out at the first meeting of the Lent term.

"There's no escape," said Brown. "We can only hope that he'll get through it all right. Perhaps he'll feel the responsibility is too much for him and ask to be excused. If so, as Pilbrow isn't here, it will devolve on you, Despard, and everything will be safe. But we shouldn't be in order in passing over Gay. The only thing remaining is to let him know at once."

Despard-Smith at once wrote a note to Gay, telling him the Master had died at 7.20 that night, explaining that it was Gay's duty to call a meeting the following day, telling him that the business was purely formal and a meeting at the usual time need only take ten minutes. 'If you feel it is too dangerous to come down to college in this weather,' Despard-Smith added, 'send me a note in reply to this and we will see the necessary steps are taken.'

The head porter was called into the combination room, and asked to take the letter to Gay's house. He was told to see that it reached Gay's hands at once, whether he was in bed or not, and to bring back a reply.

I went off to see Roy Calvert: the others stayed in the combination room, waiting for Gay's reply.

The night was starless and a cold rain was spattering down. As I looked round the court, I felt one corner was strangely dark. No light shone from the bedroom window of the Lodge.

I found Roy alone, sitting at his table with one of the last pages of the proofs.

"You know, of course?" I asked.

"Yes," said Roy. "I can't be sorry for him. He must have gone out without knowing it. But it's the others who have to face what death means now, haven't they?"

Soon Joan came into the room, and he had to devote himself to her and her mother.

I returned to the combination room, where Brown, Winslow and Despard-Smith were still waiting.

"It is nothing less than a disaster," Despard-Smith was saying, "that our statutes entrust these duties to the senior fellow." He proceeded to expound the advantages of a permanent vice-master, such as some colleges had; from Winslow's expression, I guessed this ground had been covered several times already.

Before long the head porter arrived, his top hat tarnished from the rain. He handed Despard-Smith a large envelope, which bore on the back a large red blob of sealing-wax.

"Did you find Professor Gay up?" asked Brown.

"Certainly, sir."

I wondered if there was the faintest subterranean flicker behind that disciplined face.

Despard-Smith read the reply with a bleak frown. "This confirms me in my view," he said, and passed the letter to us. It was written in a good strong nineteenth-century hand, and read:

Dear Despard,

Your news was not unexpected, but nevertheless I grieve for poor Royce and has family. He is the fifth Master who has been taken from us since I became a fellow.

I am, of course, absolutely capable of fulfilling the duties prescribed to me by statute, and I cannot even consider asking the college to exempt me from them. It was not necessary for you to remind me of the statute, my dear chap, nor to send me a copy of the statutes: during the last weeks I have regularly refreshed my memory of them, and am now confident of being able to master my duties.

I do not share your opinion that tomorrow's proceedings are purely formal. I think that such a meeting would not show sufficient respect for our late Master. However, I concur that the meeting need not detain us overlong, and I therefore request that it be called for 4:45 p.m. I have never seen the virtue of our present hour of 4:30 p.m. I request also that tea be served as usual at 4:00 p.m.

Yours ever,
M. H. L. Gay.

"The old man is asserting himself," said Brown. "Well, there's nothing for it but to obey orders."

Next afternoon most of the society, apart from Gay, arrived later than usual for tea in the combination room. They ate less and talked more quietly. Yet most of them were quiet through decorum, not through grief. The night before, there had been a pang of feeling through many there; but grief for an acquaintance cannot last long, the egotisms of healthy men revive so quickly that they can never admit it, and so put on decorum together with their black ties and act gravely in front of each other. All the fellows were present but Pilbrow; but only three bore the marks of strain that afternoon. There was Chrystal, brusque and harsh so that people avoided his company; Roy Calvert, who had dark pouches under his eyes after a night in the Lodge; Jago, whose face looked at its most ravaged.

Even of those, I thought, Jago was tormented by anxiety and hope. Perhaps only two mourned Royce enough to forget the excitement round them.

At half-past four many of us began to sit down in our places, but Gay finished his tea at leisure, talking loudly to anyone near. The clock struck the quarter before he said:

"Ah. The time I fixed for our meeting. Let us make a start. Yes, this is the time."

He took the chair, and looked round at us. The hum died away. Then slowly and with difficulty Gay rose unstably to his feet, and supported himself by gripping the table with his hands.

"Remain seated, gentlemen," he said. "But I should like to stand, while I speak of what I have summoned you to hear today." He looked handsome and impressive; his beard was freshly trimmed, it took years from his age to be presiding there that day. "I have grievous news. Indeed I have grievous news. Yesterday evening our late Master passed away. In accordance with the statute I have requested you to meet on this the following day. First I wish to say a few words in honour of his memory." Gay went on to make a speech lasting over half an hour. His voice rang out resonantly; he did not seem in the least tired. Actually, it was a good speech. Once or twice his memory failed him and he attributed to Royce qualities and incidents which belonged to earlier Masters. But that happened seldom; his powers had revived that afternoon; he was an eloquent man who enjoyed speaking, and he remembered much about Royce which was fresh to many of us. The uncomfortable nature of the speech was that he made it with such tremendous gusto; he was enjoying himself too much.

"And so," he finished, "he was stricken with the disease, which, as my old saga-men would say, was his bane. Ah indeed, it was his bane. He bore it as valiantly as they would have borne it. He had indeed one consolation not granted to many of them. He died in the certainty of our Christian faith, and his life was so blessed that he did not need to fear his judgment in the hereafter."

Then Gay let himself back into his chair. There was whispering round the table, and he banged energetically with his fist.

"Now, gentlemen," he said briskly and chidingly, "we must set ourselves to our task. We cannot look back always. We must look forward. Forward! That's the place to look. It is part of my duties to make arrangements for the election of a new Master. I will read the statutes."

He did read the statutes, not only that on the election of the Master, which he kept till last, but also those on the authority, qualifications, residence and emoluments. He read very audibly and well, and a good many more minutes passed. At last he came to the statute on the election. He read very slowly and with enormous emphasis " 'When the fellows are duly assembled the fellow first in order of precedence attending shall announce to them the vacancy . . .' " He looked up from his book, and paused.

"I hereby announce to you," said Gay resoundingly, "a vacancy in the office of Master."

He went back to his reading.

" '. . . and shall before midnight on the same day authorise a notice of the vacancy and of the time hereby regulated for the election of the new Master, and cause this notice to be placed in full sight on the chapel door.' "

"Cause to be placed! Cause to be placed!" cried Gay. "I shall fix it myself. I shall certainly fix it myself. Shall I write the notice?"

"I've got one here," said Winslow. "I had it typed ready in the Bursary this morning."

"Ah. I congratulate you. Let me read it. I can't get out of the responsibility for any slips, you know. 'Owing to the death of Mr. Vernon Royce, there is a vacancy in the office of Master of this college. The fellows will meet in the chapel to elect a Master, according to statutes D—F, at ten o'clock in the morning of December the twentieth, 1937.' "

"That seems fair enough," Gay went on, as though unwilling to pass it. "December the twentieth? No one's made a slip there, I suppose?"

"The vacancy occurred in term," said Winslow impatiently. "It is fifteen days from today."

"Indeed. Indeed. Well, it seems fair enough. Does everyone understand? Shall I sign it?"

"Is that necessary?" said Despard-Smith. "It's not in the statutes."

"It's fitting that I should sign it," said Gay. "When people see my signature at the bottom, they won't doubt that everything is in order. I shall certainly sign it."

He wrote his great bold signature, and said with satisfaction:

"Ah. That's a fine notice. Now I must fix it." Chrystal and Roy Calvert helped him with his overcoat, and as they did so he heard the clock strike. It was six o'clock. He chuckled:

"Do you know, our old friend Despard wrote to me last night and said this would be a purely formal meeting. And it's lasted an hour and a quarter. Not bad for a purely formal meeting, Despard, old chap! An hour and a quarter.

What do you think of that, Winslow? What do you think of that, Jago?"

It was raining hard outside, and we put on overcoats to follow him. Roy slipped Gay's arms through the sleeves of his gown again. We followed him out into the court, and Chrystal opened an umbrella and held it over the old man as he shuffled along. The rest of us halted our steps to keep behind him, in the slow procession across the first court to the chapel. The procession moved very slowly through the cold December evening.

When we arrived at the chapel door, it was found there were no drawing pins. Chrystal swore, and, while Luke ran to find some, tried to persuade Gay that it was too chilly for him to stay there in the open.

"Not a bit of it, my dear chap," said Gay. "Not a bit of it. There's life in the old dog yet." Luke came back panting with the pins, and Gay firmly pushed in eight of them, one at each corner of the sheet and one in the middle of each side.

Then he stood back and admired the notice.

"Ah. Excellent. Excellent," he said. "That's well done. Anyone can see there's a vacancy with half an eye."

III

NOTICE OF A VACANCY

THIRTY

JAGO THINKS OF HIMSELF AS A YOUNG MAN

The funeral was arranged for December 8th, and in the days before a sombre truce came over the college. Full term ended on the 7th, and the undergraduates climbed Brown's stairs to fetch their exeats, walked through the courts to Jago's house, more quietly than usual; even the scholarship candidates, who came up that day, were greeted by the hush as soon as they asked a question at the porters' lodge. On the nights of the 5th and 6th, the two nights which followed Gay's meeting, I did not hear a word spoken about the Mastership. Chrystal was busy arranging for a fellows' wreath, to add to those we were each sending as individuals; Despard-Smith was talking solemnly about the form of service; there was no wine drunk. Roy Calvert did not dine either night; he was looking after Lady Muriel, and she liked having him eat and sleep in the Lodge.

On the afternoon of the 7th, I wanted to escape from the college for a time and went for a walk alone. It was a dark and lowering day, very warm for December; lights were coming on in the shop windows, a slight rain was blown on the gusty wind, the wind blew down the streets as though they were organ-pipes, umbrellas were bent to meet it.

I walked over Coe Fen to the Grantchester meadows, and on by the bank of the river. There was no one about, the afternoon was turning darker; a single swan moved on the water, and the flat fields were desolate. I was glad to return to the lighted streets and the gas flares in Peas Hill, all spurting furiously in the wind.

While I was looking at the stalls under the gas flares, I heard a voice behind me say: "Good Lord, it's you. What are you doing out on this filthy day?"

Jago was smiling, but his face was so drawn that one forgot the heavy flesh.

"I've been for a walk," I said.

"So have I," said Jago. "I've been trying to think straight."

We walked together towards the college. After a moment's silence, Jago broke out:

"Would it be a nuisance if I begged a cup of tea in your rooms?"

"Of course not."

"I've been trying to collect my thoughts," he smiled, "and it's not a specially pleasant process. It hurts my wife to see me, very naturally. If I inflict myself on you, you won't mind too much, will you?"

"Come for as long as you like," I said.

In the first court, Brown's windows gleamed out of the dusk, but on the other side of the court the Lodge was dark behind drawn blinds.

"It is very hard to accept that he is dead," said Jago.

We went up to my sitting-room, I ordered tea. And then I asked, feeling it kindest to be direct.

"You must be worrying about the election now?"

"Intolerably," said Jago.

"You couldn't help it," I said.

"I should be on better terms with myself if I could."

"You wouldn't be human," I said.

"I haven't been able to forget it for an instant this afternoon. I went out to clear my head. I couldn't put it aside for an instant, Eliot. So I've been trying to think it out."

"What have you been trying to think out?"

"How much it means to me."

He burst out:

"And I'm quite lost, Eliot, I don't know where I am." He looked at me in a manner naïve, piercing and confiding. "I can tell you what I shouldn't like to tell Chrystal and good old Arthur Brown. There are times when it seems absolutely meaningless. I'm disgusted with myself for getting so excited about something that doesn't matter in the slightest. There are times when I'd give anything to run away from it altogether."

"And those times are when——"

Jago smiled painfully:

"When it seems quite certain I shall get it," he said. "Often I feel quite certain. Sometimes I think it will be taken from me at the last. Whenever I think that," he added, "I want it more than anything in the world. You see, I've no use for myself at all."

"I should be the same," I said.

"Should you? Do you really know what it is to have no use for yourself?"

"Oh yes," I said.

"You seem more sensible than I am," said Jago. "Perhaps you wouldn't want so badly to run away from it altogether."

"Perhaps not," I said.

"Chrystal ought to be standing himself. He would have enjoyed it," said Jago with a tired and contemptuous shrug.

I was thinking: it was the core of diffidence and pride flaming out again. He would have liked, even now, to escape from the contest. He told himself 'it did not matter in the slightest'. He assured himself of that, because he could not bear to fail. Then again he revolted from the humiliations he had consented to, in order to gain an end that was beneath him. He had been civil to Nightingale, for months he had submitted himself to Chrystal's lead. He had just revealed something I had already guessed, something I believed that had worried Arthur Brown all along. Jago had always been far away from Chrystal. In the course of nature, as Chrystal ran the campaign, Jago liked him less. He came to think that Chrystal was a soulless power-crazed business man, and it irked him to bow: his temper over the candidates' vote had been an outburst of defiance. Yet even that night he had been forced to retract, he could not bear to ruin his chances, he needed this place more even than he needed his pride.

"We must get it for you," I said, with a feeling I had never had for him before. There was a pause. Jago said:

"I think I want it more than anything in the world."

"It's strange," he added in a moment. "It's extremely strange. When I was a young man, Eliot, I was ambitious. I wanted everything that a man can want. I wanted honour, riches and the love of women. Yes, I was ambitious. I've suffered through it. And now this is what I have come to want. It can't be long now——"

He passed on to talk, with a curious content, of some appointments he would make as Master. He was enjoying in advance the pleasure of patronage: in his imagination the future was golden: for a moment he pictured the college in years to come looking back upon his reign—'the greatest of our Masters'. Then that vision left him. He glanced at me almost fiercely and said:

"You'll be surprised how splendid my wife will turn out in the Lodge. She always rises to the occasion. I couldn't bear to lose it now, on her account. She's looking forward to it so much."

I felt he wanted to say more about her, but he could not manage it. It had been a relief to talk of his ambition; perhaps it would have been a greater relief to let someone see into his marriage. But it was impossible. Certainly with me, a friendly acquaintance, a supporter, a much younger man. I believed that it would have been impossible with anyone. I believed he had never laid bare his heart about her. He had many friendly acquaintances, but, despite his warmth and candour, he seemed to have no intimate friends. I had the impression that he had not spoken even of his ambition so nakedly before.

Over tea, though he could not confide about his own

marriage, he talked of one that would never happen. He had seen that Joan Royce longed to marry Roy. Jago switched from that one challenging remark about his wife to talk of them. Perhaps the switch showed what he was feeling in the depth of his heart. She ought to have been right for Roy, said Jago. Jago had once hoped that she would be. But she simply was not. And so it would be madness for Roy to marry her. No one outside can tell who is right for one. There are no rules. One knows it without help. Sometimes the rest of the world thinks one is wrong, but they cannot know.

Then his thoughts came back to himself. December 20th.

"It can't be long now," he said.

"Thirteen days."

"Each day is a long time," said Jago.

Next afternoon, the bell tolled and the chapel filled up for the funeral. Lady Muriel and Joan sat in the front rows with their backs like pokers, not a tear on their faces, true to their Spartan training: they would not show a sign of grief in public and it was only with Roy that they broke down. All the fellows attended but Pilbrow, from whom there was still no news; even Winslow came into the chapel, for the first time since Royce's election. Many of the heads of other colleges were there, all the four professors of divinity, most of the orientalists and theologians in the university; and also a few men who went by habit from college to college for each funeral.

The wind had dropped, but the skies were low outside and a steady rain fell all day. Every light in the chapel was burning, and as they entered people blinked their eyes after the sombre daylight. The flowers on the coffin smelt sweet and sickly. There was a heavy quiet, even when the chapel was packed.

Despard-Smith recited the service, and Gay, less dispirited than anyone there, chanted his responses with lusty vigour. "Lord, have mercy upon us," cried Despard-Smith: and I could distinguish Roy Calvert's voice, light, reedy and abnormally clear, as he said Amen.

Despard-Smith put into the service an eulogy of Royce. On the night the news of the death came to the combination room, Despard-Smith had spoken simply and without thinking: 'he was a very human man'. But by now he had had time to think, and he pronounced the same praise as he had done so often. "Our first thoughts must go to his family in their affliction. . . . Greater as their loss must be, we his colleagues know ours to be so catastrophic that only our faith can give us hope of building up this society again. We chiefly mourn this day, not the Master whom we all venerated, not the leader in scholarship who devoted all his life to searching for truth, but the kind and faithful friend. Many of us have had the blessing of his friendship for a lifetime. We know that no one ever turned to him for help in vain; no one ever found him to hold malice in his heart or any kind of uncharitableness; no one even believed he was capable of entertaining an unkind thought, or heard him utter an unkind word."

I glanced at Roy. He had loved Royce: his eyes lost their sadness for a second as he heard that last singular piece of praise; there was the faint twitch of a smile on his lips.

In the even and unfaltering rain, a cavalcade of taxis rolled out to a cemetery in the suburbs, rolled past the lodging-houses of Maid's Causeway, the blank street fronts of the Newmarket Road. The fellows were allotted to taxis in order of seniority: Francis Getliffe, Roy Calvert, Luke and I shared the last. None of us spoke much, the heaviness rested on us, we gazed out of the streaming windows.

At the cemetery, we stood under umbrellas round the grave. Despard-Smith spoke the last words, and the earth rattled on the coffin.

We drove back, more quickly now, in the same group. The rain still pelted down without a break, but we all felt an inexplicably strong relief. We chatted with comfort, sometimes with animation: Francis Getliffe and Roy, who rarely had much to say to each other, exchanged a joke about Katherine's father. There were wild spirits latent in each of us just then, if our conventions had given us any excuse. As it was, when the taxis drew up at the college, knots of fellows stood in the shelter of the great gate. The same pulse of energy was passing round. I expected one result to be that the truce would be broken by dinner time that night.

THIRTY-ONE

"A GOOD DAY FOR THE COLLEGE"

Actually, it took twenty-four hours for the truce to break in earnest. Then a rumour went round that Nightingale had threatened to 'speak out'. It was certainly true that Francis Getliffe spent the afternoon arguing with Luke; I heard of the conversation from Luke himself, who could not bear to be separated for an hour from his work just then. His fresh skin had lost most of its colour, there were rings under his eyes, and he said angrily: "You'd have thought Getliffe was the last man in the bloody place to keep anyone away from the lab. —just when the whole box of tricks may be tumbling out."

"You look tired," I said.

"I'm not too tired to work," he retorted.

"What did you tell Getliffe?"

"Everyone else in this blasted college may change their minds twice a week," said young Luke, who was frantic with hope, who had anyway given up being tactful with me. "But *I* bloody well don't."

Francis's attempt was fair enough, and so was another by Winslow to persuade me. Neither caused any comment, in contrast to a 'flysheet' which Nightingale circulated to each fellow on December 10th. In the flysheet Nightingale put down a list of Crawford's claims to the Mastership, and ended with the sentence: 'Mrs. Crawford appears to many members of the college to be well fitted for the position of Master's wife. This is not necessarily true of a candidate's wife, and they attach great weight to this consideration.'

He said no more, but I was stopped in the court several

times between lunch and dinner:—was this Nightingale's final shot? was he going further? I was ready for an open scene in hall that night. Roy Calvert and I were the only members of Jago's party dining, and Nightingale, Winslow and Despard-Smith were sitting together. I had braced myself to take the offensive—when Jago, who had not come into hall since the Master's death, walked in after the grace. Nightingale seemed to be waiting for a burst of fury, but there was none. Jago sat through the dinner talking quietly to me and Roy. Occasionally he spoke a civil word to Despard-Smith and Winslow. Nightingale he had come there to ignore, and not a word was spoken about the Mastership, either in hall or in the combination room.

As I was having breakfast next morning, December 11th, Brown came in, pink and business-like.

"I've been wondering whether to answer Nightingale's latest effort," he said, sitting in the window-seat. "But I'm rather inclined to leave it alone. Any reply is only likely to make bad worse. And I've got a sneaking hope that, now he's started putting things on paper, he may possibly give us something to take hold of. I did sketch out a letter, but I had last minute qualms. I don't like it, but it's wise to leave things as they are."

"How are they?" I asked.

"I won't pretend to you that I'm entirely comfortable," said Brown. "Though mind you it's necessary for both of us to pretend to the other side. And perhaps"—he looked at me—"it's even more necessary to pretend to our own. But, between ourselves, things aren't panning out as they should. I haven't had a reply from Eustace Pilbrow. I sent off cables to every possible address within an hour after poor Royce died. And I sent off another batch yesterday. I shall believe Pilbrow is coming back to vote when I see him walking through the gate."

He went on:

"I had another disappointment last night. I went round

with Chrystal to make another try to lobby old Gay. Well, we didn't get any distance at all. The old boy is perfectly well up to it, but he won't talk about anything except his responsibility for presiding over the college during the present period. He read the statutes to us again. But we didn't begin to get anywhere."

"I wish you'd taken me," I said sharply.

"I very much wanted to take Chrystal," said Brown. He saw that I was annoyed (for I did not believe they had ever been good at flattering Gay), and he spoke more frankly about his friend than at any time before. "I feel it's a good idea to—keep up his interest in our campaign. He's never been quite as enthusiastic as I should like. I have had to take it into account that he's inclined to be temperamental."

The telephone bell rang. Was Mr. Brown with me? Mr. Chrystal was trying to trace him urgently. Brown offered to go to Chrystal's rooms; no, the Dean was already on his way up to mine.

Chrystal entered briskly, his eyes alight with purpose and the sense of action.

"It's a good day for the college," he said at once.

"What's happened?" asked Brown, quick and suspicious.

"I don't think I'm entitled to say much more till this afternoon," said Chrystal. He was revelling in this secret. "But I can tell you that Despard-Smith received a letter from Sir Horace by the first post today. It's very satisfactory, and that's putting it mildly. There's one thing that's a bit cranky, but you'll hear for yourselves soon enough. I'd like to tell you the whole story, but Despard showed me the letter in confidence."

"It sounds perfectly splendid," said Brown.

"Despard didn't see how we could do anything about it until we'd elected a Master. But I insisted that it would be lamentable to hold back the news of something as big as this," Chrystal said. "I had to tell Despard straight out that I wasn't prepared to let that happen. If he wouldn't summon an informal meeting himself, I would do it off my own bat."

Brown smiled affably at his friend's brisk triumphant air.

"Wonderful," he said again.

"That's how we left it. I've got the college office running round to get hold of people for this afternoon. It shocked old Despard too much to think of having an informal meeting in the combination room." Chrystal gave a tough grin. "So it will be in my rooms. I've called it for 2:30. I tell you, Arthur, we've done something between us. It's a good day for the college."

When I arrived in Chrystal's sitting-room that afternoon, it was already arranged to seat the fellows, with a dozen chairs round the dining table. Ten men turned up by half-past-two; Luke had gone early to the laboratory, did not return for lunch, and so no message had reached him; Gay was not there, and I suspected that Chrystal had taken care that that invitation had miscarried. We sat down round the table, all except Chrystal, who stood watching us, like a commanding officer.

"It's time we began," he said. "I move Mr. Despard-Smith take the chair."

Brown seconded, and there was a murmur, but Despard-Smith said: "I ought to say that I consider this meeting is definitely irregular. I find myself in a dilemma. It would be scandalous not to let the college know as soon as I properly can of a communication which I received this morning. On the other hand I cannot conceal from myself that the communication was sent to me under the misunderstanding that I still had the status of Deputy for the Master. I do not see the way clear for the college to receive any official communication during the *dies non* while there is a vacancy in the office of Master. I see grave difficulties whatever view we decide upon."

At last Despard-Smith was persuaded to take the chair

(which, as Roy whispered, he had been determined to do all the time). He began:

"The least irregular course open to us in my judgment is for me to disclose to you in confidence the contents of the communication I received this morning. I am p-positive that we cannot reply except to explain that I am no longer Deputy but that the letter will be laid before the new Master as soon as he is elected. Very well. The communication is from Sir Horace Timberlake, who I believe is a relative of one of our recent men. It will ultimately call for some very difficult decisions by the college, but perhaps I had better read it.

'Dear Mr. Deputy,

During the past year I have had many interesting talks upon the future of the college. I have had the privilege in particular of hearing the views of Dr. Jago—'" (I wondered for a second if Sir Horace had timed his letter to assist Jago in the election: he was quite capable of it) "'and frequently those of Mr. Brown and Mr. Chrystal. I should like to add my own small share to helping the college, feeling as I do its invaluable benefits to my nephew and the great part I can see it playing in the world. I am clear that the most useful assistance anyone can give the college at the present time is the endowment of fellowships, and I am clear that a substantial proportion should be restricted to scientific and engineering subjects. I wish to lay the minimum conditions upon the college, but I should not be living up to my own ideas of the future if I did not ask you to accept this stipulation. If the college can see its way to agree, I should be honoured to transfer to you a capital sum of £120,000'" (there was a whistle from someone at the table) "'which I take to be equivalent to the endowment of six fellowships. This capital sum will be made over in seven equal yearly instalments, until the entire endowment is in your hands by 1944. Four of these six fellowships are to be limited to scientific and engineering subjects and one is to be held in any subject that the college thinks fit. You will appreciate that this letter is not a formal offer and I shall crystallise my ideas further if I learn that the general scheme is acceptable to the college. I shall also be able to crystallise my ideas about the one remaining fellowship which I hope to designate for a special purpose.'" I saw some puzzled frowns and could not imagine what was coming. "'The best way to make a contribution to my purpose has not yet presented itself to me, but I am desirous of using this fellowship to help in the wonderful work of—'" —Despard-Smith read solemnly— "'Mr. Roy Calvert, by which I was so tremendously impressed. Possibly his work could be aided by a fellowship on special terms, but no doubt we can pursue these possibilities together. I am not sufficiently conversant with your customs to know whether you attach distinguishing titles to your endowments, and I should not wish in any case even to express a view on such a delicate topic.'"

Someone whistled again, as Despard-Smith finished. There were glances at Roy Calvert, who was looking serious. A rustle went round the table. The only person who stayed quite still was Winslow; he had been gazing down in front of him throughout the reading of the letter, and now he did not move.

"This is the largest benefaction the college has ever had," said Chrystal, who could contain himself no longer. "I call this a day."

"I foresee grave difficulties," said Despard-Smith. "I am positive that it will need the most serious consideration before the college could possibly decide to accept."

"Somehow, though, I rather think we shall," said Crawford, with the only trace of irony I had ever seen him show. "I must say this is a fine achievement, Chrystal. I suppose we owe this to you, and you deserve a very hearty vote of thanks. Speaking as a man of science, I can see this college taking the biggest jump forward it's ever made."

"Good work, Chrystal," said Francis Getliffe. "It's going to make a terrific difference. Good work."

"I can't accept all these congratulations for myself," said Chrystal, curt but delighted. "There's one man who's been more responsible than I have. That's Brown. He nursed young Timberlake. He looked after Sir Horace. It's Brown you ought to thank. Without him, we shouldn't have come within shouting distance."

"I'm afraid that I'm compelled to disagree," said Brown, settling himself comfortably to enjoy passing a good round compliment to Chrystal. "The sense of the college is absolutely right in thinking that we owe this magnificent endowment to the Dean, as no one is in a better position to appreciate than I am. If other fellows had been able to witness the time and trouble, the boundless time and trouble, that the Dean has bestowed upon securing this benefaction, I can assure the college that its sense of indebtedness to him would be even more overwhelming than it is. For his untiring devotion and unparalleled skill, I believe we ought to rank the Dean himself among the great benefactors of this society."

"I associate myself wholeheartedly with those remarks," said Crawford. Francis Getliffe and others said hear, hear.

"I feel we also owe the deepest gratitude to our other colleague Brown," said Jago. I joined in the applause, even Nightingale said an amiable word. Roy Calvert grinned.

"The old boy has unbelted to some purpose," he said. "I wonder how many free meals he could have taken off us before we gave him up."

"You're not in a position to complain," said Chrystal severely, provoked because Roy did not seem weighed down by his obligation.

"Certainly not." Roy was still grinning. "But it would have been very beautiful if the old boy's patience hadn't given out."

"It will make your subject, young man," Crawford reproved him.

"Just so. We'll polish it off," said Roy.

Winslow had not yet spoken. Words went to and fro across the table, expressing gratification, mild misgivings, disapproval from some that Roy Calvert had been singled out, triumphant emphasis from Brown, Jago and myself. In all of these exchanges Winslow took no part, but went on sitting with his head bent down—until at last, when the table happened to fall silent, he looked up from under his lids.

"I confess that I am not particularly confident of disentangling the sense of this remarkable letter," he said. "The style of our worthy friend is not apparently designed to reveal his meaning. But correct me if I am wrong—I gather some members of the college have been discussing this benefaction with Sir Horace?"

"In the vaguest terms you can possibly imagine," said Brown, prompt and emollient. "Put it another way: Sir Horace asked me among others one or two questions, and it wouldn't have been ordinary decent manners not to reply. I imagine the Dean was placed in the same rather embarrassing position."

"It must have been most embarrassing," said Winslow. "I take it, my dear Tutor, you were forced most unwillingly to discuss the finances of the college?"

Roy Calvert was scribbling on a piece of paper. He passed it to me along the table: it read *'Winslow will never recover from this.'*

"Naturally we shouldn't consider ourselves competent," said Brown. "No one's got a greater respect for the Dean's financial acumen that I have—but, if either of us had had the remotest idea that Sir Horace was going to make a definite proposition without giving us time to look round our first thought would have been to go straight to the Bursar."

"That doesn't need saying," Chrystal joined in.

"I recall very vividly," said Brown, "one evening when the Dean asked me what I thought was the point of Sir

Horace's questions. 'I suppose it can't mean money,' he said. 'If I had the slightest hope it might'—I think I'm remembering him properly—'our first step would be to bring the Bursar in'."

"I'm very much affected by that reminiscence," said Winslow. "I'm also very much affected by the thought of the Dean expending 'countless time and trouble' without dreaming for a moment that there would be any question of money."

"I'm sure I'm speaking for the Dean as well as myself," said Brown, "when I say that nothing would distress us more than that the Bursar should feel in the slightest degree left out. It's only the peculiar circumstances——"

"I've never had much opinion of myself as Bursar," said Winslow. "It's interesting to find others taking the same view. It looks at any rate as though my judgment remains unimpaired. Which will be a slight consolation to me in my retirement."

Despard-Smith said: "I hope you're not suggesting——"

"I'm not suggesting, I'm resigning," said Winslow. "I'm obviously useless when the college goes in for money seriously. It's time the college had someone who can cope with these problems. I should have a great deal more faith in the Dean or Mr. Brown as Bursar than they can reasonably have in me."

"I couldn't consider it," said Chrystal, and Brown murmured in support.

"This is disastrous," said Despard-Smith.

There were the usual exclamations of regret, incredulity, desire that Winslow should think again, that followed any resignation in the college. They were a shade more hurried than usual, they were more obviously mingled with relief. Despard-Smith remembered that no resignation could be offered or accepted while the college was without a Master. "In that case," said Winslow, "the new Master will have a pleasant duty for his first." His grim sarcasm was more repelling than ever now, and there was no warmth in the attempts to persuade him back. No one dared to be sorry for him. Then suddenly Jago burst out:

"This is a wretched exchange."

"I don't follow you," said Crawford.

"I mean," Jago cried, "that we're exchanging a fine Bursar for a rich man's charity. And I don't like it."

"It's not our fault," said Chrystal sharply.

"That doesn't make it any more palatable." Jago turned to his old enemy and his eyes were blazing. "Winslow, I want you to believe that we're more distressed than we can say. If this choice had lain with us, you mustn't be in any doubt what we should have chosen. Sir Horace would have had to find another use for his money. We can't forget what you've done for us. In one office or another, you've guided this college all your life. And in your ten years as Bursar the college has never been so rich."

Winslow's caustic smile had left him, and he looked abashed and downcast.

"That's no thanks to me," he said.

"Won't you reconsider it?" cried Jago.

Winslow shook his head.

The meeting broke up soon after, and Roy Calvert and I went for a stroll in the garden. A thick mist was gathering in the early evening, and the trees stood out as though in a Japanese print. We talked over the afternoon. Roy had enough trace of malice to feel triumphant; he imitated the look on some of their faces, as they heard of the bequest to him. "Sir Timberlake's a bit of a humorist," he said. "Oh dear, I shall have to become respectable and stuffed. They've got me at last."

We walked into the 'wilderness', and I mentioned Winslow. Roy frowned. We were both uncomfortable: we shared a perverse affection for him, we had not liked to watch his fall, we had admired Jago's piece of bravura at the end. But we were uneasy. Somehow we felt that he had been reckless and indiscreet; we wished he would be quiet until the election. Roy showed an unusual irritation. "He will overdo things," he said. "He never will learn sense. All this enthusiasm about Winslow's work as Bursar. Absurd. Winslow's been dim as a Bursar. Chrystal would be much better. I should be an extremely good Bursar myself. They'd never let me be. They wouldn't think I was sound."

It seemed odd, but all he said was true.

Then we saw Winslow himself walking through the mist, his long heavy-footed stride noiseless on the sodden grass.

"Hullo, Winslow," said Roy. "We were talking about you."

"Were you?" said Winslow. "Is there much to say?"

"Quite a lot," said Roy.

"What shall you do, now you've got some leisure?" I asked.

"Nothing. I can't start anything new."

"There's plenty of time," I said.

"I've never lacked for time," he said. "Somehow, I've never had the gift of bringing things off. I don't know why. I used to think I wasn't a fool. Sometimes, by the side of our colleagues, I thought I was a remarkably intelligent man. But everything I've touched has come to nothing."

Roy and I looked at each other, and knew it was worse to speak than to stay silent. It would not have consoled him if we spoke. It was better to watch him, stoically facing the truth.

Together the three of us walked in silence through the foggy twilight. Bushes and trees loomed at us, as we took another turn at the bottom of the garden. We had covered the whole length twice before Roy spoke again, to ask a question about Dick Winslow. He had just got engaged, said Winslow. "We scarcely know the girl," he added. "I only hope it's all right."

His tone was warm and unguarded. His son had been the bitterest of his disappointments, but his love glowed on. And that afternoon the thought of the marriage refreshed him and gave him pleasure.

THIRTY-TWO

THE VIRTUES OF THE OTHER SIDE

While we were walking round the garden, Roy Calvert asked Winslow to go with him to the pictures. Winslow was puzzled by the invitation, grumbled that he had not been for years, and yet was touched. In the end, they went off together and I was left to go in search of Brown.

I wanted to talk to him alone, for I still thought it might be worth while for me to go round to Gay's. But, when I arrived, Chrystal was just sitting down. He was smoking a pipe, and his expression was not as elated as it had been that morning. Even when Brown produced a bottle of madeira—'it needs something rather out of the ordinary to drink Sir Horace's health'—Chrystal responded with a smile that was a little twisted, a little wan. He was dispirited because his triumph, like all triumphs, had not been as intoxicating as he had imagined it.

He emptied his glass absently, and smoked away. He interrupted a conversation with a sharp question:

"What was your impression of this afternoon?"

"My impression was," said Brown, who sensed that his friend needed heartening, "that everyone realises you've done the best day's work for the college that anyone has ever done."

"Not they. They just take it for granted," said Chrystal.

"Everyone was full of it," said Brown.

"I believe they think we've treated Winslow badly. That's the thought they've gone away with." Chrystal added, with hurt and angry force: "Jago is *amusing*."

"He wanted to soften the blow," said Brown.

"There may have been a bit of policy in it," I suggested.

"He may have wanted to make a gesture. He's bound to be thinking of the election."

"Certainly. I was glad to see him showing some political sense at last," said Brown. He had followed my lead with his unceasing vigilance: he knew it was untrue, as well as I did: we were trying to take Chrystal's attention away.

"I don't believe it, Eliot," retorted Chrystal.

"He's not a simple character," I went on.

"I give you that," Chrystal said. "By God, I give you that. And there's something I wouldn't confess outside this room." He paused and looked at us. "There are times," he said slowly, "when I see the other side's case against Jago. He's too much up and down. He's all over you one minute. Then he discovers some reason for getting under one's skin as he did this afternoon. I say, I wouldn't confess it outside this room, but there are times when I have my doubts. Don't you? Either of you?"

"No," said Brown with absolute firmness.

"Some of what you say is true," I said. "But I thought it over when I decided on Jago. I didn't believe it mattered enough to count against him. I still don't."

"Not more than you did?"

"No, less," I said.

"I hope you're right," said Chrystal.

Then Chrystal said, with a pretence of off-handedness: "Anyway, it doesn't look as though we're going to get him in."

"I don't quite follow you," said Brown, but his eyes were piercing.

"Has Pilbrow cabled back to you yet?"

"Not yet."

"There you are. I shall expect him when I see him. Sometime next year."

"I've never known you rush to conclusions so fast," Brown said, "as you have done over this election." A deep frown had settled on his face.

"I knew we shouldn't get over it," said Chrystal, "the day I heard about Royce's cancer. People still don't know what we've lost."

"I can't regard that as a reason," Brown said, "for not settling down to play our hand."

Chrystal said: "You haven't denied the facts. You can't deny them."

"What do you mean?"

"I mean, you've had no reply from Pilbrow. It's a bad sign. And the votes are 6—6."

"There's nothing at all sensible to be done."

"Nothing at all," I added.

"Is that absolutely true?" Chrystal was talking to Brown in a tone of great reason and friendliness. "Look, I'll put up a case for you to knock down. We threatened those two prima donnas that if they didn't play we'd settle on a third candidate. The other side were only too anxious to come in. Men like old Despard and Getliffe didn't like this lamentable position any more than we did. And I don't believe Crawford did. I've got some respect for their judgment. Did you notice that they were very forthcoming this afternoon? More than some of our own side. Well, I should like to know their line of thought tonight. What do they expect? They know it's 6—6 as well as we do. Do you think they've heard about Pilbrow?"

"I should consider that it's extraordinarily unlikely."

"I should like to know," said Chrystal, "whether their thoughts have turned to a third candidate again."

Brown was flushed.

"It's possible they may have," he said, "but it wouldn't be a very profitable speculation. It couldn't get anywhere unless we were foolish enough to meet them half-way."

"I shouldn't like to dismiss it," said Chrystal.

"I'm sorry to hear you say so," said Brown.

"We should have to feel our way. We shouldn't have to give away a point. But I should like a chance to explore it."

"Have they made any approaches?" I asked.

"Not to me," said Chrystal.

"Do *you* intend to?"

He looked truculent.

"Only if I see an opening," he said.

"I very much hope you won't," said Brown sternly and with great weight.

"It's only as a last resort. If we can't get our man in." All the time Chrystal was trying to placate Brown, trying to persuade him all was well: he was working to get rid of the heavy, anxious, formidable frown that had stayed on Brown's face. "After all," said Chrystal, with his trace of the gamin, "you didn't like our last effort. But it came off."

"We were luckier than we deserved."

"We need a bit of luck."

"Nothing will reconcile me," said Brown, "to any more approaches from our side. They can only give the others one impression. And that is, without putting too fine a point on it, that we've lost faith in our man."

He looked at Chrystal.

"I realise you've always had your misgivings," he went on. "But that's all the more reason why you shouldn't have any dealings with the other side. This isn't the time to give them any inkling that you're not a whole-hogger. The only safe course is to leave them in their ignorance."

"If they make a move?"

"We ought to cross that bridge when we come to it." Then Brown relaxed. "I'm sorry Jago let his tongue run away with him this afternoon."

"That didn't affect me one way or the other," Chrystal said curtly. "It doesn't alter the situation."

"We'd better all sleep on it," said Brown. "I expect you'll agree tomorrow that we've got to sit tight. It's the only statesman-like thing to do."

"I should let you know," said Chrystal, "before I spoke to anyone."

THIRTY-THREE

THAT WHICH DIES LAST

The next day, December 12th, began for me with a letter which took my mind right away from the college. When I dined in hall that night, my private preoccupation had so affected me that I felt I was a visitor from outside. The college was full of rumours, hushed conversation, *tête-à-têtes*; in the combination room Francis Getliffe and Winslow spent several minutes talking in a corner. The chief rumours that night were that an informal meeting of the whole college was to be held to discuss the deadlock: and that Nightingale was just on the point of sending round another flysheet.

I had three impressions of extreme sharpness. The first was that Brown was deeply troubled, even more than he had been during the talk with Chrystal the previous night. Chrystal was not dining, and Brown slipped away by himself immediately after hall. I did not get the chance of a word with him. My second impression was that Nightingale behaved as though he had something up his sleeve. And the third, and much the strongest, was that Jago felt that night assured that he was in.

Perhaps, I thought, it was one of those intermissions that come in any period of anxiety: one is waiting for an answer, one goes to bed anxious, wakes up for no reason suffused with hope, suffused with hope so strong that it seems the answer has already come.

Anyway, Jago was quite relaxed, his voice easy; he did not have to clown: he did not make a remark which drew attention to himself. He spoke to Crawford with such friendliness, such quiet warmth, such subdued but natural confidence, that Crawford seemed out of his depth. He had never seen his rival like this before, he had never felt the less comfortable of the two.

I walked away from the combination room with Jago. He had promised to show me a small comet which had become visible a night or two before, and we climbed to the top of a staircase in the second court. There, looking over the garden to the east, he made me see a blur of light close to the faintest star of the Great Bear. He had been an amateur astronomer since childhood, and from the stars he gained, despite his unbelief, something close to a religious emotion.

The silence of the infinite spaces did not terrify him. He felt at one with the heavens; it was through them that he knew a sense of the unseen. But he only spoke of what he could observe. That night, he told me where the comet would have reached by the same time next day: how fast it was travelling: the size of its orbit: how long it would be before men saw it again.

Coming down the stairs, he was full of happiness. He was not even much excited when he saw Pilbrow's door open and his servant lighting a fire. I went in and asked the reason, and was told that Pilbrow had sent a telegram from London, saying that he was returning by the last train.

Jago heard the servant's answers from the landing, and I did not need to tell him that Pilbrow was coming back. "He's a wonderful old boy," said Jago. He did not say it with emphasis; for him, the news just completed the well-being of an evening. He said a contented good night, and walked at a leisurely pace along the path to his house. I had not seen him walk so slowly since that afternoon of our first party meeting, when he felt the Mastership lay in his hands.

Once at least he lifted his eyes to the stars.

It was well past one o'clock next morning, and I was writing by my fire, when I heard the clang of the great gate's bell: gently once or twice, then a long impatient ring, then another. At last the porter must have woken up. I heard the opening of a door, and finally the rattle and clash as the gate was unlocked.

There were steps through the court. I wondered who had come in late, and turned back to my writing. A few minutes later, the steps sounded on my own staircase. It was Pilbrow.

"I saw your light on my way past. I had to tidy up after the trip. I specially wanted to see you before you went to bed."

He had burst in, looking ten years younger than his age. He was ruddily sunburned, and there were one or two patches on the top of his bald head from which the skin had peeled.

"I had lunch in Split thirty-six hours ago. Split! Split! I like the Slavs——Absurd names. Much more absurd than the Italian names." He pronounced the name several times aloud, chuckling to himself. "Astonishing number of beautiful people. You sit in the market-place and watch them. . . . Also extremely prudish. Why do people get steadily more beautiful as you go south-east from the Brenner? The Tyrolese are lovely. The Dalmatians are better still. They also get more prudish as they get more beautiful. The Tyrolese are moderately prudish. The Dalmatians extremely. . . . I suppose it's a law of nature. A very stupid one too."

I could scarcely get in a word. He had been flown most of the way home. He had been travelling for two days: his cheeks shone, he did not seem in the least tired.

Soon he said, earnestly and without any introduction:

"Eliot, things are worse in Europe than they have been in my time."

"You mean politically?"

"All our friends are in danger. Everything you and I believe in is going. . . . Our people are just sitting by and watching. And dining in the best houses. Bloody fools. Snobs. Snobbery will make this country commit suicide. These bloody snobs can't see who their enemies are. Or who are their friends. When a country is blinding itself to that, it's in a bad way."

He told me of some of his doings. He had somehow managed to visit his friends in a concentration camp. He was a very brave old man. He was also an acute one, underneath the champagne-like gaiety.

"I came to tell you," he said suddenly. "That's why I was glad to see your light. I wanted to tell you before anyone else. I can't vote for Jago. I can't vote for someone who won't throw his weight in on our side. It's your side as well as mine. That's why I came to tell you first. . . ."

I was taken aback. I should not have been so surprised at the outset. I knew it had worried him, but I thought he had come to terms and satisfied himself. It would not have astonished me if he had found some reasonable excuse and stayed away. But I was not prepared for his journey home, his ebullient entry, and then this. I had not recovered myself when I asked flatly:

"What are you going to do?"

"Vote for the other man," said Pilbrow without a pause. "He's on the right side. He's always been on the right side. We can trust him in that way."

I tried to shake off the shock, and do my best. I retraced the arguments I had had with Francis Getliffe. I searched for anything that might influence him: I told him that the three youngest fellows in the college were all supporting Jago—it was not like Pilbrow, I reproached him, to leave the side of youth. But he was obdurate—sometimes a little flustered in speech, but quite unshaken.

I tried once more.

"You know I feel about the world as strongly as you," I said. "If that's possible."

Pilbrow smiled, pleased by the remark.

"You do know, don't you?"

"Of course," Pilbrow replied. "Of course. More than any of those . . ."

"No," I said. "Not more than Getliffe or young Luke. But

as much. Anyway, I take an even blacker view than you. I'm beginning to feel it like a personal sorrow."

"Yes! Yes!" cried Pilbrow. "Things outside have got to be very bad before they make one feel like that. But they are——"

"Even so," I said, "I can't believe that it ought to affect us here. We're choosing from two human beings." I waited, in the hope it would sink in. "You've always liked Jago, haven't you?"

"Yes," said Pilbrow at once. "He's warm. He's got a great gift of warmth."

"You don't care for Crawford?"

"I'm neutral to him," said Pilbrow.

"He's on the right side in politics," I said, "but you know very well that most of your kind of civilisation he doesn't begin to touch. If the books you've devoted your life to disappeared tomorrow, he wouldn't notice the difference."

"No. But——" Pilbrow's bright brown eyes were troubled.

"You've always set a value on human beings. Surely you're not going to pass over the difference between those two? You're saying that you'll just vote for a programme. Are you really ready to forget what human beings mean?"

"We've got to sacrifice something." Pilbrow had found his tongue, and spoke with vigour. "If we don't sacrifice something, there'll be nothing left at all."

I made a last attempt.

"You know what it means for Jago," I said.

"Disappointing. . . ."

"You know it will be far worse than that."

"Yes."

"For you it wouldn't have mattered much—at any time. Would it? You're not such a diffident man as Paul Jago, you know. You couldn't pin your self-esteem on to a job. You've never given a damn whether people elected you to masterships or presidencies of buffaloes' clubs. It's not people like you who are ambitious for positions, Eustace. It is people like Jago—who need some support from outside. And he needs it *intolerably*. If he doesn't get the Mastership, it will hurt him more than anyone imagines. It won't be just disappointing. It will break his heart."

I added:

"Don't you agree?"

"I'm afraid so."

"Doesn't it affect you?"

"It's a pity," said Pilbrow. "He'll recover in time. They always . . ."

He broke off. His tone was almost light-hearted, and I knew it was no good. Then he said, with extraordinary vigour, his eyes shining like brown beads, his whole body clenched with energy:

"I can't bear to have anyone say that I helped the wrong side. I can't do as much as I should like, but I shall throw in my weight wherever I can. I hope I have a few years left to do it."

I knew it was no good. There was nothing to be done. No one could move Pilbrow now. He would vote for Crawford to the end.

And I felt something else. His vigour was marvellous and enviable: I wished I could imagine being so radiant at seventy-four: and yet, for the first time, I saw him overtaken by age.

A few years before he would not have said of Jago, as though human feelings were tiresome, 'he'll recover in time'. But in fact he had come to the point where human feelings *were* tiresome—no, not tiresome, so much as remote, trivial, a little comic. That was the sign of age. Pilbrow had been a man of strong affections. But those affections died off, except the strongest of all; as he became old, he could only feel moved by the great themes of his life; all else cooled down, although he struck no one as old, certainly not himself. And where he did not feel himself, he lost his sympathy for others' feelings. They did not seem important. Very little seemed important. Just as a mature man dismisses calf love with a smile, because he can no longer feel it (though it may once have caused him the sharpest pain), so Pilbrow, that vigorous old man, smiled indifferently at the triumphs and sufferings of the middle-aged. Suddenly one encountered blankness at a point where one expected sympathy and response. He looked just as he had looked ten years before; he could still feel passionately about his deepest concerns; but those concerns were narrowing, and one knew at last that he was growing old.

At times he knew it. At times he could not help but know it. So he clung more ardently to that which moved him still. It was that which died last. For Pilbrow, who had befriended so many, who had spent a life-time in good causes, who had fought with body and mind, it was the picture of himself still 'throwing in his weight' on the side of light. That rang out of his last words. In them one heard the essence of the man: he was stripped by age of all that did not matter: and age revealed his vital core. In a sense, he was self-centred—more so than many men whose lives were selfish by the side of his. He was sweet-dispositioned, he was the most generous of men, but nothing could make him forget his picture of himself. That night I was too much upset to care, but later on it made me feel more brother-like towards him. I did not see in him the goodness that some did; but I felt the comradeship of common flesh, as well as great tenderness, for the gallant, lubricious, indomitable and generous old man, with the sturdy self-regard that nothing on earth could move.

He did not realise that I was deeply upset by his news. He went on talking about a Croatian writer, and it was getting on for four when he said that he was looking forward to a good long night.

I was too much disturbed to go to bed myself. I decided to wake Roy Calvert; it was a strange reversal of rôles, when I recalled the nights of melancholy in which he had woken me. In his sitting room the embers were still glowing. He must have had a large fire and sat up late. Proofs of the liturgy lay stacked on his lowest table, and I noticed the dedicatory page IN MEMORY OF VERNON ROYCE.

He was peacefully asleep. He had not known insomnia since the summer, and always when he slept it was as quietly as a child. It took some time to wake him.

"Are you part of a dream?" he asked. They were his first coherent words.

"No."

"Let me go to sleep. Rescue my books yourself. Is it a fire? I need to go to sleep."

He looked tousled and flushed, and, though his hair was already thinning, very young.

"I'm very worried," I said, and he shook himself into consciousness.

He jumped out of bed, and put on a dressing gown while I told him of Pilbrow.

"Bad. Bad," said Roy.

He was still sleepy, but we moved into the sitting room, and he warmed himself over the remnants of the fire.

"What is our move, old boy?"

"We may be losing. I'm afraid for Jago now."

"Just so. That gets us nowhere. What is our move?"

He took out his box of bricks and arranged the sides again. "7—6 for Crawford. That's the worst it's been."

"We've got nothing to lose if we tackle any of them. I wish we had before. We certainly ought to try everything we know on old Gay," I said.

"Just so. I like the sound of that. Ah. Indeed," said Roy. He smiled at me. "Don't be too worried, old boy."

"We'll try everything, but the chances are against us."

"I'm sorry for poor old Jago. You're frightfully sorry, aren't you? He's got hold of your imagination. Never mind. We'll do our damnedest." Roy was enjoying the prospect of action. Then he smiled at me again. "It's extremely funny for me to be consoling you."

THIRTY-FOUR

OBLIGATIONS OF LOVE

Although I had had only a few hours' sleep, I was lying wakeful when Bidwell called me. He drew the blind and let in the grey half-light of the December morning: I turned away, longing for sleep again, I wanted to shirk the day.

Bidwell had not lit the fire in my sitting room early enough; there were only spurts of flame among the great lumps of coal. Smoke blew out of the grate, and it struck cold and raw in the lofty room. I sat down heavy-heartedly to my breakfast. With an effort, I roused myself to call down the stairs for Bidwell. He entered with his usual smile, intimate, deferential and sly. I sent him to find whether Pilbrow was up yet, and he returned with news that Pilbrow had pinned a note on his door saying he proposed to sleep until midday and was not to be disturbed.

I knew that, as soon as he was about, he would be punctilious in warning his former side of his change of vote. His views were eccentric for an old man, but his manners had stayed gentle and nineteenth century; the only grumble I had ever heard him make about his young friends of the left was that, though he was sure there was some good reason for it, he could not for the life of him understand why they found it necessary to be so rude.

It was certain that Jago, Brown and Chrystal would receive his note of apology by the end of the day. I did not want to break more bad news to Brown; over breakfast, I decided to leave it, he would find out from Pilbrow's note soon enough. Then I thought I had better face the trouble, and sent out Bidwell with another message, asking Brown to visit me as soon as he came into college.

He was busy with the scholarship examination, and it was not until eleven o'clock that he arrived.

"Is it anything serious? Have you heard about a meeting?" he asked at once.

I told him of Pilbrow's visit. His face flushed an angry purple, and he cursed with a virulence I had never heard before. He ended up:

"It's all his confounded politics. I always thought that he'd never grow up. It's bad enough having people with cranky opinions in the college, saving your presence, Eliot, but it's a damned scandal when they interfere with serious things. It's a damned scandal. I shall never think the same of Pilbrow."

It was the first time in the whole year that he had lost his balance. At last he said, with regretful bitterness: "I suppose we may as well tell Chrystal. I should have hoped at one time that he would take it as much amiss as I do."

Chrystal listened to the news with attention, and received it quite differently from Brown.

"Well. That's that," he said. "I can't say I'm much surprised."

His response was mixed from the first moment—mixed, with his soft-hearted concern for his friend's misery, his guilt at his friend's anger, his delight at a hidden plan, his strong but obscure gratification.

"It's just as well I established contact yesterday," he said triumphantly. "We hadn't told you, Eliot. Brown was not happy about going on. But some people on the other side would welcome a meeting. Of everyone who wants to come. Throwing everything into the melting pot. I told Brown yesterday it was our best way out. Now I'm sure of it."

"The position was different yesterday."

"I took it for granted there were floating votes."

"I don't want a way out from Jago, and I never should," said Brown.

I asked if the meeting had been decided on.

"I don't think they'll back out," Chrystal replied. "I'm not sure if they want to."

"Not even," I said, "now that they can see a majority for Crawford? When they hear about Pilbrow, they'll feel they're winning for the first time. Why should they want a meeting?"

"They would be very foolish to contemplate such a thing," said Brown heavily to Chrystal. "Yesterday was a different situation. They stood to gain by saying yes to any approach you made. It was only decent common sense for them to draw you on. I shouldn't think much of their judgment if they hadn't welcomed any discussion you liked to suggest. They knew that we were showing our weakness."

"It's turned out right. It may save us," said Chrystal.

"I'll believe that when I see the slightest sign that they're willing to compromise—now they're sitting with the majority."

"I'll see there's a meeting," said Chrystal. "It can be done. They'll be willing to compromise."

After lunch, Roy and I were sitting in my rooms. We intended to walk out to Gay's house in time for tea; it was no use leaving the college until three, for the old man took his afternoon sleep according to the time-table which regulated all his actions and which had not varied for forty years.

I had deliberately kept back from Brown and Chrystal that we were making an attempt on Gay. Chrystal was now set on a compromise, and I did not think it safe to tell him. Unless Jago's chances were revived, there was nothing Chrystal would do to help: he was more likely to hinder.

"Just so," said Roy. "He's an interesting man. If he'd been as single-minded over poor Jago as he was about making Sir Timberlake unbelt, we should have raced home."

We talked about personal politics, of which in different places we had now seen a good deal. One point had struck us both: will, sheer stubborn will, was more effective than cunning or finesse or subtlety. Those could be a help; but the more one saw, the more one was forced to the banal conclusion that the man you wanted on your side was the man who believed without a shade of doubt that you were right. Arthur Brown was cunning and resourceful; but he had been the mainstay of Jago's cause because, more powerfully than any of us, without any qualifications at all, he was determined to get Jago in. And Crawford's side, which had so long been numerically weaker, began with Despard-Smith, Winslow and Getliffe, not one of whom ever felt a doubt between Crawford and Jago. In that they were luckier than we had been; for Chrystal, whose will could be as strong as any of theirs, had had it split throughout the entire struggle.

As we were talking, there was a tap on the door and Mrs. Jago came in. She said: "I've been up to Roy's rooms. I had to find someone——" and burst out crying. I led her to a chair by the fireplace, tears streaming down her face: there she cried aloud, noisily, with abject and abandoned misery: she laid her head on the arm of the chair, but did not try to hide her face: her heavy body shook with the tearing sobs.

Roy and I met each other's glance. Without speaking, we agreed to leave her alone. When the weeping became quieter, when the convulsions no longer tore her, it was I who stroked her hand.

"Tell us," I said.

She tried to summon up her dignity. "Mr. Eliot, I must apologise for this exhibition," she said, with her imitation of Lady Muriel—then she began to cry again.

"What is the matter?" I said.

She tried again to be grand, and then broke down.

"They're all saying—they're all saying that I'm not fit to go into the Lodge."

"Alice, what do you mean?" said Roy.

"They all hate me. Everyone here hates me. Even you"—she straightened herself in the chair, her cheeks glistening with tears, and looked at Roy—"hate me sometimes."

"Don't be foolish."

"I'm not always as foolish as you think." She put a hand

to the breast of her frock, and drew out a note. I looked at it and so did Roy over my shoulder. It was Nightingale's fly-sheet.

"What else does it mean?" she cried. "I know I'm an ugly hysterical woman. I know I'm no use to anyone. But I'm not as foolish as you think. Tell me the truth. If you don't hate me tell me the truth."

"We don't hate you," said Roy. "We're very fond of you. So will you stop hurting yourself? Then I'll tell you the truth."

His tone was affectionate, scolding, intimate. She dried her eyes and sat quiet.

"That paper means what you think," said Roy. "One or two men mean to keep Paul out at any cost. They're aiming at him through you. They've done the same through me."

She stared at him, and he added gently:

"You're not to worry."

"How can I help worrying?" she said. The cry was full of pain, but there was nothing hysterical in it.

"I should like to know how you saw this paper," I said. "Did Paul leave it about?"

"He'd never be careless about anything that might upset me—don't you realise he's always taken too much care of me?" she said. "No, this one was sent so that I could see it for myself."

"Poor thing," said Roy.

"That must be Nightingale himself," I said. "What in God's name does he hope for?"

"He hopes," said Alice Jago, with a flash of shrewdness, "that it will make me do something silly."

"It might be just malice," said Roy.

"No, it's their one chance to keep Paul out. I'm his only weakness, you know I am," she said. "I suppose they know Paul is bound to be elected unless they shout the place down." (Neither Roy nor I realised till then that she was still ignorant of the latest news.) "I'm their best chance, aren't I? I've heard another whisper—I expect I was meant to hear it—that they're not going to leave me alone. They think I'm a coward. They're saying that this note is only a beginning. They believe that I shall want Paul to withdraw."

"You couldn't help being frightened," said Roy.

"I could hear them all talking about me," she cried. "I was hysterical. I didn't know what to do. I ran out of the house, I don't know why I came to you——"

I could not be certain what had happened. She had received the flysheet: but had it actually been sent by Nightingale? I could not think of any other explanation. Had there really been other rumours? Was she imagining it all? Now she was speaking, quietly, unhappily, and with simple feeling.

"I'm so frightened, Roy. I'm terribly frightened still," she said. "I've not been a good wife to Paul. I've been a drag on him all these years. I've tried sometimes, but I've never been any good. I know I'm horrible, but I can't prevent myself getting worse. But I've never done him so much harm as this. I never thought they'd use me to prevent him being Master. How can I stand it, how can I stay here if they do?"

"Think of Paul," said Roy.

"I can't help thinking of myself too," she cried. "How can I stand seeing someone else moving into that drawing room? And I know you think I oughtn't to worry about myself, but how can I stand the things they'll say about me?"

"It may not happen," I said.

"It *will* happen."

"If it does, you'll have to harden yourself."

"Do *you* know what they'll say?" she asked me wildly. "They'll say I wasn't good enough for Paul. And instead of doing my best for him, I couldn't resist making a fool of myself with other men. It's perfectly true. Though none of them wanted anyone like me." She gave a smile, wan, innocent, and flirtatious. "Roy, you know that I could have made a fool of myself with you."

"You've always tried to make Paul love you more," said Roy. "You've never believed that he really loves you, have you? Yet he does."

"How can he?"

Roy smiled: "And you love him very much."

"I've never been good enough for him," she cried.

She was wretched beyond anything we could say to her: disappointment pierced her, then shame, then self-disgust. She had looked forward so naïvely, so snobbishly to the Lodge; she had boasted of it, she had planned her parties, she had written to her family. Could it still be taken away? We guessed that Jago had shielded her from all the doubts so far. Could it be taken away through her follies? She was sickened by shame; she had 'made a fool of herself' and now they might bring it against her. She did not feel guilty remorse, she was too deeply innocent at heart for that. She felt instead shame and self-hatred, because men spoke ill of her. She had never believed that she could be loved—that was the pain which twisted her nature. Now she felt persecuted, unloved, lost, alone. Had Paul always pretended to love her out of pity? She believed even that—despite the devotion, despite the proofs.

No one could love her, she knew ever since she was a girl, she never had the faintest confidence of being loved. If she could have had a little confidence, she thought, she might have given Paul more comfort; she would not have been driven to inflict on him the woes of a hypochondriac, the venom of a shrew, the faithlessness of one who had to find attention. He would never know how abjectly she worshipped him. All she had done was damage him (she saw the letter in her hand) so much that she could never make it up.

It was long past the time when Roy and I had planned to start for Gay's, and we had to give up our project for that day. Nothing we said was any help, but it was unthinkable to leave her alone. At last she invited us back to her house for tea. She walked between us through the courts. On our way, we were confronted by Nightingale, walking out of college. His hand moved up to his hat, but she looked away, with a fixed stare. We heard his footsteps dying away. She said almost triumphantly:

"They've cut me often enough."

In their drawing room Jago was standing, and the moment we entered he put his arm round her shoulders.

"I've been looking everywhere for you," he said. "Why didn't you leave word where you'd gone? You mustn't disappear without a trace. What is the trouble?"

"What is the trouble with you?" she cried. He had been standing in the twilight, but she had switched on the light as we went in. His face was haggard, his eyes sunken; even his lips were pallid.

"You two know by now?" said Jago. We nodded. He turned to his wife, his arm resting on her.

"Dearest, I'm afraid that I'm going to make you unhappy. It seems that I shall be rejected by the college."

"Is this my fault?"

"How could it be your fault?" Jago replied, but her question, which pierced one like a scream, was not addressed to him. I answered:

"It's nothing to do with anyone we've been talking about. It's quite different. Old Eustace Pilbrow has crossed over—for political reasons. He can't even have read the flysheet when he decided, and he'd be the last to take any notice——"

"Thank God," she said, laying her head on Jago's shoulder. "If they don't give it to you after all, Paul, I couldn't bear it to be because of me."

"Does it concern us," asked Jago bitterly, "the precise reason why I may be thrown aside?"

"Yes! Yes!" she said. She rounded on me. "Why didn't you tell me?"

I said:

"I couldn't—until I was sure Paul knew."

"Do you realise what it means? Do you realise that they're hoping to humiliate me now?" Jago cried.

"They couldn't," she said. "Nothing could. Nothing could touch you. You're big enough to laugh at anything they do. They know you're bigger than they are. That's why they fear you so."

Jago smiled—was it to relieve her, as a parent pretends to an anxious child? Or had she brought him comfort?

He kissed her, and then said to Roy and me:

"I am sorry to receive you like this. But the news has knocked me out more than I expected."

"We're not giving up," I said.

"I'm not sure," said Jago, "that I shouldn't ask you to."

He seemed suddenly tired, passive, and resigned. He sat down in his armchair as though the suffering had lost its edge but had worn him out. He enquired after tea, and Alice rang for it. Suddenly he said to her:

"Why did you ask whether it was your fault? What do you know about the flysheet?"

She began to speak, then said: "No, Paul, I can't——" and turned to us for aid. I told Jago that someone, presumably Nightingale, had made sure that she should see the flysheet: she was afraid there might be more attacks upon her: she thought they wanted her to persuade Jago to withdraw; she had been in anguish for Jago's sake.

Very softly, Jago exclaimed.

Then he spoke to her in a quiet, familiar tone.

"I expect to be rejected now. Would you like me to withdraw?"

Tears had come to her eyes, but she did not cry. She could hardly speak. At last she managed to say:

"No. You must go on."

"You knew what you had to say." Jago gave her a smile of love.

When that smile faded, his expression was still sad and

exhausted: but in his eyes, as he spoke again, this time to Roy and me, there was a flash of energy, a glitter of satanic pride.

"I've cursed the day that I ever exposed myself to these humiliations," he said. "I knew you and my other friends meant well, but you were not doing me a kindness when you persuaded me to stand. Whether the college rejects me or takes me, I am certain that I will not stand for another office so long as I live." He paused. "But I am equally certain that if those people hope to get me to withdraw through doing harm to my wife, I will stay in this election while I've got one single man to vote for me."

He added:

"And I shall leave nothing to chance. I shall tell my rival so."

THIRTY-FIVE

CRAWFORD BEHAVES SENSIBLY

After Jago cried out that he 'would tell his rival so', he asked Roy to find from the kitchens whether Crawford was dining that night. The answer was yes. "That is convenient," said Jago.

Crawford arrived in the combination room at the same time as I did, and several of his party were already there. They were drinking their sherry in front of the fire, and there was an air of well-being, of triumph, of satisfied gloating. Crawford greeted them with his impersonal cordiality, and me as well. He seemed more than ever secure, not in the least surprised by what had happened; he took it for granted that it was right.

"Eliot," Nightingale addressed me. He had not spoken to me directly for months.

"Yes?"

"I suppose you've heard about Pilbrow."

"Of course."

"I had a note from him this afternoon," Crawford announced.

"Good work," said Francis Getliffe.

"It's very civil of him to have written," said Crawford,—and went on to talk without hurry of a new theory of electrical impulses in nerves. Francis Getliffe was making a suggestion for an experiment, Nightingale was listening with the strained attention that nowadays came over him in Crawford's presence, when Jago threw open the door and said:

"Crawford. I should like you to spare me a minute."

Everyone looked up at Jago. He did not say good-evening, his eyes did not leave Crawford.

"Very well," said Crawford, not quite at ease. "Can we talk here, or would you prefer to go outside?"

"Nothing I have to say is secret," Jago replied. "I'm obliged to say it to you, because I'm not certain to whom it should be said by right."

Crawford rose and said "Very well" again. By the fire Despard-Smith and Getliffe made a pretence at conversation, but none of us could shut our ears to Jago's words.

"I do not hold you responsible for the outrages of your supporters, but I hope that you cannot be utterly indifferent to them."

"You're going too fast for me," said Crawford. "I don't begin to know what you're referring to."

"I shall explain myself."

"I should much prefer it," said Crawford, looking up into Jago's eyes, "if we could keep this business on a friendly basis."

"When you hear what I have to say," said Jago, "you will realise that is no longer easy."

Jago's temper smouldered and suddenly flared out and smouldered again. It was different from one of his outbursts of indignation; no one in that room had seen this consuming rage. As they faced it, most men would have been uneasy; Crawford may have been, but his voice was steady and sensible. Angrily, I had to confess that he was holding his own.

"If that turns out to be true, I shall be very sorry for it, Jago," he remarked.

"If you are elected, none of my friends would suggest that your wife was not entirely fit to adorn the Lodge," Jago said.

"I should be very much surprised to hear it."

"I was a little surprised to hear that my wife had received a copy of the flysheet written by your supporter Nightingale."

Jago's words were not loud, but Crawford stood silent in front of him.

"You have seen the flysheet I mean?"

"I am afraid that I have," said Crawford.

"Can you faintly imagine what it would mean to a woman?"

Crawford stirred.

"Jago, I very much regret that this should have happened. I shall write to your wife personally, and tell her so."

"That is not enough."

"It is all I can do, unfortunately."

"No," said Jago. "You can discover through what source the flysheet reached her. I may tell you that it was deliberately sent."

Jago was at the limit of his anger. Crawford shook his head.

"No," he said. "I can understand your feelings, but you exaggerate my responsibility. I am sincerely sorry that your wife should suffer through any circumstances in which I am even remotely concerned. I consider it my duty to tell her so. But I don't consider it my duty to become a private detective. I have consented to be a candidate at this election, but I have taken no part whatever in any of the personal complications which have taken place, and I might take this opportunity of saying that I deprecate them."

Jago was quietened for an instant, by the solidity of that reply. Then he said:

"This attack on my wife is intended to make me withdraw."

"I can't express any view on intentions in which I am not interested," said Crawford.

"If you are not interested, your supporters may be," said Jago. "I shall protect my wife in all ways open to reason but also, while any of my colleagues are prepared to give me their votes, I shall remain a candidate for the Mastership."

There was no reply from Crawford, and the whole room was silent, for the conversation round the fire had died right away.

The bell began to peal for dinner, and Crawford said, as though anxious for a cordial commonplace:

"Are you coming into hall, Jago?"

"No," said Jago. "I shall dine with my wife."

There was a constrained hush as he walked out. Crawford was frowning, the smooth composed impassive look had gone. He sat next to me in hall, did not speak until the fish, and then complained:

"Speaking as a reasonably even-tempered person, I have the strongest possible objection to being forced to listen to those who insist on flying off the handle."

"I'm glad he spoke to you," I said.

"It's no concern of mine. He ought to know that I have never lent an ear to local tittle-tattle. I'm not prepared to begin now, and I shall wash my hands of the whole stupid business."

But Crawford was in his fashion a man of justice and fair dealing, and he was shaken. He took the chair in the combination room with a preoccupied expression, when Despard-Smith left after hall. None of us asked for wine that night, and Crawford lit his pipe over the coffee.

"It does look," he said, "as though somehow Mrs. Jago has come into possession of that circular of yours, Nightingale. I must say that it is an unfortunate business."

"Very unfortunate—but I fancy she might have benefited if she'd learned what people thought of her before." Nightingale smiled.

"Naturally," said Crawford, "it can't have been sent to her by anyone connected with the college. Every one of us would take a grave view of an action of that kind."

His tone was uncomfortable, and no one replied for some moments. Then Nightingale smiled again.

"Is there anything to show," he asked, "that she wasn't looking through her husband's letters on the quiet, and found one that wasn't meant for her?"

I looked at him.

"I believe she did not read your note by accident," I said.

"How did you form that opinion?" he said.

"I spent the afternoon with her just after she'd read it."

"That's as may be. What does it prove?"

"She was so miserable that I believe what she said," I replied.

"Do you really expect us to be impressed by that?"

"I expect you to know that it was the truth."

His eyes stared past mine, he did not move or blench. Nothing touched him except his own conflict. Find the key to that, and one could tear him open with a word. Touch his envy, remind him of the Royal Society, his other failures, and he was stabbed by suffering. But to everything else he was invulnerable. He did not see any of his actions as 'bad'. So long as he did not feel 'put upon' as weak, he did not worry about his actions. He regarded his attempts to blacken Jago's circle as a matter of course. He was not at peace enough to go in for the luxuries of conscience.

"I can't say your claim is completely convincing, Eliot," said Crawford. "She may have enemies, nothing to do with the college, who wanted to play an unpleasant practical joke."

"Is that how you see it?" I said.

"Perhaps it is a storm in a teacup," said Crawford. "After all she is just going through an awkward time of life. And Jago has always been over-emotional. Still we must try and calm things down. I have occasionally felt that this election has generated more heat than light. We've got to see that people know where to stop."

Then he laid down his pipe, and went on:

"I always think that the danger with any group of men like a college is that we tend to get on each other's nerves. I believe that everyone, particularly the unmarried fellows, ought to be compelled by statute to spend three months abroad each year. And also—and this I do suggest to you all as a practicable proposition—I think we ought to set for ourselves an almost artificially high standard of manners and behaviour. I suggest to you that, in any intimate body of men, it is important to have the rules laid down."

I noticed that as Crawford delivered his steady impersonal reproof, Nightingale was watching him with anxious attention and nodding his head. It was more than attention, it was devoted deference.

As Crawford rose to go, he said:

"Nightingale, are you busy? You might walk part of the way home with me."

The moment he heard the invitation, Nightingale's harsh strained face broke into a smile that held charm, pleasure and a youthful desire to please.

I was to blame, I told myself, for not having seen it before. No doubt he still craved Crawford's support for getting into the Royal Society, but somehow that longing for a favour had become transmuted into a genuine human feeling. He would do anything for Crawford now.

"I hope," said Francis Getliffe, when we were left alone, "that Crawford tells him to shut up."

I could not resist saying satirically:

"I thought that Crawford was remarkably judicious."

"I thought he was pretty good. If he always handles situations as well as that, I shan't complain," said Francis, with irritation.

"Some people would have gone further."

"No responsible person could have gone further, on that evidence," said Francis. "Damn it, man, she's an unbalanced woman. Do you expect Crawford to take as absolute fact every word she says?"

"I think you do," I said.

He hesitated.

"It's more likely true than not," he said.

"You're finding yourself in curious company," I said.

"There looks like being enough of it to win," said Francis.

We could not get on terms of ease. I asked after his work; he replied impatiently that he was held up. I invited him to my rooms, but he made an excuse for going home.

THIRTY-SIX

VISIT TO AN AUTHORITY

The next morning, December 14th, neither Brown nor Chrystal came into college, and it was from a few minutes' talk with Winslow in the court that I heard there might be a meeting. "Not that any of my way of thinking were much impressed by that remarkable suggestion," he said. "We're comparatively satisfied with things as they are. But if it pleases you, it doesn't hurt us."

His grin was still sardonic, but more friendly and acquiescent than it used to be. He was on his way to the bursary to clear up his work, so that he could resign as soon as the Master was elected. Nothing, he said with a trace of sadness, would make him stay a day longer.

That afternoon Roy and I were not baulked before we set out for Gay's. We walked through the backs, going under the mourning sky, under the bare trees; Roy was in the best of spirits. It was with a solemn expression that he rang the bell of Gay's house, which stood just by the observatory. "This is an occasion," he whispered.

Gay was sitting in his drawing-room with a paper in his hands.

"Ah. Splendid," he said. "You're come to see my exhibits, I'll guarantee. I'm glad to see you, Calvert. I'm glad to see you, Nightingale."

I avoided Roy's glance.

"Not Nightingale," I said.

"No. Indeed. Tell me your name, will you?"

"I'm Eliot." It was difficult to conduct this conversation without feeling uncomfortable.

"I absolutely remember. And what is your subject?"

"Law."

"I congratulate you," said Gay with splendid finality.

Although both Roy and I had been to the house several times before, he insisted on our looking round the room and out into the garden. It was all that befitted a middle-class donnish home in Cambridge—the furniture heavier and more old-fashioned than at the Getliffes', but nothing except the difference of years to pick it out from theirs. Gay, however, regarded it with singular satisfaction.

"I always say that I built this house out of my masterpiece. Three thousand pounds I made out of that work, and I put every penny of it into bricks and mortar. Ah, that was a book and a half. I haven't any patience with these smart alecks who tell us that one can't get fine scholarship home to the reading public. Why, I shouldn't have this fine house if they didn't lap it up. Lap it up, they did, Calvert. What do you think of that?"

"Wonderful," said Roy.

He glanced at us affably and stroked his beard.

"I will give you young men a piece of advice. Satisfy the scholars first. Show them that you're better than any of them, that's the thing to do. But when you've become an authority, don't neglect your public. Why, I should welcome my books being presented by the films. I don't despise these modern methods. Fine films my sagas would make too. Nothing namby-pamby about them."

Roy then produced greetings from a letter—I did not know whether it was invented—from one of the linguistic scholars in Berlin. Gay beamed. He seized the chance to tell us again of his honorary degree at Berlin—'the great authority on the sagas'.

I made an attempt to get down to business.

"We very much wanted your advice," I said. "Now you've got this responsibility for presiding over the college till the election——"

"Ah. Indeed."

"We should value your guidance over the Mastership. It's been on our minds a good deal. Are you satisfied with the ways things are shaping?"

"December the twentieth," said Gay resonantly. "That's the great day. Six days from this morning. Splendid. I have everything in hand. I read the statutes each night before I go off to sleep. It's all in safe hands. You can be sure of that. Now you'll have been getting impatient to see my exhibits. That's something more interesting for you."

We had seen the 'exhibits' each time we had gone to the house, but it was impossible not to see them again. Gay's wife, tiny and bird-like, as old as he but very active, came and wrapped his muffler round his neck and helped him into his great coat. Then he led us at his shuffling pace to the bottom of the garden. All the 'exhibits' were connected with his life's researches on the sagas, and this first one was an enormous relief model of Iceland, at least a hundred feet long—so long, in fact, that on it he was able to make visible each farmstead mentioned in the whole of the saga literature.

"No towns my saga-men had," said Gay proudly. "Just healthy farms and the wild seas. They knew what to do with towns. Just burn the houses and put the townsmen to the sword. That was the way to deal with towns."

He remembered each farm as though he had lived among them as a child. And when we went back into the house, and his wife, coming in almost at the run, had taken off his coat again, he showed us models of Icelandic halls, longships, pictures drawn by himself of what, from the curt descriptions, he imagined the saga heroes to have looked like. His interest was as fervent, as vivid and factual, as it must have been when he was a young man. Some of the sketches had the talent of a portrait-painter: there was one of Gudrun that had struck me on my last visit, and another of Skarphedinn, pale, fierce, scornful, teeth projecting, carrying his great axe over his shoulder.

"Ah. That was a terrible weapon," said Gay. "That was an axe and a half."

He loved each detail. And that was, I thought, part of the explanation of his fabulous success. He was not a clever man in the sense that Winslow was, who had done nothing at all. He was simple, exuberantly vain, as pleased with himself as a schoolboy who has just received a prize. But he had enormous zest and gusto, unbounded delight in his work. He had enjoyed every minute of his researches. Somehow all his vitality, mental and physical, had poured into them without constraint or inhibition or self-criticism. He did not trouble himself, he had not the equipment to begin, with the profound whys of existence—but in his line he had a strong simple unresting imagination. And he had the kind of realism which exactly fitted in. He could see the houses of his saga men, their few bits of furniture, their meagre food and stark struggle for a livelihood: he could see them simply as they were, often as men puzzled, ill-adjusted, frail, trained to a code of almost Japanese courage; and at the same time he could see them as a good deal larger than life. He had thrown every scrap of himself into their existence, and won—and no one could say it was unjust—success on a scale denied to more gifted men.

He talked about each model until a maid brought in a very large tea-tray.

"Ah ha. Tea," said Gay, with a different but equal enthusiasm. "That's a splendid sight."

He appeared to eat as his daily tea a meal not much less copious than the one he put away before college meetings. He did not talk, except to ask us to pass plates, until he was well through. Then I decided to come back to our attempt.

"You're occupying an exceptional position in this election," I said.

"Ah. Indeed," said Gay, munching a slice of black fruit cake.

"You're the great scholar of the college."

"The greatest Northern scholar of the age, my Berlin friends used to say," Roy put in.

"Did they now, Calvert? Splendid."

"You're also responsible as senior fellow for seeing that this election is properly carried out," I went on. "And we've noticed that you don't interpret that in a purely legalistic sense. You're not concerned simply with the ceremony. We know that you want to see the proper choice properly made."

"Just so," said Roy.

"I shall never want to escape my duty," said Gay.

"Isn't that your duty?"

"I agree with you," said Gay, cutting another piece of cake.

"We need a lead. Which only you can give. We're extremely worried," said Roy.

"Ah. Indeed."

"We want you to advise us on the two candidates," I said. "Crawford and Jago. We want you to show us how to form a judgment."

"Crawford and Jago," said Gay. "Yes, I think I know both of them. Let me see, isn't Jago our present Bursar?"

This was baffling. We could not predict how his memory would work. Everything about the world of scholarship was clear before his eyes: but he would suddenly enquire the name of Despard-Smith, whom he had known for fifty years.

"I thought," said Roy, "that you had promised to support Crawford?"

"Perhaps I have, perhaps I have." Suddenly he seemed to remember quite well, and he nodded his head backwards and forwards. "Yes, I recollect indicating support for Crawford," he said. Then, with a kind of simple, cheerful cunning he looked at us:

"And you two young men want me to change my mind?" He guffawed: it seemed to him the best of jokes.

For a second, Roy blushed. I thought it was best to brazen it out.

"Well," I said, "you're not far off the mark."

"You see," said Gay, in high feather, "you can't pull the wool over my eyes."

"Yes," said Roy, "we want you to think again about those two. You do remember them, don't you?"

"Of course I remember them," said Gay. "Just as I remember your address in Berlin last summer, young man. Jago—that's our Senior Tutor. He's not taken quite enough care of himself these last few years, he's lost a lot of hair and he's put on too much weight. And Crawford. A very sound man. I hear he's well spoken of as a man of science."

"Do you want a scientist as Master? Crawford's field is a long way from yours," I said.

"I should never give a second's thought to such a question," Gay rebuked me. "I have never attached any importance to boundary-lines between branches of learning. A man can do distinguished work in any, and we ought to have outgrown these arts and science controversies before we leave the school debating society. Indeed we ought."

I had been snubbed, and very reasonably snubbed. The only comfort was the old man had his mind and memory working, and we were not fighting in a fog.

"What's your opinion of Jago?" asked Roy.

"Jago's a very sound man too. I've got nothing but good to say for Jago," Gay replied.

I tried another lead. "At present you're in a unique position. There are six votes for each man without you. If it's understood that you vote for Crawford, the whole thing is cut and dried and the chapel election is just a formality."

"Cut and dried," Gay repeated. "I don't like the sound of that."

"It means," said Roy, extremely quick, "that the whole thing is settled from today. It's all over bar the empty form."

Gay's faded blue eyes were screwed up in a frown.

"I certainly indicated support for Crawford. He's a very sound man. Jago is a very sound man too, of course."

"Need that be final?" I asked. "In those days it didn't look such a near thing. But you've had the opportunity, which none of the rest of us have, of surveying the whole position from on high."

"Ah. Those old gods looked down from Odin's hall."

"I should have thought," I said, "you might now consider it best to remove yourself from the contest altogether. Mightn't it be best to stand aloof—and then in your own good time decide the election one way or the other?"

"It would make every one realise how grave a choice it was," said Roy.

Gay had finished his last cup of tea. He smiled at Roy. In looks he might have been Roy's grandfather. But I thought at that moment how young he was at heart.

"You two are still trying to bamboozle me into voting for Jago," he said.

This time Roy did not blush.

"Of course we are," he said. "I very much hope you will."

"Tell me," said Gay, "why do you prefer him so much?" He was asking the question in earnest: he wanted to know.

"Because we like him better," said Roy.

"That's spoken like an honest man," Gay said. "I congratulate you, Calvert. You're much closer to these two men than I am. I may survey the position from on high"—he was actually teasing us—"but I'm too far away. And I've always had great faith in the contribution of youth. I respect your judgment in this matter, indeed I do."

"Will you vote for Jago?" asked Roy.

"I won't give you an undertaking today. But I am inclined to reserve my vote." Then he went on: "The election mustn't be taken for granted. Our founders in their wisdom did not lay it down for us to meet in chapel just to take an election for granted. Why, we might just as well send our votes by post."

"You will think of Jago, will you?" I persisted.

"I shall certainly think of Jago. I respect your judgment,

both of you, and I shall take that very considerably into account."

As we got up to go at last, Gay said:

"I congratulate you both on presenting me with the situation in this splendid way."

"We're the ones who've learned something," I said.

"I will write to Despard telling him I propose to reserve my vote. Casting vote, that's the line for me. Thank you for pointing it out. Thank you, Calvert. Thank you. Old heads on young shoulders, that's what you've got."

In the dark, Roy and I walked down the Madingley Road. He was singing quietly in his light, clear, tuneful voice. Under the first lamp he glanced at me. His eyes were guiltless and sparkling.

"Well done," he said.

"He didn't do so badly, either."

"Shall we get him?"

"I shall be surprised if we don't," I said.

"Just so. Just so."

THIRTY-SEVEN

"SIX NIGHTS TO GO"

I left Roy at the great gate, and walked round to Jago's house. Mrs. Jago received me with a hostile, angry explanation that she had not been feeling well yesterday. Perhaps she could make amends by offering me some 'refreshment'? She was so self-conscious that it was painful to be near, jarringly apologetic, more resentful of me with each apology she made.

"I badly want to see Paul this evening," I said.

"I can perfectly well understand that," she replied. "You naturally don't want to take the risk of me making an exhibition of myself again."

"You don't think I mind, do you? It would have done you more harm to stay by yourself."

"I know some people are willing to bear with me out of charity—but I won't accept it."

"You've not been offered it," I said. Perversely, I was coming to have more fellow-feeling for her. "Is Paul free? I've got something to tell him that's fairly important."

"He's very busy," she said obstinately. "I don't think he can be disturbed."

"Look," I said, "I want to tell him that this election is not lost."

"Has anything happened, has anything really happened?"

"Yes. Don't hope too much. But it's not lost."

Her face exploded into a smile. She looked like a child, suddenly made happy. She ran out into the passage. "Paul! Paul! You must come and see Mr. Eliot at once! He's got something to tell you."

Jago walked into the drawing-room, tense to his fingertips.

"It's extremely good of you to take this trouble, Eliot. Is it something—worse?"

"No," I said. "It's not impossible that Gay may finish on your side. He may not—but it's worth holding on for."

"Old Gay?"

I nodded.

Suddenly Jago broke into roars of laughter.

"Gay! He's the vainest old boy I've ever met in my life."

He went on laughing. "The vain old boy!" It was an odd response, I thought later: yet on the spot it seemed completely natural.

Then he wiped his eyes and settled down; his tension returned in a different mode.

"I'm most grateful to you, Eliot," he said. "I don't know what I should have done without you right through this wretched business. This news changes everything. I think I was just teaching myself to face the humiliation. But this changes everything."

I warned him, but it had no effect. He was always capable of being possessed by a rush of hope. Now there was no room for anything else. It all lay in his hands, the college, his whole desire. He looked at his wife with love and triumph. When I had gone, they would get busy on their plans again. He was alive with hope.

I tried once again to make him more moderate. In some ways it would have been kinder not to tell him about Gay at all.

"There is one thing you needn't warn me of, Eliot," he said with a smile. "There are still six nights to go. We've still six nights to get through."

"You've got to rest," she said.

"In a week's time," said Jago, "it will all be over."

I went from his house straight to Brown's rooms, and found Brown and Chrystal talking of the meeting. It was as good as arranged for the following night, December 15th.

To Brown's amazement, the other side had not backed out (were they so confident that they did not care? or did Despard-Smith like the last ounce of grave discussion?) They were talking of what line to begin on.

"Is that the meeting?" I asked.

"Certainly," said Chrystal.

"It may not be necessary," I said.

"What do you mean?" asked Brown very quickly.

"I think there's a good chance of Gay coming over."

"Have you seen him? I didn't know you were thinking of seeing him——"

"No, I wasn't," I said. "Roy Calvert and I happened to drop in for tea."

Brown cross-questioned me with the inquisitiveness he showed at any piece of news, but with an extra excitement and vigilance. His curiosity was always insistent; there were moments, as those sharp eyes watched one, when his company ceased to be bland and peaceful; now it was like being in the dock. Deliberately I played down the part Roy and I had taken—I was feeling Chrystal's silence on the other side of the fire. Roy had asked the old man a question or two, I said: and I gave word for word his last replies.

In the end Brown was satisfied.

"It's absolutely wonderful!" he cried. Then he turned, heavily but quickly, on his friend. "Don't you think it's wonderful?" he said.

Chrystal did not look at him, but stared challengingly at me.

"Are you sure of this, Eliot?" he asked.

"I'm sure of what I've told you."

"That doesn't get us very far. He didn't even say he might vote for Jago."

"Not in so many words."

"It's not good enough, Eliot. You're being led away by your optimism. Wishful thinking," said Chrystal. "Remember, I've had a shot at him myself. I know Gay."

"I trust Eliot's judgment," said Brown. His voice was comfortable and rich, as always—but I heard a stern, angry note.

"It's not good enough," said Chrystal. "I daresay the old man will withhold his vote. Just to have a bit of fun. What's to stop him coming down for Crawford at the end?"

"I trust Eliot's judgment," said Brown. The stern note was clearer now.

"I can't be sure," I said. "No one can be sure. But I don't think so for a minute. Neither does Calvert."

"I don't give twopence for Calvert's opinion. He's not lived long enough. He hasn't seen anything yet," Chrystal replied.

"I should bet at least 4—1," I said, "that when we go into chapel Gay will write down Jago's name."

"I accept that absolutely," said Brown, still watching his friend.

"Well, we disagree," said Chrystal. "This is all *amusing* about Gay. But I don't see that it can alter our plans."

"We may have this election in our hands," said Brown.

"We may not."

"I believe we have. Have you stopped listening to reason?" Brown's friendly blandness had broken at last, he spoke with a mixture of menace and appeal.

"I'm afraid we disagree, Arthur."

"You can't disagree that the sensible course is to get out of this meeting," said Brown. "Anything else is ridiculous."

"I wish I didn't disagree. I'm afraid I do."

"I want an explanation," said Brown.

"Yes. Well, I don't believe that Gay will come over. I expect Eliot has got everything he said right. But I've seen Gay myself."

"A lot of water has flowed under the bridges since then," cried Brown. "These two may have been better at handling the old man than we were."

"They wouldn't claim that themselves," said Chrystal. "I'm sorry to seem ungrateful for Eliot's efforts, but I don't believe in Gay. Even if I did, there's another point. I think we're bound to keep our understanding with the other side. They were willing to hold this meeting. They didn't try to back out when they seemed to be sitting pretty."

"Did they ever mean business?" asked Brown, his voice no longer comfortable at all, but full of scorn.

"I think they did, Arthur."

"I think you deceived yourself. I think you've deceived yourself over many things you've done in this election. I know you've always wanted to find a way out from Crawford. I've never doubted that. But you've also been glad of a chance to find a way out from Jago. That's why you're giving me reasons that aren't anything like reasons, they're ridiculous after everything we've brought off together. You said yesterday that you'd stay with Jago if I could get him in. Now you're finding an excuse for spoiling it, just when we've got our last chance."

"It won't spoil it, Arthur. If he does stand a chance," said Chrystal. "Very likely nothing will come out of this meeting. Then if old Gay remembers we might still be all right."

"I keep thinking of the things we've brought off together. We shouldn't have managed them alone. We couldn't even have begun getting that benefaction alone. And that's been true for a good many years. It's a pity to find us divided now."

"Do you think I don't feel that?" said Chrystal brusquely. He had been buoyed up, exhilarated, master of his plans, conscious that others were waiting for him, pleased perhaps to escape from Brown's steady imperceptible guidance. Yet he was moved by the reminder of their comradeship, by the call on his affection. His manner, which had been conciliatory, became at once tough and aggressive. He was angry to be so moved.

Brown, too, was moved. His composure was riven, he had spoken more jaggedly than I had known him. Through the rifts one saw the formidable core of the man. He had great feeling for his friend, he was warm and expansive—but that did not matter to him now. He was moved by the thought of defeat, by losing the struggle for Jago, by the sheer blank fury of losing. I was sure that he had called deliberately on their friendship, knowing that it would affect Chrystal far more than himself.

"Aren't you prepared to stop this meeting?" asked Brown.

"I don't see how I can," said Chrystal.

"I regard it as a major disaster," said Brown.

THIRTY-EIGHT

A CAVE IS FORMED

There was a large gathering in hall on the night of December 15th: and afterwards, without waiting for wine, we moved off by twos and threes to Chrystal's rooms. As we turned under the light at the bottom of the staircase, I noticed Chrystal walking with Despard-Smith and Getliffe. Jago and Crawford appeared out of the darkness together: then Brown alone.

Everyone was there but Gay. Luke, who had not been dining but hurried in after, was apologising to Despard-Smith for not being able to stay. He made the same apology to Brown, in his smooth, youthful, deferential way. I was sitting near the door, and he had a word with me on his way out. "I've got an experiment to finish," he said in a whisper, forgetting all about tact, "and I'm going to finish it if I sit up the whole blasted night. I've told these uncles that I'm going to vote for Jago. I've been bloody well telling them that ever since I can remember."

Despard-Smith showed his usual hesitation before taking the chair ("Some day," said Roy half-audibly, "we'll take him at his word. Then he'll be dished."). He explained solemnly that some fellows were 'increasingly exercised about the serious position' in which the college found itself over the election. He thought he could, without breach of confidence, mention that within the last twenty-four hours he had received two letters from Professor Gay. One he was not at liberty to disclose, since it was addressed to him as having presided over the caucus for one of the candidates, "but I think I may say, in fact I think I must say, that our senior colleague in that letter expresses his intention to reserve his vote. The other letter refers to this meeting, and I propose to read it." As always when reading, Despard-Smith passed into his chapel voice.

" 'Dear Despard,

" 'I learn with interest of your intention to have an informal pow wow' "—Despard-Smith repeated the word with extraordinary and depressed gravity—" 'pow wow before the great day of our election. I thoroughly approve of this little venture, and you may go ahead with my blessing. Did not my saga-men discuss cases in their booths before they came to the great debates in the Thing? I congratulate you on this attempt to clear your heads. Clear heads, those are what you most require. I do not, however, consider that it fits my present position of responsibility to take a hand in your little pow wow. You appear to suggest that I may not want to stay out at night because I am not so young as I was. Pray do not worry on that account. I can outlast some of you younger men yet. If I absent myself, it is on completely different grounds. I am entrusted with the grave responsibility of being at the helm while the college plunges through this stormy crossing. And I should further say that some of our colleagues have represented to me that I have an added trust because of such little distinction as I may have been fortunate enough to attain.

" 'Weighing these responsibilities in my mind, I have reached the conclusion I must stand aloof from any discussions among yourselves up to the great day of the election. I shall then cast my vote as my conscience guides me, and I hope to lead you all on that same course, so that we may make a worthy choice.

" 'Good luck to your little pow wow.

" 'Ever sincerely yours,

" 'M. H. L. Gay.' "

"This does *not* make our task lighter," said Despard-

Smith, looking up from the letter. "So far as I am entitled to judge the intentions of the fellows, we have not yet attained a firm majority for either of our candidates. Some of us think this may lead us into a position which is nothing short of disastrous. I have never known anything comparable during my long association with the college. By this stage we have always been certain before who was going to win our suffrages. We were certain"—he said, with one of his funereal anti-climaxes—"who was going to draw the lucky n-number. But this time we have not been so wise. I should like to hear the Dean's views on this most unfortunate dilemma."

"It's lamentable," Chrystal began, and went on to make a brisk, reasonable, friendly statement. It had been bad for the college to go through this prolonged suspense. He disliked being separated from his friends on the other side, and he hoped they disliked it too. Either of the candidates would be an excellent Master whom the college would be lucky to get. It was a sign of something wrong that the college should become unfit to live in just because they could not choose between two excellent men. But apparently they could not choose. "I'm just pointing out the snags," said Chrystal. "It's lamentable. I don't pretend to see the solution. But I just want to ask one question: has the time come to forget our disagreement? Has the time come to find a way out?"

From that moment the room was electric with attention. This was not just a talk: something was in the air. Even those who had not followed Chrystal's progress knew something hung on these minutes. Brown's face was lowering: Jago sat as though he did not hear.

We looked at each other, waiting for someone to begin. At last Crawford spoke. He was even more deliberate than his habit, not so impregnably assured: he was choosing his words.

"I wish this was such a pleasant occasion as the last time

we met in this room. I should much prefer to hear the Dean explain again how he and his friend Brown had brought off their great coup for the college. The more I reflect, the more chances I think that coup of theirs opens up in front of us. As for the present position, I agree with a good deal of what the Dean says. But I don't consider this is the right time to act. I know this long wait hasn't improved some of our tempers. But it won't be much longer. Speaking as a fellow, I don't see any alternative to waiting. I didn't quite understand the Dean's suggestion. I do not know whether he thinks that other names ought to be canvassed now. Speaking as a candidate, I can't be expected to accept the view that other names ought to be considered at this late stage. I hope that the Senior Tutor agrees with me."

"Utterly."

"My advice is," said Crawford, "leave it until the day. One of us will be elected unless someone decides to throw away his vote. If neither of us is elected, then it will be time for us to have a talk."

Jago had only spoken that one word since he entered the room. Now he roused himself. He had been keeping unnaturally still. By this night, even Crawford's expression bore a trace of worry: but it was nothing to Jago's. Yet he spoke with dignity.

"If the college votes in chapel and cannot reach a majority for either my colleague or myself, it will be necessary for us all to meet together," he said. "It is not fitting either for me or my colleague to say more now. If the need should arise, we shall give what help we can to find a solution for the college. It would be our plain duty to do so."

His eyes had rested in turn on Chrystal, Despard-Smith and Brown. Now he looked at Crawford.

"If the others wish to continue with their discussion," he said, "I think we must remove ourselves. There is nothing left for us to add."

"I agree," said Crawford, and they left the room.

We listened to their footsteps down the stairs. Chrystal said sharply to Despard-Smith: "I should like to hear what other people think."

There was a pause. Pilbrow burst out that he was solid for Crawford, despite the lateness of his change, for reasons some of us knew. Another pause. Nightingale said with a smile that he would never vote for anyone but Crawford. Then Brown spoke, and during his whole speech his gaze did not leave Chrystal.

"I'm glad to have this opportunity of explaining to most of the college," he said, "that I think we're in danger of making a terrible mistake. Some people already know the strength of my views, but perhaps those of our number who support Crawford have not heard them. I should like to assure them that I believe Jago will be the best possible Master for the college, and I believe it with more absolute certainty than I have ever felt on such an occasion. Any departure from Jago would be a loss that the college might not be able to recover from for many years. During the rest of my time here, I should not be able to forget it."

Everyone was looking at him and Chrystal. Many were puzzled, they did not know what was going on. Some saw the struggle clear. Yet everyone was looking at those two faces, the benign one, now flushed with anger, and the domineering.

No one spoke. Chrystal was regarding Brown as though there were a question to ask: there came an almost pathetic smile on Chrystal's firm mouth.

Suddenly Chrystal looked away.

"We're not getting far," he said with a harsh, curt bravado. "I believe several of us are not satisfied with either candidate. Some of us never have been. I can speak out now they've gone. There's something to be said for Jago: I've been resigned to voting for him, as you all know. There's something to be said for Crawford: I've seen things in him lately that

I like, and I understand his supporters' point of view. But we're not tied to either of them. I believe that's the way out."

"What are you proposing?" said Despard-Smith.

"I want to bring it to a head," said Chrystal. "I'm ready to form a cave. Will any of you join me? I should like to find another man altogether."

IV

MORNING IN THE CHAPEL

THIRTY-NINE

A GROUP TALKS TILL THE MORNING

"I want to bring it to a head," Chrystal said again. "I should like to find another man altogether. This is the time. We might get somewhere tonight."

He leaned forward over the table, with an eager, alert, dominating smile.

There was a shuffle of feet, a cough, the squeak of someone's finger on the table top. Some moments passed, and then Pilbrow got to his feet.

"I don't think it's any good my staying, Despard," he said. "If you're going to find another man, which I suppose you are. I don't want to run away, but . . . I know I've wobbled disgracefully, but I don't feel like changing again. I'm content as I am."

He had not left the room when Nightingale began talking. He was so excited that he had no politeness left.

"I always said it would happen. I always knew that that precious clique wouldn't let well alone. They were bound to put up one of themselves in the long run."

"Are you going to stay, Nightingale?" said Despard-Smith bleakly. "If you stay, you will hear what names are being discussed."

"Stay!" Nightingale smiled. "Do you think I want to hear the names? I could tell you them now."

As he closed the door, Roy commented:

"I'll bet anyone that he rings up Crawford within five minutes."

Solidly, heavily, Brown stood by the table, looking down on those of us still there.

"I can't see my way to remaining in this discussion," he said to Despard-Smith. "I've gone as far as I can to turn you all from it. In my judgment, it is completely ill-considered, and I should have nothing useful to add if I stayed with you."

He gave Chrystal one glance, angry, troubled, unwavering, yet steady and still intimate: he walked out, and we heard his deliberate tread down the stairs.

Chrystal was frowning—but he shrugged his shoulders and said, with confidence and zest:

"It's time to get down to it."

There were only six of us now sitting round the table, Chrystal himself, Despard-Smith, Winslow, Francis Getliffe, Roy Calvert and I. It was not a good beginning for Chrystal: even if he could persuade us all, he still needed another for a majority. But his confidence was extreme, his energy flowed out just as when he had made us coerce the candidates in October. When someone mentioned that we were not much of a cave, Chrystal said:

"I don't mind that. We can bring others in. There's Luke. There's even Crawford. And the others—they may not want to stay out in the cold."

Promptly he brought out his first candidate.

"I'm not going to be coy," he said. "I have someone in mind. In my view the time has come to look outside the college. I want you to think of Lyon."

Most of us knew Lyon; he was a Reader, a fellow of another college, a man of good academic standing and a bit of a university politician. In a few minutes it was apparent that he would get no support. We all gave reasons for half-heartedness—but the reasons were a matter of courtesy, a way of saying we were not disposed to fall in.

Chrystal, still undeterred, canvassed another name, also from outside the college, and then another. Different reasons were brought against them, but there was never a chance that either would be looked at: at the sound of each name, everyone there was saying no. It was not that we had anything special against them; simply, we did not want to find them suitable. By now I was sure that Chrystal would get nowhere. I had seen him in October carry us, by sheer force of will, into dragooning the candidates to vote for each other. But then we had all been ready to be convinced, and now the reverse was true. He was exuding just as much will, and few men had more than Chrystal. But in our hearts we were not persuadable; and in all the moves of politics, dexterity is meaningless, even will itself does not avail, unless there is some spot in one's opponent ready to be convinced. "Most reluctantly," said Despard-Smith, after we had discussed the third name, "I am coming to the conclusion, Dean, that it is too late in the day to look outside the college."

"I accept that for the moment, Despard," said Chrystal, still brisk and good-tempered. "But we've not finished. In that case we must look inside."

It was late at night, the room was hot, smoke was spinning slowly under the light: the older men were sleepy, and once Winslow's eyes had closed. But, at the sound of that last remark, they were awake, vigilant, ready once more for the long cautious guarded talk. Winslow lit his pipe again; as the match flared, a trick of the shadows smoothed out the nutcracker lines of nose and chin, and his eyes gleamed, deep, bright—and anxious. Yes, anxious. Was there still a remnant of hope? "We must look inside," said Chrystal.

"Of course," said Despard-Smith, "all of us gave serious thought to the possibilities when we heard the disastrous news last spring. Or if we didn't we were very seriously negligent."

"Never mind," said Chrystal. "I want to go over them once more. We shan't get the chance again. It's no use having second thoughts after Thursday."

"Some of us," said Despard-Smith, "are always coming to bolt the stable door after the horse has f-flown."

"They won't this time," said Chrystal. He stared round at us all. "Well, we've got to look inside. I'm going down the fellows in order of seniority. Gay. Pilbrow. You, Despard. The statutes won't let us have you."

"I supported the new statute about the retiring age," said Despard-Smith solemnly. "I've often asked myself whether I did right. Some men of seventy are still competent to hold any position of responsibility——"

"You would be," interrupted Chrystal. In his brusque way he was placating the old man. And he was looking two moves ahead: I thought I guessed his intention now. "You would be. No one doubts it. But it can't happen." He paused. "Going on down the list." He added in a tone which he kept casual and matter of fact: "Winslow. Winslow, you're the next."

"Curiously enough," said Winslow, also trying to be casual, "I was aware of that."

"Do you think," said Despard-Smith in a hurry, "that you'd feel satisfied to take on such an office for a very short time? I doubt whether it is fair to ask a man to take an office with only five years to run."

"I should actually have seven years. I was sixty-three in October," said Winslow.

"You'd just learn the job. Then you'd have to go. I agree with Despard," said Chrystal, looking at Winslow with a bold, embarrassed smile.

"I seriously doubt," said Despard-Smith, "whether it would be *fair* to ask you."

"When is it fair to ask anyone?" said Roy Calvert. His eyes were glinting with mockery: he was moved for Winslow.

Before he could say more, Francis Getliffe put in:

"On general principles, there is something to be said for a younger man. We ought to have someone with at least ten years to go. I know you'd take that view yourself, wouldn't you?" He spoke to Winslow directly.

Francis had got on better with Winslow than most of the college, and the question was kind. But it did not soften the fact. Winslow's eyelids had drooped, he was staring at the table.

He said at last:

"No doubt you're right."

"I was certain you'd see it that way, Winslow," said Chrystal, with relief, with excessive heartiness. I was watching Roy Calvert, half-expecting him to say more: but he gave a twitch of a smile, and let it slide. It was too forlorn a hope even for him.

Chrystal proceeded down the list.

"Crawford. Jago. Already dealt with. Brown. The next senior is Brown," he said. "Brown. I'm asking you to think carefully about him. Isn't he the man for a compromise candidate?"

Winslow looked up for a second.

"That's a very remarkable suggestion, Dean," he said with savage sarcasm, with a flicker of his old spirit.

"Isn't he much too young? I don't see how the college could possibly consider anyone so junior," said Despard-Smith.

"He's forty-six," said Chrystal.

"It's dangerous to have young men in these positions," said Despard-Smith. "One never knows how they'll turn out."

"Brown won't alter till he dies," I said. It seemed strange that anyone, even Despard-Smith, should think of Brown as young.

"I don't think his age is a reason against him," said Francis Getliffe. "But——"

"I know everything you're going to say," said Chrystal. "I know all about Brown. I know him better than any of you. He's been my best friend since we were up together. He's not brilliant. He'll never set the Thames on fire. People would think it was a dim election. But there are things in Brown that you don't see until you've known him for years. He'd pull the place together."

"My dear Dean," said Winslow, "it would mean twenty years of stodge."

"I should have considered," said Despard-Smith, "that if we were to take the serious step of looking at such junior fellows, we should want to consider you yourself long before Brown."

"I couldn't look at it," said Chrystal. "I'm not up to it. I know my limitations. I'm not fit to be Master. Brown is. I'd serve under him and think myself lucky."

He spoke with absolute humility and honesty. It was not put on, there was none of the stately mannered mock-modesty of college proceedings. This was the humility and honesty of his heart. It was so patent that no one challenged it.

He pressed on about Brown. I said that I would prefer him to any other compromise candidate. Less warmly, Roy said that, if the first vote in chapel did not give Jago a majority, he would not mind transferring to Brown on the second turn. Francis Getliffe said that, if the first vote were a stalemate, he would consider doing the same as Roy. With that kind of backing, such as it was, Chrystal argued with the other two into the early morning: he was not touchy, he did not give way to pique, he just sat there and argued as the quarters went on chiming away the night; he sat there, strong in his physical prepotence, persuading, browbeating, exclaiming with violence, wooing and bursting into temper.

Everyone in the room but himself knew that he must fail. Winslow was mostly silent, but every word he spoke was edged with unhappy contempt. Despard-Smith was solemnly obstinate. Everyone knew but Chrystal that neither would ever consent to vote for Brown. The last hope of compromise had gone. Yet Chrystal seemed undiscouraged. By midnight the rest of us would have given it up as useless, but he kept us there till after two o'clock.

At the last he won one concession through the others' sheer fatigue. He got them to admit that Brown was the only possible third candidate.

"It's obvious," he said. "Several of us here have said they might come round to him. Do you quarrel with that, Despard?"

Despard-Smith wearily shook his head.

"That's good enough for me," said Chrystal. "It means that Brown must be asked whether he'll stand. It may come to it. We can't leave it in the air. I'll speak to him in the morning."

His face was fresh, he was smiling, he was obscurely satisfied. He looked at his clock on the mantelpiece.

"I shan't have to wait long," he said. "It is the morning already."

FORTY

"I HAVE HAD A DISAPPOINTING LIFE"

Chrystal had kept us up so late that I slept until the middle of the morning. It was December 17th, a dark and stormy day: the wind was howling again, for the westerly gales had returned; it was not cold, but the heavy clouds hung over the roofs, and in the afternoon Roy and I built up the fire in my sitting-room for the sake of the blaze. We compared impressions of Chrystal's tactics and manner on the night before. Why had he persisted against all rational sense? Why had he gone away so pleased? Was it because he wanted to prove to Brown that, whatever he did in this election, he was still completely affectionate and loyal? That was part of it, we felt sure: but we did not believe it was the end.

As we were talking across the fire, a double and deliberate knock sounded on the door. "Uncle Arthur in person," said Roy, and we both smiled as Brown came in. But Brown's smile in return was only formal.

He sat down, looked into the fire, and said in a constrained tone:

"I wanted to see you both. I am told that, without my consent, I was mentioned as a candidate last night. Did you have anything to do with this?"

He was grimly indignant. We told him what we had each promised.

"I was glad to do it," I said. "I should enjoy voting for you. It would be admirable to see you in the Lodge."

He did not respond. After a time he said:

"I suppose you all intended it kindly."

"I don't know about kindly," I said. "It was intended to show what we feel about you."

"I hope you all intended it kindly," said Brown.

"Chrystal wanted the chance to say you ought to be Master," said Roy.

"So he told me."

"It's quite true."

"It should have been obvious to him that I could not conceivably be a candidate in these circumstances," said Brown. "The only result of my name being mentioned is to stand in Jago's light. It can only mean dissensions in Jago's party and no responsible man can see it otherwise. I am very sorry that Chrystal should have seen fit to use my name for that purpose. And I am obliged to tell you that I am sorry you two associated yourselves with it."

"You ought to believe that we mean what we say," I replied.

"I realise you didn't mind paying me a compliment," said Brown, as though making an effort to be fair. "What I can't make out is how anyone as astute as you can have lost your head and behaved in this irresponsible fashion. Surely you can see that nothing is gained by paying useless compliments when things are as delicate as they are now, three days away from the event. It is nothing more nor less than playing into the hands of the other side. It looks as though I was being made a tool of."

"Have you told Chrystal?"

"I have. I'm not prepared to have people think that I'm being made a tool of."

I had never seen him so completely shaken out of reason and tolerance and charity—not even when Pilbrow defected. His whole picture of 'decent behaviour' had been thrown aside. He liked to think of himself as the manager of the college, the power behind the meetings; but, as I had often noticed, as for instance in the first approach to Luke, he was always scrupulous in keeping within the rules; he was not easy unless he was well-thought-of and in good repute. It upset him to imagine that people were now thinking that he had planned an intrigue with his friend, so as to get in as a last-minute compromise. It upset him equally if they thought he was just a catspaw. In the end, he had an overwhelmingly strong sense of his own proper dignity and of the behaviour he wanted the world to see.

He was also, of course, the most realistic of men: he saw the position with clear eyes, and it made him angrier still with Chrystal. He knew very well that he was not being offered even a remote chance: he felt he was just being asked to save Chrystal's conscience. And that was the most maddening of his thoughts: that was the one which made him come and reproach Roy and me as though he could not forgive us. For Brown could see—no one more sharply—the conflict, vacillation, temptation and gathering purpose of his friend. He could not control him now; for the first time in twenty years he found his own will being crossed by Chrystal. Chrystal might do more yet: in moments of foresight Brown could see the worst of ends. When Chrystal came to him with this gesture, Brown felt that he had lost.

He went away without any softening towards Roy or me, telling us that he must write round to each fellow, in order to say that in no circumstances would he let his name be considered. I suspected that he had shown his anger more nakedly to us than to Chrystal. He had controlled himself with Chrystal—then had to come and take it out of us.

As soon as he had gone, Roy looked at me.

"Old boy," he said. "I fancy Jago's dished."

"Yes."

"We need to do what we can. If we can entice someone over, we might save it."

We decided to try Despard-Smith and Pilbrow that same day, and went together to Pilbrow's rooms after tea. We had no success at all. Roy used all his blandishments, the blandishments which came to him by nature, but which he could also use by art. He was as lively and varied as he was to women, in turns teasing, serious, attentive, flattering, mocking. He invited Pilbrow to visit him in Berlin in the spring. Pilbrow enjoyed the performance, he liked handsome young men, but he did not give a foot: it seemed to him impossible now to vote for anyone but Crawford. I took up the political argument, Roy lapped the old man with all his tricks of charm. But we got nowhere, except that he pressed us both to dine with an exiled writer in London, the night after the election.

We walked through the court. Roy was grinning at his own expense.

"I've lost face," he said.

"You're getting old," I said.

"You'd better try Despard by yourself," said Roy. "If I can't get off with old Eustace, I'm damned if I can with Despard."

It was a fact that Despard-Smith looked on him with mystified suspicion, and so after hall I went alone. Despard-Smith's rooms were in the third court, on the next staircase to Nightingale's and near Jago's house. He had not been to hall that night, and on the chest outside the door lay the dishes of a meal sent up from the kitchen. His outer door was not closed, but there was no one in his main room, and the fire had gone out. I tapped on the inside door: there was a gruff shout 'who's there?' When I answered, no reply came for some while: then there were movements inside, and a key turned in the lock. Despard-Smith looked out at me with bloodshot, angry eyes.

"I'm very busy. I'm very busy, Eliot."

"I only want to keep you five minutes."

"You don't realise how busy I am. People here have never shown me the slightest consideration."

His breath smelt of liquor; instead of being solemn, grave, minatory, he was just angry.

"I should like a word about the election," I said. He glared at me.

"You'd better come in for two minutes," he said in a grating tone.

His inner room was dark, over-furnished by the standards of the twentieth century, packed with cupboards, tables, glass-fronted cases full of collections of pottery. Photographs, many of them of the undergraduates of his youth, in boaters and wearing large moustaches, hung all over the walls. By his old armchair, which had projecting head-rests, stood a table covered with green baize, and on the table were a book and an empty tumbler. Bleakly he said: "Can I offer you a n-night cap?" and opened a cupboard by the fireplace. I had a glimpse of a great array of empty whisky bottles; he brought out one half-full and another glass.

He poured me a small whisky and himself a very large one, and he took a long gulp while we were still standing up.

He was not drunk but he was inflamed by drink. There had been rumours for years that he drank heavily in private, but he had no friends in college, his life was lonely, no one knew for certain how he lived it. Gossip had a knack of not touching him closely; perhaps he was too spare and harsh a figure to be talked about much. His natural authority seemed to protect him, even in his absence.

"I wondered if you were happy about the election," I said.

"Certainly not," said Despard-Smith. "I take an extremely grave view of the future of this college."

"It isn't too late——" I began.

"It has been too late for many years," said Despard-Smith ominously.

I said something about Crawford and Jago, and for a moment my hopes sprang up at his reply.

"Jago has sacrificed himself for the college, Eliot. Just as every college officer has to. Whereas Crawford has not sacrificed himself, he has become a distinguished man of science. On academic grounds his election will do us good in the outside world. I needn't say that I've always been seriously disturbed at the prospect of electing a bolshevik."

I had not time to be amused by that term for Crawford, the sturdy middle class scientific liberal: I had seized on the gleam of hope, was forcing the comparison between the two, when Despard-Smith brushed my questions aside, and stared at me with fierce bloodshot eyes.

"The college has brought it upon itself," he said. "They've chosen not to pay attention to my warnings, and they can only expect disastrous consequences. They did it with their eyes open when they chose Royce. That was the f-first step down the slippery slope." He put a finger inside his dogcollar and then took it out with a click. He said in a grating, accusing tone: "They ought to have asked me to take on the burden. They said I wasn't known outside the college. That was the thanks I got for sacrificing myself for thirty years."

I said a word or two, but he emptied his glass and faced me with greater anger still.

"I've had a disappointing life, Eliot," he said. "It's not been a happy life. I've not been given the recognition I had a right to expect. It's a scandalous story. It would not be to the credit of this college if I let everyone know how I'd been treated. I'm looking back on my life now, and I tell you that it's been one long disappointment. And I lay it all to the blame of the people here."

From another man, the cry might have been softened by pathos. But there was nothing soft about Despard-Smith at seventy, drinking in secret, attacking me with his disappointment. 'I've had a disappointing life': he did not say it with the sad warmth of self-pity, but aggressively, certain that he was in the right.

"You're going to let them elect Crawford now?" I said.

"They ought to have asked me to take on the burden ten years ago. I tell you, this college would have been a different place."

"Wouldn't Jago be more likely to take your line?"

"He's done better as Tutor than I bargained for," said Despard-Smith. "But he's got no head for affairs."

"That needn't rule him out——"

"Royce had no head for affairs, and they chose him," said Despard-Smith.

"I'm still surprised you should vote for Crawford."

"He's made a name for himself. That's good enough for a Master. They wouldn't choose me because I wasn't known outside the college. Crawford will do. No one can deny that he will do. And if people don't like him when they've got him," he said, "well, they'll have to l-lump it for the next fifteen years."

He fetched out the bottle again and poured himself another drink. This time he did not offer me any. "I don't mind telling you, Eliot, that I've got a soft spot for Jago. If I were just voting on personal grounds, I would choose him before the other man. But the other man has made his name. And Jago hasn't. He's sacrificed himself for the college. If a man takes a college office, he makes a disastrous choice. He can't expect people to recognise him. Jago ought to be prepared to face the consequences of his sacrifice. He ought to know what happened to me."

My hope had faded. At last I understood something of why he had stuck to Crawford from the beginning—Crawford, the 'bolshevik'. Despard-Smith had loved power so much in his austere fashion: it thickened the blood in his veins. He had loved his years as bursar, he had done what pleased him most, even though he believed that he was 'sacrificing himself'. But it rankled still that they had not made him Master. It seemed to have struck him as a surprise, as a physical shock. I wondered whether it was from those days, ten years ago, that he started his solitary evenings with the whisky bottle.

Unluckily for Jago, the old man saw in him his own misfortune re-created. He did like Jago; he was starved of affection, he was not without the power to enjoy friendship, though he could not take the first steps himself. But seeing that Jago might retrace his old distress, Despard-Smith wished simply and starkly that it should happen so. He wished it more because he liked the man. It was right that Jago too should sacrifice himself. He thought of his own 'disappointing life'. He thought of Jago, treated as he had been. And he felt a tinge of sadic warmth.

FORTY-ONE

TWO CIGARS IN THE COMBINATION ROOM

There was nothing to do but wait. Both Roy and I had a sense of the end now, but we were tantalised by a fluctuating hope. On paper (if Gay did not fail us) we could still count a majority for Jago. If it were to be broken, we must get news at any hour. It could not be long. What was Chrystal doing, now that even he had to abandon the notion of a third candidate? He had to face the struggle of Jago and Crawford again. No news seemed good news. Throughout the morning of December 18th, forty-eight hours from the election, throughout that whole day, we heard nothing. I did not see either Chrystal or Brown, although Brown's letter arrived. It was much more mellifluous and stately than his outburst in the flesh, and said that 'though any member of the college ought to be honoured even to have his name mentioned as a possible candidate for the Mastership, I must after prolonged consideration and with many expressions of thanks ask my friends and colleagues to permit me to withdraw.'

That was all the news that day. It seemed that bargainings and confidential talks had ceased.

In the evening Jago came to my room.

"Have you heard any thing fresh?" His tone was jaunty, but under his eyes the skin was stained and dry.

"Nothing at all."

"I want you to tell me anything you know. The very moment it happens," he said, menacing me with the force of his anxiety. "This is a bad enough business without having to wonder whether one's friends are keeping anything back."

"I'll keep nothing back," I promised.

"I must be an unendurable nuisance to you." He smiled. "So there really isn't any news? When I lay awake last night, I thought of all the absolutely inexplicable things I had watched the college do——"

"Can't you sleep?"

"Never mind," said Jago. "I shall sleep in a couple of nights. So good old Arthur Brown wasn't prepared to be made a convenience of. That takes us back where we started. They really have got to make the bizarre choice between me and my opponent. And nothing has happened to upset the balance, so far as you know?"

His moods were not stable, he was strained and expectant, fervent and hostile, at odd moments sarcastically detached, all in the same excitement of the nerves. Above all, his optimism had not left him. To his wife I was certain he maintained that he would get in. Some men would have defended themselves by saying that they expected the worst. Jago in his proud and reckless spirit was not able to protect himself by such a dodge. There was something nakedly defenceless about his optimism. He seemed quite without the armour, the thickening of the skin, that most men take on insensibly as the years pass.

I wanted to guard him, but he resisted the slightest word of doubt. He listened and thanked me, but his eyes were flashing with an excitement that I could not touch. He knew very little about what had happened at the meeting in Chrystal's room, and even less about the cumulative disagreement between Brown and Chrystal. He did not want to know of it. That evening he still had hope, and as he lay sleepless through the long night to come it would steady his heart.

We went into the combination room together before hall;

there were several men already waiting, but no one spoke. The constraint took hold of us like a field of force. Despard-Smith was there, Francis Getliffe, Nightingale, Roy Calvert. It was not that they had been talking of Jago, and were embarrassed to see him. It was not the constraint of a conversation left in the air—but simply the paralysing weight that comes upon men at a late stage of their struggle. Even Roy's sparkle was borne down under it. When we took our places in hall, there was still almost no word spoken. Despard-Smith sat at our head, solemnly asking for toast, muted and grave by contrast to the inflamed old man of the night before.

Then Luke bustled in late. He hurled himself into the seat next Roy Calvert's, and swallowed a plate of soup at an enormous pace. He looked up and smiled round at us indiscriminately—at me, at Francis, at Nightingale. I had never seen a face more radiant with joy. One did not notice the pleasant youthful features: all one saw was this absolute, certain and effulgent happiness, and it warmed one to the bottom of the heart.

"Well?" I could not resist smiling broadly back.

"I've got it out! I know for sure I've got it out!"

"Which part of it?" said Francis Getliffe.

"The whole damned caboodle. The whole bloody beautiful bag of tricks. I've got the answer to the slow neutron business, Getliffe. It's all just come tumbling out."

"Are you certain?" asked Francis, unwilling to believe it.

"Of course I'm certain. Do you think I'd stick my neck out like this if I weren't certain? It's as plain as the palm of my hand."

Francis cross-questioned him, and for minutes the technical words rapped across the table—'neutrons', 'collision', 'stopping power', 'alphas'. Francis was frowning, envious despite himself, more eager to find a hole than to be convinced that Luke was right. But Luke was unperturbed, all faces were friendly on this day of certain joy; he gave his explanations at a great speed, fired in his homely figures of speech, was too exhalted to keep back his cheerful swear-words; yet even a layman came to feel how clear and masterful he was in everything he said. Gradually, as though reluctantly, Francis's frown left his face, and there came instead his deep, creased smile. He was seeing something that compelled his admiration. His own talent was strong enough to make him respond; this was a major work, and for a moment he was disinterested, keen with admiration, smiling an experienced and applauding smile.

"Good work!" he cried. "Lord, it's nice work. It's one of the most beautiful things I've heard for a long time."

"It's pretty good," said Luke, unashamed, with no pretence of modesty though his cheeks were flushing scarlet.

"I believe it's wonderful," said Jago, who had been listening with intense interest, as though he could drown his anxieties in this young man's joy. "Not that I understand most of your detestable words. But you do tell us that he has done something remarkable, don't you, Getliffe?"

"It's beautiful work," said Francis with great authority.

"I'm more glad than I can say," said Jago to Luke. Nightingale had turned his head away and was looking down the hall.

"When did you know you'd made a discovery?" cried Jago.

"I thought a week ago the wretched thing was coming out," said Luke, who used a different set of terms. "But I've thought so before a dozen bloody times. This time though I had a hunch that it was different. I've been pretty well living and feeding at the lab. ever since. That was why I didn't come to the meeting on Monday," he added affably to Despard-Smith, who gave a bleak nod.

"The little pow-wow," Roy said to Despard-Smith, by way of explanation.

"I could almost have sworn it was right that night. But

I've been bitten by false bloody dawns too many times. I've not been to bed since. I wasn't going to leave off until I knew the answer one way or the other.

"It's wonderful," he burst out in a voice that carried up and down the table, "when you've got a problem that is really coming out. It's like making love—suddenly your unconscious takes control. And nothing can stop you. You know that you're making old Mother Nature sit up and beg. And you say to her 'I've got you, you old bitch.' You've got her just where you want her. Then to show there's no ill-feeling, you give her an affectionate pinch on the bottom."

He leaned back, exhausted, resplendent, cheerful beyond all expression. Getliffe grinned at him with friendly understanding. Jago laughed aloud, Roy Calvert gave me half a wink (for young Luke's discretion had vanished in one colossal sweep) and took it upon himself to divert Despard-Smith's attention.

In the combination room, Jago presented a bottle to mark 'a notable discovery completed this day by the junior fellow', as he announced for the formal toast. Hearing what was to happen, Nightingale rushed away before the health was drunk. Despard-Smith, who had his own kind of solemn formal courtesy, congratulated Luke and then settled down to the port. Luke took one of the largest cigars and smoked it over his glass, drowsy at last, his head humming with whirling blessedness. And Jago, with a gentle and paternal smile, did what I had never seen him do, and took a cigar himself. The two sat together, the square ruddy boy, happy as he might never be again, and the man whose face bore so much suffering. As each listened to the other, the tip of his cigar glowed. They were talking about the stars. It was thirty-six hours before the election.

Francis Getliffe and I left them together, and walked to the gate. I hesitated about asking him up to my rooms, and then did not.

"That's very pretty work of young Luke's," he said.

"I gathered as much from what you said."

"I doubt if you know how good it is," he said. He paused. "It's better than anything I've done yet. Much better."

He was so quixotic, so upright, so passionately ambitious: all I could do was pretend to be ironic.

"It's time we two had a bit of luck," I said. "These boys are running off with all the prizes. Look at Roy Calvert's work by the side of mine. I may catch up if I outlive him twenty years."

Francis smiled absently, and we stopped under the lantern.

"I ought to say something else, Lewis."

"What's that?"

"I thought Jago showed up very well tonight. There's more in him than I allowed for."

"It isn't too late," I said very quickly. "If you vote for him——"

Francis shook his head.

"No, I shouldn't begin to think of altering my vote," he said. "I know I'm right."

FORTY-TWO

THE LAST NIGHT

The day before the election, December 19th, passed with dragging slowness. Throughout the morning there was no news: only Roy visited me, and as we chatted we were waiting for the next chime of the clock: time stretched itself silently out between the quarters. It was not raining, but the clouds were a level dun. Before lunch we walked through the streets and Roy bought some more presents; afterwards he left me alone in my room.

There Brown joined me in the middle of the afternoon. It was a relief to see him, rather than go on trying to read. But there was something ominous in his first deliberate question.

"I was wondering," he said, "whether you had Chrystal with you."

"I've not seen him since the meeting," I said.

"I've not seen him," said Brown, "since he approached me afterwards in the sense that I've already given you my opinion of. But I thought it might not be unwise if I got into touch with him today. I've called round at his house, but they said that they thought he'd gone for a walk early this morning."

I looked at the darkening window, against which the rain had begun to lash.

"It seems an odd day to choose," I said.

"I've tried his rooms," said Brown. "But it looks as though they had been empty all day."

"What is he doing?"

Brown shook his head.

"I'm afraid that he's in great distress of mind," he said.

It was for one reason alone that he was searching for Chrystal: he might still be able to influence him: using all the pressure of their friendship, he might still be able to keep him to Jago. On that last day, Brown had no room for other thoughts. He knew as well as I did where Chrystal had been tending. But Brown was enough of a politician never to lose all hope until the end, even though it was forlorn. One could not be a politician without that kind of resilient hope. When Chrystal asked him to be a candidate, Brown had felt for a time it was all lost. But now he had got back into action again. Chrystal was undecided, Chrystal was walking about in 'distress of mind'—Brown was ready to throw in all his years of understanding of his friend, there was still a chance of forcing him to vote for Jago next morning.

"I am rather anxious to see him before tonight," said Brown, looking at me with his acute peering glance.

"If I see him," I said, "I'll let you know."

"I should be very much obliged if you would," said Brown. "Of course, I can always catch him at his house late tonight."

His manner was deliberately prosaic and comfortable. He was showing less outward sign of strain than any of us; when he was frayed inside, he slowed down his always measured speech, brought out the steady commonplaces like an armour, reduced all he could to the matter-of-fact.

"Well," he said, "I think I'd better be off to my rooms soon. I've still got some letters to write about the scholarships. Oh, there's just one thing. I suppose you don't happen to have talked to Jago today?"

I said that I had seen Jago in hall the night before.

"How did you think he was?"

"Hopeful. So hopeful that it frightened me."

"I know what you mean. I had an hour with him this

morning. He was just the same. I tried to give him a little warning, but I couldn't make any impression at all."

"If he doesn't get in?—" I said.

"If he doesn't get in," said Brown steadily, "I don't believe he'll ever be the same man again."

He frowned and said:

"It's annoying to think that, if we were certain Chrystal was going to be sensible, we should have a decent prospect of tomorrow turning out all right. It's a tantalising thought."

Then he left me, and I went to have tea with Roy. I returned to my rooms through rain which had set in for the night, and I settled by the fire, not wanting to move until dinner time. But I had not been there half an hour when the door opened.

"Good evening, Eliot," said Chrystal in his sharpest parade ground voice. He was wearing a mackintosh, but it was only slightly damp at the shoulders, and his shoes were clean. He had not been walking much that day.

"I want a word with you."

I asked him to sit down, but he would not even take off his coat.

"I'm busy. I've got to have a word with Brown." He was brusquer than I had ever heard him.

"He's in his rooms," I said.

"I'll go in three minutes. I shan't take long with either of you. I shan't stay long with Brown."

He stared at me with bold, assertive, defiant eyes. "I've decided to vote for Crawford," he said. "He's the better man."

Like all news that one has feared hearing, it sounded flat.

"It has been a lamentable exhibition," said Chrystal. "I tell you, Eliot, we've only just missed making a serious mistake. I saw it in time. We nearly passed Crawford over. I never liked it. He's the right man."

I began to argue, but Chrystal cut me short:

"I haven't time to discuss it. I'm satisfied with Crawford. I went round to see him this morning. I've been with him all day. I've heard his views on the college. I like them. It's been a satisfactory day."

"I remember you saying——"

"I'm sorry, Eliot. I haven't time to discuss it. I've never been happy about this election. It's been lamentable. I oughtn't to have left it so late."

"It's very hard to leave our party at this notice," I said angrily.

"I joined it against my better judgment," he snapped.

"That doesn't affect it. You're contracted to Jago. Have you told Brown?"

"I didn't want to write to Jago until I'd told Brown. I owe Brown an explanation. We've never had to explain anything to each other before. I'm sorry about that. It can't be helped." He looked at me. "You don't think I mind sending a note to Jago, do you? He would never have done. Not in a hundred years. I'm saving us all from a calamity. You don't see it now, but you'll thank me later on."

He kept his coat on, he would not sit down, but he stood talking for some time. He did not wish to face Brown, he longed for the next hour to be past, he was putting off the struggle: not through direct fear, the fear that some men are seized with when they cross their wills against a stronger one, but because he was too soft-hearted to carry bad news, too uncertain of his own part to display it before intimate eyes.

He did not like the part he had insensibly slipped into. Just as Jago hated the path of ambition which, once he had begun it, led him from step to step, each one springing naturally from the last, until he was tempted to humiliate himself in front of Nightingale—in the same way Chrystal hated the path of compromise, which, step by step, each one plausible, enjoyable, almost inevitable, had brought him now to quarrel with his friend and break his contract. It was all so natural. Angrily he justified himself to me, said 'you'll all thank me later on'. He had been torn one way and the other, he had drifted into the compromise. He had never been master of the events round him. It was that which he could not forgive.

He had never been fond of Jago, had never liked to think of him as Master, had only joined in to please Arthur Brown. Then, liking the feel of power, he had tried to find ways out. He had revelled in making the candidates vote for each other. Yet even so he had not struggled free from his indecisions. Was he too much under Brown's influence? His affection was hearty and simple; but his longing to be masterful was intense. Was he right in sacrificing his judgment, just to please Brown? Even here, where he felt each day that Brown had made a mistake?

For Chrystal had come to feel that electing Jago would be a mistake; it would hinder all that Chrystal wanted, for himself and for the college. With Jago, there would be no chance of the college gaining in riches and reputation among solid men.

As the months went on, Chrystal found he could endure the thought of Jago less and less. He felt free in the conferences with the other side: in the pacts with them, the search for a third candidate, he could assert himself. Every time he was with the other side he felt that the whole election lay in his hands. In those meetings, in the hours at night with Jago's opponents, he came into his own again.

And how much, I wondered, was due to hurt vanity—urgent in all men, and as much so in Chrystal as in most? Had he been piqued so intolerably when Jago defended Winslow and laughed at Sir Horace and the benefaction—had he been piqued so intolerably that it turned the balance? Envy and pique and vanity, all the passions of self-regard:

you could not live long in a society of men and not see them often weigh down the rest. How much of my own objection to Crawford was because he once spoke of me as a barrister manqué?

I did not know, perhaps I never should know, on what day Chrystal faced himself and saw that he would not vote for Jago. Certainly not in the first steps which, without his realising, had started him towards this afternoon. When he began the move to make the candidates vote for each other, his first move to a coalition with the other side, he could still have said to himself, and believed it, that he was pledged to Jago. He did not make any pretence of enthusiasm to Brown or me, and to himself his reluctance, his sheer distaste, kept coming into mind. Yet he would have said to himself that he was going to vote for Jago. He would still have said it when in search of a third candidate—he was going to vote for Jago unless we found another man. On December 17th, when he approached Brown, he would have gone on saying it to himself. He would have said it to himself: but I thought that there are things one says to oneself in all sincerity, statements of intention, which one knows without admitting it that one will never do. I believed it had been like that with Chrystal since the funeral. He believed he would vote for Jago, unless he brought off a coup: in some hidden and inadmissable way, he knew he never would.

Yet it was probably less than forty-eight hours before this afternoon when at last he saw with explicit certainty that he would not vote for Jago. He had tried Brown as a third candidate, to give himself an excuse for throwing away his vote. Brown had turned him down. There would be no third candidate. It must be Jago against Crawford to the end. Chrystal was caught. There was nothing for it now. So, within the last forty-eight hours, it had come to him. Everything became clear at one flash. With relief, with release, with extreme satisfaction, he knew that he would vote for Crawford. It was what he had wanted to do for months.

It was astonishingly like some of the moves in high politics, I thought afterwards when I had a chance of watching personal struggles upon a grander scale. I saw men as tough and dominating as Chrystal, entangled in compromise and in time hypnotised by their own technique: believing that they were being sensible and realistic, taking their steps for coherent practical reasons, while in fact they were moved by vacillations which they did not begin to understand. I saw men enjoying forming coalitions, just as Chrystal did, and revelling in the contact with their opponents. I saw the same impulse to change sides, to resent one's leader and become fascinated by one's chief opponent. The more certain men are that they are chasing their own concrete and 'realistic' ends, so it often seemed to me, the more nakedly do you see all the strands they could never give a reason for.

Such natures as Chrystal's are more mixed in action than the man himself would ever admit—more mixed, I sometimes thought, than those of stranger men such as Jago and Roy Calvert. Chrystal thought he was realistic in all he did: you had only to watch him, to hear his curt inarticulate outbursts as he delayed breaking the news to Brown, to know how many other motives were at work: yet it was naïve to think he was not being realistic at the same time.

In a sense, he was being just as realistic as he thought. He had his own sensible policy for the college: that was safer with Crawford than with Jago. He wanted to keep his own busy humble power, he wanted his share in running the place. For months, every sign had told Chrystal that with Jago it would not be so easy. His temper and pride over Nightingale, his fury at having his hand forced over his vote, the moods in which he despised riches and rich men—

Chrystal had noticed them all. He noticed them more acutely because of his other motives for rejecting Jago: but he also saw them as a politician. He had come to think that, if Jago became Master, his own policy and power would dwindle to nothing within the next five years. And he was absolutely right.

He still stood in his mackintosh in front of my fire. He could not force himself to go out.

"You'd better come with me, Eliot," he broke out. "Brown's got to be told. He'll want to talk to you."

I refused.

"There's nothing for me to say," I told him. I was too downcast: why should I help spare his feelings?

"Brown's got to be told. I shan't take long about it," said Chrystal, standing still.

"It's late already—to tell him what you're going to."

"I accept that," said Chrystal. "Well, I'll do it. You'd better join us in a few minutes, Eliot. You see eye to eye with Brown on this. He'd like to have you there. I shall have to go. As soon as I've told him. I've got plenty to do tonight."

As he spoke he started out of the room. Half-an-hour later I followed him. Brown was sitting deep in his habitual armchair; his face was sombre. Chrystal, his mackintosh unbuttoned, stood with his back to the fire, and his mouth was drawn down into lines unhappy and ill-treated. When I entered, it seemed as though neither had spoken for minutes past; and it was a time before Brown spoke.

"I gather that you have an inkling of this change in the situation," he said to me.

I said yes.

A moment later, there were light and very rapid footsteps on the stairs. In burst Jago, his eyes blazing.

"I'm extremely sorry," he said to Brown. His tone was wild, and he turned on Chrystal with a naked intensity. His skin was grey, and yet the grimace of his lips was for all the world as though he smiled. "It was you I wanted to find," he said. "It is necessary for me to see you. This note you've been good enough to send me—I should like to be quite certain what you mean."

"I had not realised," said Brown in a quiet, measured voice, "that you had informed Jago already. I rather got the impression that you were speaking to me first."

Chrystal's chin was sunk into his chest.

"I wrote before I came," he said.

FORTY-THREE

EACH IS ALONE

For an instant—was it an illusion?—they seemed quite motionless. In that tableau, Brown was sitting with his fingers interlaced on his waistcoat, his eyes fixedly watching the other two: Chrystal's head was bent, he was staring at the carpet, his forehead shone under the light, his chin rested on his chest: Jago stood a yard away, and there was still a grimace on his lips that looked like a smile.

"I must have got hold of the wrong impression," said Brown.

"Many of us," Jago flared out, "have got hold of wrong impressions. It would have been extraordinary if we hadn't. I've seen some remarkable behaviour from time to time——"

Chrystal raised his head and faced Jago with a bold assertive gaze. What had passed between him and Brown I did not know; but I felt that he had said little, he had not tried to explain himself, he had stood there in silence.

"I'm not taking those strictures from you, Jago," he said.

"At last I can say what I think," said Jago.

"We can all say what we think," said Chrystal.

"This isn't very profitable," said Brown.

At the sound of that steady, monitory voice, Jago frowned. Then quite suddenly he began to talk to Chrystal in an urgent, reasonable-seeming, almost friendly manner.

"I think we've always understood each other," Jago said to Chrystal. "You've never made any pretence that you wanted me as Master on my own merits, such as they are. You were presented with two distinctly unpleasing candidates, and you decided that I was slightly the less unpleasing of the two. You musn't think it was a specially grateful position for me to be placed in—but at any rate there was no pretence about it. We both knew where we stood and made the best of it. Isn't that true?"

"There's something in it," said Chrystal. "But——"

"There's everything in it," cried Jago. "We've had a working understanding that wasn't very flattering to me. We both of us knew that we had very little in common. But we managed to adjust ourselves to this practical arrangement. You disliked the idea of my opponent more than you did me—and we took that as our common ground. It's lasted us all these months until tonight. And it seems to me sheer abject folly that it shouldn't last us a few hours longer."

"What do you mean?"

"This will all be over tomorrow morning. Why have you suddenly let your impatience get the better of you? I know only too clearly that you're not very pleased at the idea of me as Master. We've both known that all along. Chrystal, I know we don't get on at heart. I'm not going to pretend: I know we never shall. But we've made shift for long enough now. It's too serious for us to indulge our likes and dislikes at the last minute. I'm ready now to talk over all the practical arrangements that we can conceivably make for the future. I'm asking you to think again."

"There's no point in that."

"I'm asking you to think again," said Jago, with feverish energy. "We can make a working plan. I'm prepared to leave certain things in the college to you. It won't remove the misunderstanding between us—but it will save us from the things we want most of all to avoid."

"What do I want most of all to avoid?" asked Chrystal.

"Having my opponent inflicted on you."

"You're wrong, Jago." Chrystal shook his head.

"How am I wrong?"

"I don't mind Crawford being Master. I did once. It was my mistake. He'll make a good Master."

Jago heard but seemed not to understand. His expression remained strained to the limit of the nerves, angry and yet lit by his nervous hope. It remained so, just as when one reads a letter and the words spell out bad news, one's smile takes some time to go. Jago had not yet realised in his heart what Chrystal had said.

"You know as well as I do," said Jago, "that seeing him elected is the last thing any of us want."

"I take you up on that."

"Do you seriously deny it?"

"I do," said Chrystal.

"I'm very much afraid that you're——"

"I'm sorry, Jago," said Chrystal. "I'd better make it clear. Crawford will be a good Master. You've got the advantage over him in some respects. I've always said that, and I stick to it."

He paused. He kept his gaze on Jago: it was firm, satisfied and curiously kindly.

"That's not the whole story," he went on. "I don't like saying this, Jago, but I've got to. You've got the advantage over him in some respects—but by and large he will make a better Master than you would have done."

Jago gasped. It seemed that that was the moment when he began to know and suffer.

"Don't worry too much," said Chrystal, with his curt, genuine, almost physical concern. "It isn't everyone who's suitable to be a Master. It isn't always the best——"

"Now you want to patronise me," said Jago, very quietly.

A faint flush tinged the thick-skinned pallor of Chrystal's cheeks. It was only then, when Jago was defeated, beginning to feel the first empty pang, knowing that the shame and suffering would grow, that he succeeded in touching Chrystal.

"You never give anyone credit for decent intentions,"

snapped Chrystal. "If you had done, you might have more support."

"I regard it as useless," Brown intervened, "for either of you to say more."

The two confronted each other. For an instant it felt as though they would clash with accusations of all they found alien in each other. They were on the point of denouncing what they hated because they could not share.

But those words were not spoken. Perhaps Brown had just managed to stop them. They confronted each other: Chrystal's face was fierce and sullen, Jago's ravaged by the encroaching pain: it was Chrystal who turned away.

"I'm going into hall," he said.

"I rather think they're expecting me at home," said Brown.

"I shall see you in chapel then. Tomorrow morning," said Chrystal.

Brown inclined his head. Chrystal gave a short good-night, and went out.

Jago threw himself, as though both restless and exhausted, on to the sofa.

"So this is the end," he said.

"I'm afraid it is, Paul," said Brown steadily. "Unless something very unexpected turns up to help us—and I couldn't let you hope anything from that."

"I've got no hope left," said Jago.

"I'm afraid we must resign ourselves," said Brown. "I don't need to tell you what your friends are feeling."

"It's bitter," I said.

"Thank you both," said Jago, but his tone was far away. Suddenly he cried, as from a new depth of pain: "How can I inflict this on my wife? How can I face seeing her being so much hurt?"

Neither Brown nor I replied. Jago twisted on the sofa, drew up his knees and turned again. The bell began to ring for hall.

"I can't dine with them," said Jago. "It would be intolerable to let them see me."

"I know," said Brown.

"I do not see," said Jago quietly, "how I am going to stay here. I shall be reminded of this for the rest of my life."

"It sounds trite," said Brown, "but these wounds heal in time."

"I've got no money," said Jago. "I am too old to move. Every time they see me, I shall be ashamed."

He added:

"I shall have to watch another man in the place I should have filled. I shall have to call him Master."

It was not a conversation. For minutes together he lay silent: then came a broken outburst. It was painful to hear the spurs of defeat wound him in one place, then another. Will the other side know tonight? Are they celebrating in hall at this very moment? When will the news go round the university? Has it got outside the college yet? Who would be the first of his enemies to laugh? Why had he allowed himself to be a candidate?

His grief became so wild that he rounded on Brown.

"Why did you expose me to this danger? No one has ever done me so much harm before."

"I misjudged the situation," said Brown. "I regard myself as very much to blame for lack of judgment."

"You oughtn't to take risks with your friends' happiness."

"I shall always be sorry, Paul," said Brown with affectionate remorse, showing no sign that he resented being blamed.

After an interval of quiet Jago suddenly sat up and faced us.

"I want to ask you something. Is it quite certain that this man will get a majority tomorrow?"

"I'm afraid it is. So far as it's given to us to be certain."

"Is it?" cried Jago. "Why should I vote for him? Why should I make up his majority? I was coerced into it by Chrystal. Why should I do it now?"

"I think you're bound by your promise," said Brown.

"That is for me to say," said Jago.

"Yes, it is for you to say," said Brown in the same even tone. "But there is another reason why I hope you won't break your promise. If you do, people will say that Crawford would never have done so in similar circumstances. And that this was the best proof that they had been right all the time."

"Do you think now that they have been right all the time?"

"I am as sure they are wrong as I've ever been."

"Even though I've shown you that I'm prepared to break my promise?"

"I know," said Brown, "that you feel temptations that I'm lucky enough to escape. But I also know that you don't give way to them."

"You're a good friend, Arthur," said Jago. It was his first familiar touch that night.

He stared at us with his eyes distraught, and said:

"So I'm asked to sign my own rejection tomorrow morning. That's something else I have to thank Chrystal for—I know he's been your friend, Arthur. But he's more detestable than any of the others."

"It's natural for you to say so," said Brown. "But it isn't true."

"Are you going to trust him again?"

Brown gave a sad, ironic, firm-hearted smile: I thought it meant that he would trust Chrystal as much or as little as he had trusted him before. For Brown loved his friends, and knew they were only men. Since they were only men, they could be treacherous—and then next time loyal beyond belief. One took them as they were. That gave Brown his unfailing strength, and also a tinge, deep under the comfortable flesh, of ironic sadness.

"How are *you* going to live in this college?" said Jago.

"Paul," said Arthur Brown, "I've failed in the thing I've most wanted to bring off here. You're right to blame me, but perhaps you will remember that it isn't going to be pleasant even for me yet awhile. I don't welcome having this difference with Chrystal. And I abominate the thought of Crawford as Master more than anyone in the college. After you, I believe I'm more affected than any of our friends."

"I'm sure that's true," I said.

"Still," said Brown, "I'm not prepared to become a hermit because we've lost. We've shown some bad management and we've had some bad luck, and I don't forgive myself for what it's going to mean to you. But it has happened, and we've got to make the best of it. We're not children, and we must go on living decently in this place."

"For myself," he added, "I propose to try and make the college as friendly as possible. We ought to be able to heal some of these rifts. I admit that it will take time. It will be a few years before we stop being more divided than I should like."

Jago looked at the most devoted of his supporters. Each of them took calamity according to his nature. To Jago, those last words were meaningless, were nothing but a noise that sounded outside his distress. He felt inescapably alone.

Brown saw Jago look more than ever harrowed, and yet could not begin to console him again. He had done all he could. He said to me: "I always insisted that it wasn't a foregone conclusion. I expect you remember me giving you occasional warnings. I'm afraid they've turned out more than justified."

He was moved for Jago to the bottom of his heart; he was defeated on his own account; and yet, I was all but sure, there came a spark of comfort as he thought how far-sighted he had been.

The telephone rang. It was Brown's wife, asking why he was half an hour late for dinner. Brown said that he did not like to leave us, but I offered to take Jago into my rooms and find him food.

FORTY-FOUR

DEEPER THAN SHAME

Jago sat down by my fire. The flames, flaring and falling, illumined his face, left it in shadow, at times smoothed out the lines of pain. He gazed into the fire, taking no notice of me. I smoked a cigarette, and then another. At last I went quietly, as though he were asleep, to see what I could give him to eat.

There was not much in my gyproom. Bidwell had seen to that. But there was a loaf of bread, cheese and butter, and, very surprisingly, a little jar of caviare (a present from a pupil), which Bidwell happened not to like. I put them on the little table between us, in front of the fire. I went out again to fetch some whisky and glasses. When I returned, Jago had already begun to eat.

He ate with extreme hunger, with the same concentration that a man shows when he has been starved for days. He did not talk, except to thank me when I filled his glass or passed a knife. He finished half the loaf and a great wedge of cheese. At the end he gave a smile, a youthful and innocent smile.

"I was glad of that," he said.

He smiled again.

"Until tonight," he said, "I intended to give a celebration for my friends. Of course it would have been necessary to keep it secret from the rest. They mustn't—it would have been fatal to let them feel there were still two parties in the college. But we should have had a celebration to ourselves."

He spoke very simply and freshly, as though he had put the suffering on one side and was able to rest. I was certain that he was still *hoping*. In his heart, this celebration was still going to take place. I knew well enough how slow the heart is to catch up with the brute facts. One looks forward to a joy: it is snatched away at the last minute: and, hours later, there are darts of illusory delight when one still feels that it is to come. Such moments cheat one and pass sickeningly away. So, a little later, the innocence ebbed from Jago's face. "There will be no celebration for my friends," he said. "I shall not even know how to meet them. I don't know who they are."

It was worse for him than for a humbler man, I thought. A humbler man could have cursed and moaned among his friends and thrown himself without thinking upon their love. Jago could not lower himself, could not give himself away, could not take pity and affection such as soften fate for more pedestrian men. It was the fault of his pride, of course —and yet, one can be held back by one's nature and at the same time long passionately for what one cannot take. Jago could bring sympathy to young Luke or me or Joan Royce or twenty others; but he could not accept it himself. With him, intimacy could only flow one way. When he revealed himself, it was in the theatre of this world, not by the fireside to a friend and equal. He was so made that he could not bear the equality of the heart. People blamed him for it; I wondered if they thought it enviable to be born with such pride?"

"Do you think for a moment," I said, "that it will make a difference to any of us?"

"Thank you for saying that," said Jago, but none of us was close enough. We were allies, young man to be helped, protégés whom it was a pleasure to struggle for: we could not come closer. That was true of us all. Brown had a strong, protective affection for Jago—but I had just seen how Jago could not receive it. To him, Brown was another ally, the most useful and dependable of all. He was never easy with Brown. So far as he found ease with men at all, it was with his protégés.

"Do you think," I persisted, "we value men according to their office? Do you think it matters a damn to Roy Calvert or me whether you're called Master or not?"

"I wanted to hear it," said Jago nakedly. His imagination turned a knife in his bowels. He could not keep it from running after all the humiliations to come. They passed before his eyes with the sharpness of a film. He could not shut away the shames of his disgrace. He was drawn towards them by a morbid attraction. He had to imagine Crawford in *his* place.

His place: he had counted on it with such defenceless hope. He had heard himself being called Master: now he would hear us all call Crawford so. Among the wounds, that rankled and returned. He saw—as clearly as though it were before his eyes—Crawford presiding in hall, taking the chair at a college meeting. He could not stand it. He could not go to dinner, with that reproach before him in the flesh.

He thought of meeting his acquaintances in the streets. The news would hush round Cambridge in a week: people would say to him, with kindness, with a cruel twinkle 'I was surprised. I'd always hoped you'd be elected yourself'. Others would see the announcement in *The Times*. Had he kept his hope strictly to himself? He had dropped words here and there. The stories would go round; and they would gain colour as time passed, they would not be accurate, but they would keep the frailty and the bite of human life. Crawford's election—that was the time when Jago thought he had it in his pocket, he had actually ordered the furniture for the Lodge—Chrystal changed his mind on the way to the chapel, and said it was the wisest decision he ever made in his life.

They were the ways in which Jago would be remembered. Perhaps the only ways, for there would be nothing that did not die with the flesh; he would never get high place now, there was no memorial in words, there was no child.

The evening went on, as Jago sat by my fire: the chimes

clanged out, quarter by quarter, hour by hour; the shames bit into him. They pierced him like the shames of youth, before one's skin has thickened. Jago's skin had never thickened, and he was at their mercy.

Shames are more acute than sorrows, I thought as I sat by him, unable even to soften that intolerable night. The wounds of self-consciousness touch one's nerves more poignantly than the deepest agonies of the heart. But it is the deep agonies that cut at the roots of one's nature. It is there that one suffers, when vanity and self-consciousness have gone. And Jago suffered there.

It was not only that he winced at the thought of seeing his acquaintances in the streets. That wound would mend in time. He had also lost something in himself, and I did not see how he could get it back. He was a man diffident among his fellows in the ordinary rub-and-wear of life; it was hard for him to be a man among ordinary men; he was profoundly diffident about his power among men. That diffidence came no one knew from where, had governed so many of his actions, had prevented him from reaching the fame and glory which he believed was his by right. Very slowly he had built up a little store of confidence. Somehow men had come to respect him—he nearly believed it at the age of fifty. This Mastership was a sign for him. That explained, as I had already thought, the obsessive strength of his ambition. The Mastership meant that men esteemed him; they thought of him as one of themselves, as better than themselves. Listening to Brown and Chrystal when they asked him to stand, Jago had felt that he could have had any kind of success, he felt infused by confidence such as he had never known. It was one of the triumphant moments of his life.

He had become obsessed by the ambition; he had hated the path along which it had led him; the disappointments, the anxieties, the inhibitions, the humiliations—they corroded him because they brought back his diffidence again. But always he was buoyed up when he thought of his party and the place they would win for him. Above all, he was buoyed up by the support of Brown and Chrystal. He did not like Chrystal; they were as different as men could be; but that antipathy made Chrystal's support more precious. He resented Chrystal's management, he thought Chrystal was a coarse-minded party boss—but even when he wanted to quarrel, he thought with wonder and delight 'this man believes in me! this man is competent, down-to-earth—and he's ready to make me Master! If such a man believes in me, I can believe in myself!'

That night Chrystal had drained away the little store of confidence. Would it ever be refilled? It would be harder now than when Jago first became ambitious, first wished to prove himself among men.

It was eleven o'clock, the clock was just striking, when he began to speak about his wife. She had been his first thought in Brown's room. He had not brought himself to mention her since.

"She will be waiting up for me," he said. "I shall hurt her beyond bearing when I see her. I've tried hard all my life not to hurt her. Now I can't see a way out."

"Won't she guess there's something wrong?"

"That won't make it easier—when she hears it's true."

"She'll bear it," I said, "because it comes from you."

"That makes it a hundred times worse."

"For you. But not for her."

"If I brought bad news from outside," said Jago, "I should not be afraid for a single instant. She is very brave in every way in which a human being can be brave. If this place shut down and we'd lost every penny, I'd tell her the news and she'd start getting ready to work the next minute. But this is horribly different."

I did not question him.

"Don't you see," he cried, "that she will accuse herself?" He added quietly:

"She will be certain to think it is her fault."

"We must tell her it isn't," I said. "Roy and I must explain exactly what has happened."

"She will never believe you. She'll never believe any of you." He paused. "I'm very much afraid that she will not believe me."

"Is it no use our trying?"

"I'm afraid that nothing will reassure her," said Jago. "I think she trusts me—yet she can't believe me when it concerns herself. I've not brought her peace of mind. If she'd married another man, she might have found it. I don't know. I hoped I could make her happy, and I haven't done."

"I know what you feel," I said.

"So you do," said Jago—a smile, evanescent but brotherly, shone for an instant through his pain.

"I don't believe anyone else could have made her as happy."

"I've seen her in the worst hours," said Jago. He went on in despair: "Yet I've never done anything to hurt her until now. If I'd been the cruellest of men, I couldn't have found a way to hurt as much as this. I cannot bear to see her face when I tell her. She will be utterly beside herself—and I shall be no good to her."

With his chin in his hands, he looked into the fire. For many minutes he was silent. At last he spoke as though there had been no pause.

"I think I could endure it all," he said, "if it were not for her."

FORTY-FIVE

THE ELECTION

On the morning of the election, I woke while it was still dark. There were knocks at the great gate, the rattle of the door opening, the clink of keys, voices in the court; it was six o'clock, and the servants were coming in to work. Although I had been late to bed, telling Roy the final news, I could not get to sleep again. The court quietened, and the first light of the winter dawn crept round the edges of the blind. As the grey morning twilight became visible in the dark room, I lay awake as I had done in other troubles and heard the chimes ring out over the town with indifferent cheerfulness. I was full of worry, though there was nothing left to worry about.

The light increased; there were footsteps, not only servants', passing through the court; I recognised Chrystal's quick and athletic tread. Why was he in college so early? It was a solace when Bidwell tip-toed in. After his morning greeting, he said:

"So the great old day has arrived at last, sir."

"Yes," I said.

He stood beside the bed with his deferential roguish smile.

"I know it's wrong of us to talk among ourselves, sir, but we've had a good many words about who is to be the next Master."

"Have you?"

"They're two very nice gentlemen," said Bidwell. "A very popular gentleman Dr. Jago is. I shouldn't say there was a servant in the college who had ever heard a word against him." He was watching me with sharp eyes out of his composed, deliberately bland and guileless face.

"Of course," he said when I did not reply, "Dr. Crawford is a very popular gentleman too." He hurried a little, determined not to be on the wrong side. "Between ourselves, sir, I should say they were equally popular. We shall drink their healths all right, whoever you put in."

I got up and shaved and put on my darkest suit. It was curious, I thought, how strongly ritual held one, even though one was not given to it. Out of the window, the court looked sombre in the bleak morning, and one of the last leaves of autumn had drifted on to the sill. Bidwell had switched on the light in my sitting-room, and for once the fire was blazing strongly in time for breakfast, though the air still struck cold.

I ate some breakfast without much appetite and read the morning paper: the news from the Spanish war seemed a little better. Roy ran up the stairs and walked about the room for a few moments.

"Hurry up, old boy," he said. "You musn't miss the show."

He was dressed with more than his usual elegance, and was wearing a black silk tie. When I asked him why, he said it was a sign of loss. He was less disturbed, more excited and far gayer than I was. He told me that he had met Chrystal in the court, and commiserated with him for being cursed with his temperamental indecision.

" 'It must be a grave handicap,' I said." Roy's face became impassive. " 'It must make active life an impossible strain,' I said."

I grinned. "How did he take it?"

"He looked rather puzzled."

"It wasn't very wise."

"Just so," said Roy. "But it was remarkably pleasing."

He left to send a telegram before he went into chapel: he was off to Italy next day.

I stood by the window, and set my watch by the clock

across the court. It was just ten minutes to ten. The chapel door stood open, and the head porter, his top hat gleaming in the grey morning, was waiting to give the signal for the bell to peal. But he had not done so when, through the great gate, appeared old Gay. He was wearing mortar board and gown, as he always did when he came to college; he was wrapped up in a new, heavy coat and padded thick with scarves; his beard looked as though it had been cut that morning. Step by step, foot and a half by foot and a half, he progressed towards the chapel. Two under porters walked behind him; I thought he must have commanded them, for they seemed mystified and had nothing to do. Before he was half-way round the court, the bell began to ring. At the first sound, Gay looked up at the tower and gave an approving and olympian nod.

As the old man drew near, Brown emerged from the chapel door. His face glowed pink, and I guessed that he had been bustling about seeing that all was in order. Gay beckoned him, and he went along the path. Before they met, Gay called out a resounding good-morning that I could hear even across the court and through my windows; when they came close enough, Gay enthusiastically shook hands.

At that moment, Chrystal and Despard-Smith were approaching from the second court, and Winslow came through the gate. The bell rang out insistently. It was time for me to go.

When I went into the chapel there was complete silence, though most of the college were already sitting there. A long table had been placed in the nave; it was covered with a thick rich crimson table-cloth I had never seen before; and there, with Gay at the head, Pilbrow on his right hand, Despard-Smith on his left, the others in order down its length, the fellows sat. The bell clanged outside: in each pause between the peals, there was complete silence. The chapel was solemn to some by faith; but others, who did not believe, who knew what the result of this morning must be, to whom it was just a form, were nevertheless gripped by the ritual magic.

The lights shone down on the red cloth. In the silence, one noticed more than ever the smell of the chapel—earthy, odorous from wood, wax, fusty books. Along with that smell, which never varied, came a new concomitant, a faint but persistent tincture of pomade. It must have been due, I thought, to old Gay's barber.

The bell still clanged. Ten o'clock had not yet struck. There were three empty places at the table. One was on my left, where Luke had not yet come. There was another between Despard-Smith and Brown, and a third between Winslow and Chrystal. Then Jago walked in, slowly, not looking at any of us. He stared at the table, took in the empty places. He saw where his must be. He took the chair between Winslow and Chrystal. No word was spoken, he made no indication of a greeting: but Brown, opposite to him, gave a slight kind smile.

Luke came to his place, and we were still quiet. The bell gave its last peal: the chimes of ten were quivering above the chapel: Crawford moved, swiftly but without heat or fuss, to the last seat.

"I apologise if I'm late, Senior Fellow," he said equably. They were the first words spoken since I went in.

The last stroke of ten had sounded, and there was no whisper in the chapel. Gay sat upright, looking down the table: Pilbrow and Despard-Smith faced each other: Winslow and Crawford: Jago and Brown: Chrystal and Nightingale: Getliffe and me: Roy Calvert and Luke. In front of each of us, on the crimson cloth, was a copy of the statutes, a slip of paper, and a pen. Down the middle of the table ran a series of four silver inkstands—one for Gay alone, one for each group of four.

Gay climbed to his feet.

"Ah," he said. "I propose to carry out the duties conferred on me by our statutes." He began at once to read from his leather-covered copy. " 'At ten o'clock in the morning of the appointed day the Fellows shall assemble in the chapel, and of the fellows then present that one who is first in order of precedence shall preside. He shall first read aloud——' " Gay looked up from the book. "This is the appointed day, there's no doubt about that. And I am the fellow first in order of precedence. Now is the time to do my duty."

In his strong and sonorous voice he read on. The words echoed in the chapel; everyone sat still while the seconds ticked past; I kept my eyes from Jago's face. The quarter struck, and Gay was still reading.

At last he finished.

"Ah," he said, "that's well done. Now I call upon you to stand and make your declarations."

Gay vigorously recited: "I, Maurice Harvey Laurence Gay, do hereby declare that I have full knowledge of the statutes just read and will solemnly observe them. I do also hereby declare that without thought of gain or loss or worldly considerations whatsoever I will now choose as Master that man who in my belief will best maintain and increase the well-being and glory of the college. I vow this in sincerity and truth."

In the ordinary elections, of a scholar or a fellow, it was the practice for each of us to repeat in turn the seven words of the promise. But now we heard Eustace Pilbrow go through the whole declaration, and Despard-Smith after him.

Despard-Smith's voice died away.

Winslow thrust out his underlip, and said:

"I vow this in sincerity and truth."

Despard-Smith immediately whispered in Gay's ear. Gay said:

"The senior fellows consider that everyone should read the whole declaration."

"Am I bound by the decision of the senior fellows?" said Winslow.

"We mustn't leave anything to doubt. No indeed," said Gay. "I have to ask you to comply. Then everyone else, right down the line. That's the proper way."

"I do it under protest, Senior Fellow," said Winslow sullenly, and read the declaration in a fast monotone.

When it came to Jago's turn, I felt the strain tighten among us as we stood. His voice was muffled but controlled. When he ended his promise, he threw back his head. His shoulder was almost touching Chrystal's.

The declaration passed across the table, came to the young men. At last Luke had completed his: we all stayed on our feet.

"Is that everyone?" said Gay. "I want to be assured that everyone has made his declaration according to the statutes. That's well done again. Now we may sit down and write our votes."

For some minutes—perhaps it was not so long—there was only the sound of the scratch of pens on paper. I noticed Chrystal, who was using his fountain pen, push towards Jago the inkstand that stood for them both to use. Someone higher up the table was crossing out a word. I finished and looked at Francis Getliffe, directly opposite: he gave me a grim smile. Several people were still staring down at their slips. Gay was writing away.

He was the last to look up. "Ah. All ready? Pray read over your votes," he said.

Then he called out:

"I will now request the junior fellow to collect your votes and deliver them to me. I shall then read them aloud, as prescribed in the statutes. I request the two next senior fellows to make a record of the votes as I announce them. Yes, that's the work for them to do."

Pilbrow and Despard-Smith sat with paper in front of them. Young Luke walked down the nave, arranging the votes in order, so that they could be read from the juniors upwards.

"Well done," said Gay, when Luke placed the little pile in his hands. "Well done."

He waited until Luke was once more in his seat.

"Now is the time to read the votes," Gay announced. Once more he clutched the table and got to his feet. He held the slips at arm's length, in order to focus his faded, long-sighted eyes. He recited, in the clearest and most robust of tones:

"Here they are.

" 'I, Walter John Luke, vote for Dr. Paul Jago.'

" 'I, Roy Clement Edward Calvert, elect Paul Jago.' "

My vote for Jago. There was no fixed form of voting, though Roy's was supposed to be the most correct. It struck me irrelevantly how one heard Christian names that one had scarcely known.

" 'I, Francis Ernest Getliffe, elect Redvers Thomas Arbuthnot Crawford.'

" 'Ronald Edmund Nightingale votes for Dr. Crawford.'

" 'Charles Percy Chrystal elects Dr. Thomas Crawford.' "

As Gay's voice rang out with Chrystal's vote, there was a quiver at the table. There may have been some, I thought, to whom it was a shock. Had the news reached everyone by ten o'clock?

" 'I, Arthur Brown, elect Paul Jago.' "

I waited anxiously for the next.

" 'I, Paul Jago, elect Thomas Crawford.'

" 'Redvers Thomas Arbuthnot Crawford chooses Paul Jago.'

" 'Mr. Winslow elects Dr. Crawford, and signs his name as Godfrey Harold Winslow.'

" 'Albert Theophilus Despard-Smith elects Redvers Thomas Arbuthnot Crawford.'

" 'I, Eustace Pilbrow, elect Redvers Thomas Arbuthnot Crawford.' "

Someone said: "That's a majority."

There was still Gay's own vote to come.

Gay read with doubled richness:

" 'I, Maurice Harvey Laurence Gay, Senior Fellow of the college and emeritus professor in the university, after having performed my duties as Senior Fellow in accordance with the statutes and heard the declarations of the fellows duly assembled in chapel, do hereby cast my vote for Paul Jago as Master of the college.' "

There was a movement, either of relaxation or surprise. I caught Roy Calvert's eye.

"There we are," said Gay. "There are the votes. Have you counted them?"

"Yes," said Despard-Smith.

"Mind you count them carefully," said Gay. "We mustn't make a mistake at the last."

"Seven votes for Dr. Crawford," said Despard-Smith bleakly. "Six for Dr. Jago. Seven votes makes a clear majority of the college, and Dr. Crawford is elected."

"Ah. Indeed. Remarkable. Dr. Crawford. I understood—You're certain of your records, my dear chap?"

"Certainly." Despard-Smith was frowning.

"I think I must scrutinise them. I ought to make sure." Still standing, the old man held the list of votes two feet from his eyes, and checked each one beside the written slips.

"I agree with you," he said genially to Despard-Smith. "Well done. Seven votes for Dr. Crawford. I must declare him elected."

For the last time, a hush fell in the chapel. Gay stood alone, smiling, serene and handsome.

"Dr. Redvers Thomas Arbuthnot Crawford," he called. Crawford rose.

"Senior Fellow," he said.

"I declare you elected this day Master of the college," said Gay.

He added, with a superb and natural air:

"And now I give the college into your charge."

"I thank you, Senior Fellow," said Crawford imperturbably. "I thank the college."

Without a word, Jago leaned across the table, shook Crawford's hand, and walked out of the chapel. Everyone watched him go. It was not until the outer door swung to that chairs were pushed back and men surrounded Crawford. We all congratulated him. Nightingale smiled at him, admiringly. Chrystal said: "I'm very glad, Crawford." Brown shook him by the hand with a polite, formal smile. Crawford was good-humoured and self-assured as ever while people talked to him. It was strange to hear him for the first time called Master.

FORTY-SIX

THE MASTER PRESIDES

I went away from the chapel with Roy Calvert, and we stood in the great gate, watching women bustle by to their morning shopping: the streets were full, the buses gleamed a brilliant red under the slaty sky.

"Dished," said Roy. "Old boy, one never feels the worst until it happens. I'm deflated."

"Yes."

"Why does one mind so much about things which don't matter? This doesn't matter to us."

"It matters to Jago," I said.

"Ought we to see him? I should be frightened to, you know. Did you see how he looked?"

"I did."

"I should be frightened while he's so wretched. It's more in your line, Lewis." He smiled, mocking both me and himself.

Soon he left me to get some money for his journey, and I turned back into the court. There was a knot of people at the chapel door, and I went towards them. Gay, Brown, Despard-Smith and Winslow were standing together, with the head porter a yard away: I saw that they had been pinning a notice to the door.

"What do you think of that, Nightingale?" Gay greeted me.

"Not Nightingale," said Brown.

"What do you think of that?" said Gay. There's a notice and a half for you. There's no doubt about that. If they want to see who's been elected, they've only got to come and read. And they can see my signature at the bottom. I like a good bold signature. I like a man who's not ashamed of the sight of his own name. Well, my friends, it's all gone like clockwork. You couldn't have a better election than that. I congratulate you."

"I've taken part in four elections," said Despard-Smith. "I don't expect to see another."

"Come, come," said Gay. "Why, there is plenty of time for one or two more for all of us. I hope to do my duty at another one or two myself."

He waved a jocular finger at Winslow.

"And there'll be no slackness, Winslow, my dear chap. Declarations in full, mind. I can see I shall have to keep you up to the mark."

Winslow smiled caustically.

"I still maintain I was right," he said. "I want it discussed. I've never believed in multiplying mummery——"

He flanked Gay on one side, Despard-Smith on the other, and they kept pace with his shuffle as they moved off arguing. "Good-morning to you," said Winslow to Brown and me. "Good-morning, my dear chaps," Gay shouted to us behind him.

I remained with Brown, and asked him what Roy had asked me: ought one of us to look after Jago? Would he go round himself? "I should be useless to him," said Arthur Brown. "I'm very much afraid that I shouldn't be acceptable. I must reconcile myself to the fact that my company will distress him for a long time to come. He won't want to be reminded of our disaster."

Brown spoke evenly, with resignation but with deep feeling. His concern would not flag, would not be snubbed away: his was not a nature to forget. Yet it was like him to have stayed behind with Gay to make sure that the formalities were properly complied with. No one else of Jago's party would have cared whether or not the notice was affixed: Brown could not help scrutinizing the ceremony to the end: even though Crawford was elected, the ceremonies must be performed, the college must be carried on. And now, standing by the chapel door, he said:

"I suppose everyone will want to drink some healths tonight. I'd better see that they're not forgetting to have a few bottles ready."

For the rest of the day, until dinner, I heard only one more comment. It was from Chrystal, whom I met as he was walking out of college after lunch.

He looked at me with bold eyes, and gave his brisk good-afternoon.

"I tell you what, Eliot," he said sharply, "I didn't like Jago's behaviour this morning. He oughtn't to have gone off like that."

"He's had something to put up with."

"I know what he feels. I shouldn't like it myself. But one's got to put a face on things."

It was true, I thought: he did know what it was like to be wounded.

"It makes me feel justified in the line I took," said Chrystal. "I know you disagree with me. I wasn't happy about it myself. But he's not dependable enough. He's a likeable man. But he wouldn't have done."

I did not want to carry on the argument.

Before we parted, he said:

"You'll come and thank me in time, Eliot. I shouldn't be surprised if he doesn't turn up tonight. That won't be so good."

By custom, all fellows came in to drink the new Master's health on the night of his election; it was to provide for this occasion that Brown had gone to the cellars.

Roy was busy packing and getting ready his note-books for the Vatican library, so I spent the afternoon alone. I went out for tea in the town, and on my way ran straight into Mrs. Jago. I began to tell her how distressed I was. She cut me dead.

In my rooms that evening, I kept thinking of that strange incident. It was easy to see it as a joke—but I had come to feel fond of her, and it was no joke at all. What state must she be in? How completely was she possessed? I tried to write her a note, but thought of the meanings she would read behind each word. I was more upset than I should have confessed even to Roy.

I went into the combination room some time before dinner, and found Crawford, Getliffe and Nightingale already there. Nightingale had accepted a glass of sherry from Crawford, and was as coy with it as a girl over her first drink. He had not touched a drop, he was saying, since Flanders. Crawford asked me to have a drink with impartial cordiality, and spoke to us all:

"Speaking now as Master," he said, "I expect one will have to exercise considerable selection over the meetings one addresses. I don't want to parade opinions which part of the college vehemently objects to but, speaking as a responsible citizen, I can't remain entirely quiescent in times like these."

The room was filling rapidly. Despard-Smith, Chrystal, Brown and Winslow joined the group round Crawford. Francis Getliffe took me aside.

"Well, it's over," he said.

"It's over."

"I'm sorry if you're too disappointed, Lewis."

"I don't pretend to be overjoyed,' 'I said.

"It will shake down." He smiled. "Look, I need your advice. Come out and see us tomorrow night."

I said yes as spontaneously as I could.

"Good work," said Francis.

Nearly all the fellows had arrived. Each time the door opened, we looked for Jago. But first it was Pilbrow, sparkling with delight because he had received an invitation to go to Prague in the spring—then Gay, although he was breaking the routine of his nights. "Ah, Crawford, my dear chap," he said. "I thought you would feel the gilt was off the gingerbread unless I put in an appearance. Master I must call you now. I congratulate you."

We were still waiting for Jago when the butler announced to Crawford that dinner was served.

"Well," said Crawford, "this seems to be the whole party. Gay, will you take my right hand? Eustace, will you come in on my left?"

He sat at the head of the table in hall, looking slightly magnified, as men do when placed in the chief seat. His face was smooth and buddha-like as he listened to old Gay through dinner. Down the table, I caught some whispers about Jago, and a triumphant smile from Nightingale. None of Jago's friends referred to him. We could not explain why he had not come. We said nothing: Luke looked at me and Brown, hurt that no one could put up a defence.

When we returned to the combination room, there were several decanters on the table, the glass glittering, the silver shining. Near them stood a pile of peaches in a great silver dish, which was reflected clear in the polished wood. Gay's eyes glistened at the sight. As he was congratulating the steward, Crawford started to arrange us in our seats.

"I think we must have a change," said Crawford. "Gay, you must take my right hand again. That goes without saying. Chrystal, I should like you up here."

Just as we were seated and Crawford had filled Gay's glass and his own and was pushing the first decanter on, the door opened and Jago came into the room. He was pale as though with an illness. All eyes were on him. The room was quiet.

"Jago," said Crawford. "Come and sit by me."

Chrystal moved down one, we re-arranged ourselves, and Jago walked to the place on Crawford's left.

"I am so very sorry," he said, "to have missed your first dinner in hall. I had something to discuss with my wife. I thought I might still be in time to drink your health."

The decanter was still going round. As glasses were being filled, Jago said, in a voice to which all listened:

"I think I can claim one privilege. That is what my wife and I have been discussing. We feel you should be our guest before you go to anyone else. Will you dine with us tomorrow"—Jago paused, and then brought out the word—"Master?"

He had got through it. He scarcely listened to Crawford's reply. He raised his glass as Gay proposed the health of 'our new Master'. Jago did not speak again. He went out early, and I followed him, but he did not wish to say a word or hear one. He did not even wish for silent company along the path. In the blustering night, under the college lamps, he walked away. I watched him walk alone, back to his house.

THE END

APPENDIX

REFLECTIONS ON THE COLLEGE PAST

Often, during that year of the Mastership election, I thought how much the shape of our proceedings was determined by the past. Coming back for that first college meeting in January, I began thinking about the agenda, and wondered how long that rigid order had stay unchanged. The minutes were, of course, a recent innovation; within living memory there had been no record of any decisions except for the most formal acts, such as elections and the sale of land. It had been left to the recollection of the senior fellows—which suggested some not uncolourful scenes. But first the livings, second money: it seemed our predecessors had kept that order for at least two hundred years.

Many forms had stayed unchanged in this place for much longer still. Fellows had elected their Master, as we had to do that year, by a practice that scarcely varied back to the foundation. The statute Despard-Smith had recited at that January meeting was dated 1926, but the provisions were the same as those of Elizabeth. And the period of thirty days after the death, if the vacancy happened out of term, was a safeguard to prevent a snap election without giving men time to ride across country to Cambridge.

The forms had stayed so much unchanged that it was sometimes hard to keep one's head and see the profound differences between us and our predecessors. It was very hard in a college like this, where so much of the setting remained physically unchanged. True, the college antiquaries told us that the windows had been altered in the seventeenth century, that the outer walls all over the college had been at least twice refaced, that the disarray of the garden was an eighteenth century invention, that no one could trace the internal arrangement of the rooms. But those were small things: a sixteenth century member of the college, dropped in the first court now, would be instantaneously at home. And we felt it. However impervious one might be to the feeling of past time, there were moments when one was drugged by it. It was a haze which overcame one as one walked on the stones of the first court, touched the panelling in a room such as mine, looked over the roofs to King's: all these had been so long the same.

One felt it even in the streets of Cambridge. Walking as Roy and I had done on a rainy night, we passed through streets whose shape would have been comfortably familiar to our predecessors. The houses, the buildings, except for the colleges and churches, had all gone; but the colleges and churches defined the streets, and it was hard not to think of other men walking as we did, of the chain of lives going back so long a time, of others walking those same narrow streets in the rain.

As I said, this physical contact with past time made it hard to keep one's head. It was so easy to imagine our predecessors as they walked through the same court, dined in the same hall, drank their wine in the same combination room, elected a Master according to the same forms. It was easy to go a step further and think the election of a Master two or three hundred years ago was almost indistinguishable from ours now: it was easy to think that our predecessors and ourselves could be exchanged with no one noticing. One lost one's sense of fact. Of course, there would be resemblances between any elections to the Mastership; take a dozen men, ask them to elect their own head, and they will go through the same manœuvres as we are going through now; put an ambitious man like Jago in the college three hundred years ago, and he would have wanted the Mastership—put Brown there too, and he would have tried to work it for him.

But there would have been one deep difference between then and now. The dozen fellows would have been mostly youths in their early twenties. The core of solid, middle-aged, successful married men who now gave the college its strong and adult character—of these there could be no trace. The Winslows, Browns, Chrystals, Jagos, Gays, Getliffes, Crawfords could have no counter-parts at all. Of the present society, one might expect to find in a seventeenth or eighteenth century college one or two old bachelors like Despard-Smith and Pilbrow—and apart from them only the very young. The average age of the fellows in 1937 was over fifty. In 1870 it was twenty-six. In 1800 it was twenty-seven. In 1700 it was twenty-five. For 1600 the figures are not so certain, but the average age seems to have been even less.

This juvenile nature of the society meant incidentally that the Master had a predominance quite unlike the present day. He was often elected as a young man (Francis Getliffe or I would have been a reasonable age for a seventeenth century Master), but his dividends were much greater then the fellows', he did most of the administration of the college, including the work of the modern bursar, he remained in the post for life and could be married. It was not an accident that the Lodge had its stately bedroom, while fellows' sets, even those as handsome as mine, contained as sleeping places only their monastic cells. The Masters down to 1800 lived a normal prosperous adult life in the midst of celibates, young and old: and they inclined in fact to form a separate aristocratic class in Cambridge society.

By now that segregation had disappeared. The Mastership which Jago longed for would not make him rich among the fellows: as Brown calculated, he would lose a little money on it: in the comfortably middle class Cambridge of the 'thirties, most dons drew in between £1,000 and £2,000, Masters as well as the rest. The old predominance and powers had gone. The position still had glamour, repute, a good deal of personal power. It carried a certain amount of patronage. But its duties had faded away. Anyone who filled it had to create for himself the work to do.

This was one of the signs which showed how the college itself was changing. The forms remained, but the college was changing now, as it had changed in essence before in its six hundred years.

Few human institutions had a history so continuous, so personal, so day-to-day, I thought one night, listening to the rain on the windows. The cathedral schools of Milan and the like have histories of a kind which take one back to the Roman Empire; but they are not histories like the college's, of which one could trace each step in the fabric, in the muniment-room, in the library, in the wine books, in the names scratched on the windows and cut into the walls. Over the fire-place, a couple of yards from my chair, there were four names cut in the stone: in the sixteenth century they had shared this room, and slept in bunks against the panelling: those four all became (it is strange that they came together as boys) leaders of the Puritan movement: they preached at Leyden, wrote propaganda for the Plymouth plantation, advised Winthrop before he went to Boston. Two of them died, old men, in America.

It was astonishing how much stood there to be known of all those lives. The bottles of wine drunk by each fellow were on record, back almost for two hundred years.

I looked at the names carved into the fire-place, and I reverted to my thought of a few moments before. All this physical intimacy with the past could fill one's imagination as one sat before the fire; but there were times when it intoxicated one too much to see what the past was like. It was hard to remember, within these unchanging, yard-thick walls, how much and how often the college had changed, in all it stood for and intended to do.

It had begun as nothing very lofty. It had begun, in fact, as a kind of boarding-house. It was a boarding-house such as grew up round all the medieval universities; the universities drew students to the town, and there, as quite humble adjuncts, were houses for students to lodge—sometimes paid for by their clubbing together, sometimes maintained by an older man who paid the rent and then charged his lodgers.

The medieval universities came to full existence very quickly. They happened, it seems, because the closed, settled, stagnant world of the dark ages was at last breaking up; the towns, which had become small and insignificant in the seventh and eighth centuries, were growing again as—for some reason still not clear—trade began to flow once more over Europe, though still nothing like so freely as under the Antonines. By the twelfth and thirteenth centuries, the exchange of trade was becoming lively; and there was a need for an educated professional class to cope with affairs that were daily growing more complex. This seems to have been the reason why western Europe suddenly broke out in universities—Bologna, Salerno, Pisa, Paris. In England Oxford became in the thirteenth century a university of European reputation; Cambridge, which originated by the simple process of a few masters leaving Oxford, setting up in the little fen market-town, and starting to teach, was not a rival in the same class for a long time.

In these universities, students attended to hear the teachers lecturing in the schools. The lectures began early in the morning, finished at dusk, in the cold, comfortless, straw-strewn rooms. The stuff of the lectures, the Quadrivium and the Trivium, seems to us arid, valueless, just word-chopping; but out of it the students may have gained plenty of zest and facility in argument. The course was a very long one, and many did not stay it. At the end there was a sort of examination; as with a modern Ph.D., everyone who stayed the course seems to have passed.

But this somewhat unattractive prospect did not put students off. They scraped money to come to Cambridge, some of them lived in bitter poverty and half starved. There was one main motive; if they could get their degree, jobs lay ahead. Jobs in the royal administration, the courts, the church; jobs teaching in the schools—the fees were not light, and the teachers made a good living. The training was in fact vocational, and jobs lay at the end.

And the students liked the life. It was wild, free, and entirely uncontrolled. Some came as men, some as boys of fifteen or sixteen, some as children of twelve. They looked after themselves, and did as they wanted. The university offered them nothing but lectures, to which they went if they pleased. They found their own lodging, often in the garrets of the little town. Their time was their own, to talk, gamble, drink, fornicate. They seem to have been unusually active with their knives. They must have felt the wild hopes of youth, reeling hilariously through the squalid streets. Some of them wrote poems in silver Latin, full of ardour, passion, humour and despair.

The students liked their life, but no one else did. Certainly not the townspeople; nor the students' parents; nor the teachers; nor possibly the more bookish and domesticated of the students themselves. So, almost from the origin of the university, there were attempts to get them out of their lonely lodgings into boarding-houses. Boarding-houses were cheaper, they could live four or five to a room and have meals in common—the salt meat, salt fish, beer and bread of a medieval Cambridge winter. It was possible to get a university teacher to live in the same house and keep an eye on them.

These boarding-houses had nothing to do with teaching: the students just lodged there, and went off in the morning to the schools. They were simply a sensible means of keeping those youths from the wilder excesses. Some of them were given money, rules, and became known as colleges, but their purpose remained the same.

They were a mixed crowd of people who endowed the first colleges—ecclesiastical politicians and administrators, country clergymen, noble ladies, local guilds, kings and lords. Behind the kings and noble ladies one can usually find the hand of some priestly adviser who had himself attended in the schools; those who knew the needs from direct experience set about getting money, and went as high as their influence could take them. And those who were persuaded, and provided a little money and the rents of a bit of land (for the gifts were small): what moved them? Possibly the sensible recognition of a need: not a specially important need, but one on which their confessor seemed to lay some stress. Possibly a spark of imagination. Certainly the desire to allay anxiety by having a few young clerks obliged to say each day in perpetuity a mass for the founder's soul. Certainly the desire to have their names remembered on earth: no one likes to leave this mortal company without something to mark his place. They were the same motives, rationalised into different words, as might now have moved Sir Horace Timberlake.

The endowments were small (no founder spent anything like the equivalent in medieval money of what Sir Horace was contemplating now). These glorified boarding-houses were not ambitious affairs. They were called colleges, for that was the jargon of the day for any collection of men—there were colleges of fishmongers, cardinals and undertakers. A large proportion of the endowments went into buildings, as is the usual wish of benefactors, since buildings are easy to see and give a satisfactory impression of permanence. They were good stout simple buildings, though not as a matter of fact as stout as they looked; for the money was never enough, there was a good deal of jerry-building, and the yard-thick walls of my rooms, for instance, contained two feet of rubble. In these buildings there were just the bare necessities of a medieval community: a kitchen; a large room to eat in; stark unheated rooms where the young men could live in twos and threes and fours; a set of rooms for the university teacher who was paid to look after the college and was called the Master (he was, of course, an unmarried priest till Elizabeth's time, and the Master's quarters in the early colleges were nothing like the great Lodges of later years). The only luxury was the chapel, which was larger than such a small community required; it was built unnecessarily large to the glory of God, and in it masses were celebrated for the founder's soul.

The community was usually a very small one. This college of ours was founded, by taking over a simple boarding-house, towards the end of the fourteenth century. It was given rents of a few manors in order to maintain a Master (usually a youngish teacher, a master of arts who lectured in the schools), eight fellow-scholars, who had passed their first degree and were studying for higher ones (they were normally youths of about twenty) and thirty-six scholars, who were boys coming up for the courses in the schools. These were the college; and it was in that sense that we still used the arrogant phrase 'the college', meaning the Master and fellows. 'The governing body' was a modern and self-conscious term, which betrayed a recognition of hundreds of young men, who liked to think that they too were the college. The eight fellow-scholars elected their own Master; the number stayed eight until the college received a large benefaction in the 1640's.

This was the college when it began. It was poor, unpretentious, attempted little save to keep its scholars out of mischief, counted for very little. It had the same first court as now, a Master, some of the same titles. In everything else it was unrecognisably different.

Then three things happened, as in all Oxford and Cambridge colleges of that time. Two were obvious and in the nature of things. The third, and the most important, is mysterious to this day. The first thing was that the Master and the young fellow-scholars took to looking over the young boys' studies. They heard their exercises, heard them speak Latin, coached them in disputing. Instead of staying a simple boarding-house, the college became a coaching establishment also. Before long, the college teaching was as important as the lectures in the schools. The university still consisted of those who lectured in the schools, conducted examinations, gave degrees; but, apart from the formal examination, the colleges took over much that the university used to do.

That was bound to happen. It happened in much the same fashion in the great mother university of Paris, the university of the Archpoet, Gerson, William of Ockham, and Villon, and in Bologna, Siena, Orleans, the universities all over Europe.

It was also natural that the colleges should begin to admit not only scholars to whom grants were paid, but also boys and young men who paid their own way—the 'pensioners'. These young men were allowed into the colleges on sufferance, but soon swamped the rest in numbers. They added to the power and influence of the colleges, and considerably to their income—though the endowments were always enough, from the foundation down to the time of Brown and Chrystal, for the fellows to survive without any undergraduates at all.

That raises the question of the third process which gave Oxford and Cambridge their strange character and which is, as I said, still unexplained. For some reason or by some chance, the colleges flourished from the beginning. They attracted considerable benefactions in their first hundred years; this college of ours, which started smaller than the average, was enriched under the Tudors and drew in two very large benefactions in the seventeenth century (it then became a moderately prosperous college of almost exactly the middle size). The colleges became well-to-do as early as the Elizabethan period; old members gave their farms and manors, complete outsiders threw in a lease of land or a piece of plate. Astonishingly quickly for such a process, the colleges became wealthy, comfortable, in effect autonomous, far more important than the university. And the process once properly started, it went on like the growth of a snowball; the colleges could attract the university teachers to be Masters or fellows, because they could pay them more. The university was poor; no one left it money, it was too impersonal for that, men kept their affection and loyalty and nostalgia for the house where they had lived in their young manhood; the university had just enough to pay its few professorships, to keep up the buildings of the schools, where the relics of the old lectures still went on; the university still had the right to examine and confer degrees. Everything else had passed to the colleges. Quite early, before the end of the sixteenth century, they did all the serious teaching; they had the popular teachers, the power, the prestige, the glamour, and the riches. As the years passed, they got steadily richer.

And so there developed the peculiar dualism of Oxford and Cambridge. Nowhere else was there this odd relation between the university and the colleges—a relation so odd and intricate, so knotted with historical accidents, that it has always seemed incomprehensible to anyone outside.

It remains a mystery why this relation only grew up in England. Why was it only at the two English universities—quite independently—that the colleges became rich, powerful, self-sufficient, indestructible? At Paris, Bologna and all the medieval universities, boarding-houses were transformed into colleges, just as in England; at Paris, for example, they were endowed, given much the same start in property, and almost exactly the same statutes and constitution. Yet by 1550, when the Cambridge colleges were already dwarfing the university, those in Paris were dead.

At any rate, I thought, this college was, except in detail,

typical of all the middle-sized English ones, and had gone through all their changes. By the sixteenth century it had long ceased to be a boarding-house, and become instead a cross between a public school and a small self-contained university. The boys up to seventeen and eighteen were birched in the college hall (which would have been unthinkable in less organised, less prosperous, freer days). The young men went out, some to country livings, some to the new service of administrative jobs required by Tudor England. The Masters were usually married even now, the Lodge was enlarged, the great bedroom came into use; the fellows were predominantly, as they remained till 1880, unmarried young clerics, who took livings as their turn came round. Their interests were, however, very close to the social conflicts of the day: the active and unrebellious, men like Jago and Chrystal and Brown, were drawn into the Elizabethan bureaucracy: the discussions at high table, though put into religious words, must often have been on topics we should call 'political', and many of the idealistic young threw themselves into calvinism, were deprived of their fellowships by the government, and in exile led their congregations to wonder about the wilderness across the Atlantic sea.

The seventeenth century saw, really for the first time, some fellows busy with scholarship and research. The times were restless and dangerous: trade was on the move, organised science took its place in the world. A few gifted men stayed all their lives in the college, and did solid work in botany and chemistry. Some of my contemporaries, I sometimes thought, would have fitted into the college then, more easily than into any time before our own.

The country quietened into the eighteenth century peace, there was a lull before the technological revolution. For the first time since its foundation, the college, like all others, declined. In 1540 the college had been admitting 30 undergraduates a year, in 1640 the number had gone up to 50 (larger than at any time until after the 1914-18 war). In 1740 the number was down to 8. No one seemed very much to mind. The dividends stayed unaffected (about £100 a year for the ordinary fellow), the college livings did pretty well out of their tithes; it just remained for one of them to come along. The college had for the time being contrived to get cut off from the world: from the intellectual world of the London coffee-houses, from the rough-and-ready experiments of the agricultural revolution, from any part in politics except to beg patronage from the great oligarchs. The college had stopped being a boarding-house, a school; had almost stopped being in any sense a place of education; it became instead a sort of club. Most people think affectionately now of an eighteenth century Cambridge college; it was a very unexacting place. Most people have a picture of it—of middle-aged or elderly men, trained exclusively in the classics, stupefying themselves on port. The picture is only wrong in that the men in fact were not middle-aged or elderly, but very young: they were trained first and foremost, not in classics, but in mathematics; and they drank no more than most of their successors. Roy Calvert would have joined one of their harder sessions, and gone off without blinking to give a lecture in German on early Soghdian. But they had the custom of drinking their port twice a day—once after dinner, which began about two o'clock, and again after supper at seven. They must have been sleepy and bored, sitting for a couple of hours on a damp, hot Cambridge afternoon, drinking their wine very slowly, making bets on how soon a living would fall vacant, and how long before the last lucky man to take a living got married or had a child.

By the nineteenth century, the deep revolution (threatened faintly by seventeenth century science: acted on, in the nineteenth century factories) was visible everywhere. There had never been such a change so quickly as between the England of 1770 and the England of 1850: and the college felt it too.

Something was happening: men wanted to know more. The country needed scientists. It needed every kind of expert knowledge. It needed somewhere to educate the commercial and industrial middle class that had suddenly grown up. Between 1830 and 1880 the college, like all Cambridge, modernised itself as fast as Japan later in the century. In 1830 the young clergymen still sat over their port each afternoon; in the '80's the college had taken on its present shape. Nine English traditions out of ten, old Eustace Pilbrow used to say, date from the latter half of the nineteenth century.

The university courses were revolutionised. The old rigid training, which made each honours student begin with a degree in mathematics, was thrown away. It became possible for a man, if he were so adventurous, to start his course in classics. In 1860 it even became possible to study natural science; and the Cavendish, the most famous of scientific laboratories, was built in 1874. Experimental science was taught; and the new university laboratories drew students as the old schools had drawn them in the middle ages; here no college could compete, and university teaching, after hundreds of years, was coming back to preeminence again.

The college kept up with the transformation. It made some changes itself, in others had to follow the Royal Commissions. Fellows need not be in orders; were allowed to marry; were no longer elected for life. At a step the college became a secular, adult, settled society. For five hundred years it had been a place which fellows went from when they could: at a stroke, it became a place they stayed in. By 1890 the combination room was inhabited by bearded fathers of families. The average age of the fellows mounted. Their subjects were diverse: there were scientists, oriental linguists, historians—and M. H. L. Gay, one of the younger fellows, had already published two books on the historical basis of the Icelandic sagas. The scholarly work of the college became greater out of all knowledge.

The college suddenly became a place of mature men. They were as frail as other men, but they won respect because of their job, and they had great self-respect. They were men of the same make as Winslow, Brown, Chrystal, Crawford, Jago and Francis Getliffe; and Gay and Pilbrow had lived through from those days to these. From those days to now, the college had been truly the same place.

Gay and Pilbrow, as young fellows, had seen the college, the whole of Cambridge, settle in to the form which, to Luke for example, seemed eternal. Organised games, bumping races, matches with Oxford, college clubs, May week, competitive scholarships, club blazers and ties, the Council of the Senate, most Cambridge slang, were all nineteenth century inventions. Gay had been elected at a time when some of his colleagues were chafing for the 1880 statutes to become law, so that they could marry. He had been through four elections to the Mastership. They were all elections dominated by the middle-aged, like this one about to come. He had seen the college move to the height of its prosperity and self-confidence. And now, his memory flickering, he sat with us and heard of another election, the last that would come his way.

There was one irony about it all. Just as the college reached its full mature prosperity, it seemed that the causes which brought it there would in the end change it again, and this time diminish it. For the nineteenth century revolution caused both the teaching of experimental science and the college as we knew it, rich, proud, full of successful middle-aged men, so comfortably off that the Master no longer lived in a separate society. The teaching of experimental science had meant the revival of the powers and influence of the university; for no college, however rich, not even Trinity, could finance physics and engineering laboratories on a modern scale. To cope with this need, the university had to receive contributions from the colleges and also a grant from the state. This meant as profound a change as that by which the colleges cut out the university as the prime source of teaching. It meant inevitably that the reverse must now happen. The university's income began to climb into £1,000,000 a year: it needed that to provide for twentieth century teaching and research: no college's endowment brought in more than a tenth the sum. By the 1920's the university was in charge of all laboratories, and all formal teaching: it was only left to colleges to supplement this by coaching, as they had done in their less exalted days. There were, by the way, great conveniences for the fellows in this resurrection of the university; nearly all of them had university posts as well as college ones, and so were paid twice. It was this double source of pay that made the income of Jago, Chrystal, Brown and the others so large; everyone between thirty and seventy in the college, except for Nightingale, was earning over £1,000 a year. But it meant beyond any doubt whatever that the colleges, having just known their mature and comfortable greatness, would be struggling now to keep their place. It sometimes seemed that the time must come when they became boarding-houses again, though most superior ones.

I regretted it. They had their faults, but they had also great humanity.

However, that change was in the future. It did not trouble the fellows as I knew them. Of all men, they had the least doubts about their social value. They could be as fond of good works as Pilbrow, as modest as Brown, but still they were kept buoyed up by the greatest confidence and self-respect in their job. By the 'thirties, the conscience of the comfortable classes was sick: the sensitive rich, among my friends, asked themselves what use they were: but that was not a question one would have heard in the college. For everyone, inside and out, took it for granted that the academic life was a valuable one to live; scientists such as Crawford, Francis Getliffe, and Luke had become admired like no other professional men, and the rest of us, with a shade of envy, took a little admiration for ourselves. In England, the country with the subtlest social divisions (Pilbrow said the most snobbish of countries), Oxford and Cambridge had had an unchallenged social cachet for a long time; even Lady Muriel, though she did not feel her husband's colleagues were her equals, did not consider them untouchable; and so a man like Francis Getliffe, when asked what was his job, answered with a double confidence, knowing that it was valued by serious people and also had its own curious place among the smart. Many able men entered the academic life in those years because, with a maximum of comfort, it settled their consciences and let them feel that their lives were not utterly without a use.

For many it was a profound comfort to be one of a society completely sure of itself, completely certain of its values, completely without misgivings about whether it was living a good life. In the college there were men varied enough to delight anyone with a taste in human things: but none of them, except Roy Calvert in one of his fits of melancholy, ever doubted that it was a good thing to be a fellow. They took it for granted, felt they were envied, felt it was right they should be envied: enjoyed the jokes about dons, which to some, such as Chrystal, Brown and Francis Getliffe, as they thought of their busy efficient lives, seemed peculiarly absurd: wanted to grow old in the college, and spend their last years as Gay and Pilbrow were doing now.

When I arrived in the college, I had already moved about a good deal among the layers of society; and I had not come to the end of my journey yet. I had the luck to live intimately among half-a-dozen different vocations. Occasionally, among men who had never been near the place, I thought that a good many of them would have found in the college the least anxious and the most comforting lives, and some, more surprisingly, the freest.

END OF APPENDIX